Broken Fae

BROKEN FATE

Copyright © 2024 by Sabrey Moiraine

Library of Congress Control Number: 2024901828

Paperback ISBN: 979-8-9898195-0-8
eBook ISBN: 979-8-9898195-2-2

First paperback edition March 2024

Cover Artist: Brooklyn Bertagnole
Map Artist: Shepengul
Editor and Formatter: Ariana Tosado
eBook Formatter: Mckenna Rowell
Published by Standard of Light Publishing

To Kayla.

I started writing Broken Fate *for myself, but I finished it for you.*

SABREY MOIRAINE

© Sabrey Moiraine | Standard of Light Publishing

Table of Contents

PART ONE

Four Years Ago — 17

Chapter One — 23

Chapter Two — 30

Chapter Three — 35

Chapter Four — 41

Chapter Five — 49

Chapter Six — 59

Chapter Seven — 68

Chapter Eight — 75

Chapter Nine — 83

Chapter Ten — 90

Chapter Eleven — 96

Chapter Twelve — 101

Chapter Thirteen — 107

Chapter Fourteen — 116

Chapter Fifteen — 122

Chapter Sixteen — 130

Chapter Seventeen — 136

Chapter Eighteen — 144

Chapter Nineteen — 150

Chapter Twenty — 164

Chapter Twenty-One — 177

Chapter Twenty-Two — 184

Chapter Twenty-Three — 191

Chapter Twenty-Four — 203

Chapter Twenty-Five   206
Chapter Twenty-Six   212
Chapter Twenty-Seven   221
Chapter Twenty-Eight   228
Chapter Twenty-Nine   234
Chapter Thirty   239
Chapter Thirty-One   248

PART TWO

Chapter Thirty-Two   257
Chapter Thirty-Three   265
Chapter Thirty-Four   272
Chapter Thirty-Five   280
Chapter Thirty-Six   287
Chapter Thirty-Seven   293
Chapter Thirty-Eight   303
Chapter Thirty-Nine   309
Chapter Forty   317
Chapter Forty-One   327
Chapter Forty-Two   339
Chapter Forty-Three   346
Chapter Forty-Four   357
Chapter Forty-Five   370
Chapter Forty-Six   377
Chapter Forty-Seven   383
Chapter Forty-Eight   390
Chapter Forty-Nine   398
Chapter Fifty   405
Epilogue   414

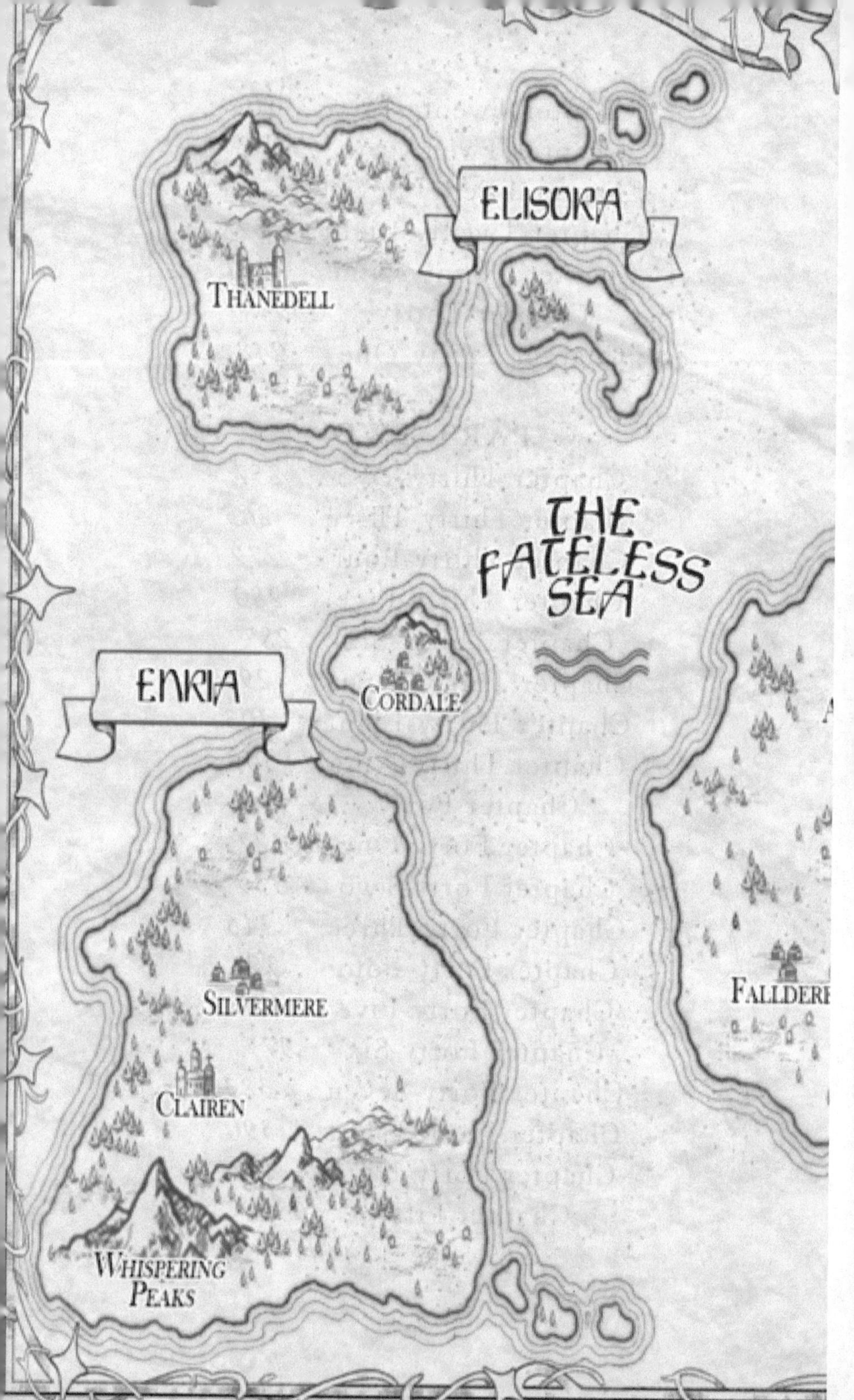

ELISORA
THANEDELL
THE FATELESS SEA
ENKIA
CORDALE
SILVERMERE
FALLDERE
CLAIREN
WHISPERING PEAKS

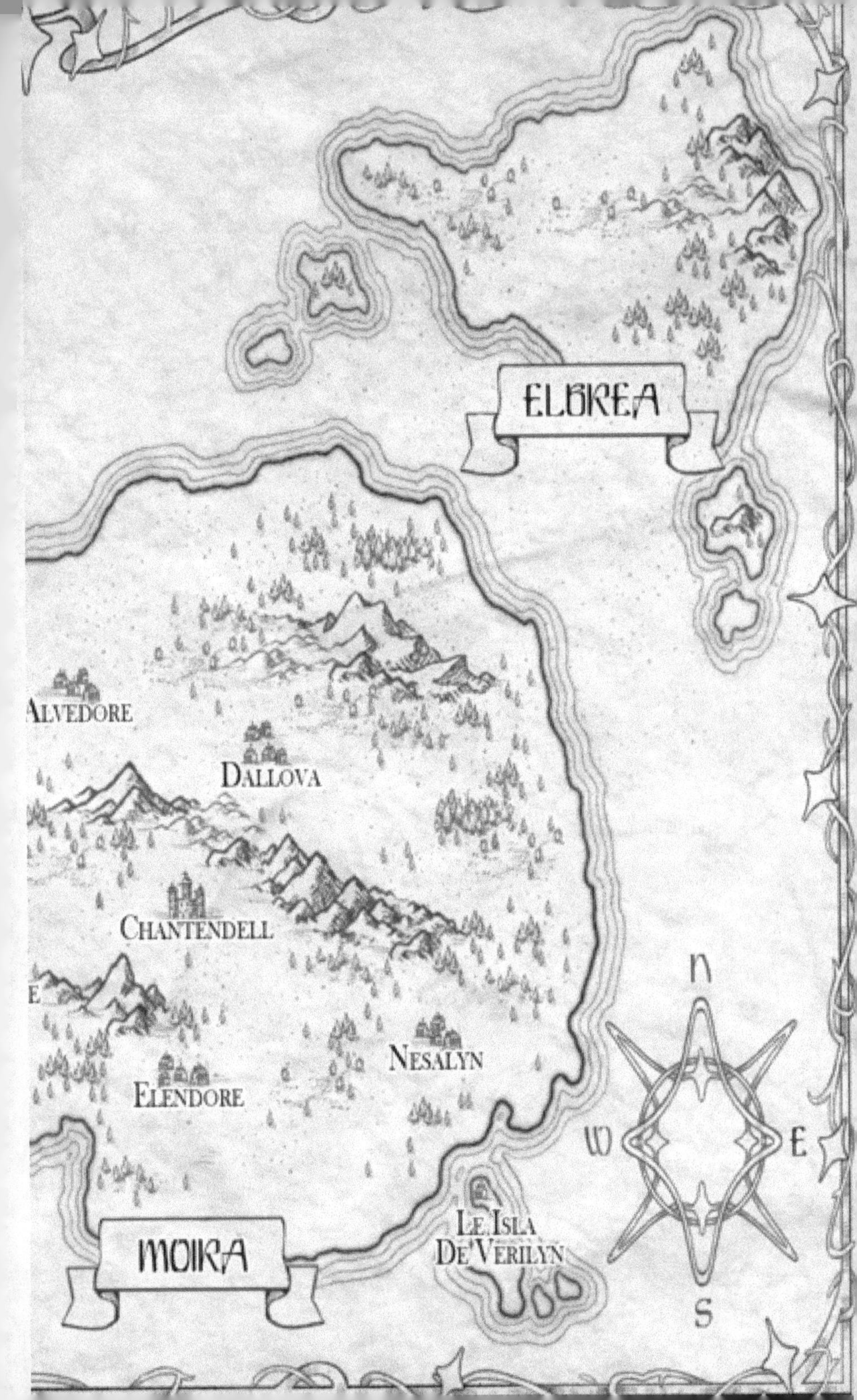

ELBREA
ALVEDORE
DALLOVA
CHANTENDELL
NESALYN
ELENDORE
LE ISLA DE VERILYN
MOIRA
N
W
E
S

PREFACE

Broken Fate, at the surface, is a story about defying fate and choosing destiny. It's about freeing ourselves from the idea of the inevitable and embracing a life comprised of choices we make, resulting in one we control. And while every story has an overarching theme at its surface, every story also has a thousand smaller ones hidden beneath.

So, *Broken Fate* is also a story about love, hope, confusion, change, friendship, and dedication.

Every story you read, watch, or hear may seem like a single idea, but I believe that stories are mosaics of countless lessons, experiences, and truths that writers are aching to share.

I wrote *Broken Fate* during a time spent choosing who I wanted to be. But who we are is not a single choice or title. We choose who we are every time we make a decision.

Broken Fate, at its heart, is a story about deciding, defining, and refining who you want to be, and then always remembering who that person is.

Dear reader, remember who you are.

Sincerely,

Sabrey Moiraine

PART ONE

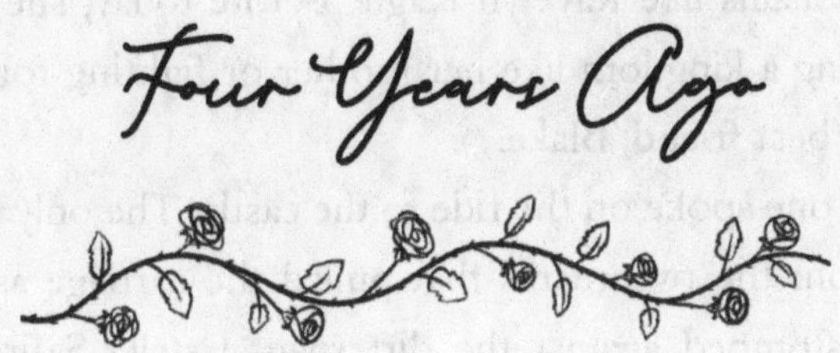

VILLAIN. THE FATE GIVER'S DECLARATION HUNG IN THE air like a taunt.

Looks of disapproval danced around the room. Xenia Safire's heart sank and her head spun at the buzz of whispers that filled the air—whispers about her.

Closing her eyes, she willed everything around her to stop. But she wasn't that fortunate. In only a moment, her life continued, leaving her scrambling to figure out the next part.

From across the dome, Xenia's mother glared at her, lips in a tight line. The sharp click of her heels against the marble floor echoed around the room as she neared. She grabbed Xenia's pale wrist and pulled her from the chair. "We will be leaving now," she said.

Xenia fumbled over her feet as her mother pulled her towards the exit. She pushed the door open, and blazing light flooded into room. Xenia followed her mother to their carriage and clambered in behind her.

Tension swarmed the small space between them. How could any of this be real? How could her fate be the same as terrible villains like Ravelyn Kage? Before today, she imagined ruling a kingdom like her mother or fighting for good with her best friend, Blake.

No one spoke on the ride to the castle. The only sound came from the two mares that pulled the carriage as their hooves stomped against the dirt road. Estelle Safire said nothing, though her eyes communicated her feelings well enough: confusion; worry; and, even if she never admitted to it, disappointment.

Sensing her mother's unwavering stare, Xenia turned to look out the window. She didn't live far from the Hall of Destiny, and already the stone towers that made the Dwelling of Royals appeared in the distance.

Her mother's fate had earned her a spot in the settlement. Estelle was a queen in her story, but in Chantendell, that didn't make Xenia a princess. Only a villain. Everyone born in Chantendell received a fate they would one day fulfil by living out a story that would then be published for anyone to read.

Xenia spent her fourteenth birthday the same way everyone in Chantendell did—in the Hall of Destiny waiting for the single word that would change her life forever.

The carriage stopped in front of her mother's dark, stone castle. Xenia jumped out and ran through the castle to the tower that held her bedroom. The walls blurred around her as she climbed the spiral stairs and pushed open the wooden door.

Xenia locked her bedroom door and then leaned against it, taking in her round bedroom. The canopy above her bed fluttered in the wind from the open window. Books lined the shelves against her wall. The dresses she had decided against wearing still cluttered the wooden floor in varying shades of scarlet. Nothing to indicate that a villain lived there.

Tears spilled down her cheeks, ruining the makeup her mother had spent so much time perfecting. *What am I?*

She couldn't hurt anyone. How was she supposed to be a villain? Xenia's body trembled as she fell onto her bed, curling into herself as she cried.

A demanding knock came from her door. Despite her desire to ignore it, she forced herself towards the door. She pulled her dark, wavy hair out of her face and then opened it.

Blake Cedar stood in the doorframe, wearing a smile that quickly vanished when he saw her. He had received his fate a few months earlier: Hero's Allegiant.

Xenia didn't want him to know what she was. Her fate made them enemies. He would never want to continue their friendship once he knew. But after she'd known him for so long, would fate be strong enough to break their relationship?

"Nia?"

She couldn't meet his gaze.

"You're the villain, aren't you?"

Once again, tears shook her. Blake closed the gap between them and wrapped his arms around her. "It's going to be okay," he whispered. "You're going to be okay."

Xenia wanted to believe him, but she didn't think he believed himself. Her entire future had been redirected down a path she never wanted to walk; how would anything be okay?

Taking a breath, she stepped back. She turned away from Blake and crossed the room to her bookshelf. She pulled out a book with a dark, leather cover and uneven pages. In golden ink, the front read, "The Seekers"—her mother's story. Xenia opened the book to chapter forty-one. Tears blurred her view of the words. This was the chapter that marked the end of her father's life. The villain had killed him.

"You're not like her," Blake said, coming up behind her.

"I could become like her."

"You won't."

"I *have* to." She pushed the book back on the shelf and faced Blake.

"Do you want to talk about it?"

She shook her head. It was a topic she wanted to ignore for as long as possible. She knew she couldn't, but she had a choice now. And those moments she spent pretending nothing had changed couldn't have meant more.

The start of term approached quickly, and today Xenia would move into the Training Center to begin preparing for her story. Her mother waited outside with the carriage as

Xenia grabbed the last of her things and took them outside to meet her.

Outside, the sun was setting and a cool breeze ruffled her hair. Before Xenia could climb into the carriage, her mother gently pulled her close, a sad smile touching her lips. "I'll miss you here," she said, and then sighing she added, "I love you, Xenia."

They exchanged goodbyes. Xenia took her seat in the carriage, and the brown mares pulled her away from the castle.

She would reside at the Training Center until she earned permission to enter her story. Then, she could enter at any time until she turned twenty-four. Most would suffer arrest after ten years, but resisting a major fate, like hers, meant execution. The law ensured that no one neglected their fate.

The sun had set by the time Xenia arrived at the Training Center. The gravel street switched to cobblestone and lanterns lined the path, lighting up the night. Dozens of students filled the courtyard, exchanging excited conversation.

A large, brick building, fashioned similarly to a castle, sat in the center of the premise. On either side of the building were hundreds of individual towers covered in bricks.

The carriage stopped at the stables, and Xenia took her things and started right, towards the women's towers. No one paid her any mind as she crossed the courtyard. No one knew who she was yet. What would change once they learned her fate?

Her tower, number seven, didn't lack the rest of the school's beauty, wrapped in dark-gray bricks and tangled vines. She took a deep breath, unlocked the door, and pulled it open.

Her steps echoed around the empty tower as she entered. Xenia took a few steps farther before stumbling over an uneven floorboard. The board was thicker than the others, as if made to stand out. She nudged it with the tip of her boot and it shifted, revealing a dusty chest. She picked it up and brought it to a table farther into the tower.

Inside the chest lay a book worn at the edges with lavish embellishments that should have earned it a spot in a museum. Thick, yellow pages and tattered binding exposed its old age. A thick strap held it closed, and golden letters at the top spelled "FORBIDDEN."

Chapter One

I AM A VILLAIN.

After four years of training, Xenia still couldn't say those words out loud. "Once you admit it to yourself, it's easier to accept," Ravelyn Kage had always said. Xenia knew she was right; that was why she hadn't said it.

A mirror hung on the wall in front of Xenia. Through it she could see herself, Ravelyn Kage, and the two Training Center escorts who stood in the back of the room.

"You need to listen to me." Ravelyn's voice was softer and steadier than the other villains she had met. Her eyes were sharp, but she looked at Xenia through a gentle lens. "You cannot do this forever, the sooner you accept yourself, the sooner you can enter your story."

"How long did you wait to enter?"

She shook her head and placed a hand on Xenia's shoulder. Xenia tensed at the touch. "Things were different when I was young."

Ravelyn never talked about herself—something other villains did gladly. She hardly seemed like the same villain everyone had come to know through her story. Allegedly, she was one of the greatest villains to ever live. She had fought Samuel Liftson, and despite her defeat, her name became a part of history.

"I think that's enough for today," Ravelyn said, turning her back on the mirror. Xenia followed her to the front of the house, the escorts just behind them.

Ravelyn lived in a house that was more prison than home. The walls were made from rough cement, the furniture simple and unpolished, and she had no decorations.

Xenia stepped outside and waited as the guards locked Ravelyn inside before climbing into the carriage. The men sat on either side of her, enclosing her in the small space. The velvet door swung closed, and the carriage rattled from the impact. It stopped, only to be swayed again as the horses carried them away from the house.

Ravelyn lived far out of the kingdom. The rulers claimed it was for the safety of the people. One day, Xenia would be confined to a small home away from everyone else as well. The law added to the long list of reasons she wished she could forsake her fate. The thought of living alone all her life carved a hole inside her.

The curtain blew in the wind, revealing the deep-green trees surrounding them. A city had been built upon the forest Chantendell once was. And as buildings went up, the land was ridden of its natural beauty. Here, no buildings filled the space that belonged to nature. Flourishing green burst from the trees the whole way back to Chantendell.

Even if Chantendell's inner streets weren't polished with trees, the kingdom held its own glamor. After riding through miles of trees, the horses pulling the carriage kicked up dust from the gravel roads as they approached the stone buildings that made up Chantendell's shopping quarter. From one, a group of girls a few years younger than Xenia ran out giggling. Each girl carried an elegant dress—likely for the upcoming Yule Celebration.

After the War of Chantendell, the nation celebrated the first snow as a symbol of the peace and purity to come. Other nations adopted the tradition over the years, and now it was celebrated in nearly every region—aside from Enria.

The carriage pulled into the Training Center's stable and came to a stop. Xenia clambered out of the carriage behind her escorts and into the dim stall. He offered a stiff nod, excusing her. She returned it and hurried out.

Outside of the stable's protection, Gale's merciless wind whipped her hair into her face, blocking her view with dark locks. She pushed her hair behind her ears and continued towards the courtyard.

After training sessions, Xenia would ignore the usual crowds that gathered in the courtyard and go to her tower. Since Blake had entered their story, she had no one to spend her evenings with. He had received permission to enter years ago and didn't wait to leave. Xenia had hoped that after spending most of their time together from a young age, if anyone could see beyond her fate, it would be him. Blake claimed he wasn't leaving because of her or her fate, but he hadn't stayed for her, either.

Will anyone ever stay?

Xenia had to train with Ravelyn Kage to earn permission. She could enter when *she* thought she was ready. Xenia imagined she would be stuck in Chantendell until she turned twenty-four. If she failed to enter before then, she would be executed and replaced by a past villain. In Chantendell, not fulfilling her fate made her worthless.

In the center of the courtyard, where two cobblestone trails met near a water fountain, more students gathered than usual. Xenia tried to ignore the excited whispers and kept her head down as she walked towards her tower.

When she reached the fountain at the center of the courtyard, applause and shouts of approval sliced the air. *What's going on?* Xenia hesitated. Could staying to find out hurt? If she slipped into the crowd, she might stay unnoticed. Instead of continuing to her tower, she joined the thick of the crowd by the fountain.

Silence fell over the courtyard as a man at the front called to the crowd. Xenia straightened herself to peer past shoulders, but the man stayed hidden.

"My name is Samuel Liftson! Thank you for welcoming me to your school! Every time I visit, I'm filled with the great sense of purpose that this school holds. Each of you has a vital fate and promising future, and I'm honored to be here with you now!"

Xenia frowned as people around her shouted praise and applauded his flattery. Several years ago, she might have joined them, but now a sickly feeling gripped her at the thought of Samuel Liftson and what he'd done to Ravelyn. She had done horrible things—every child in Chantendell was haunted with her stories—but still, Ravelyn seemed to *understand* her. That thought hurt Xenia's stomach even more.

"Most of you, I know, are familiar with my story," he continued. "Back then, not only that world, but Chantendell also were at stake. I fought for you then, and I still dedicate every day to making this kingdom a better place.

"As I'm sure you know, the nation will welcome a new ruler in only a few weeks. The choice is one we must be careful while making. Few people are worthy of ruling our nation. And few people fighting for your choice are honest."

Xenia tensed. Her mother was taking part in the selection this year. If she won the throne, Xenia would become Princess of Chantendell. No one would want a villain so close to the throne, so they did what they could to keep her fate from being publicized and used against them. Some people knew, of course—and from his words, Xenia worried that Samuel Liftson was one of them. His influence had the ability to turn the nation against them.

"Change is approaching—not only in Chantendell but all around," Samuel said. "Rumors of war against western countries are spreading. Light in our lives is needed now more than ever before. You have the power—each of you— to change the world you live in. It doesn't always take a hero to make a difference. I encourage you to be a light in someone else's life as times grow darker. I want to be a light that illuminates your life! Tonight, I'll be here at your school to give you the chance to get to know me the way I want to know you!"

The crowd erupted into roars of applause at his closing line.

Complaints mingled with the cheers as several students pushed through the crowd. Several of the villains that currently lived at the Training Center led the group. One of the girls, Merrie, snagged Xenia's wrist as she passed, pulling her along.

"Hey!" Xenia twisted her arm.

"Do you know the plans?"

"No, what plans?" Xenia's heart sped up.

"Why do you think we're here?" she asked, stopping to let Xenia answer. When she didn't, she added, "Can you think of a better time to establish who we are? Neither can I."

"What—?"

"Liftson!" another girl shouted, cutting off Xenia's response.

The crowd of people in front of them parted as they turned to look at the girl who had shouted. The courtyard became quiet.

"Do you ever think your success might have come from your name? Your victory is hardly memorable. If Ravelyn was really so terrible, why is she no longer a threat? What did you do to stop her?"

Xenia's breath caught as Samuel made his way towards them. Everyone had turned to watch her. She wanted to run as far away from the courtyard as she could before he reached them, but she couldn't now.

Samuel's eyes rested on Xenia and clawed into her as if she was the one who had harassed him. His stare tore through her and grabbed hold of her heart. She took a deep breath to regain control of her body.

"I've found *incredible* villain victories! They really get too little attention, wouldn't you agree?" the girl continued.

"Villains, are you?" He looked between them. "I don't want to engage in any arguments, but I don't think you fully understand the importance of the battle I fought." His voice turned cold. "Ravelyn's intentions were far worse than anyone here realizes."

The countless eyes on her made Xenia dizzy, but anger fought the feeling, and she surprised herself by speaking next. "Ravelyn is no different than any other villain—she's no worse! Just as you're no better than any other hero!"

Laughter rang behind Xenia, and she glanced over her shoulder to find it: Samuel's youngest son smiled back at her.

"I think it's best if you return to your towers," Samuel said. "You are not wanted here tonight."

Xenia breathed out, relieved as he turned his attention back to the rest of his audience, and stormed to her tower.

Chapter Two

XENIA THREW A MATCH INTO THE STOVE AND WATCHED the fire flicker to life. She cooked her own meals most nights, but today she couldn't think of a place worse than the dining hall for a villain to spend her time. Heroes would be priding their nonexistent victories while condemning villains and people like Xenia who held the title.

Her fate affected so much more than her story. Royals like her mother worked in the palace and competed for the Moiran throne every ten years. Heroes were idolized while villains were treated like a curse. *Avoided.*

Xenia filled her pot with water and hung it above the flames. Everything about the opposite life seemed more appealing. What could her future possibly hold for her to fulfill her fate?

Magic is never wrong. I am destined to be a villain.

A sharp knock snapped her out of her thoughts. *Oh no!* She couldn't think of any good reason anyone would come to see her.

She left the counter where she'd been cutting vegetables and hurried to the door. Headmistress Grimmlyn stood outside, a stern expression painted across her features.

Panic stirred inside Xenia; Mrs. Grimmlyn didn't visit students without a reason. Had she heard about the incident with Samuel Liftson?

"Can I help you?" Xenia asked, trying to mask her concern.

She shook her head. "I was sorting through files and realized you still don't have a roommate. With our limited space, it would be best for you to share this tower. I've already spoken to Karielyn Height about it."

Xenia's thoughts spun at the proposal. Karielyn was her allegiant, though they hadn't spoken outside of class for several seasons. Xenia had always wished her tower weren't so lonely. Now she tried to imagine what living with Karielyn would be like. She didn't imagine anything good.

"I don't need a roommate, do I?"

Mrs. Grimmlyn's sharp features were concealed in the dark, and the candles inside the tower didn't provide enough light to see her expression clearly. "We have far more students currently enrolled than living space. I can't let you keep this entire tower to yourself."

"She can't stay with someone else?"

Grimmlyn sighed. "No, Xenia, I think that the two of you should be together. She is your allegiant," she said with a final edge in her voice.

"When—?"

"She'll be here tonight. Expect her any time after I leave."

Xenia opened her mouth and then closed it, deciding against arguing with the headmistress further.

"Good night, Xenia," she said as she turned to leave.

The door fell closed behind her, and Xenia turned around, leaning against it. She wasn't ready for anyone to move in tonight—especially not Karielyn.

She put out the fire and then took the stairs closest to the door. Each tower had two rooms on the upper floor. Two sets of stairs wrapped around the tower, leading to a narrow hallway guarded by a waist-level railing. She used the spare room as a place to keep her books and drawings. Now she needed to find a place for all of it in her bedroom.

She moved the furniture and decorations from the extra room into her bedroom and swept the floor in Karielyn's soon-to-be room. She wanted to leave no small details for her to complain about; somehow, she always managed to do so.

The door opened downstairs and Xenia groaned, leaving the room to greet Karielyn. She stood in the door frame, struggling to keep the door open while carrying her things. Long locks of rose-gold hair cascaded down her petite figure. Her blue eyes jumped to Xenia as she stepped inside, letting the door close. She slumped from the weight of the boxes in her arms.

"Oh, Xenia, there you are. I was just dropping off my things—I hope you don't mind." Before Xenia could respond, Karielyn set all the boxes at her feet but one, which she took into the kitchen.

"Were you trying to cook?" Karielyn called.

Xenia followed her under the landing into the kitchen. She had left the vegetables out to clean the bedroom. "I got distracted—"

"I suppose I'll have to cook dinner," Karielyn mumbled, setting her box onto the counter. "Just let me finish getting my things from my old tower."

Xenia said nothing. She didn't need Karielyn to cook for her, but nothing would change her mind now.

"I can't imagine what you planned to make with *those*— I'm surprised I don't see you in the dining hall more often."

Karielyn didn't wait for a response before returning to the living room for another box, muttering to herself about Xenia's decorations.

"I think I'll take a walk and let you get settled," Xenia said, following Karielyn to the door. She wasn't ready to counter any of her remarks and already longed for fresh air.

The cool air stung her face as she made her way through the maze of towers. *At least it's not snowing.* She tugged at the sleeves of her black blouse. *If only I had worn a sweater.* Chantendell's brutal winters often left the kingdom white with snow for several seasons. Most of the snow from the last storm had melted, making room for the next storm to arrive.

Laughter and conversation from the dining hall sounded across the courtyard. The windows glowed from the candle light. Xenia stopped when she reached the fountain. Part of her longed to be inside laughing with the rest of the students instead of outside alone.

She sighed, and her breath froze in the air. The cold tempted her to turn around, but she couldn't bring herself to go back yet. Instead, she followed the cobblestone trail around the premises. She passed the Villain Studies building, the library, and eventually stood in front of the dining hall. With her eyes fixed on the path, she nearly walked into the door, but it opened, slamming into her. Losing her balance, she fell onto the cold ground. Her head throbbed and she reached for her temple, groaning. She glanced up to see who had hit her.

Felix Liftson stood in the doorway, holding out his hand to help her up.

Chapter Three

"I AM SO SORRY! ARE YOU HURT?"

Xenia accepted Felix's hand and pulled herself to her feet. "I'm fine," she mumbled, avoiding his gaze. When she glanced at him, his stare still lingered on her. Something in his light-brown eyes calmed her irritation. At the thought, her heart froze, and she pulled her hand from his.

His eyes fell to the ground for a moment. "You're the villain of our story. Xenia, isn't it?" His voice wasn't laced with fear when he addressed her as a villain like most people's.

She nodded, already anticipating the snide comment that would follow. Still sensing his eyes on her, she flashed her stare in his direction. He stood several inches taller than her, and his caramel hair lay brushed over one side. She had seen him before, though not often. He was the hero.

"You weren't planning on going in, were you?" he asked. "It's hardly suitable for a villain in there, especially after what you said earlier."

Xenia's cheeks burned. "No, I wasn't going in. I—I know I shouldn't have said anything. I just—"

"Don't apologize." Felix laughed. "He needs people like you to keep him humble."

Her brow creased, and her face grew warmer as she struggled to find a response. "I should get back now," she said, taking a step away from Felix.

"Would you like me to walk with you?"

Her stomach twisted. *He wants to walk with* me? "Why? Your father hosting dinner tonight."

"He is. But it's getting late, and you won't be safe alone while all the people he's encouraged are out."

Spiders raced across her skin. "But I can trust you?"

He smiled. "Well, I am a hero. Unfortunately, most seem to think that means they can treat villains however they please. I won't hurt you."

Xenia strained to find the hidden meaning in his offer. No one spoke to her—heroes least of all. Why would he do this? She wanted to enjoy someone's company for a change, but she couldn't keep from worrying that this was a sort of tease.

"Well?"

"My tower is this way," she said finally, turning to face the women's side of the premises. She began walking away from the dining hall, and Felix fell into step at her side.

"Why *are* you out alone so late?" he asked as they reached the section of the stone path that split toward the towers.

Xenia crossed her arms for warmth. "I'm avoiding my roommate, I guess."

He snickered. "Who's your roommate?"

"Karielyn Height."

"Karielyn is your roommate?"

"As of tonight." She slowed as they approached her tower, looking carefully for the number seven.

Each tower housed two people, but until now Xenia had lived alone despite there not being enough towers for everyone training. People with more significant fates, such as heroes and villains, were guaranteed rooms, while others had to wait for an available spot.

She used to imagine that having a roommate would combat her constant loneliness, but now that she had to share a tower with Karielyn, she wasn't sure it would help.

Would anyone make a pleasant roommate? Most people were wary of Xenia because of her fate. The select people she once called friends no longer spoke to her.

"This is it," she said, stopping in front of her tower. She pulled open the door and stepped inside. It always felt dull when she entered, like her house had when she left town for a few days. Maybe it was because there was never anyone there—or maybe because she had never accepted it as home.

Karielyn sat by fire at the front of the tower, reading a thick book. She looked up, and her eyes skipped from Xenia to Felix. "Oh. Liftson, hello."

Felix's expression shifted.

"Xenia," Karielyn said, closing the book in her hand. "Why do you have a book in Elisoran?"

She narrowed her eyes. "Elisoran? Are you sure?"

Karielyn nodded, holding up the large book.

Xenia immediately recognized it as the one she had found her first night at the Training Center. She stormed into the tower and snatched it from Karielyn. "Why were you in my room?" she demanded. "And how do you know it's in Elisoran?"

Karielyn glared, her lips pursed. "My mother has books on the Elisoran language. I've studied them. I know a bit of it."

"My father has a book in Elisoran," Felix added quietly, as if to himself. Distracted by Karielyn, Xenia had almost forgotten about him.

"Why is it forbidden?" Karielyn added.

"I don't know. It's not even mine, I found it in the tower when I got here."

Felix moved deeper into the tower. "Forbidden?" he asked.

Butterflies traveled through Xenia's chest. Would he turn her in for having it?

Karielyn nodded irritably, tossing him a cruel look.

"Can I see?" he asked, ignoring her annoyance.

Xenia froze. If she gave it to him, what would he do with it?

He'll think I have something to hide if I keep it from him.

Reluctantly, she handed him the book. She could get in trouble for having a forbidden book at school. What if he told someone?

"1403," he whispered to himself as he fanned through

the pages. He closed the book and handed it back to Xenia, and then he beamed, easily brushing off the serious expression he wore previously. "I should get back now. Good night." He reached for the door and pulled it open. Before leaving, he gave her a final glance and something close to a scowl to Karielyn.

"Why was he here?" Karielyn snapped, breaking the silence Felix had left behind.

"We ran into each other in the courtyard and he offered to walk with me. Is that a problem?"

She cocked her head and stayed silent for a moment. "You should be more careful with people like him." With that, she stormed up the stairs to her room and slammed the door behind her.

Xenia understood their contradicting roles, but she had only spent a few minutes with him. Nothing harmful. She didn't know why he wanted to walk her home; they were supposed to be enemies, not friends. The line that drew them apart was bold.

Before retiring to her room, Xenia assured that the kitchen was clean for the morning and then blew out all the candles downstairs. After moving all of her things into one room, the space seemed to shrink. She wove between her bed and drawer and set the book onto her nightstand.

Blake had suspected it was just an old journal, but Xenia had never been able to pull herself away. She flipped through the yellowed pages, studying the foreign characters that lined each one. She knew little about it, aside from the information scattered on notes throughout the pages.

On one page "Last time successfully performed 1403" was scribbled into the corner. On another, a small note read, "Jewel of," but she couldn't read the rest of the smudged ink. The most interesting note stuck between the pages rose a question of whether fate was truly inevitable.

Blake may have been correct, but the possibility failed to waver her fascination for the book.

Chapter Four

THE NEXT MORNING, XENIA WOKE TO WARM SUNLIGHT on her face. Something sweet filled the air.

Karielyn must be baking.

She pushed off her heavy comforter and pulled herself out of bed. Hastily, she straightened the ruffled sheets, and then she stepped towards her door and reached for the handle, yawning.

Light bled through the high window above the living room, filling the tower. Downstairs, Karielyn Height stood in the kitchen below the landing, humming softly to herself. Her head snapped in Xenia's direction as she entered the room. "Good morning, Nia," she said with a smile.

Xenia blinked. No one had called her that since Blake left four years ago. "Good morning," she returned.

Atop the counter, Karielyn had a small carton of strawberries marked with a stamp from a local fruit farmer. With her tight training schedule, Xenia only stopped there on occasion, but she had bought those a few days prior.

"I didn't want to use your things," Karielyn said, "but you were still asleep, and I was hungry."

Xenia reddened from embarrassment. *How late is it?* "How long have you been awake?"

Karielyn smiled. Dimples appeared on her clear face, and the morning light danced across her skin. "Nearly three hours. I wanted time to unpack my things." She narrowed her eyes at Xenia. "Aren't you going to put on proper clothes?"

Xenia looked down at her night slip and blushed harder. Karielyn already wore a rosy, lace dress that clung to her figure. It couldn't have come from Chantendell. All of Xenia's dresses were locally sewn and consisted of dark-red and black velvets and silks.

Karielyn turned back to her dish. She had made a flakey pastry topped with white sugar and chopped berries. "Would you like me to make you breakfast as well?"

Xenia's brows pinched in thought. "No, thank you. I think I'll eat in the dining hall." Most days the last place Xenia wanted to be was in the dining hall with the other students, but this morning their indirect disapproval seemed more bearable then Karielyn's blatant criticism.

Before Karielyn had a chance to make another comment, Xenia hurried back to her room to change. She dressed in a simple, black dress that laced up the front, paired with a pearl bracelet her mother had gifted her for her eighteenth birthday. She studied her appearance in the mirror that hung on her back wall before returning downstairs.

Karielyn stood in the living room, her eyes narrowed. "Have you thought about redecorating? The colors in here are a little dull," she said.

The sitting room had a gray couch and oak end table provided by the Training Center. Some of Xenia's things lined the fireplace mantle, though the tower still looked mostly like it had when she moved in.

"I think it's fine," she replied.

"Well, I don't like it," Karielyn said distractedly.

A wooden box sat on the end table, filled with small items that lay between cuts of silk. Karielyn took a white vase from the box and set it onto the mantle, where Xenia had previously kept a painting of Chantendell's symbol: a crown in a circle of seven stars.

Karielyn faced the fireplace, her eyes narrowed.

"I think it looks fine," Xenia said.

Karielyn's lips rose, though she didn't smile. "Oh, Xenia, nothing about this tower is *fine*."

She picked up a small, marble sculpture; turned it around in her hand; and then returned it to its place. "Most everything in this room needs to go."

Xenia no longer watched to see what else she would move or change. "I'm going to the dining hall now," she said, crossing the room and placing her hand on the door.

"Okay," Karielyn said.

Xenia pulled open the door and stepped into the cool air. The sun was high, but dark clouds threatened to mute it. The normally brilliant-green grass faded to a faint yellow. Flowers guarding the tower doors had lost their petals and withered. The end of the year was approaching, draining Xenia of her time to enter her story.

She walked over to the stone path and started for the dining hall. Though Karielyn didn't treat her as badly as others, she knew how to crawl beneath her skin.

Xenia reached the doors to the dining hall, and the loud buzz of conversation greeted her inside. Seven rows of long tables stretched across the room, each one filled nearly completely. Xenia kept her head down as she wove between students, searching for an empty spot far enough away from anyone that wouldn't appreciate her company.

"Xenia?"

She stilled at Felix's voice before turning to face him.

"I don't see you here often." He smiled. "Would you like to sit with me?"

Her forehead creased and she took a step back. "I shouldn't—"

"It won't hurt anything. Come on, we're over here," he said, motioning towards the farthest table to the right.

Unsure what to say to dissuade him, she followed him to his table.

People gave her scolding looks as she passed—aside from the girls who had shouted at Samuel last night; they smiled at her with a laugh following closely.

Felix reclaimed his seat and Xenia sat opposite him, next to a strong boy with mangled, black hair. He grimaced when he noticed her sitting beside him.

A few of the students silenced themselves at her presence. Felix seemed not to notice the change and motioned to a young, dark-haired boy. "This is Merrick, he's the hero of the class beneath ours," he said.

Turning to a girl with dark skin and thick curls, Felix said, "That's Victoria. She's the queen of our story."

Xenia already knew Victoria: they used to be friends when they both lived in the Dwelling of Royals, but she hadn't talked to Xenia since she turned fourteen. Since she got her fate.

"Why are you talking to *her*?" Victoria asked, brushing her hair over her bare shoulder. The silky, red dress she wore molded to her thin figure and showed off more of her chest than Xenia was comfortable seeing.

"Why shouldn't I?" he returned.

Victoria narrowed her eyes. Xenia sensed her anger towards her, but she couldn't decide if it was because Felix was talking to her or because she was there at all.

"I haven't seen you in so long. Don't you do anything without Blake?" she said, leaning in enough for Xenia to catch the scent of her flowery perfume.

To calm herself, Xenia started fiddling with the hem of her velvet sleeve. "I just…" She turned away from Victoria's dark-brown eyes. "I've been busy."

Victoria hummed in response and shook her head. "You should have stayed away." Her voice lowered. "You don't belong around people like us."

Felix frowned and glared at Victoria but said nothing.

Xenia took even breaths to keep her cheeks from coloring. The table's other occupants were all listening to Victoria. A few of them whispered in one another's ears.

Don't listen! It didn't matter what they thought. *My fate doesn't define me!* She tried to convince herself that that was the truth, but it wasn't. Her fate did define her.

"I should leave," she said. "Something's come up."

A grim smile spread across Victoria's face. "But nothing came up." She placed a hand on her exposed chest. "Unless I'm mistaken."

"I… I'm really busy today."

"Really? Well, then, if you must."

"You haven't even eaten yet," Felix said.

"I know, but I have somewhere to be." It was a lie. Xenia knew it sounded just as fabricated to everyone else as it felt to her.

She stood and, without giving him time to respond, passed the tables full of students who wanted nothing to do with her. In quick strides, she exited the dining hall.

She attempted to push the exchange from her mind but had no luck. It didn't matter what Victoria thought of her. She had more important things to worry about.

Her attention shifted finally when she remembered what Karielyn had said the day before. Xenia didn't want her going through her room, but a part of her thanked her for it because she had answered one question about the mysterious book: it was in Elisoran.

The reminder of the book and the notes scribbled in it brought to mind a new thought. What happened in the year 1403? The year written into the book?

The Training Center campus was composed of multiple brick buildings—the dining hall; hero and villain classrooms;

the main building, where they met for other classes; and the library. Xenia started towards the latter.

The library had tall spires and stained windows that caught the morning sun as the clouds concealing it shifted. Xenia pulled open one of the double doors and entered the library.

Inside, endless rows of leather-bound volumes lined the large hall. Between shelves sat oak tables and chairs. Tall windows between aisles let in enough light to read during the day, and glass chandeliers lit the library at night.

Xenia approached the librarian behind the desk at the front of the room.

"How may I help you?" he asked, looking up from the musty catalogue he'd been studying.

"I'd like to look at the story from 1403."

The librarian nodded and flipped through the catalog. "That book is in the forbidden library—do you have permission?"

Her heart fell; she didn't want to go into the forbidden library, but now she wanted to know what had happened that year to have earned it a place there.

The books kept in the forbidden library were the ones that didn't have happy endings. Not all heroes won. Their stories were kept in the most secure areas of libraries and bookstores in Chantendell. Xenia had only been there once before, when one of her teachers gave her a list of books with successful villains to read for homework. The book had left her stomach churning.

After a few seconds of hesitation, she said, "No, can I

get permission?"

Again, he nodded and reached for a paper log with a short list of names. He handed it to her and she signed it, and then he gave her a slip with written permission to access the forbidden section. She held her breath as she took it from him. The school monitored who requested permission. Her trainers would likely be notified. It wasn't hard to obtain permission, but she imagined purchasing a forbidden book would be more difficult.

She brought it to the entrance of the forbidden library at the back of the room, and a guard took the slip from her and unlocked the door.

The forbidden section was colder than the rest of the library. There were no windows to let in sunlight, and fewer candles had been relit after burning out. Another librarian worked from a desk in the center of the room. She requested the story from 1403, and he led her down a shadowed aisle.

"Well, it should be right here," he said, gesturing towards an opening on the otherwise tight shelf. "But someone else requested the same title just this morning, and it appears he borrowed the only copy."

Xenia's heart sank.

Books lined shelf after shelf and row after row. A blanket of dust dulled nearly every volume. Why would someone choose the same day as her to look for this one? Whoever had taken it must have had the same thoughts as her. Karielyn and Felix were the only ones around to hear last night, and Karielyn never left the tower—had Felix taken the book she wanted?

Chapter Five

"I'M SORRY, MISS," THE LIBRARIAN SAID. "IF YOU'D LIKE I could—"

"Thank you," Xenia said, already turning around. "I'll come back another time."

She returned to the main library, relieved to no longer be surrounded by haunting tales, and started for the exit.

"Xenia!" Karielyn's voice made her heart jump.

She spun to face her. Karielyn stood near a shelf a few aisles back.

Xenia walked towards her. "What are you doing here?"

"You hardly eat in the dining hall since Blake left. I knew you'd be here. You want to translate your book now that you know what language it's in."

"Actually—"

"I'll help you if you'd like."

Xenia hesitated. She *hadn't* come here to translate the book, but now that Karielyn proposed the idea, she couldn't bring herself to turn her down.

"Fine. But I don't have my book—"

"I do!" Karielyn smiled and brushed past her towards the front desk. Xenia hardly had time to process her words before hurrying to join her.

"What can I help you with now?" he asked.

"I need books on the Elisoran language," Xenia answered, already peering around the shelves as if she might find them upfront. She wouldn't, of course; Elisora wasn't very populated, and people that could speak the language were scarce in Moira.

"This way," he said, motioning behind them.

Xenia followed him to the back of the library, and he pointed at a small section of paper-bound books. Xenia smiled at the small collection. She had longed to uncover the book's secrets for years.

"Thank you," she said to the man as he began walking away.

Reaching for a few of the denser books, she pulled them off the shelf and then sat at a wooden table with a chair on either side. She and opened the first book, glancing up at Karielyn. "So, you know Elisoran?"

"More than you," Karielyn snapped, tossing a book onto the table. "My mother is a linguist. She owns books on all different languages—I've read books on all different languages. I may not speak Elisoran fluently, but I know enough to get further than you have."

Xenia didn't mention that she hadn't gotten *anywhere* yet. All she had were the past owner's notes.

And it may be related to Fate, she thought, keeping herself from thinking too deeply about the note. Fate was inevitable—Xenia would disappoint herself by hoping otherwise.

Karielyn pulled Xenia's book from her bag, and it fell open. As she bent over it, whispering beneath her breath, Xenia began reading the books she'd taken from the shelf. Each book had similar information, but she looked through each one diligently.

As they worked, she found herself doing little more than juggling books for Karielyn as she studied the flowy symbols in the book. When she found something, she made more notes on the pages.

After what felt like hours, Xenia closed another book and rested her head between her hands. They were making slow progress, but they had managed to translate a few sentences. She glanced at what they'd written so far: *Two willing to change the way written on the scrolls. To find the jewel hidden higher than the clouds or lower than the sea, it lurks where magic is the most. Then climb above the clouds and do the unspeakable deed.* It was the passage below one of the old notes.

Karielyn gasped. "Let me see the paper, I've got something else!"

She dipped her pen into ink and wrote quickly. Xenia leaned closer to watch the words appear, her chest seizing. *The Jewel of Fate—ability to switch the fate of two willing personages. WARNING: highly dangerous, if failed may result in imprisonment or death.*

The air became hot as Xenia stared at the words. Her head spun until she felt sick. Was her fate as unavoidable as she had formerly believed?

As she read it again, her excitement fell. *Two willing personages. Who would be willing to switch fates with me, especially if it's illegal?*

"I also found a passage that someone wrote in," Karielyn said. "'Last time successfully performed 1403' and 'very illegal.' That must have been the last year someone successfully switched their fate."

Xenia couldn't manage more than staring at the words while she tried to get her thoughts in order.

"What 'came up'?" Felix asked from behind the table.

Xenia jumped at his sudden arrival and slammed the book closed. Had he overheard what they'd said? She didn't want to give him another reason to report her. They should have gone back to their tower, but no one ever came to talk to Xenia.

While she scrambled for an answer, Karielyn muttered something and left her at the table alone. Hesitantly, she explained a seemingly harmless lie. "I have a lot of homework." She moved her hand to cover the title of one of the books so he couldn't see what she was actually doing.

That made him smile. "Well, I don't have any. If you want, I could help."

She almost choked, staring at him in disbelief. "*You* will help *me* with homework?" Even repeating what he had said felt wrong. "This is for *Villain Studies.*"

"I assumed as much." Something like a smile flickered across his features. Without any further convincing he slipped into the seat next to hers. "Show me what you have."

Taking a deep breath, Xenia grabbed her bag off the ground and took out her papers. As she reached for a quill, Felix picked them up.

He examined the page and ran his finger down the line of points as if counting the questions. "This shouldn't take us long. You've read *The Way of a Villain*, haven't you?"

Setting the quill onto the table, she said, "Only for class, yes." She reached for the papers, but Felix pulled away.

His brows drew together and his light-brown eyes narrowed. "You don't like your Fate?"

"Not in the slightest." The words left her mouth with swift regret. Should she have told him that? Many people knew how she felt about her fate, she couldn't pretend she enjoyed it. But… could he use that against her in their story?

Butterflies beat against her chest. Was all he wanted information to use against her later? Her teachers had told her that knowing Felix's weaknesses would be an advantage, though she never cared to learn them. She knew Blake—she didn't want to know another enemy.

"Well, then…" Felix said after a moment. She waited for more, but it never came.

"Let's start," he said, setting the paper down onto the table between them. He took the quill and began writing. His hand flew across the page as he wrote, as if the answers came from memory.

"What are you doing?" she asked. "You're supposed to *help* me, not do it for me!"

He laughed under his breath. "But you don't want to do it, right?" He continued writing answers, stopping occasionally as if reconsidering what he had written, yet he never changed anything. "I'll just do it for you."

Was this his way of mocking her? A wave of panic swept over her. Had she been too vulnerable? Maybe he wanted her to fail and all his answers were incorrect. Why else would he help her? *He's supposed to be my enemy!*

"I can't cheat." The words formed, but she didn't fully comprehend what she had said.

His hand glided across the sheet as the paper absorbed the ink leaving gracefully formed letters. Even if she let him do this, her teacher would never believe it to be her writing.

"You're not, I am. And even if you were, cheating isn't the worst thing a villain could do. I'm sure your teacher would love to hear you've been cheating."

Xenia groaned. Why was he doing this? Why did he *want* to do this?

She leaned over the table and watched him write. "Felix, this isn't right." She needed to leave. Heroes didn't help villains. Not for any good reason. She never should have agreed to this.

"I'm not making you… uncomfortable, am I? I don't mean to, I just thought I might get to know you better." He said it in such a kind way. But what did he mean by it? Why would he want to know anything about her?

It's a tactic. If he knows more about me, he'll use it against me later.

Xenia glared sadly at the ground from the thought. Would anyone want to know her genuinely?

"We're not supposed to…"

"In case you ever change your mind, I'll be available to simply *help*."

"I really shouldn't. But—thank you anyway." She couldn't understand why he wanted to help her, but she knew not to let herself get close to him. Blake being her destined enemy was already hard enough. "I'm really sorry, I wish I could stay longer, but our fates—"

"I understand, it's fine."

When she finished packing her things into her bag, Felix stood up and offered to lead her to the door. He once again offered to walk her home, but she declined and left the library alone.

She didn't know Felix Liftson well, but Blake used to mention him. "There's something wrong with him," he had told her when Felix first moved in. "He never talks."

She had struggled to believe it. Felix was always busy with someone. He didn't fit the descriptions Blake had given her.

She didn't think much longer about Felix. Her thoughts were still stuck on her and Karielyn's finding in the library. If this Jewel of Fate truly existed, could she use it to evade her fate?

Karielyn's morning tea filled the air, and her light-color scheme swept across the tower. When Xenia woke and joined her downstairs, she hardly recognized it. Nothing was left the way it had been when she went to sleep, and nothing looked like hers.

Karielyn's light decorations now sat in place of the small things Xenia once kept on the fireplace mantle. The only thing that hadn't been moved was a drawing of Blake from five years ago.

"What happened to my things?" she asked, stopping at Karielyn's side.

As she arranged pink roses in the vase on the mantle, Karielyn said, "I moved them. I thought you could keep your things in your room."

Xenia clenched her teeth, fighting back a foul comment about Karielyn's things or sharing the tower. Karielyn knew it wasn't fair; she didn't need Xenia to tell her. She wanted to elicit a reaction, that was it. Why, Xenia didn't know. Had she ever done anything to Karielyn?

Without arguing, Xenia took her things from a pile formed on the couch and set them in her room.

While Karielyn continued decorating downstairs, Xenia pulled out her homework and glanced at the page. It was mostly finished—thanks to Felix—but there were a few questions left. She meant to answer the remaining questions but instead found herself reading Felix's writing. A knock on the door finally tore her from the page.

Karielyn got to the door before Xenia could reach the bottom of the stairs.

"Why are you here?" Karielyn snapped.

"Certainly not to see you," Felix Liftson returned. "Is Xenia here?"

Before Karielyn could answer, Xenia met him at the

door. "Yes, I'm here."

"I was wondering if I could borrow your book."

Her brow fell. "The one in Elisoran?"

"Yeah, that one," he said with a trace of a smile.

He must have been recalling her fight with Karielyn. *Why did he have to see that?*

"Do you know something about it?"

His eyes flashed away from hers. "Not enough, unfortunately. I'm doing some research and thought your book might have an answer for me."

Karielyn cocked her head as her eyes narrowed on him. "No. Her answer is no."

Xenia held up hand to stop her. "Researching what?" She wanted it to sound more demanding, but it came out soft. She took a deep breath and regretted it immediately when she caught a trace of his papery-fresh smell and felt her cheeks grow hot.

He hesitated. "It's complicated. I… never mind that."

What didn't he want to tell her? Did he plan on giving the book to someone at the school? Was he already trying to get her in trouble?

"Well, we're reading it and we aren't done yet, so you'll have to wait," Karielyn told him. She spoke to him with a certain confidence, as if she expected him to dance across her words on invisible strings. No one else spoke to him in such a way. Xenia didn't want to give him the book, but she couldn't bring herself to tell him that, so she silently thanked Karielyn.

"But—is there anything else you need?" Xenia asked,

trying to break the tension that swarmed around the room.

Felix glared, silent. After several moments, he said, "Actually, yes. Xenia, would you speak to me outside? Alone?"

Before she could respond, Karielyn gave a warning glance. "Xenia, don't. He's not—"

"Yes," Xenia said, ending Karielyn's protests.

He moved aside to let her out of the tower and gave Karielyn a final glance before he turned and left. The room rattled as he closed the door.

His features were set like stone—his eyes narrow and his lips straight. Worry poured into her as he faced her. She couldn't stop her heart from beating in a warning-like rhythm.

"What—what did you want?"

"I heard what you were talking about yesterday, at the library. If that's something you want, meet me at the fountain tonight."

Chapter Six

SOMEONE SUCCESSFULLY SWITCHED THEIR FATE.

Those words refused to leave Felix Liftson's thoughts.

"Maybe that was the last year someone successfully switched their fate." That was what Karielyn had said.

He smiled.

In the locked room in his tower, Felix sat at his desk, scribbling notes on old story. He found the villain in the story quite intriguing—but he had always found the schemes of the villains more fascinating than the heroes that messed them up.

He had stayed up deep into the night to read the story from 1403, and by the time the sun came up, he had finished it. Already he had started reading a second time. This story had brought him closer to hope than he'd come in so long.

He found more hidden between the lines than an average good-versus-evil battle. More than once he found himself reading over the same line until it took on a new meaning. The difference was subtle; someone had intended to cover it up. Still, Felix noticed.

The villain in this book had *traded* her fate with the hero.

And as he read deeper into the book, he found himself wishing he could do the same. His father constantly boasted about his victories, telling Felix that he would be the next *Great Liftson*—but being the next Liftson hero wasn't on the list of things that he wanted to be.

Forsaking his heroic title had seemed like a fantasy—until yesterday at the library. He had enough information already to know that Xenia's book had everything to do with the switch of fate in this one.

"Felix, we'll lose our carriage if we don't leave now!" Merrick, his roommate, called from outside his door.

Felix groaned. Couldn't he have one night to stay in his room alone? He spent nearly every night with his *friends* finding lavish, new places to dine or dance. He lived a life that others longed for. But he didn't want it. If he could erase his name from every paper and blend into a crowd the way others could, he would choose it over what he had. Because what he had wasn't *glamorous* or *freeing*. Most days it felt like a prison. He couldn't escape the people that acted like they knew him better than they did. Or the way women treated him and men spoke to him. Everyone wanted to be *something* to him. And often, he wanted no part of them.

He closed his book and hid it in a drawer and he blew out his candles.

If his father weren't a famous hero, no one would care about him. And that made all the attention and praise harder to handle. The people who really knew him didn't love him like that.

After forcing himself from his room, he left the tower with Merrick and they met Victoria Vanday and Warren, one of her fated guards, by the stables. Together, they climbed into the carriage prepared to take them to the tavern.

The ride through Chantendell was beautiful. The kingdom was alluring, but Felix wanted to live in the country. It seemed simpler. He could sacrifice the lit buildings and old architecture if it meant he could spend his nights alone.

Beside him, Victoria spoke about her favorite places. He appeared to be listening, though he wasn't. When she made a point, he would nod, even if he didn't understand enough to agree. She didn't seem to notice and didn't stop to let him speak the entire trip.

They arrived at a large, dimly lit building that resembled a stone castle chamber. Inside, performers played music on a wooden platform with instruments Felix couldn't name. A host led them to a table close to the stage, and a woman dressed in all black came to serve them.

Felix requested the same dish he had the last time he spent the night out. The woman scribbled down the order on a piece of paper and looked at the others expectantly.

"I'll have the same thing," Victoria said in a flirtatious tone. The others ordered, and the server took her notes back to the kitchen.

"So, Felix," Victoria asked, tracing her varnished nail along the rim of her glass. "Why were you with Safire?" She drawled the words as if she expected his answer to be something misleading.

Felix wished he were spending the evening with Xenia instead. Not because she had a pretty face or a good reputation, simply because she was interesting—she was a villain.

Shaking his head, he said, "We were only talking, no reason." A part of him urged to say more, something that would remind Victoria of his fate. That was what his father would have done. Felix had stopped listening to that part of him too late.

"Well, you should be more careful. You know how your fates contradict—I would hate to see you hurt."

Felix restrained from rolling his eyes. He knew Xenia wasn't bad. She was far from it. It made him wonder why she would be a villain. Then again, he also questioned his own fate—what made him *heroic*? "I'm not afraid of her."

Merrick and Warren laughed at his comment as if it had been a joke. Felix assumed they had taken it to degrade Xenia. He forced himself to smile and join them.

The server returned to their table before Victoria could make another comment, carrying steaming plates of food. Felix thanked her, and the woman blushed as she left to the next table.

"Have you thought more about when you'll enter our story?" Victoria asked him.

He watched the steam drift away from the tender slices of meat as he struggled to find an answer. He had earned permission years ago, but he wasn't looking forward to fulfilling his fate. Unfortunately, waiting as long as he could to enter his story wouldn't change his fate.

But maybe something else will. His mind went back to the book. Back on Liz Eveyon, the girl who had undoubtedly changed her fate.

"I don't know yet, I'll enter eventually," he said in attempt to bring his mind back to the tavern, which smelled incredible. He could practically taste the steak burning on the fire in the room behind him.

"Well, I was planning on entering in Yule. We could enter at the same time!" Victoria had recently earned permission to enter their story, and Felix had yet to hear the end of it.

"I don't think I'll be ready by then," he said. Even if he would be, he would wait just to spare himself the extra time with Victoria. Their relationship was nothing that her behavior implied.

He turned back to the table and tried to focus on something other than his current circumstances. Days like these— over many years—had equipped him with a strength for acting. These and the times his father told him about his battle against Ravelyn Kage. Hiding his true emotions had simply become a need. Though, lately, he had been testing his limits. When everyone respected him because of something an ancestor did, it proved hard to lose that respect.

Felix ate slowly, his mind not quite where he wanted it to be, but he still finished faster than the others, who spent more time talking than eating.

After dinner, they joined the group of dancers by the stage. The smile on Felix's face was nothing more than a mask of his emotion. *Smile, even when they're harassing you. Smile.*

It was part of the advice given to him from his father during one of his many lectures on how to deal with the people that never let him breathe… as well as one of the only bits of his advice Felix willingly followed. He found it easier to wear a smile as a mask than to face the insincere questions he'd receive when he showed anything else.

Victoria danced to the music as if she knew the song, though he doubted she had even heard it before. She moved to face him and lifted her finger, tracing the line of his jaw. Then she clasped her hands behind his neck. He tensed at her unwelcome touch, smiling slightly to cover his discomfort. She swayed to the song's rhythm.

Sensing Merrick's and Warren's gaze on them, he put his hands on her waist. His body was rigid despite the years he had spent appeasing Victoria.

As soon as the song ended, he pulled away and suggested they leave. Smiling, Victoria agreed. He had done what she wanted. She knew what he felt when she touched him, and she knew who was in control, because despite his position, she knew he could never stop her. It would break his perfect façade.

Outside the tavern, the music faded, and the laughter and conversation that filled the street took its place. They passed the stables, where their carriage waited. Felix longed to return to it and end the night early, but without discussion, they kept walking along the strip of buildings. His chances of being recognized and stopped would only increase the longer they spent out. Most people had no way to recognize him, but enough had seen family portraits or attended an event that he had. Even people who didn't know him would often stop and stare. His finely tailored clothes and air of confidence was enough to indicate he was of *importance*.

Victoria led the way through the people gathered on the streets, paying no mind to who stood in her way and forcing the crowd to part as they passed. Once they left the busier streets and it became quiet, the three others resumed their trivial conversation. Felix kept his eyes fixed on the cobblestone, excluding himself. Fire from the streetlamps cast unsteady shadows across the rocks.

"Felix?" Victoria said, shaking him from his thoughts.

"Hmm?"

"You haven't been listening," she commented. "I said you should ask your father to visit the Training Center more often."

"Everyone loved his dinner the other day," Warren added.

Not everyone, Felix thought. Irritation sparked inside of him at the mention of his father and his unexpected visit. *He can show up for dinner unannounced, yet he can't remember my birthdate.*

Despite himself, Felix could have laughed at Victoria's request. Nothing he said would have any influence over his father.

"If I even see him before his next visit," he said, masking his honesty with a laugh. He likely *wouldn't* see Samuel until they both ended up at the same event.

"You left early," Merrick said as they turned down a dark alley. "Did something happen?"

Felix shook his head. "I needed fresh air and got a bit distracted. Nothing happened."

"We missed you," Victoria said.

"You see me every day," he teased.

She rolled her eyes and then draped her arm over his shoulder. "How late is it?"

"Late enough," he said. "We should head back now." The earlier he could get back to his tower, the happier he would be, though he would be fine with anything so long as he was back at the Training Center by midnight.

They left the alley and turned down another main street, back towards the stables.

At the carriage, Felix spoke to the coachman, requesting a ride back to the Training Center. Then he joined the others in the warm cabin.

The Training Center courtyard was quiet when they returned. The cobblestone path was lit by yellow-tinted lanterns that lined the path. Felix and Merrick walked back to their tower, and Victoria and Warren separated to go to theirs.

Once they were back, Felix went up to his room and stayed there until he was sure Merrick was asleep. If he saw Felix leaving alone in the middle of the night, he wouldn't let him go unquestioned.

Avoiding Merrick didn't inconvenience him. Even with his former roommate, Blake Cedar, he spent as many nights as he could get away with locked upstairs.

While he waited for the clock ticking on his desk to chime midnight, he pulled out his book and flipped through the worn pages. Though he had learned a lot from it, he wanted to read Xenia's book. Then he could know more about the strange subject—more about trading fates.

If Xenia didn't come, he would never have another chance like this. But he had done all he could to persuade her. Shortly before leaving for dinner, he had left a reminder at her door. She likely hadn't forgotten, but he needed her to know how important this was to him. If she didn't show up, he would be stuck with his unanswered questions and unwavering fate.

Chapter Seven

THE CLOCK IN XENIA'S ROOM TICKED CLOSER TO MID-night. She needed to leave now if she wanted to make it in time. Some part of her wanted to meet Felix enough to keep her up until midnight, watching the clock, yet unsurety stopped her from leaving the tower.

Couldn't they have met before midnight? Felix had acted strange before, but did that make him untrustworthy? Even though she wanted to meet him and trust him, she still had a reoccurring thought lingering in her mind.

He's a hero. He's my destined enemy.

Anything they did together would come to a violent end. And he would be seen as the hero no matter what he did to her. What if he only wanted to mess with her? That was what she thought when he had offered to walk her home, but nothing happened. Surely nothing would happen now. She kept telling herself that until she found the courage to leave.

Frost iced the windows, so she grabbed a cardigan and then walked to the door. She hesitated before opening it and letting the cool air rush in. Without further thought, she stepped into the dark night and closed the door behind her. The last of the candlelight that spilled out of the tower vanished, and the moon became the only thing that lit her path.

Xenia crossed the courtyard, straining to see in the dark. No windows were lit, and the lanterns that lined the path had burned out.

The fountain water rushed in the distance, still working when the rest of the school had quieted. Xenia followed the sound to the center of the courtyard.

She stopped at the fountain, but Felix wasn't there. Her stomach turned. Would he come? Fear numbed her with the possible reasons he hadn't shown up. He might not be coming alone. Or maybe he wanted to send her out alone just to disappoint her.

Or maybe he's just late. He might be afraid too.

She breathed in the crisp air and then sat at the base of the water fountain. Waiting a few more minutes wouldn't hurt.

The moon's reflection rippled on the surface of the water. On her first week of training, someone told her and Blake that the fountain was filled with liquefied diamond in place of water. She didn't believe it, but it made her believe she shouldn't touch it.

"Xenia?"

She jumped up and spun around to face Felix. He stood behind her, just off of the path to the men's towers.

"Hi," she said quietly.

"Hi," he echoed, smiling.

Despite the cold, Xenia felt her anxieties melt away. Something about this felt right. Like fate had had this moment planned from the very second they met.

Felix reached her side, and his smile faded. "You're trembling, here, take my jacket," he said, pulling it off and resting it on her shoulders.

She opened her mouth to argue, but his heavy jacket did much more against the cold than her cardigan. Instead, she thanked him.

He sat on the fountain, and she sat back down beside him. "About what I overheard at the library—"

"I'm not even sure it's real," Xenia said. The concern had nagged at her all night.

"I am," Felix said, "I believe, if you give me time, I can present proof."

Proof? How would he be able to prove it—especially without a translated version of the book?

"Tell me exactly what it said," he said, moving closer to her.

"It mentions this jewel—the Jewel of Fate." As she spoke, his eyes lit despite the dark. "It said it has the power to switch the fates of two willing personages."

"So, if you found this jewel, all you would need is someone to switch with." His voice was filled with enthusiasm. "I would switch with you."

His words caught her off guard. Why would he want to switch with *her?* She couldn't imagine a Liftson villain. Or a

Liftson that wanted to be a villain.

"Why?" she managed to ask.

His smile wavered slightly. "I'm not the fondest of my fate, either."

"But you're a *Liftson*, how can you not be happy with your fate?"

He grimaced. "It—it's complicated. But I can't be another hero. I can't be like my father."

His answer left her more confused than she had been before the question.

"Is the jewel somewhere in Chantendell?"

"I don't know. We only have a small bit translated. It's mostly in Elisoran." Xenia hadn't thought about the jewel's location. What if it was somewhere else, like Elisora? Or somewhere guarded like the palace?

"I could help you translate it."

Her brows wrinkled. "I don't understand why you want this."

He breathed out and looked down. "I can't give you a reason, but I *need* this, Xenia. Please, if you want it to, will you take this chance?"

She closed her eyes. She imagined her life if she weren't a villain and her future if she wasn't exiled. She longed to have a different fate. Did Felix truly want the same thing?

She met his gaze. Sincerity painted his expression and filled his eyes.

"You really want this?" she asked, her voice failing.

He nodded once. "More than anything else."

"Me too."

A gentle smile played at his lips. "Then we'll look for the jewel."

Xenia's blood turned to ice, but now that the possibility hung so close, she couldn't risk giving it up. "The book might tell us where to look, if we can translate the whole thing."

"Then we'll do that," Felix decided. He hesitated. "Can we keep this between the two of us?"

"I have no one to tell."

He shook his head. "I mean Karielyn. If we translate the book, I want to do it without Karielyn."

Did he think Karielyn would tell someone and they'd get in trouble? Something told Xenia that she wouldn't. In a way she couldn't understand, she trusted her with this secret.

"I'm not sure if I'll be able to translate it without her."

His lips tightened and he turned away, looking up at the moon. "We can find a way to translate it without her. I think it will be… easier that way."

"Easier?" Karielyn was the only reason Xenia knew what she did about the book.

"Yeah, a lot easier. Trust me," he assured.

"Fine. It will stay between us," she said. "But we can't hide it from her forever, she is my allegiant."

The last part felt odd on her tongue. She meant it to be a hint, letting him know she still wanted Karielyn's help—but she'd never cared about her before.

He clenched his teeth, fighting the cold. "We'll tell her eventually, but it can wait, we need to figure it out ourselves first."

"Yeah, of course."

A chill breeze passed through their hair. She glanced at Felix again, his eyes remained warm despite the bumps coating his skin. "Are you cold?" she asked, reaching for the jacket, but he shook his head and pulled her hand from the sleeve.

"I'm fine."

"Are you sure?"

"Yes, I'm fine," he confirmed. Then, as if denying his previous words, added, "Is it snowing?"

Xenia squinted. Dust-like snow fell from the sky, sparkling as if it were glitter dancing away from a spinning skirt.

He picked up her hand, catching her off guard. "If we succeed, this will change the course of our lives forever. It might if we fail too. Will you risk that?"

She held her breath. This could give her everything she wanted, but it could also take away everything she had. She could continue her life as she had without risking anything but remaining a villain. Or she could accept Felix Liftson's offer to take her place. The latter option risked everything and could leave her with nothing. But becoming a villain would do just the same. And right now, she didn't know what she was risking, only what she would gain if they succeeded. Was the possibility enough to commit to the unknown challenge ahead?

"I will."

Felix's eyes bored into hers, silently communicating that his thoughts mirrored hers. By attempting this, they subjected both of their lives to dangers they would likely never face if they didn't.

Do I have more to lose than gain? She wondered if he was thinking the same thing.

"I hope this works."

He rose to his feet. "I believe it will."

Chapter Eight

XENIA TURNED TO STONE AS SHE PULLED OPEN THE DOOR to her tower. Karielyn sat by the lit fire, arms crossed.

"Really, Xenia?"

"I just—"

"I heard you leave. And I found the note. Do you know what kind of risk that was?"

Xenia hugged her arms for warmth. Felix's jacket fit her loosely, and the sleeves covered her fingers. "I know I shouldn't have, but he…"

"He's charming and persuasive. But you're a villain and he's a hero. Whatever it is he wants from you will only be to his advantage."

Xenia didn't need to hear Karielyn vocalize the concerns she already had. She knew Felix didn't have good intentions. No one willing to become a villain would. But she could make a deal with him without it becoming anything more. "I know. I'll be careful."

"I don't think you understand. There's no good reason for Felix to speak to you. He's a bad person. I know you think you're being careful, but please, don't take any chances with him."

What was there for Xenia to misunderstand? She knew the danger that engaging with him involved. "I won't do anything reckless."

"What did he say?"

"It was nothing," she said, biting back the truth.

Karielyn rolled her eyes and pushed herself off of her couch.

"What?" Xenia asked.

"Well, I find him kind of… *deceitful*."

"Karielyn, he's a *hero*—"

"You're a villain, are you bad?" she asked.

Xenia didn't respond but felt her cheeks grow hot.

"Well? I don't think your fate changes you, so why can't he be an untrustworthy hero?"

What did she have against him? He hadn't done anything wrong. "He isn't untrustworthy, I don't understand what you see in him." She stood still and met her gaze.

Karielyn crossed her arms. "It's not what *I* see in him, it's what you *don't*," she snapped.

"And what do you know about him that I don't?" Xenia asked, mimicking her and folding her arms.

Why am I defending him?

Karielyn's cheeks glowed pink, matching her hair. She turned for the stairs and disappeared inside her room, slamming the door closed.

Xenia scoffed. She didn't need Karielyn to tell her what to do or who to be wary of. She had lived alone for four years at a school full of people who didn't like her; she didn't need her now.

In the morning, a film of frost coated the windows, and sparkling snow covered the ground outside. The endless white looked like a fresh start. Xenia bit her lip, covering her smile. For the first time, she felt like she had also been granted a fresh start.

She dressed for the cold day and tied her hair in a braid. Before leaving the tower, she slipped on Felix's oversized jacket.

Breakfast lasted an hour each morning, she hoped to find Felix there now. She could return his jacket and maybe speak more about the switch before class started.

The snow along the path to the dining hall was nearly melted from the stream of students going to breakfast. Xenia walked slowly, watching for patches of ice.

She reached the dining hall and pulled open the heavy door. The cavernous room was full of lively chatter and laughter. Some people quieted as she passed; others gave her a quick glance but kept talking.

She spotted Karielyn sitting alone at the farthest table from the door and decided to speak to her first. Karielyn's face hardened when she saw her.

Xenia frowned and slid onto the bench beside her. "I'm

sorry about last night."

Karielyn shrugged. "Oh, I was only being overly cautious." She stood up and added in a bitter tone, "Have fun with Felix."

Xenia turned as she stomped off and *almost* walked into Felix.

"Hello, Height, you might want to watch where you're going," he said briskly.

She groaned. "Thanks, I wouldn't want to keep running into *you*, would I?" she replied.

He walked past her and filled the seat next to Xenia. "Why didn't you come sit with me?"

"I wanted to tell Karielyn something. We can move to your table if you want."

"No," he said, shaking his head. "I like it over here, it's not as loud. Let's stay right where we are."

"Okay—oh, and here's your jacket, thanks for letting me borrow it."

He took it and folded it in his lap.

"You have his jacket?" Karielyn asked from behind them. Apparently, she hadn't left yet.

Xenia rolled her eyes. Hadn't she seen it last night?

"That does not concern you. Go find Morea and leave us alone," Felix snapped.

"Fine. I don't have time to waste around you, anyway," she said, crossing her arms.

"Not anymore, huh?"

Karielyn straightened herself, and her face became heartless. "No, not anymore. *This* is a waste of time. *That* was a waste of time." As she stomped off, she added, "Have fun, hero."

"Sorry about that," Felix apologized once Karielyn was out of earshot.

Xenia leaned closer to him, her voice dropping to a whisper. "Did something… happen between you two?" she asked, hoping she wasn't prying. The question could have had a simple answer. She was a villain. He was a hero. Though, the way he treated Xenia convinced her that their contention came from something else.

"It's complicated. Something I—said—upset her, I suppose," he answered. Before Xenia could question him further, he turned to the plate of food he'd carried to her table.

"Should we meet soon to study the book?" she asked, attempting to move the focus off Karielyn.

Her question brought a smile to his face. "Of course. I'm not sure when yet, there always seems to be something happening. But I'll make sure I find time."

"Whenever you're ready."

Careful, she reminded herself when she heard the eagerness in her voice. *I need to be careful.*

The sea of students began to drain out of the hall as everyone dispersed to their classes. Xenia left Felix and walked alone through the courtyard to the building that held Villain Studies. It was in a separate building at the far end of the school for *students' safety*.

The resistance she felt each time she pressed her skin against the door was only subtle today. Occasionally, a past villain would teach their class. Today Ravelyn would teach.

She couldn't say she liked her, but she was never as harsh as the other teachers.

The classroom was small and empty: nothing but seats and desks to avoid any violence. Even the small room felt too big with the number of students. Villain Studies and History of Heroes would never have more than ten students, and there had never been that many to Xenia's memory. This year there were only her and three others.

She sat across from Merrie and pulled out her notebook. She folded back the leather cover and stared at the last words she had written.

Twenty-seventh day of Gale—Villain Studies
"Evil isn't a game, it's an art." –Silvia Bell.
- *Dedication is key.*
- *Determination keeps you in line.*
- *Hope is for those too weak to stay on top.*

The papers that lay above the page had been reduced to a rigid border where she'd torn out past notes. She tore out the top page and shoved it into her bag.

The door swung open, and several guards raided the room, followed by Ravelyn. Her hands were bound behind her back, and several more guards trailed behind her. Xenia wrinkled her brow. Having villains in class meant guards, but never anything this extreme. They stood by every door and window, making escaping nearly impossible.

Xenia shifted uncomfortably in her seat as Ravelyn passed a glance around the room. She always had a strong grace to her expression and posture. The other students must have felt the same strange feeling Xenia had the first time she met her.

Ravelyn wasn't the woman people claimed—she appeared gentle, but Xenia knew her resilient side too. When people spoke of her, they danced around the fact that she was human.

"Good morning," Ravelyn said, offering a smile. The woman closest to her glared at her as if she had issued a threat. "I'm Ravelyn Kage, I'm here today to share my experience as a villain and to help you on your path to becoming one."

The class stayed silent, although she hadn't yet tried to grip their attention. Not really.

Ravelyn breathed in deeply as if preparing to sing a long song. "What drives a villain? Power? Perhaps they're acting on purely evil intentions. Or maybe the true reasoning is something a bit more personal. When I received my fate, I hated it. I was constantly trying to figure out what could possibly motivate a person to harm another—physically or emotionally. My trainers told me I had a villain inside me, I just needed to find it. That made me feel excluded from my peers when I was no different. Over time I realized that passion is how I would fulfill my fate." She stared numbly in the distance as if recalling painful memories.

"Passion can be found through many things—love, fear, hate. I thought I knew what I was doing—and what was best for me, but I didn't. Once I focused my attention on the hatred I felt towards the people who took away everything I cared about—hurting them wasn't that hard."

Xenia felt empty, like someone was squeezing out her

insides, leaving her with nothing. *I won't become like her*, she told herself. If only Fate's plans aligned with her own.

Ravelyn continued her lesson, though Xenia hardly listened. She wished she didn't have to hear any of the terrible things taught in Villain Studies.

Relief flooded her when class was dismissed. She had Chantendell History next. She preferred it to her training classes. Most of the classes at the Training Center taught how to use weapons, fight, hunt, anything that might be useful in a story. To gain permission Xenia only needed Ravelyn's permission, but she would consider her scores in all of her other classes.

After Chantendell History, Xenia attended her skill training classes. She shared most of them with Karielyn, who communicated only with icy glares. When training ended, Xenia joined her to walk back to their tower. Karielyn refused to speak, and as soon as they arrived, she locked herself in her room, leaving Xenia wondering what she had said last night that upset her so much.

Chapter Nine

XENIA STARTED THE FIRE IN THE LIVING ROOM FOR LIGHT as the sun began to drop and set her book onto the end table, along with a stack on notes. Karielyn still hadn't left her room, and Xenia planned to use this time to review the progress they'd made in the library without her interference.

Keeping the secret from Karielyn would be hard if she expected to translate more. Xenia hoped if she stopped speaking of the book around her, Karielyn would forget long enough to move on.

Xenia sat on the gray settee, leaning against the arm to see her papers. Once the golden sunlight disappeared, she would need a candle to see the words.

A knock pulled her from her thoughts. She stuffed the notes inside the book and closed it before hurrying to the door.

The young woman outside frowned at the sight of her. It was Morea Mailazee. She was a fateless from the story below Xenia's. Most people were born without a major fate and took on their own roles in their story. Xenia recalled Morea studying journalism.

"Oh, Xenia… is Karielyn here?"

"Yes, she's in her room, but I don't think she wants to talk right now."

Morea forced a large smile. "Oh, maybe not to you, but she'll talk to me," she said, pushing her way past her and into the tower. Once she left her sight, Xenia rolled her eyes.

Morea crossed the tower and climbed the stairs to Karielyn's room. Karielyn let her in and, once she was inside, secured the lock again.

Sighing, Xenia closed the door. She didn't want to risk Morea discovering the Elisoran book.

Or reading the notes. She grabbed them from the end table and carried them back to her room.

The blinds were drawn, leaving the room in darkness. Xenia pulled them open, letting in enough light to find her matches. She set the book onto her dresser and lit the candles lining her desk.

The note from Felix still sat on her desk. She grabbed it and set it into a small jewelry box encrusted with rubies.

When she finished putting everything away, she went to the washroom to clean herself for the night. The stone walls and tile floors only added to the bitter chill of the room. A framed mirror hung above a basin filled with water. Xenia took the matches from her room and used them to light the candles surrounding the basin and the light hanging from the ceiling.

She untied her braid and set the ribbon aside. Then she dipped her hands into the water and rinsed her face.

In the next room over, Morea's voice seeped through the walls. Xenia froze. "He's insufferable. Honestly. It's hard to believe the two of you lasted as long as you did."

Karielyn's voice followed. "I should have left sooner." She paused. "I just wish he would stay away. Now Xenia is falling into the same trap, and she won't listen to me."

They must be talking about Felix. Xenia hadn't been around anyone else.

"Maybe she won't care, she is a villain," Morea said.

"Xenia's not—she isn't like that. Felix is worse than her. You remember what he did. He's rude and he always acts so fake. It makes me sick."

Xenia left the basin and stepped closer to the wall next to Karielyn's room.

"It seems Safire can't tell a real villain from a hero."

Felix is the rude one? Of course Xenia knew to stay wary of Felix.

"Apparently not." Karielyn scoffed. "He's been here every day since I moved in."

"I'm sure he's obsessed with her because of her fate too."

Karielyn paused, or her words failed to reach the washroom. Then she said, "I wish I hadn't wasted so much time with him."

How much time could she have possibly wasted with him? Xenia's heart skipped a beat. Had they been together before?

She pulled open the door and stepped into the hallway. This was a bad idea. A terrible idea. Yet she couldn't stop herself. She approached Karielyn's door and, after a few unsteady heartbeats, knocked.

"What do you want?" Morea called from inside.

While Xenia worked up the courage to ask, she froze. She had no idea how to explain that she had overheard them. That she had *listened* to them. Karielyn would be so much angrier when she found out she had eavesdropped.

Before she had time to forget the question, the door flung open. Morea leaned against the doorframe, scowling.

"I wasn't trying to listen," Xenia started, already stumbling over the words. Karielyn sat on her bed, her face turning red as if she already knew her next words. "Karielyn, were you and Felix Liftson together?"

Karielyn stood from her bed and stared vacantly, her teeth clenched. After a few moments, Xenia thought she would leave the question hanging in the hot air between them.

Xenia turned to leave the room and spare herself a few more seconds of the painful silence, but Karielyn opened her mouth to speak. "Yes, we were, and I strongly wish we hadn't been." Her voice rang with bitterness.

Xenia's heart skipped a beat. "I'm sorry I—"

Karielyn's hand cut her off. "It's fine—but now that you know will you listen to me? Felix is not a good person."

The way his name slipped past her lips like a curse rattled in Xenia's mind and formed an unreachable itch of anger. "Because he doesn't want the pressure of being a hero?"

Karielyn looked as if Xenia had struck her. "Is that what he told you? He *wants* to be a villain!"

"Maybe he would take any other fate!" Xenia's fingers formed tight fists that hung limply at her sides. What had he done for her to keep defending him?

Karielyn shook her head. "No, he wants to be *the villain.*"

"You don't know him, Xenia," Morea said, shaking her head. "He's incredibly rude when he isn't acting."

Karielyn nodded her agreement.

"When were you with him?" Xenia asked, ignoring Morea.

Karielyn's eyes dimmed. "We started seeing each other almost a year ago, and we split up six seasons ago now. I really did like him in the beginning. But his father didn't want people to know about us since I'm a villain."

Xenia remembered the way Samuel had looked at her when she saw him at dinner. She could only imagine his reaction towards his son being with a villain.

"I didn't care at first, but it wasn't all that easy since people were always around him—around us. Morea knew, but Felix treated her terribly. He wasn't trying to be the person everyone knows him as around us. One night he told me that he wanted to be a villain. I tried not to let this bother me since I am… *by fate* a villain, but I thought it was strange that Felix *wanted* to be one."

Xenia found it strange too, but she didn't think it was the title of a villain he wanted. Surely not. No one with a well mind could want that.

"We—we planned to spend the warm seasons together. But then he… he called me terrible things. He said he never knew me." Emotion broke Karielyn's speech, but it was anger that carved her words. "I'm begging you, Xenia, stay away from him. That bit of friendliness he's shown you—it's not him and it's not real."

"I'm sure if he didn't have a status to maintain, you'd find him drinking in the shadows with the rest of the villains," Morea said, breaking the string of thought that held what Karielyn had said.

Xenia's body stiffened. She felt like this comment wasn't only referring to him. She was about to argue that she'd never tasted a sip of anything stronger than tea, but she stopped herself and kept on topic. "Felix isn't like that, he…"

"He's what? You don't know him. Not like I do," Karielyn said, shaking her head.

"He could've changed."

"Could've, but he hasn't."

She was right. Xenia barely knew him, so why was she so defensive?

Because I need him, she thought. *I need him if I want to switch my fate.* But she didn't need to befriend him.

"After an argument, we split up. I still haven't told anyone and I prefer it that way—but now that you know, I hope you'll keep my advice and stay away from him."

Karielyn glanced at Morea, and the pair of them brushed past Xenia, leaving her alone to think about everything said.

Karielyn knew him better than her, but still—something wasn't right. Xenia had a feeling Karielyn had left out a vital detail.

Chapter Ten

THE FRONT DOOR SLAMMED SHUT AS KARIELYN AND Morea left. Xenia sat on Karielyn's bed and stared, motionless, at the ground. Was she wrong to have ignored Karielyn's warnings? She really did know him better than her.

She looked around the room. Since Karielyn moved in, she hadn't given the room more than a glance. Delicate decorations filled the room, and it displayed no sign of life. Each ornament and vase sat neatly upon pristine dressers and shelves. Most of the decorations appeared to be from foreign kingdoms.

The room seemed to glow pink. Maybe it was from the sun's evening hues—or maybe it was the lack of other colors.

The room was more proof that they had nothing in common. Aside from both being villains—both not wanting to be villains. Since Xenia turned fourteen, she thought no one truly knew how she felt. She'd been so caught up wishing for a different fate, she never stopped to think that her own allegiant might feel the same way. Everyone else seemed satisfied with their fate. Xenia was even envious of people like Morea, who didn't have specific fates.

She stood up and left the room for her own. Reminders of her deal with Felix filled the air. She could work with Felix without anything forming between them. Forming a relationship would only put her at risk. The less he knew about her—and she knew about him—the better. There was no reason they needed to speak when they weren't studying the book.

For the next few weeks, Xenia tried her best to stay on a different path than him. He proved to be hard to avoid. He took advantage of every moment he saw her between classes and in the courtyard. He was like hot water in the winter snow—warming her for a fragment of a second and then freezing her without consent.

Though she wanted to keep their relationship minimal, she couldn't bring herself to tell him to stay away. He was still company in a place she seldom had any.

However, Karielyn had begun talking to her over the next season—more than rude comments. Despite their constant conversations, Xenia never told her about the deal she had made at midnight with Felix.

The Yule celebration was fast approaching, and the snow wasn't missing its chance to fill the dry air with its cold spirit. The Training Center always hosted a large feast the day before. Xenia had never gone, but Karielyn had insisted she go with her and Morea. Since her mother wouldn't be available for the holiday, she agreed. Estelle had been selected as a finalist in the selection, and she hadn't seen her since.

"Xenia, can you get the door?" Karielyn shouted from the kitchen. She had spent the entire morning baking. The tower smelled wonderful, like childhood memories and cinnamon. But she wouldn't let Xenia try anything.

"Yeah, I'll be right there." Xenia hurried downstairs to open the door, but when she opened it, no one waited outside. The only proof that anyone had knocked was the trail of footprints breaking the surface of the freshly fallen snow and a small package wrapped in black paper. A note in Felix's neat script was stuck to the top.

"Who is it?" Karielyn asked.

Xenia picked up the package and decided against telling her who it had come from. "No one. Must have been…" She trailed off as she pulled the top off the perfectly wrapped package. Inside lay a book with a cover made of plain, brown paper. Where a title would be printed, there was nothing but the word *forbidden* in tiny letters. On the back, she found the date in small black numbers.

1403.

Felix had bought her a copy of the book from 1403.

Her head spun from a mix of emotions. Before Karielyn could ask anything else, Xenia crept quietly to her room and placed it with her other book. Then she walked back to the kitchen before Karielyn could grow suspicious.

"I'm going to deliver these, there are some for us on the counter if you'd like," Karielyn said as she grabbed her plates of treats and walked towards the door. Xenia opened it for her, and she walked out into the cold.

Xenia's thoughts continued to race, but the most reoccurring one was that there must be something very important in the book for Felix to have given it to her.

She picked up one of Karielyn's cookies from the plate she had left in the kitchen and took a bite. The cookie was perfectly round and, despite its sweet properties, had a salty flavor.

Distracting her, someone knocked on the door. It couldn't be Karielyn, surely. Xenia pulled open the door, and Felix Liftson welcomed himself inside.

"Enjoying the cookies?" he asked.

Swallowing, she nodded but said nothing.

"We still haven't made plans," he commented. Xenia tried to find his unspoken words. Was he ready to study the book?

He stepped closer. "It's been nearly a season."

She took a step back. "Have you got any time?"

He eyed her for a moment. "I do, actually. I'll be free over Yule break."

"You won't be spending it with your family?"

"No. Will you?"

She exhaled. She didn't want to explain why she would be spending the holiday alone. "My mother will be away due to the selection. She's one of the finalists. There's no one else here who wants to spend it with me."

Felix smiled. "I heard about that. Would you like to spend it with me? We could have dinner at my tower."

Her breath caught at his proposal. "You—you want to spend it with me? Felix, I'm not sure this is a good idea. You and I aren't—"

"I know. Believe me, I know what our fates mean."

Xenia looked away from him and focused on the wooden floor. They needed to work together eventually. He wasn't inviting her as a friend.

"That sounds nice. Let's do that."

He smiled. "Wonderful." He led himself into the kitchen and picked up one of Karielyn's cookies. They sat down at the table, and he handed her a thin envelope.

Xenia frowned as she took it. "What is this?"

"I read the book from 1403," he said. "The hero and the villain switched fates. After reading it I did some research on the once-was villain of the story—the one who became the hero, Liz Eveyon—I found this."

Xenia took the paper. What could he possibly have found? She pulled out a slip of paper and read.

Vivian Red (1350–1429)—Villain + Trude Liftson (1350–1430)—Villain's Allegiant

Bentlix Liftson (1382–1459)—Villain + Liz Eveyon (1384–1461)—unavailable

Sizian Arie (1412–1480)—Hero Allegiant + Trude Liftson Jr. (1410–1482)—Hero

Morea Elva (1455–1529)—Hero + Ericson Liftson (1454–1524)—Hero

Ella Seastell (1430–1500)—Hero's Allegiant + Heardon Liftson (1430–1505)—Hero

"What is this?" Xenia asked, reading over the names again. The list went on and on. Each line featured a Liftson. It continued all the way until 1812: **Felix Liftson—Hero.**

"It's part of the Liftson family tree. My family is a hero family. We're all heroes."

Xenia nodded without saying anything so he would continue.

"But upon research, I discovered it wasn't always that way—we used to be villains, Bentlix, Trude, all their siblings, they were *all* villains—until Liz Eveyon switched her fate and married Bentlix. The line switched to heroes. There hasn't been a non-hero Liftson since." He took the paper back and stuffed it into his pocket. "If you're still interested in switching your fate, read the book I gave you, and we'll meet for Yule."

Xenia couldn't find any words. Of course she was still interested, but that didn't stop her from being terrified. And what did Felix's discovery mean?

Before she could say anything else, he stood up to leave, and she followed him to the living room.

The door burst open, and Karielyn stopped in the doorway. Her hair had wet drops where snow had melted, and the fur-lined hood she wore lay neglected around her neck. Her eyes flickered in their direction. The pleasant smile that once creased her face vanished.

"Hello, Karielyn," Felix said calmly.

"What are you doing in my tower?"

"Visiting Xenia, it is her tower too, and since we're friends you can't expect me to stay away forever. Can you?"

Xenia's stomach turned when he called her his friend. Karielyn took a deep breath and shot her a look. Felix smiled, said goodbye, and then left her alone with Karielyn.

 Chapter Eleven

"YOU BROUGHT HIM HERE?" KARIELYN SAID THROUGH gritted teeth.

"I didn't invite him over—he just came in!" Xenia returned.

"Oh, he let himself in and made himself tea too, didn't he?"

Xenia ignored her and crossed the room to the door. She pulled on her jacket and stormed out of the tower, slamming the door shut. She tracked through the snow to the stables and ordered a carriage to take her to her mother's manor.

A few minutes later a small carriage pulled up, and she clambered into the back seat. If she didn't visit her mother soon, she wouldn't see her until after the holiday. And with the selection at the end of the season, it could be a while after.

After taking multiple detours because of the snow,

Xenia pulled back the curtains as they approached the Dwelling of Royals. Snow crowned the stone castles and hid the ground. The carriage stopped in front of Estelle's castle. Xenia climbed out hastily and thanked the coachman. A few guards nodded at her as she made her way through the snow to the castle. The guards next to the door pulled it open to allow her entrance.

She passed through the stone arch that led into the living room. Estelle's seamstress, Madame Hezlyn, sat at the end of the room, pouring over a sketchpad. Aside from her the room was empty.

No one sat on the black, velvet sofas or at the marble table with Hezlyn. Xenia relished in the silence the estate hosted. So much went on at the Training Center, it felt good to get away. And the silence here wasn't like the silence her tower once held. This silence carried peace.

Her mother emerged from beneath the stone arch that separated this room from the next. Worry painted her face, but when she saw Xenia, she smiled and ran across the room to greet her. She wrapped her in a hug. "Xenia, I was worried I wouldn't see you before the holiday! What brings you here?" she asked. Her kind words didn't cover the tire in her voice.

"I needed to get away from the tower. I have a new roommate, my allegiant, Karielyn Height." She wanted to tell her about Felix, but seeing the concern in her eyes, she decided to wait. "How have you been?"

She frowned and handed Xenia a copy of the *Chantendell Post*. Xenia took it, unfolded it, and read the front page.

Queen finalist, Estelle Safire, mother of a villain?

During an interview last night, hero Samuel Liftson warned of the dangers the possible queen of Chantendell possesses. "If chosen, the villain will be in line for the throne—we cannot let Chantendell slip from us!" Liftson's words lead us to wonder, what are Estelle's true intentions? As the day to decide our next ruler draws near, we can only hope those who represent our voice will make the decision that is for the better of Chantendell and its people.

Xenia stared at the paper in disbelief—but what couldn't she believe? Samuel Liftson would do everything in his power to keep her mother from the throne—keep Xenia from the palace. To him she was nothing more than a troubled villain. And he had a lot of power.

"I'm so sorry," she whispered as she handed her mother back the paper. If her mother won, Xenia would be the princess—she would be one of the seven Moiran representatives. Moira's seven kingdoms each contributed one person to represent their nation in court. No one would trust her to make decisions for their nation.

"Now that the public is fully aware of your fate, they'll be less willing to accept us as leaders. I know you aren't bad, but they don't—you're the only one who can change their minds."

At her words Xenia's heart sank to her stomach. She shook her head. "No, there's nothing I can do, no one will listen to me—"

"Xenia, if I win you will be their princess, you can give a speech before they decide a ruler. I suggest you use that to our advantage."

She buried her face into her hands and slowly exhaled. "I can't."

"You have to. Please." Estelle brushed the hair from Xenia's face, and she lifted her head up to look at her. "I trust you. You've hidden your fate for as long as you could, but maybe it's better this way. We need to be honest to the people."

"Okay, I'll give a speech… but I can't say it will be good."

Estelle shook her head and mouthed the word *no*. "It will be perfect."

Xenia decided not to tell her mother about Felix; she tried not to think about him herself. She longed to tell her mother about the deal she had made with him as well, but Estelle would shoot down the idea quicker then she could present it. It needed to stay between her and Felix.

The selection was at the end of this season and her mother needed every moment she could get to prepare, so Xenia didn't stay much longer.

The Training Center brimmed with life when she returned. She watched as students poured into the dining hall. Part of her wanted to find Felix's table again, but she couldn't—she wasn't sure she'd be able to look at him. Not after reading his father's article.

When she returned, Karielyn and Morea laughed by the door as they pulled on their coats. Xenia didn't say a word to them, and they returned the favor.

The first thing she noticed when she got to her room was the empty space on her dresser, where her Elisoran book had been. She sorted through her drawers rapidly, leaving piles of clothes and papers sprawled across the room.

"Karielyn!" she shouted.

"What?" she called back. The stairs creaked, and Karielyn appeared at her door, followed closely by Morea. "Well?"

"Did you take my book?" Xenia asked impatiently without ceasing to sort through her things. Karielyn had been through her room before, and Xenia didn't put her above taking her things, either.

Karielyn's eyes narrowed and her lips tightened. "Why? Did you lose it?" she asked. "I don't have it," she added before spinning to face the stairs and storming out of the tower.

Where is it? Xenia searched through more drawers and looked through her closet, but never found the book. *I can't believe I lost it! I've had it for four years and now it's gone.*

Chapter Twelve

"IT CAN'T BE THE ONLY COPY," FELIX SAID, PUSHING A book back onto the shelf. Xenia hadn't meant to run into him, but he had managed to find her hidden behind a tall stack of books in the library's forbidden section. He had also managed to get her to tell him what happened.

"You don't know that!" she snapped, tossing a book back onto the stack.

"And neither do you."

She turned away. After reading the article, she didn't want to talk to him, but he wouldn't leave. And she couldn't bring herself to ask him to.

"Nia, calm down."

Xenia straightened. No one had called her that for four years. Not since Blake left. Somehow, hearing it in Felix's voice didn't bother her.

"This doesn't have to be the end. Are you sure you looked *everywhere*?" he said, lingering on the last word, mocking her outburst from a few minutes earlier.

She nodded and continued to look through the books, though she knew she wouldn't find another copy.

He sighed. "I could go to your tower and help you look for it."

"It's not there, I've looked everywhere!"

"Do you really think someone stole your book?"

It sounded extreme, yet a part of her believed that.

"Maybe we can take a trip into the kingdom before the holiday and try to find a copy," Felix suggested, grabbing another book from her pile and returning it to the shelf.

"I don't know, I'm really busy," she said. "I have to give a speech next week, you know. My mother is one of the finalists…" She cleared her throat. "Oh, but I'm sure your father already told you, didn't he?" She shouldn't try to guilt him. It wasn't *his* fault his father had attacked her mother.

Is it?

Felix's confusion quickly turned to realization. "Xenia, I'm so sorry, my father, he…" He trailed off, abandoning whatever attempt he had to justify Samuel's words.

When she was sure he wouldn't start talking, she said, "My mother has worked *so hard!*" she screamed. "We've tried so hard to keep my fate a secret—she'll make a wonderful queen, but no one will see that now because they're blinded by *your* father's article!"

The nearby librarian held a finger to his mouth, but she didn't need to listen to his command because she was already storming out the door.

"Wait—"

"No," Xenia said through gritted teeth. "I don't care what you have to say!"

She reached the door, pulled it open, and let it fall on Felix as he tried to hurry after her.

The door slammed behind him as he ran through the courtyard after her. He wrapped his hand around her arm with a steady grip. "I truly am sorry—my father gets caught up in being a—hero—he thought he was helping the people… I'm so sorry."

"I don't want to talk about it right now. Not with you," she said, pulling her arm away from him.

"All right, fine." He let go of her arm and turned to walk away.

Xenia walked alone to her tower and took advantage of the silence. Karielyn was still at the dining hall with Morea, leaving the tower empty. Xenia skipped dinner to put her room back together and think about the speech her mother had requested.

She finished returning everything to its proper spot and then turned her attention to the speech.

Her school bag was filled with books and quills. She reached for the top one and opened to the first blank page. How was she supposed to start a speech as important as this one?

The candles burning on her desk offered her just enough light to see the page. She dipped her quill into ink that dripped onto the paper as she considered what to write. She sat at the desk and stared pensively at the paper. The page remained blank for nearly an hour before she wrote one sentence.

Good morning, I'm Xenia Safire. But wouldn't the selection be after dark? With irritation, she crossed a line through it. She moved her wrist to write *ladies and gentlemen* but pulled her hand away, dripping more ink onto the page. *Too simple.*

The stairs creaked when Karielyn returned, but Xenia didn't go to greet her. She couldn't lose focus now. She wrote a few more attempts at an opening, scratching all of them out before making it past the introduction.

She wrote deep into the night until her paper looked worse than it had when blank.

~~*Good morning, I'm Xenia Safire.*~~ *Welcome to the selection ceremony, everyone, I'm Xenia Safire. Today is* ~~special~~ *important for a collection of reasons. By the end of the night, we will have a new ruler, and Chantendell deserves someone good. I know some of you may believe what Samuel said to be true and it is, but that shouldn't affect my mother. My fate may be a villain, but I would never mean Chantendell any harm.*

She tore out the paper and threw it onto the floor. Tears filled her eyes, and she groaned. Why couldn't she write a simple speech? Because it *wasn't* simple.

She hid her face in her knees. *Why does she think I can do this? I've never given a speech before!* She groaned and turned back to her paper.

Something hit her window, and she dropped her quill into the ink pot. Warily, she rose from her desk and crept towards it, pushing the curtain out of the way. After she wiped the fog off the window, she peered into the darkness. The outer edge of the glass had been chipped. A rock flew against her window, hitting it with a thud.

Someone was trying to get her attention. She darted downstairs and ran outside.

"Hello?"

The icy snow seeped into her bare feet. She shivered. *What am I doing? This could be dangerous!*

She peered through the darkness, searching for whoever had thrown the rock. In front of her, Felix Liftson's figure separated from the darkness.

"What are you doing?" she demanded.

"I came to apologize. Again."

Xenia pursed her eyes and tried not to think about the sincerity in his voice. *This isn't his fault.* "Felix, I—"

"No, no, I'm sorry. Is there anything I can do to—?"

She shook her head. "It's not your fault and there's nothing you can do."

"Please, there has to be something."

The wind whistled as it moved through the trees in the distance before sweeping their faces. The moon hid behind threatening, dark clouds, leaving only a small amount of light from her tower left to illuminate Felix's features.

"There's not. Good night," she said, turning back to the door.

"Okay…" He released a breath that froze in the air. "Good night."

She didn't look back to see him walk away.

Her room felt cold and unwelcoming when she returned—maybe because now she knew how alone she was.

She hesitated before slipping back into her chair and

picking up the quill. Before she had the first word down, she dropped the quill, and ran back downstairs. She flung open the door and ran out, not bothering to close it behind herself.

"Felix!" she called, hoping he was still close enough to answer. She called his name again as she ran. Finally, she spotted him ahead and gasped for breath before calling him again. She trembled from the cold. Snow seeped between her toes and numbed her bare feet.

Felix turned around and rushed to her. "Yes?"

She held her breath. *Am I asking too much?* "Actually, there is one thing."

Chapter Thirteen

"WHAT HAVE YOU WRITTEN SO FAR?" FELIX ASKED, reaching for Xenia's book, but she didn't hand it to him. Instead, she took a moment to stall by holding a finger to her lips. Karielyn was likely sleeping just down the hall, and Xenia didn't want her to find out Felix was *here. In her room. Now.*

"Nothing yet, just some rough drafts," she whispered, tossing a glance at the paper on the floor.

Felix's smile didn't match his voice as he said, "Well, lucky for you I grew up with five professional speech writers."

Xenia stifled a laugh.

He crossed the dark room and leaned next to the chipped window, examining it. After a moment he said, "Sorry, did I do that?" He dropped the black curtain, covering the glass.

"Yeah. Why didn't you just knock?"

"I didn't want to wake Karielyn."

She shook her head. "So, you threw rocks at my window?"

He shrugged. "Are you ready to start?"

Nodding, Xenia opened her book and set it onto the desk. The candle flames flickered from the disturbance. "What are you trying to get out of this speech?" He dipped the quill into the ink and held it above the page.

"I don't know. The opposite of what your father was trying to get."

He smiled. She was relieved he hadn't seemed to take offense from her words. She watched his hand glide across the paper as he explained different ways to relay messages, and how she should get hers through.

He wrote a few drafts with her help, and after reading the last one, she took the book from him and wrote it herself.

It took several attempts before she was confident in what she had written. Unlike before, the words flew easily and they sounded *right*. A feeling of peace, previously foreign to her, slipped into her chest, easing the heavyweight from earlier. *I can do this.*

She continued scribbling words until the speech was finished. Then she set the quill down and flipped to the beginning of the speech. She read over it and hoped it would be enough.

When she finished, Felix had passed out in the wrong direction across her bed. She touched his arm and shook him awake. "Felix, I'm done!" she said.

"Oh… great," he said, suppressing a yawn. He rolled over and fell back asleep.

Xenia shook her head, smiling. She slipped downstairs and sat at the kitchen table. Her eyes poured over the speech until the words stuck in her brain and she found herself quoting it to herself more than reading. Then she laid her head next to the journal and closed her eyes.

"Xenia, wake up," Karielyn said, shaking her shoulder softly. Xenia glanced up at her, squinting. "Why are you sleeping at the table? How late did you stay up?"

Did Felix go home?

Rubbing her eyes, Xenia said, "I had to…"—a yawn broke her speech, and she stretched her arms and took a deep breath—"write a speech."

"A speech for what?" Karielyn asked.

"The selection," Xenia said, closing the book in front of her and pulling it towards her chest. Karielyn must have read Samuel's article by now—most of Moira must have. What did she think of it? She had expressed on multiple occasions she didn't think of Xenia as a villain.

Karielyn looked as though she had another question, but she didn't ask it.

The wooden stairs creaked behind them, and Felix fumbled down. He wore a half-smile on his face and held the stair's rail.

"*Felix!*" Karielyn's voice was filled with disgust. "Get

out! *Now!*" she shrieked, pointing towards the door.

Felix looked at her with his brows drawn as if he were confused, though Xenia knew he wasn't. He passed the door and walked towards her instead. His hand fell to her shoulder, and he moved his mouth to her ear. Butterflies beat against her chest. [Title]

"Sorry, I didn't mean to outstay my welcome. I'll see you later."

"Yes. Later."

Once the front door closed, Karielyn released her full temper. "He *slept* here!" She paced between the kitchen and living room, complaining to herself—or possibly Xenia. She wasn't listening.

"Why are you so upset?" Xenia asked, rubbing her eyes again.

Karielyn didn't answer, but she did stop shouting. Then, without another word, she left the tower.

Xenia returned her attention to the journal still in her hand. And the sheets of Felix's crisp writing. She read over the speech one more time before taking it to her room and stuffing it away.

Training was canceled for the Yule festivities, and that left her schedule entirely open. Most days Xenia didn't know how to spend her free time, but this time she didn't remember thanking Felix for his help.

She grabbed her jacket off the couch and pulled it over her shoulders before leaving the tower. The path to the men's towers was slick from the ice that had formed from last night's half-melted snow. Xenia sorted through her mind trying to remember his tower number.

Forty. Blake's old number. His tower was identical to every other one at the Training Center: tall and dressed in brown and beige stones. Xenia knocked on his door and waited for him to pull it open.

Felix had already changed into different clothes, and his hair dripped with beads of water. "Is everything all right?"

"I didn't get to say thank you."

"There's no need. We're even now."

Xenia frowned. "It was never your fault. I'm sorry for how I treated you."

He moved aside to let her into his tower. It looked nearly the same as it had the last time she visited four years ago, only now Blake's possessions were gone and replaced with Felix's new roommate's things.

"I still felt terrible," he said, leading her to the couch. "He treats too many people unfairly because of their fate."

Xenia eyed the couch with uncertainty. *I can't stay long.* Reluctantly, she sat beside him, crossing her legs.

The end table in front of them was empty, aside from a torn envelope. Felix followed her eyes to it. "Oh," he said. "That's from my parents—I meant to tell you."

Xenia frowned. "Tell me what?"

"They want me home for the holiday. I—we can still spend it together if you don't mind my family."

Xenia's skin turned hot. He wanted her to spend the Yule holiday with his family? With Samuel Liftson?

"I shouldn't. I'm sure your family would prefer—"

"They don't care. It's—if they say anything... *irrational,* ignore it."

"You mean, if they mention my fate?"

"Well, yes, but you aren't a bad person, they might understand." He had an odd tone in his voice, convincing her that Samuel wasn't okay with her coming over in the slightest. He likely didn't even know yet.

"Felix, I'm used to it. I don't need to come over."

"No, it will be fine. My father will be fine. My family will be fine. I just wanted to warn you. We still need to work on the book."

The only thing Xenia had gathered from his reassurance was that Samuel was absolutely *not* fine with this. She didn't want to spend the holiday with Samuel Liftson, but she didn't know how long after it would be until they could work together.

"Okay, thank you. I'll be there."

The stairs creaked behind them, and they turned to see Merrick making his way down stairs. His brow creased when he saw Xenia. "What's going on?"

"We were just talking," Felix answered.

"About…?"

"The Yule Celebration."

"I see. Speaking of which, I'm going to my parents' house for the week. I'll see you after Yule," he said, pulling open the front door, a breath of cold air filling the warm tower. He slammed it, and the small items on the mantel rattled.

"Sorry about him," Felix said.

"Why are you apologizing?"

"He interrupted us."

"I don't mind," Xenia said softly, narrowing her eyes. Merrick didn't do anything wrong. But Felix had apologized just as he did when she yelled at him about the article. His father's article, not his. He seemed to take the blame for a little more than necessary.

As silence settled between them, she caught herself wondering how many times Karielyn had come over to his tower to visit. Her mind danced across the thought of the two of them sitting together, and her stomach twisted.

"What's on your mind?" Felix asked, snapping her out of her daze.

"I was just thinking."

He drew his brows together. "What were you thinking about?"

Despite how much she wanted to hear the story from him, she didn't want to bring up Karielyn. "Nothing."

"Nothing? Are you sure?"

"I—I was thinking about Karielyn… and you," she said quietly, hoping he might not hear.

He nodded, and she noticed him move closer until their bodies were less than a span apart. She tensed. "So, she told you?"

She nodded. If it were her secret, she would feel as if he were invading her privacy by knowing. But he didn't seem bothered.

"And that's why you were avoiding me last season, wasn't it?"

What Karielyn said had motivated her to keep herself

distant from Felix, but Xenia wasn't doing it for Karielyn. She couldn't let herself get any closer to him than she already was regardless.

I'm making a mistake. Already she and Felix were too close.

"I'm sorry," she mumbled.

"You don't have to be. I'm sure she told you nasty things about me… I'm not—I'm not what she says." His voice stayed gentle despite the harsh topic.

"Was it serious?" she asked. Choosing her words felt like stepping onto a scale and trying to keep it level. "Your relationship?"

"Right before the end, I suppose." He shook his head and leaned back. "But she always liked Cedar, anyway."

"Cedar?"

"Yeah, Blake Cedar."

Xenia's heart skipped a beat. "She dated him too?" she finally managed. *How could Blake keep something like that from me?* The answer hurt to think about.

An amused grin swept Felix's face, and he let out a quick laugh. "No, but she wanted to."

Her chest eased. "What makes you think that?"

He laughed again. "Fate, it was obvious. You didn't notice?"

Xenia's brow furrowed. "What did she say about him?"

"It's not only what she said. She tried visiting when Blake was still my roommate. How did you not notice?"

"I don't know, we didn't talk much until she moved in with me," she said quickly, hoping he would keep talking.

"Well, that was before we were together—she didn't talk about him after that." He paused for a moment. "You knew him well, didn't you? Did he ever say anything about her?"

Blake had never talked about Karielyn, though now Xenia remembered she would try to fit into their conversations. Or push Xenia out of them. "Not really."

"Hmm."

Her thoughts reeled as they fell into silence. She turned over the pieces Felix had given her and tried to fit them with the ones from Karielyn. "I should go home now," she said, rising to her feet and attempting to stop her thoughts from delving too far into Felix and Karielyn's past. "Thank you."

He stood. "Of course, I understand needing to get away from Karielyn. Will I see you at dinner?"

"I don't have other plans."

"Then I'll see you tonight." He led her towards the door. "And I'm looking forward to Yule dinner with you. Maybe then we'll know more about switching fates."

She didn't remind him that she had lost the book. His comment had turned her head numb. He seemed to want this switch as much as her. She couldn't tell if that excited or frightened her. Or something between.

Chapter Fourteen

XENIA STILL FELT SHAKEN BY THE TIME SHE REACHED her tower. Her mind replayed all the unnecessary moments she'd spent with Felix. Their relationship needed to remain minimal. How could she keep it at that?

She had agreed to seeing him again at dinner—if she started the book he gave her, she could keep their conversation focused on their goal by discussing it.

She hurried upstairs to grab the book—her bed was made, but the sheets were ruffled where Felix had lain the night before. She adjusted the curtains in her room to let in enough light to read. Slipping into the chair at her desk, she grabbed the book.

The first page contained a warning message. Xenia winced, preparing herself for whatever had earned this story a spot in the forbidden section, and then flipped the page.

Chantendell stories often took years of buildup before anything notable happened. Xenia's own story had started nearly four years ago, when people began entering. Once the stories were released, however, they were reduced to only the vital information.

The story opened with the hero, Rendon Counterstart, and villain, Liz Eveyon. Xenia narrowed her eyes as she flipped the page. If they were together already, how had their story progressed to give the book so many pages? She read deeper, waiting for one of them to attack, but soon she realized they had an alliance. And because of Felix's interest in the book and the notes she had found, she could assume it would end with them switching their fate.

Xenia read over a hundred pages before her clock chimed, reminding her of dinner. Reluctantly, she set the book down. The story felt like a puzzle. The writer had tried to mask vital things. It left the book with confusing gaps and hidden meanings between the lines, keeping her locked in a state of trying to uncover every message.

The sun sank deeper beyond the horizon, and Xenia glanced at her clock. She would need to leave now if she intended to meet Felix for dinner.

She hurried downstairs and left the tower. Cold wind stung her face as she crossed the courtyard. She reached the hall and pulled open the door; warmth rushed around her as she stepped inside.

Xenia scanned the rows of tables for Felix and spotted him standing amidst a group of people beside his usual spot.

"Felix," she called, making her way towards him through the cluster of students.

He turned at her voice and cut through the crowd in a

straight path towards her. Victoria looked as if she wanted to chase after him, but seeing Xenia stopped her.

"It's good to see you again," he said with a smile. Xenia followed him to a long food table at the end of the hall and grabbed steaming bowls of stew and rolls. Then they sat down at Felix's usual table.

Stares jumped to her as she filled the space beside him. Whispers broke out across the table, accompanied by harsh stares. Xenia looked at her bowl.

"I started the book," she said once the whispers faded.

"It's interesting, isn't it?"

"It is. I'm not that far in, but it's very... different."

He shot a glance behind his shoulder before saying quickly, "The strange part is, the villain failed."

"Isn't that a good thing?" She regretted the words almost instantly, even though she meant them. Felix wanted to be a villain; wouldn't he want villains to succeed as well?

Dread washed over her like a wave from behind. He wanted *her* to fail.

He lowered his voice so only she could hear. "The strange part is, the villain failed and it was still labeled a forbidden book."

"Do you think it's because—?"

Victoria strode over to the table and stopped behind Felix, placing an arm around his shoulders. He motioned with his hand to silence Xenia. "Yes, I think it's because," he whispered.

Victoria leaned forward, speaking against his ear. "You're coming to my party this weekend, right?"

He tore her arm away from him and turned to Xenia. "I don't know, are we, Nia?"

Why was he asking *her*? Xenia was silent for a few seconds, before saying under her breath, "I don't think she wants me there."

"Of course she does." He turned around again to face Victoria. "Right, Victoria? The invitation extends to Xenia, I assume?"

Xenia's face flushed; Victoria hadn't talked to her in four years. She *did not* want her at the party.

Victoria turned to her and cocked her head. "Of course. Why wouldn't I? Dusk, the day after the celebration, dress formally."

Xenia frowned. Victoria didn't mean it, but she wouldn't fight Felix.

Without another look or word, she left the table and found a spot on the opposite side of the hall.

Xenia lowered her voice and moved closer to him. "Are you two…?" Her mouth didn't form the last word.

His eyebrows turned in confusion. "Are we… what?"

When she didn't answer he flashed a glance in Victoria's direction. His eyes fell back on Xenia, and he grinned. "Are we together?" He shook his head in a way that fell between disgust and laughter. "No. We're not. She'd love to make people believe that, though."

Xenia scolded herself for the way her heart fluttered at his answer. He was a hero. They could never be together. He'd been smiling since her question. Her heart repeated the flutter when she noticed.

"I'll pick you up at your tower around sunset, okay?"

Victoria's party. Right. "That will work." She didn't want to go, but apparently he had decided for her. Victoria would be furious.

Felix's eyes narrowed, and he turned back to his stew. "Karielyn will be there too," he said. "Makes her parties that much better."

They finished eating, and she and Felix sat in the Dining Hall, talking well after the other students had left. She knew they needed to find more time like this to talk if they wanted to succeed in translating the book and switching their fates. But conversation kept straying further and further from the topic.

Countless times Xenia's teachers encouraged her to learn Felix Liftson's weaknesses and strengths—to learn *him*. And she had the unsettling impression that his had said the same thing and he was following directions.

The deeper his conversation led her into her own life, she imagined his kind words a disguise for the weapon he was creating. And yet, she couldn't bring herself to leave. Being in Felix's company felt so much better than being alone, whatever his intentions were.

She left the dining hall when staff returned to clean the building. The sun had gone, leaving her path obscured. She watched the ground, avoiding slick patches of ice.

Snow crushed behind her, and Xenia spun around. The dark sky made it hard to see the woman nearing her.

Victoria wore a short dress despite the cold. "Xenia," she said, drawing out the name.

"What do you want, Victoria?"

"You know what I want," she said, stepping closer. "I want you to stay away from Felix. And there's no point showing up at my party. You know no one wants you there."

"Felix wants me there."

As if the words froze in the cold air before reaching her, Victoria didn't respond.

Then, she leaned close, and the icy air turned hot. "I'm afraid that wasn't a suggestion—it was a warning. You are not welcome there."

Xenia stepped back but held her gaze. She wouldn't let Victoria see her shaken. "You've never been a good hostess, anyway."

Before Victoria could say more, Xenia spun around and started towards her tower.

"He doesn't care about you, Xenia! He's *messing* with you! You mean nothing to him—nothing more than entertainment!"

Her throat became taut as she quickened her step. Why would she listen to anything Victoria told her? Her words meant less to her than anyone else's at the Training Center. She knew not to trust her, yet she felt sick.

And why does it bother me? I know he doesn't care.

Despite how much she wanted to forget what Victoria had said, the words echoed in her mind the entire way back.

Chapter Fifteen

RELIEF FLOODED THROUGH XENIA WHEN SHE REACHED her tower. She pulled open the door, finding it dark and quiet. Karielyn sat alone by the fire, folding a letter and slipping it into an envelope.

She looked up when Xenia entered. "Is everything all right?"

Xenia frowned, feigning confusion. "Yeah, I—I'm fine. Why?"

"You look upset. Did something happen?"

She pulled off her coat and joined Karielyn on the couch. "I got in a bit of an argument with Victoria."

Karielyn narrowed her eyes and cocked her head. "What did she tell you?"

Xenia eyed the ground as she thought of something easier to explain. If she told her what Victoria had really said, she would probably agree. Wasn't that what she was trying to tell her all along? That Felix didn't really care about her?

"Xenia, tell me what happened," Karielyn urged, setting her book aside.

Xenia shook her head. "It doesn't matter. Felix invited me to Victoria's party, but on my way home, she told me I'm not welcome. And that Felix doesn't care about me." She mumbled the last part, hoping Karielyn wouldn't touch on it.

"You're going to Victoria's party with Felix?"

"I told you—"

"You'll need to borrow a dress, won't you?"

This made Xenia hold back her explanation. "No. I—what?"

Karielyn set her letter onto the small table in front of the couch and positioned herself to face her. "Sorry—you *need* to borrow a dress."

"No, I—"

She cut her off again, signaling for her to stop talking. "Sorry. You *need* to borrow one of *my* dresses because *you* don't have one suitable for a party."

Xenia buried her face in her hands. "Karielyn, I have a dress—"

"Not one like you need."

"I can't go now—"

"Why? Because Victoria told you not to? You can't let people treat you like that."

Xenia threw her head back. "I don't even want to—"

Karielyn laughed. "Of course not, that's beside the point. Why do you think I'm going? You go anyway to show Victoria that you don't care what she tells you. The only thing she wants is to feel important and in control. Don't let her get that." She rose to her feet and offered Xenia her hand. "After all, you're still a villain. She can't expect you to follow orders."

Xenia took her hand and rose from the couch. She attempted to hide her smile so Karielyn wouldn't know the idea pleased her.

Karielyn led her up to her room and to her closet and then lit a few candles, illuminating the rows of hanging dresses. "Hmm. Pink isn't your color and this one cost me a fortune, I would need your head if anything were to happen to it… How do you feel about gold?" She ruffled through her closet, mumbling to herself about Xenia's complexion.

Xenia smiled, crossing her arms. "Karielyn, I have a dress—"

"Not one for a party," she said, tossing her a lacy, white dress. "Try that one."

Before Xenia could fully survey the dress, Karielyn spun around and snatched it from her. "Wait, don't—take this one," she said, shoving another dress into her arms.

Xenia tried it on, and when she returned, Karielyn muttered something about how it didn't complement her eyes. Finally, she settled on loaning her a short, black dress with sheer sleeves. A different style then she usually wore, but Karielyn was right: she needed something suitable for Victoria's parties. The dresses she wore around her mother's noble guests wouldn't work now.

"Thank you," she said, admiring the one in her arms.

Karielyn smiled. "Well, of course. I couldn't ride to the

party with someone dressed like you usually are."

"You're coming with me? I'm already riding with Felix."

Karielyn nodded. "There should be enough room."

How would she explain this to Felix? He certainly wouldn't want to ride with Karielyn.

"Are you sure you don't want to ride with Morea?"

Her smile grew, turning mischievous. "She can come too!"

Xenia groaned. Clearly, Victoria's night wasn't the only one Karielyn intended to crash. "Well—"

"Great!" She closed the closet door and then said, "Good night, Xenia."

"Good night, Karielyn," she echoed, her voice strained from irritation. "Thanks for your help."

She returned to her room and tossed the dress into her closet. She tried not to think about Victoria's party. Between Victoria's threats and Karielyn's determination to rattle Felix, she imagined the night would go horribly wrong.

In the morning, the air smelled of cinnamon and sugar. Karielyn had made a traditional Yule bread for the feast tonight. The celebration wasn't until tomorrow, but the Training Center held their feast the day before to allow students to both attend and celebrate with their families. Though, Xenia would be with the Liftsons.

Xenia took a seat at the counter in the kitchen. Karielyn leaned into it on the other side. "Are you going over to... his house tomorrow?" Concern pulled her brows together. Perhaps she had the best intentions in trying to deter Xenia from Felix, but until recently, she had never cared about Xenia. What had changed when she met Felix?

Xenia nodded, avoiding her stare.

Karielyn sighed and turned back to the unfinished bread.

Just before the sun fully set, they began walking to the feast, accompanied by a stream of students doing the same.

They arrived to a dazzling version of the dining hall. Sparkling silver garland hung from the ceiling, dangling intricate snowflakes above the seven long tables. Girls in fine dresses danced to music from a band in the corner by the door. Displays of pastel-blue cakes twirled towards the arched roof, spaced evenly at every table.

Xenia made her way down the aisle between benches, admiring each detail. The windows were frosted, dimming the moonlight and leaving the large hall illuminated by white candles.

At the back of the hall, the food table was covered end to end in decadent dishes. It held everything from plum pies crowned in delicate lattice to traditional stew, warm enough for steam to float from the pot. In the center of the table was a carefully carved ice sculpture of an elegant doe.

Xenia sat where she and Felix had yesterday so he could find her when he arrived. The table now had a pale-blue liner stretching from one end to the other.

The hall filled rapidly with students and overlapping conversation until the music faded under all the noise. Felix arrived and joined her, attracting a swarm of people that followed him to his seat. He wore a white button-up paired with a black coat trimmed with silver thread. Xenia's own dress was a simple cut made from black velvet paired with a necklace that dangled seven small stars in a line down her chest.

Victoria, Warren, and Merrick arrived and sat across from them at the table, communicating with snide expressions and whispers.

"It's loud in here," Felix said. "I need to get out. Would you like to come?"

"Please," Xenia said, grateful for an opportunity to leave the rest of Felix's friends. Without Karielyn's persuasion she never would have come to the feast.

They stood, and Felix led the way down the aisle to the door. He pulled it open, letting the cold wind sting their faces. Xenia stepped into the moonlit night, Felix a step behind her.

They made a path in the already packed snow as they walked across the courtyard. The sky was clear, and millions of stars sparkled overhead.

Xenia risked a glance in Felix's direction. His posture had relaxed since leaving, and he watched the ground, frowning.

"Is everything all right?"

He nodded and snapped his head up to face her. "Just the crowds and parties… it always feels like too much."

"But you always go," she said. "Why?"

He shrugged. "I have to. It's part of being a hero, I suppose." His gentle, brown eyes glistened in the pale moonlight. He fell silent, his jaw tensing.

Xenia's heart fluttered, and she looked away. She hadn't meant to stare. "I'm nearly done with the book you gave me," she said.

Felix eased, and his steps slowed. "Good. It must be connected to your book. I think if we really plan to switch our fates, their story will be important."

"Do you think we'll get in trouble?" she asked.

Before he could answer, she slipped on a patch of ice and lost balance, landing flat on her back. She groaned as cold snow seeped into her dress and down her neck. Felix moved to help, double-stepping on the slick ice. He reached for her hand but fell on top of her instead.

"Only if we get caught," he said through a grin. His hands were pressed against the ground on either side of her head, and his breath froze in the small space between them before she took it in herself. Her heart hitched and her head spun.

He grabbed her hand and pulled her to her feet as he stood. She brushed the ice from her dress and shivered as the melting snow trailed down her back. "How do we keep our fates a secret?" she asked, acting as if the last moment had never happened.

"There has to be a way. Liz Eveyon was never punished." Felix turned to face the Dining Hall. From here the candle-lit windows were the only sign of the party inside. "We should get back. I don't want anyone to come looking for us."

Xenia agreed, and they made their way—more carefully

now—towards the dining hall.

The music inside sounded faintly outside when they reached the door. She grabbed the cold, metal handle and pulled it open. Light spilled against their faces. She took a step inside, but Felix grabbed her by the arm and spun her around to face him.

He looked up and then stared into her eyes. "Mistletoe."

Chapter Sixteen

HE TRIED TO KISS ME. XENIA'S HEAD STILL SPUN WHEN she made it back to her room.

What should she do now? She had rejected him under the mistletoe! She didn't try to wipe her tears as they streamed down her face. Would he still want to see her after this?

She had never kissed anyone before—she'd never come close. Tonight, she declined her first chance. Would things be better this way? Villains weren't supposed to love, right? Especially not heroes. She could never love a hero.

She pulled back the black curtain and leaned her face into the window. Her breath fogged the surface as she stared at the neighboring towers. They were all dark—no doubt their residents were still at the party dancing.

Maybe getting stopped under the mistletoe.

Had Felix gone home? She had run away as soon as he tried to kiss her and left him under the mistletoe alone. He could have left the party early after she rejected him, but was he even disappointed? Given his place, he could likely get a kiss from any other girl he wanted.

Xenia swiped at her eyes and took a deep breath. No matter what had happened—or hadn't happened—tonight, she could never have Felix.

She left the window and changed out of her dress and into her silk slip. When she finished, she crawled into bed, but despite her tiredness, she couldn't sleep. Her thoughts kept her up late, taunting her and reminding her of the night's events. Would Felix bring them up tomorrow when she went to his parents' house? She shut her eyes, willing sleep to take her. The night was nearly over when it finally did.

Despite the sleepless night, Xenia woke as soon as the sun was bright enough to shine through her window. She pulled her sheets off and climbed out of bed. Butterflies rushed to her stomach as she remembered her plans for the day. Even her wildest dreams had never taken her to dinner with the Liftsons. Let alone spending the Yule Celebration with them.

Xenia changed into a black dress with white lace at the hems and tied her hair back. Then she sorted through her ruby-encrusted jewelry box for a pair of diamond earrings and a thin matching bracelet.

After she dressed, she left her room and stopped at the top of the stairs, overlooking the tower. The early sun seeped through the window far above the fireplace, illuminating the still tower. It was a perfect Yule morning. Crisp snow coated the grounds, sunlight bleeding through the windows.

"You're already up?" Karielyn asked, closing her bedroom door behind her. She came to Xenia's side at the top of the stairs.

"I couldn't sleep." Xenia started downstairs, Karielyn following behind.

"I see."

They stepped through the archway into the kitchen, and Karielyn took a seat at the counter. "I got you a present." She motioned to a small, white box beside her.

Xenia's eyes widened. "You didn't have to—"

"Just open it," Karielyn said, handing her the box.

She took it and removed the top. Inside, a few papers lay on top of a layer of silk.

She picked up the thin stack of paper. "What is this?"

She expected Karielyn to be disappointed by her lack of enthusiasm, but instead her smile grew. "It's your book," she answered. "The one you lost."

"What do you mean?" Xenia demanded, rifling through the pages.

"Well… technically you never lost it, I took it—"

"But you said you didn't have it."

Karielyn had taken it to give it back to her? And what had happened to the original copy?

"I didn't. My mother did, she still does. You asked me for help, so I gave it to her. I told you, she's a linguist. She's familiar with Elisoran. It isn't finished yet, I gave it to her with little notice, but she said she'll send more as she works."

Xenia didn't know what to say. "Karielyn, this is perfect.

Thank you!" She examined the papers closer. They were in Moiran. Her heart fluttered just looking at the familiar characters.

Karielyn's smile faded as she handed her a smaller box with a golden ribbon tied in a small bow. "It's for tonight, when you go to the Liftsons'," she said as Xenia pulled open the box, revealing a necklace with a squared, black gem resting on a tiny, silver plaque.

Xenia looked up for a moment but glanced away before long. "You aren't going to tell me not to go?" she managed.

Karielyn shook her head. "I don't like him very much, but you do. I shouldn't make you feel miserable because of that." Tears glazed her eyes. "And I feel terrible. I've always been rude to you, and you don't deserve that. I… I guess I've always been a little jealous of you."

Xenia frowned. Silence stretched between them as she searched for a response. "Why were you jealous of me?"

The last moment of silence felt long, but not compared to this one.

Karielyn's eyes brimmed with tears ready to stream down her cheeks if she didn't blink them away. When she finally spoke, her voice trembled. "Because you were something that I always wanted to be."

"What's that?"

"You were close to Blake Cedar." She closed her eyes, and tears trickled down her cheeks, streaking them with her liquefied makeup. "Ever since I met him, I wanted to know him. He never wanted to talk to me—he always had to find you. You two were always together, I never got the chance."

She paused again, letting out a shuddering breath. "Now it's too late."

Xenia took a breath and held it in. For a while, it seemed every girl liked Blake. But Blake had never spoken of them, and she never considered what it would be like once he found someone

She couldn't find any words that sounded right, but she couldn't stand and ignore Karielyn, so she cleared her throat and said, "Why?"

Karielyn's brows pinched together, so she continued. "Why is it too late?"

She brushed a tear from the corner of her eye. "I'm a villain now. I knew that if he didn't know me before our story, then after, it would be too late after. He would know me as a villain and nothing else."

"Blake never judged me because of my fate." Xenia meant it to comfort her, but she wasn't sure if she still believed it herself. Blake had left as soon as he could.

Karielyn shook her head, more tears streaming down her face. "Because he *knows* you! He knew you weren't bad! He doesn't know me—he will only ever know the villain in me! My fate has taken *so much* from me. My entire life has been compromised because of a fate that hardly defines me! It isn't fair."

Once again, Xenia had nothing to say, so instead, she closed the space between them and wrapped her arms around Karielyn. She returned the embrace and took a deep breath, easing her body.

"I'm sorry," Karielyn whispered. She pulled away from

the hug. "I didn't mean to…"

"You don't need to apologize." Hardly anyone spoke to Xenia, and it had been so long since she had a conversation like this. *If only I knew what to say.* "Being a villain…" Her words stopped. Taking a deep breath, she tried again. "Being a villain is hard… Everyone thinks we're something we're not. It isn't fair, the way people judge us… I used to spend every day worrying that my old friends would never accept me. That even Blake wouldn't accept me. But even though it's hard, I think if someone can't see who we really are, then we don't need them.

"I haven't given up on Blake, and I don't think you should, either. He's wonderful… but if he can't see that you are more than your fate, then he doesn't deserve you."

Karielyn released a shaky breath. "Thank you, Xenia." She hesitated. "Life has been so hard since I got my fate. It feels good to talk to someone who understands me." Her blue eyes locked on Xenia's. "Can we start over? And be friends?"

"Yeah, I like that. Friends."

Chapter Seventeen

THE SUN GLOWED BRIGHT ORANGE, REFLECTING OFF THE snow as Xenia walked to the stables. They were full today. Most students needed to take a carriage to their parents' house for the holiday. Xenia stood in the stall and watched her frozen breath drift away as she waited. The sunlight seeped away quickly, and the blue moments before dusk filled the time between carriages.

After nearly an hour, a carriage came for Hero Village. She climbed in quickly, eager to escape the cold, and closed the door behind herself. She was the only one taking this carriage, as most of the heroes' children had taken private carriages hours ago.

The small cabin had parallel plush benches. It was dark inside. The lantern that hung overhead swayed gently, the candle inside was still melted in the center, and the wick blackened. The wind must have blown it out.

Xenia breathed against her hands and then crossed her

arms for warmth. The carriage left the stables, and she rode away from the Training Center premises.

The horses pulled the carriage through the kingdom's streets. Every window on the buildings she passed was lit and full of people gathering for dinner. She kept the curtains open despite the cold to see the city reinvent itself for the holiday. All the shops were closed; the streetlamps burned, illuminating the frosted grounds; and for once the streets were quiet, as most people were inside with loved ones.

The trees grew thicker and the roads darker from the lack of streetlamps as she neared the village. When the trees weren't coated with snow, they were lush and rich in color, adding to the community's beauty.

The carriage stopped at a tall, iron gate guarded on both sides. Before continuing, the coachman repeated a password to the men standing guard. They pulled open the gate, allowing them access to the village.

Once inside, Xenia felt like she had been transported to a different world. She passed sophisticated houses and yards, each one possessing a unique dash of character to represent the heroes they housed.

The Liftson Mansion was in the heart of the village. It sat on acres of tall, snow-covered trees. Every bush was carefully trimmed and shaped. Pale-brown bricks covered the outside, complemented by ornate, black trim that outlined the roof. The carriage stopped outside a gate, and Xenia climbed out.

A guard stepped towards her. "Please state your name."

"*Xenia Safire*," she said. "I'm a friend of Felix, he invited me over."

"Yes, we were told to expect a visitor. I need to check you for weapons, and then you may go in," he said.

"Of course," Xenia replied as the man began searching her. The only thing she had brought was the thin box of translations. She froze as he reached for it. If he read even one page, her and Felix's plan could be ruined.

He opened the box as a gust of wind tore through the trees. The pages flew out of the box, and the wind carried them down the street.

"No!" Xenia spun around to chase after the papers. They fluttered in the air before they dropped and the wind dragged them down the pavement. She caught what she hoped was the last one. Tears stung her eyes. The wet snow muddled the words, though she managed to make them out, but she didn't know what order they went in.

She carried them back to the mansion and put them into the box.

"I'm terribly sorry, miss, the wind has been foul today."

She just nodded as he opened the gate to let her inside. The path leading to the mansion was paved and clear of any snow. She followed it to a short set of stairs up to the door, breathing deeply to settle herself before knocking.

The door swung open, and a servant welcomed her inside. Xenia followed him in and gaped.

The foyer hardly looked like a home. Light-beige marble tiles spread across the wide hall, and the celling arched far above her. Long display tables lined both walls, showing off delicate vases and sculpted art pieces. At the far end of the foyer, a grand spiral staircase disappeared into a second floor.

Xenia had grown up in a castle—she was familiar with luxuries, but the Liftson Mansion stole her breath. She wandered to the tables, examining the elegant items on displayed.

A hand closed around her upper arm. Her heart jumped into her throat as she spun to face the man who had grabbed her.

Samuel Liftson glared down at her, his lips pinched and his eyes narrow. Xenia tried to pull her arm free, but his grip only tightened.

"What are you—?" she managed before he shouted, cutting her off.

"Felix Liftson!" He pulled her closer to the stairs, careless as if she were a rag doll. Fear numbed her head and muddled her thoughts.

Footsteps sounded from the hall upstairs, and Felix appeared on the spiral staircase, looking down at her. His eyes widened, and he ran down to her side.

"What are you doing?" he demanded. "Don't touch her!"

"*This* is the friend you invited? Safire?"

He met his father's gaze, his jaw set. "Yes."

Samuel dropped Xenia's arm, pulling his hand back as if she had burned him. She stumbled away from him and stood at Felix's side.

Samuel took a step towards his son and lowered his voice. "This needs to stop. I won't see her here again."

Xenia's cheeks burned. Felix hadn't told his father to expect her.

Before Felix could respond, Samuel turned on them and left the foyer.

"Fate." Felix cursed. "I'm so sorry. He never should have touched you…" His words fell apart, and he sighed.

"I'm used to it," she mumbled, reaching for the hem of her sleeve.

"I shouldn't have asked you to come. I knew he would—I knew this would happen. Fate, I'm sorry." His throat tensed and he tilted his head back, facing the ceiling.

Xenia watched him as he dropped his head and glared at the ground. She imagined him growing up in this house. Fate would never let her forget his upbringing, but her mind had only grazed over this part of him. He was just as beautiful as everything else in this mansion.

Her heart stopped. "Should we go to dinner now?" she asked, hoping to distract him—and herself. *What is wrong with me?*

Felix glared ahead as if the last thing he wanted was to follow his father to dinner, but he agreed anyway and led her through the foyer. They crossed through a brightly lit hall, where he stopped at a door and pushed it open, holding it for her.

Xenia's chest fluttered, and she resisted gaping as she stepped inside. The dining hall was a long, rectangular room, sharing the marble tiles from the rest of the mansion. The celling ascended higher, deeper into the room; and from the highest point in the middle, a sparkling chandelier dropped above a grand table set with golden-rimmed china and crystal glasses.

Despite the twelve seats on each side, only six were filled. Felix led her to the end of the table beside his family and took a seat. She filled the spot beside him.

The table was quiet as they settled. Felix cleared his throat. "This is my friend Xenia. Her mother is away campaigning for the selection, so I invited her to spend the holiday with us."

His brothers stared, their eyes narrowing or brows creasing.

Felix smiled despite the tension his last statement left. "Xenia," he said, motioning to the brother sitting at his left. "This is Lance. Beside him is Elden." He motioned across the table. "That's Trey and his wife, Lichelle. You're familiar with my father, and beside him is my mother."

Each brother shared Felix's caramel hair and golden-brown eyes.

"It's a pleasure to meet you," Xenia said. Her words felt like trapped tiles and stepping on the wrong one would cost her.

"It's wonderful to meet you as well," Trey said finally. "You're in Felix's year?"

"Yes, I am."

"You're the villain, aren't you?" Elden asked.

She opened her mouth to speak but didn't reply in time.

"Yes, this is Safire," Samuel said.

Lance's lips parted. "*This* is your friend? The girl from the article? Felix, this is your second—"

Before he could finish, Felix threw a dark glance in his brother's direction, and he stopped.

Xenia shifted uncomfortably in her seat. Why had Felix thought this would be a good idea? *Why did I?*

Elden's frown deepened and his brows drew together. "Karielyn was also a villain. Felix—"

"Please stop," Felix muttered. He turned back to Xenia, shaking his head. "I'm sorry about that, Nia."

"It's fine." Coming to the Liftson Mansion, she had to expect something of the sort.

He slid his arm over her shoulder, and she grimaced in surprise. She didn't pull away, though. She had no intentions of deepening their relationship, but his touch made her feel safer around his family.

A door at the back of the room opened and a line of kitchen servants in black aprons trailed into the room, carrying silver trays and glass pitchers. A server placed a platter of glazed and seasoned meat onto the table in the center of them. Tendrils of steam drifted from the meat as Samuel sliced it into thick pieces. Beside it more servers placed dishes piled with roasted vegetables, potatoes, and candied fruit. A woman filled each of their glasses with bubbly juice.

Xenia lifted her glass and took a sip. She had never had it before, but she liked it. Felix watched her empty the cup and then poured his into her glass.

After the main course, the servers returned with an array of pies and cakes in the bright shades of fruit and dark shades of chocolate.

Once everyone finished eating, Samuel led everyone from the dining room as they laughed in conversation.

Felix led her back through the foyer, up the spiral

staircase and down a wide hall with a marble floor and long, scarlet carpets. "This is my room," he said, opening a door to let her inside.

The room wasn't filled with the lavish luxuries she had expected to find. He had a bed with a wooden frame and simple, white sheets; an empty desk; and shelves lined with books. The curtains were drawn, and none of the candles on the desk had black wicks. The wooden floor was polished and colored a deep brown, the walls were paneled with dark wood, and a large chandelier illuminated the room.

"There's not much to see," he said. "I took most of my things with me to the Training Center." He crossed his arms and leaned against the desk. "What's in the box?"

"It's translations from the book!" she said, handing him the box.

He grinned. "Then let's start reading!"

Chapter Eighteen

FELIX OPENED THE BOX AND PICKED UP THE TRANSLA-tions. "What happened?" he asked.

Xenia grimaced. "The wind blew them away, I caught them, but they got a bit mixed up."

He nodded. "Then I guess we'll have to sort them out first," he said. He began spreading the papers out on his desk. "How did you get these? I thought your book was lost."

"Karielyn gave them to me. She took the book and gave it to her mother, since—"

"So, Karielyn's mother has your book?"

"Karielyn must trust her with it."

"And you trust Karielyn?"

Xenia frowned, glancing at the pages. She had done all this for Xenia. "I do. And I think we should tell her what we're doing. She's finding ways to help regardless. Wouldn't it be easier to work together?"

144

Felix sighed. "Fine. But I don't think she'll be interested. Not when she finds out I'm involved." He leaned over the desk, narrowing his eyes. "What's this?"

Along with the translations from Karielyn's mother, Xenia had also put all the notes they already had into the box. "That's one of the passages that Karielyn and I translated. I don't know what it means, though."

He picked it up and read aloud. "*Two willing to change the way written on the scrolls. To find the jewel hidden higher than the clouds or lower than the sea, it lurks where magic is the most. Then climb above the clouds and perform the unspeakable deed.*" He read over it again. "*It lurks where magic is the most…*" he whispered under his breath. He set down the note and reached for one of the papers. "*To change the path chosen for you, to jump beyond the stones laid carefully for you, to clear your title from your name, find the jewel within the story designed for your feet.*"

Her heart skipped a beat and continued faster than before. "We haven't read that part yet."

Felix handed her the paper. "Look, it comes after the passage you translated."

"What do you think it means?"

"It sounds like this jewel must be somewhere inside our story. Once we enter, we need to find the jewel… hidden higher than the clouds, but lower than the sea." His brow creased. "What is higher than the clouds, but lower…?"

Xenia read over the passage again. "It lurks where magic is the most." *Where magic is the most.* "All stories are different," she said, setting the paper down. "They never take place in the same world, which means it can never be in the same place twice, but it will always be where the most magic is. Every story must have one!"

"But if there are so many of them, why has no one switched their fate in so long? What if the jewel doesn't exist anymore?"

"It has to," she said. "It's magic."

Felix had touched on a good point. If no one had used the jewel in so long, could it be used at all? She didn't want to consider it.

"It's forbidden, and it could be guarded by magic," she said, trying harder to convince herself than him. "People might have tried, they might have succeeded, but the leaders of Chantendell found a way to keep it quiet."

"That's possible. We shouldn't doubt yet," he said, placing a hand on her shoulder. "Unless we find proof that the jewel doesn't exist, we're going to look for it."

She shrugged away from his touch; it reminded her too much of the previous night.

He continued as if nothing had happened. "Even if we enter and the jewel no longer exists, at least we tried. We need to enter our story either way, whether we keep our fates or not."

Xenia picked up her notes. "We also found a passage that said that using the jewel may result in imprisonment or death, do you think that will happen to us?"

He frowned in thought. "Not if we succeed, Liz wasn't punished. Maybe they can't interfere after it's done."

"Liz Eveyon switched hundreds of years ago. The laws could be completely different now."

"I think it's worth the risk."

Was it worth the risk? If Xenia stayed a villain, she would be imprisoned anyway.

A grin split across Felix's face. "And if anything goes wrong, hopefully, your mother will be queen. She won't let you be executed."

Xenia laughed and Felix joined her.

She jumped as the door flew open and stumbled back into him. His eyes twinkled as he swept her back up.

"What are you doing up here?" Lance asked.

"Nothing that concerns you," Felix snapped.

Lance shook his head. "Father wants you downstairs, and Trey is getting ready to leave."

"Thank you, we'll be down," Felix said, pushing the door closed on his brother. When they were alone, he turned to her. "About last night—"

Her heart fell. "I don't want to talk about it," she said quickly, her eyes falling to the ground.

"I'm truly sorry, I didn't mean to make you uncomfortable. You left right after, I didn't think you were going to come over tonight, but I'm glad you did."

"Me too. And please forget about last night." She meant it for him but took note herself.

"It never happened. Oh, are we still meeting for Victoria's party tomorrow?"

Xenia's chest tightened at the mention of the party. What Victoria had said didn't matter anymore. She had already made up her mind—she would go to the party, and Felix never had to know about their fight.

"Yes, I'll be waiting for you at sunset. And thank you for having me over tonight."

"I know it must have been miserable with my father—I'm sorry."

"It's fine," she assured.

Felix turned and grabbed the door handle. "Before you leave, you should try my mother's hot chocolate."

"I'd love to!"

Felix opened the door and hurried down the hall. Xenia chased him down the stairs and through an unfamiliar corridor. Staff gave them disapproving stares as they passed, but Felix paid no mind, so Xenia tried not to, either.

They stopped in a large room filled with plush rugs and sofas, where the Liftson's had gathered. Wide windows filled the back wall, flaunting the snow-covered garden. The Liftsons' property looked like a forest from all the tall trees.

In the back of the room was a curved bar, but instead of alcohol, cups of rich, melted chocolate topped with cream lined the surface. Felix grabbed one and handed another to Xenia.

The hot chocolate was rich and smooth, and the server gave Xenia an extra glass for the ride back to the Training Center. She rode in one of the Liftsons' fancy carriages, and by the time she arrived, she was convinced the night had been sped up.

Karielyn waited in the living room when she returned. She was deep into a newly released book and had nearly every candle out.

"You aren't celebrating with your family?" Xenia asked,

joining her on the couch.

Karielyn shook her head. "We don't celebrate."

"Oh." Xenia had met very few people who didn't participate in the celebration. But Karielyn had attended the feast with her yesterday—she had assumed she would have festive plans for tonight as well.

Xenia waited a moment before speaking again. Finally, she cleared her throat to get Karielyn's attention, and she snapped her head up from the book. "Karielyn, you've helped so much by translating the book. Me and Felix, we've been studying it together, we—we want to switch our fates. Will you work with us?"

Xenia braced herself for Karielyn to snap and unleash her anger. She waited for her to shout about how she was making a mistake and the trouble she would land herself.

But Karielyn only a smiled. "I'd love to."

Chapter Nineteen

KARIELYN KNOCKED LOUD ENOUGH TO WAKE XENIA the next morning. She stumbled lazily out of bed to get to the door. "Yeah?" she asked, covering a yawn with her hand and then rubbing her eyes.

"Seriously? Are you seriously still sleeping? It's past noon!"

"We're on break," Xenia said, pulling a strand of hair from her mouth. She hadn't made it to sleep until well into the night. She kept replaying last night in her mind. Over and over.

"Well, I've been up for hours. Victoria's party is tonight, remember? You need to get ready."

Xenia rolled her eyes and brushed past Karielyn down the stairs.

"What are you doing?" Karielyn asked from behind her.

"I'm getting breakfast."

"Breakfast was *hours* ago—"

150

"Fine, then, lunch," she corrected briskly.

Karielyn massaged her temple with her hand as she continued down the stairs. Was she always this stressed before a party?

Xenia grabbed a loaf of bread and a jar of jam.

"You're still going to be in your nightgown by the time we leave!" Karielyn said, coming up beside her.

She set the remaining bread back onto the counter. "I'll be fine."

She let out a stiff laugh. "And you still need to bathe, fix your hair, do your makeup—"

A demanding knock cut Karielyn short, and she ran to answer it. Morea followed her back inside, wearing a short, strapless dress. Her burgundy hair lay in neat waves at her shoulders, and heavy makeup covered her tan face.

As the girls greeted each other, Xenia ran upstairs to the bathroom to get ready. She slipped on the black dress, which fit well, considering Karielyn was several inches shorter than her. She brushed through her thick hair and pulled it into an intricate bun. She hadn't planned to wear makeup, but Karielyn insisted. Even then, she finished well before it was time to leave.

Felix arrived as the sun began to set. "You look amazing!" he said when she opened the door.

"Thank you!" she said, blush staining her cheeks. "So do you!"

He wore a finely tailored, black blazer, and his golden-brown hair was parted to the side. He resembled a younger, handsomer version of his father.

"All right, let's go," Karielyn said snidely as she walked past them.

"Look who decided to join us," Felix said, turning to leave.

They walked through the courtyard to the stables, where Felix's carriage waited. It wasn't the same one she had taken yesterday—it was, if possible, even nicer. It had a pale-blue and gold scheme, matching the Liftson family emblem. Unlike most carriages, this one had a chandelier in place of a lantern. That wasn't even common in *houses*. The windows were fully closed off with glass and concealed with curtains. Xenia had been in similar carriages before—her mother's wasn't far from it.

She and Felix sat side by side on one end, and Karielyn and Morea sat opposite them.

"Why are we using this carriage?" Karielyn asked.

"I just came from my father's house. If you'd rather take one from the Training Center stables, you are perfectly welcome to."

She sneered, leaning back in her seat.

Xenia must have forgotten how long the trip to the Dwelling of Royals was, though it might have seemed longer because of the tension between Karielyn and Felix. If they were to work together, something would need to change, but Xenia wasn't even sure what had happened between them.

Every time she looked at Morea, she remembered what Karielyn had told her. *Morea knew, but Felix treated her terribly.* She tried not to think about what might have been. Maybe he was rude to Karielyn, but he certainly wasn't rude to

Xenia. If he was rude then, he had changed.

The ride was silent, aside from Karielyn and Felix's occasional bickering. Xenia pulled back the curtains as they passed her mother's castle.

They arrived at the Vandays' castle, and Victoria greeted them at the door. "Felix, I'm so glad you're here!" she said, throwing her arms around him. He pulled away quickly and grabbed Xenia's hand.

"Xenia, you made it… lovely," she said tersely.

They entered the castle before Victoria could say anything else. Even though it had been five years since the last time Xenia visited, the inside looked the same as it had, only now it was filled with food tables and the buzz of people talking and laughing.

"Victoria is entering our story this week—this party is in honor of that," Felix explained irritably.

"Are you all right?"

"Why wouldn't I be?"

"You sounded… Never mind."

The Vandays' castle closely resembled Estelle's. The walls were made of the same dark-gray stone, and polished and stained wood stretched across the floors. Though, Xenia had never seen her mother's castle filled with so many people.

A group of girls approached Felix, giggling as they tried to engage him in conversation. Victoria pushed past them to reach his side. "Felix, would you like to dance?"

He turned to Xenia. "Sure. Nia, let's go dance."

Xenia smiled and followed him to the center of the

room. He picked up her hand and twirled her around. Victoria's annoyance gleamed in her eyes. Xenia's face colored when she noticed her staring, and she tried not to look at her.

The song slowed, and Felix placed his hand on her waist, then guided hers to his shoulder. He pulled her into him so she was leaning against his chest. She closed her eyes and let him lead her slight steps. His heart beat fast, and she heard every steady thump. She blocked out every other noise and focused on the rhythm.

Too soon the music changed, and Felix spun her around again. Had he enjoyed the last moment the way she had? Already, she missed the last moment so much that she wanted to ask the pianist to play the song again. Her chest tightened. Why had she enjoyed it so much?

"Are you hot?" he asked, twirling her around again. "I can find you a drink."

"Sure, but I don't need anything special."

"I'll be back," he said, dropping her hand and turning for the kitchen.

Xenia spun around to find Victoria's face inches from hers. "You need to leave," she said.

Xenia took a step back. "I… What did I do?"

Victoria shook her head. "I told you not to come. Xenia, you're making the other guests uncomfortable."

Xenia's cheeks flushed bright pink. "But I'm not doing anything!"

"What's going on?" Warren said, rushing to Victoria's side.

She took a deep breath and then turned to face him,

tears filling her eyes. "She's scaring me! I asked her to leave but she refuses. I—I told her not to come. I don't know w—what else to do."

Xenia's brows pulled together in confusion. What was she doing?

"She told you to leave!" Warren shouted. The crowd around her quieted and watched. He leaned close to her. "If you don't go now, I'll make you wish you never came," he hissed.

Blood pounded in Xenia's ears as she tried to figure out what to do. Karielyn might have told her to stay, but she wasn't Karielyn, and she couldn't bring herself to stay any longer.

"Fine!" she shouted. The crowed turned to look at her as she stormed out of the castle, into the chilly air. She tore through the night, darting for her mother's castle. The cold air stung her face as she ran across the snow-covered path to the iron gate that surrounded the backyard. Two men stood next to the gate, guarding the entrance. Her mother had many guards and servants. Xenia knew them all. They nodded when they saw her face and moved clear of the gate. She pulled it open and fumbled towards a frozen pond. She sat down on the bench beside it, sobs shaking her.

A series of worried thoughts spilled into her mind. She thought of the way Victoria wrapped her arm around Felix each time she saw him. Was it possible that what Karielyn had told her about Felix acting could be true? If she weren't in his sight, would he forget her and find another girl? And even if he did, why would it matter? Once again, she reminded herself of their contradicting fates. But for once she let herself wonder what her relationship with Felix would look like if they didn't have fates. Would she let herself want him? Did some part of her want him now?

She cried harder.

Shouts echoed in the distance. Xenia tensed. After another round of shouting, she identified Felix's voice. She darted towards the gate and demanded it open. One guard opened it while the other held Felix's arms behind his back.

"What are you doing?"

"He was trying to get in, miss. Started shouting and demanded entrance."

Xenia shook her head. Felix had grown up in a home with high security; surely he knew how to behave around guards.

"He's my friend," she explained.

The guard let him go, and she rushed to his side.

"Are you okay?" Felix asked.

"I'm fine."

"Karielyn told me you left after Warren and Victoria yelled at you. What happened?"

She let out a quiet sigh, focusing on the distance. "Victoria doesn't like me. We used to be friends, but we haven't talked since I got my fate. She told me I was making others uncomfortable and I should leave… so I left." She hesitated a moment before telling him the rest. "She told me not to come at all. That no one wanted me there."

Felix groaned. "I'm sorry I brought you into this. I was selfish for bringing you—I thought it might make the night more bearable."

Xenia's skin turned hot at his words.

"If you had told me, I never would have brought you." He leaned in so the guards couldn't hear and whispered, "I don't like her, either."

Xenia swiped at her eyes, biting back a smile.

"Come here!" he said, grabbing her wrist. They ran out of the yard and down the slick, cobblestone path.

They reached Victoria's house, but he didn't go for the door; instead, he climbed into the back seat of the carriage that had taken them to the party. "Let's get away from here. I have somewhere I want to show you."

Xenia climbed in next to him, and he whispered something to the coachman. He nodded and then climbed out of the cabin. The horses started moving towards the busy streets of Chantendell, leaving the Dwelling of Royals behind. They passed marketplaces, taverns, and many other buildings, but they didn't slow for any.

"Where are we—?"

"It's a surprise."

"Felix—"

"Don't worry, we'll be there soon."

The carriage didn't stop until they were outside the city. Fear had begun to trickle inside her. There were no streetlamps, leaving the road in darkness, and her company was a boy she wasn't sure she could trust.

Felix pulled open the door and she climbed out and gasped: Felix had brought her to an old palace ruin. It was made from dazzling, white stone that sparkled in contrast to the black sky. Half of the palace still stood tall, but the other side looked like remnants of war. Pieces were thrown across the site, and the walls were crumbled.

"What is this place?" Xenia asked, breathless.

"Hasn't your mother taken you here before?"

She shook her head.

"This used to be where the rulers of Chantendell lived."

"Really?" She had heard stories about this palace. It was destroyed by Enria during the War of Chantendell.

Moonlight glinted off the untouched snow around them. All Xenia could do was stare.

"I thought you might like it," Felix said behind her. "Come on, I want to show you the inside." He broke the snow in a path towards the entrance. Xenia hurried after him.

Inside they wandered through a dark corridor and up a set of damaged stairs that led to a high balcony. From where she stood, she could see the entire kingdom. Lights glittered like stars in the distance.

"This is beautiful!" she cried.

Felix folded his arms over the edge of the rails. "It's always peaceful out here," he said, gazing into the kingdom.

Xenia leaned against the edge next to him. She could see miles of snow-covered ground and the lit windows in the kingdom—it was breathtaking.

They didn't talk, but they didn't need to, the serene silence was enough to carry them. Just standing alone in the moonlit night with the wind stinging their faces and lifting their hair felt perfect.

"Follow me, I want to show you something else," Felix

said finally.

They turned back inside, and he guided her through the dark hallways. "This was the throne room." His words bounced from wall to wall. He stopped in a room with high ceilings and rusted chandeliers that hung by the single bolts that remained attached. They swayed in the wind, threatening to come loose and send shattered crystals in every direction.

Each wall hid behind a series of murals featuring dim colors faded from weather. Tall risers for seating wrapped around the walls, providing room to hold an entire court. On the back wall, wide stairs led to a narrow landing. The ceiling was crumbling, leaving an opening to the stars and letting the moon's rays illuminate the room.

All the walls were lined with tarnished torch holders, Xenia imagined each one roaring to life with fire and bringing light to the now abandoned castle. Two large pillars stood by the rotting base of a severely weathered throne that looked as if it might turn to dust at a touch.

"Felix, this is incredible," she said, examining the room. "I can't imagine what this place looked like before— I can't believe people lived here!" She walked up the risers and ran her fingers across one of the murals, paint chipped away at her touch.

"Well, every princess needs a castle," he said, coming up next to her.

"I'm not a princess."

"Not yet."

She turned to face him. "You think my mother will be

selected?" She had tried not to think too much about the selection after she had finished her speech. The other two finalists were Vanday and Dendilor. Xenia wasn't sure she could handle it if her mother lost to Victoria's father.

"Why do you think Victoria is leaving before the selection?" His laughter echoed off the crumbled walls and danced in the cool air. "She knows her father won't win, and she doesn't want to be here to see your mother take the throne."

Xenia stepped back down, short of a response.

Felix's hands snagged her waist, and she staggered backward into his arms. "Careful," he said with a wide grin that spread to the corners of his eyes. He swept her back up, keeping one hand on her back for support. He spun her around like he had at the party, until she fell into step and they began to dance. He guided her steps, and occasionally dipped her and let her rest in his arms.

Before, she didn't think she could dance, but with Felix, every move felt natural. She fell back when he dipped her and spun around with ease into his arms. Even without music, they both seemed to know what beat to move to.

He slowed, pulling her closer to him. His eyes locked on hers as they swayed slightly. "Are you afraid of me?" he asked evenly.

Xenia froze, no longer able to hold his gaze. "W—what?"

His jaw was set, and a frown pulled his eyes. When he spoke, emotion cracked his words. "I know you are. I don't want to hurt you, Nia."

"It's just, our fates—"

"I would never want to hurt you."

But you're going to.

Spiders ran across her skin as he held her. This man would be her demise.

"Fate is cruel," he whispered. "I would never choose you as an enemy."

After their dance, they sat down on the cold risers. "I don't understand why you want my fate," she managed. She didn't think she could continue without an answer. "Why would you *want* to be trapped and alone?"

"I'm already trapped and alone," he bristled. He looked down, avoiding her gaze, and sighed. "I suppose I owe you an explanation. My fate… it's hardly as glorious as it appears, and coming from my family—I do feel trapped. There are so many parts of my life I can't escape because of my fate. Everyone thinks they know me because of a name and a title. No one knows who I really am, sometimes it feels like that person doesn't exist at all."

Xenia propped her elbow onto the riser behind her and leaned back. Tears stung her eyes. "I—I understand that. No one cares to know me, either. They know my fate, and for them, that's enough."

"It isn't fair," Felix said. He leaned back beside her. "We'll get ourselves out of this."

Wind whistled through the trees. Xenia blinked away her tears and looked up at the stars scattered across the sky. The remains of the marble ceiling obscured her view.

They stayed in the throne room, talking deep into the

night. The air grew colder, and the wind blew harder, but Xenia hardly cared. Here, away from the kingdom, she could close her eyes and imagine she didn't have a fate to fulfil. She imagined her life without the ties of Fate.

Felix bolted up, his face growing pale. "We have to go—now. I forgot Karielyn and Morea are taking my carriage back to the Training Center. The party will be over by the time we get there."

She frowned. Was the night really over—did it have to be over?

Victoria seemed the type to throw a party that lasted until the early hours, but Xenia knew she couldn't handle a night that long.

He held out his hand to assist her up. She took it, rose to her feet, and then said, "I'm sure they can find another ride. Everyone's going to the same place."

He hesitated. "I… I need to get back." His words were uneven, and any trace of a smile had disappeared.

She didn't argue further.

They left the ruins and climbed into the back of the carriage. Felix relit the chandelier, illuminating the small space. The golden accents that lined the walls glistened in the light. She leaned her head against the cushioned walls, and if it weren't for Felix keeping her heart beating at a quick pace, she would have drifted asleep in the warm, swaying cabin.

Karielyn and Morea stood in front of the Vandays' castle when they arrived, each with heated expressions on their cold-brushed faces. "You left us!" Karielyn shouted before the horses came to a complete stop. "Where did you go?"

"It's freezing out here!" Morea said as she traipsed through the snow behind Karielyn.

"It wasn't any warmer where we were," Felix said as they clambered in.

"I hardly care," Karielyn snapped, her voice uneven from a shiver. She climbed in, followed by Morea, and they reclaimed their spots on the velvet bench.

Karielyn continued to curse Felix as the horses pulled the carriage out of the Dwelling of Royals.

"You chose to ride with me, Height. Perhaps you should find a different escort next time," Felix said.

Karielyn took a deep breath and then turned to look out her window. The four of them remained silent for the remainder of the trip.

Even when they returned home, Xenia stayed up for hours longer, lying in bed. Despite its flaws, tonight had been perfect.

Chapter Twenty

FELIX WOKE BEFORE THE SUN HAD FULLY RISEN. CONsidering how late he had stayed out the previous night, he should have slept late into the day. But sleeping was never easy after making an altering decision.

What have I gotten myself into?

He sat at his desk, staring at the stack of books threatening to topple. He needed something to distract himself from her. But nothing would.

"Felix, are you ready?" Merrick shouted from outside his door.

"Ready for what?" he called back.

"We're meeting Victoria at the library—she's entering her story today, remember?"

He suddenly didn't crave a distraction. He could handle being alone with his thoughts—though they weren't ideal. Could there be a worse way to spend his morning? He listed a few, but not many, and with his current state of mind, going

164

to see Victoria now wouldn't end well.

"Oh, right. I think I've caught something. I'm nauseous… and… I'll have to skip."

"Are you sure? Felix, she's *entering* today, can't you make it for her?"

"I really don't feel well, I can't think straight. Please tell her I'm sorry." At least one part of that was truthful.

"Of course. I hope it passes. Do you need anything?"

"I'll be fine. You should go, I don't want to make you late."

"I'll see you tonight, then."

Merrick's steps quieted as he reached the bottom of the stairs. Felix waited by his bedroom door to hear him leave. A few minutes later, the door slammed shut, leaving him alone.

Perhaps he received too much enjoyment from the moments he found himself alone. Most people didn't understand him. And even if they wanted to, most never could because they already had an idea of him in their minds. If he told them he dreamed of being a villain, they would laugh as if he were joking. His name far preceded his actions.

He grabbed his copy of Liz Eveyon's story and went downstairs to the kitchen for breakfast, though he wasn't hungry. What he told Merrick had only been a partial lie. He wasn't sick, but since last night his stomach wouldn't stop turning.

Am I doing the right thing? He had waited years to make the choice he made last night. How could he question it?

He sighed. No matter his afterthoughts, he couldn't

change his mind. Not with her. She wouldn't offer him the chance to change it. The deal was final.

Even if he could reverse his actions, would he? If his plans with Xenia failed, he would have this.

He opened the book and skimmed through the pages. After reading it twice, he formed a theory. Liz Eveyon was his ancestor. Among research, he discovered that no Liftson he could account for were heroes until Liz married into the family. Every member of his family from Liz's line was a hero.

Late last night he had concluded that when Liz switched her fate, it cursed her blood. And every one of her descendants'. There hadn't been a non-hero Liftson since. He also looked at Rendon Counterstart's line. It died shortly after, but they were all villains.

He stared at the veins in his wrist, hoping for an answer. He wished he had someone to tell. He couldn't tell Xenia yet. If he messed it up, he might frighten her out of switching. He could never tell his father. His brothers wouldn't listen, and neither would his mother. Who could he talk to about his blood being cursed if not his family? He didn't have friends—not real ones. However, there was one person in his family that seemed to understand him slightly more than the rest. His grandfather no longer spoke to the rest of the family, yet Felix came to visit him when he could.

He packed a few items into a bag, including the book, and left the tower. He paid no attention to the gray storm clouds swirling overhead, or the foul wind as he darted to the Training Center stables and climbed into a carriage.

"Hero Village, please," he ordered.

The coachman nodded, and the horses began moving.

Felix fiddled with his fingers, something he seldom did. His heartbeat crept up, and his sweat dampened his hands despite the cold.

He shivered as the wind blew the curtains open and passed through the cabin. His family's carriages were of much finer quality. He tried to ignore the open window and resecured the curtain.

Once he arrived, snow had begun to fall and stick to the ground. He darted past the gate for the door and hoped his grandfather would be home. Unlike Samuel, his grandfather didn't have somewhere to be every day. At one point, he certainly had, but not of late.

Felix knocked on the door and waited for him to open it. Even though he didn't know as much about his grandfather as he wanted to, he knew a few things: his grandfather didn't like hiring guards or servants, so he lived alone.

Footsteps neared the door. Before it opened, Felix took a deep breath to calm himself.

"Grandfather, can we talk?" he asked when the door opened.

Eugene Liftson smiled. "Of course. I don't talk to anyone anymore."

Felix followed his grandfather into the house as he complained about the lack of company, something they didn't have in common. The room he led him to had a large window overlooking the garden. Layers of rugs in a variety of dull reds, blues, and greens covered the wooden floors.

Eugene took a seat in a green chair near the bookshelf, and Felix filled the seat next to him. Eugene mumbled complaints under his breath until Felix cut him off. "Grandfather, this is important."

He went silent and stared at Felix with expecting eyes.

Felix took another breath. "I've been doing some… research…" He never struggled to speak clearly, but now his words refused to form. "Family research, and I… I think our blood is… cursed."

His grandfather stared at him for a moment, brows drawn. The silence stretched longer and longer until Felix wanted to disappear inside of himself. Would he not even consider the idea?

He pulled the book from his bag and tried to hand it to him, but Eugene waved it off. "Please, look, this book, I think—"

"Well, of course," Eugene said finally. He rose to his feet and walked over to the shelf lined with stories from his ancestors. He pulled down a book that was an identical copy of the one Felix had brought and flashed it so Felix could see as he took back his seat. "Didn't your father ever tell you?"

Felix shook his head slowly. "Tell me what?"

"Our family's secret," he whispered.

Felix narrowed his eyes. "No."

"Well, then, I'll have to talk to him about that." He laughed bitterly at his own comment. "Before I start, you must promise not to repeat this outside of the family."

"I promise," he said, eager to hear what his father had kept from him.

"Our family wasn't always heroes. Centuries ago, we were nearly all villains. Liz Eveyon was born a villain, but she used an old method to illegally switch her fate—something that could have cost her life if she failed, but she didn't."

Felix squeezed the arm of his seat. Did his family really know all along what he and Xenia had researched for weeks? Why had Samuel never told him?

"Why wasn't she punished?"

"They couldn't execute or arrest her—it would raise too many questions. Not many people knew of the strange method, and the king intended to keep it that way. Liz vowed to never let the secret reach another's ear. After she switched, she married our Bentlix, cursing every one of her descendants' blood with the magic that made her a hero."

Felix had already discovered most of this on his own. Still, his grandfather's story held his complete attention. He didn't want to lose a single detail.

"Why is it kept a secret?"

Eugene fought a laugh. "Fate switching is illegal. Very few people have gotten away with it. The king forced Liz to never speak of it. The secret has been kept in our family for centuries. There cannot and will not be a non-hero Liftson. It's impossible."

"What if one of us switched, would it not work?"

Eugene quieted for a while. "I can't say I have an answer."

Felix glanced at the books lining his grandfather's shelf. Each one told the story of a Liftson. His would accompany them soon, but would he be the hero of his story? Even if so, he wouldn't be considered a hero for long after. Not when people found out what he did. What he planned to do.

"Thank you, grandfather," Felix said, returning his book to his bag and rising to his feet. He had confirmation now. He needed to tell Xenia, but first he needed to speak to his father.

"Thank you, Felix, for visiting—I don't get much company anymore."

Eugene's sincere voice pierced Felix's heart. Years before he was born, Samuel and Eugene got into a heated argument over villain rights, resulting in Samuel severing their relationship. Felix didn't meet his grandfather until he was ten years old. Samuel rarely mentioned him, so Felix had assumed him to be dead.

"I'll come back soon," he promised, pulling open the door. Instead of letting it drop, he closed it slowly behind him, savoring the moment.

Samuel's house could be seen from Eugene's door. The village wasn't small, but all the Liftsons lived near each other. *Village* was an understatement for his family's neighborhood. Every street was lined with beautiful mansions. The name of the settlement made the heroes seem humble. Maybe most of them were—even some in his family—but he had never witnessed it.

The snow was deep enough now that Felix's shoes left imprints in the ground in a trail leading to the front door. He knocked hard on the door, forgetting his parents' busy schedule.

"Fate, be home," he whispered under his breath.

A servant opened the door to let him in, but he stayed outside. "I need to see my father. Is he home?"

"Yes, shall I tell him you're here, sir?"

"Tell him I want to speak with him. I'll be waiting here."

The servant nodded, albeit hesitantly, and hurried through the foyer and up the spiral stairs. Felix's heart raced as he prepared to confront his father.

Samuel stalled his arrival, leaving Felix shivering in the falling snow. Yet he couldn't bring himself to go inside. He would wait in the cold for his father.

When Samuel finally arrived at the door, his eyes were narrowed and his jaw set. "I am busy preparing for an event tonight—what could possibly be so important that you must speak now?"

Felix didn't move or speak. He had spent years bending to his father's will. He thought that was what he should do. But he couldn't bear to continue. Doing so had already taken enough from him.

"We can talk, if that's what you need, but I'm giving a speech tonight and I don't have a lot of time to spare," he said, his tone slightly gentler now.

Because your last speech went so well. Xenia's furious face flashed through his mind like a taunt. *What I'll do will hurt her worse.*

"Are you all right?" Samuel asked.

"You never told me!" he screamed. How could he keep something so important from him for so long? Our family secret, you never told me! Did you tell my brothers? Am I not part of this family?

Samuel glowed red. "I don't know… Who told you?"

"Grandfather."

Samuel buried his face into his hand. "Listen, Felix, I didn't want to tell—I'm sorry—I thought it had been long enough, and if I didn't tell you, the story would be forgotten. It benefits no one."

"You want everyone to forget about Liz? Why?"

"I'm not the fondest of the idea that we come from villains. We're heroes now, we have a status to maintain. The less we know about our past, the easier it will be."

Felix scoffed. "That's all you care about! It's all about how we appear to everybody else, it's always been about that, I'm tired of it! Everything you do, you do for the public, that's all you've ever cared about!"

"Felix—"

"No, Father! I won't hear it! And I discovered the curse before going to Grandfather!" He turned red and hot despite the snow blowing in his face. He ran a hand through his hair to distract himself from Samuel.

"Then how—?"

"I was researching our family. History can't be erased."

"Of course not. I'm only covering up our ancestors' mistakes."

Felix shook his head. Had he forgotten he had a life outside fame? *Did* he have a life outside fame? "Why are you so afraid of people finding out? It happened four centuries ago!"

"What's going on? Why are you yelling?" Felix's eldest brother, Trey, asked, making his way to the door through the foyer.

"What are you doing here?" Felix demanded.

"Father and I are attending an event in the kingdom together. Why are you so angry?"

Samuel gave Felix a stern look.

Felix ignored him and turned his attention to his brother. "I was talking to Father about our family secret—"

"Felix," Samuel started, a scolding frown spreading across his face.

Felix peered past his father to avoid his gaze. The house had been cleaned to perfection. Every vase was polished and held flowers shipped in from the warmer regions. The only visible fault was the melting snow by the doorway, where Felix still stood outside.

"What family secret?" Trey asked, glancing from Samuel to Felix.

"You shouldn't worry about it. Father believes it's too dangerous to share family stories with his children."

Trey glanced between his father and younger brother, waiting for an answer that Felix knew he would never get from Samuel.

Samuel glared at Felix. "There is far more than you will ever understand—"

"Then why don't you explain?" he snapped.

Trey stared in confusion as if they spoke different languages. "One of you, tell me what in Fate's name is going on!" he shouted, grimacing at his own use of Fate's name.

At Trey's raised voice, his wife darted to the door and grabbed his arm. "Is everything all right?" she asked quietly.

"Yes, everything is fine." Samuel assured her. He grabbed his temple. "Come inside and we'll discuss this further. You're only making a mess by leaving the door open."

Felix followed him through the house to a seating room with plush sofas and a view of the forest. Samuel sat on one of the sofas, and Trey and Lichelle sat beside him. Felix took a seat in a chair opposite them, glowering.

"What is this family secret?"

Felix felt a spark of annoyance at how his older brother was now getting an explanation. He only wanted to confront his father about keeping it a secret.

Samuel sighed. "For hundreds of years, Fate has gifted our family with the honor of being heroes. However, it hasn't always been this way. Many of our ancestors were villains. A woman in 1403, Liz Eveyon, was destined to be a villain. Instead of fulfilling her Fate-given calling, she used a forbidden method to switch her fate with the hero, cursing her blood."

Lichelle gasped and grabbed Trey's hand.

"Fates can be switched?" he asked, his voice failing.

Samuel's eyes flickered to Felix. "Yes, assuming two people are willing to trade places and understand how to do so."

"What did the curse do to her?" Trey asked.

"When she switched her fate, it cursed her blood—though the effected was her kin. She married a man from our lineage, and each of their children grew up to be heroes. And theirs after that, continuing all the way to each of my children."

"We're heroes because of a *curse?*"

"You are a hero in every right. Do not forget all that you did in your story to earn that title."

Felix rolled his eyes. It seemed he had found a worse way to spend his morning than with Victoria. "I'm going back to the Training Center," he said, standing.

"I don't think you'll make it back." Felix's mother stood in the doorway, snow melting in her hair. "The streets are icy and the speech has been canceled due to the storm."

"I have to go back—I can't stay here!" He grabbed his bag as if preparing to leave, even though he knew it was pointless. The coachmen wouldn't take him anywhere if it were to put him in danger.

"You should be back before your training starts again. Besides, we hardly see you. It will be nice to spend time together." Sybella Liftson filled the seat on her husband's other side and smiled at Felix.

"No, I need to get back. I need to talk to someone, it's important."

"It wouldn't happen to be about Eveyon, would it?" Samuel asked. His wife closed her eyes as if the very mention of such a thing was a disgrace. And apparently, to everyone else in the room, it was.

Felix clenched his teeth. He didn't care how much his father wanted it to remain a secret, he planned on telling Xenia as soon as he got back.

"Whatever it is must wait, you can't go out in this condition," his mother said.

"Lichelle and I can walk home," Trey said.

Felix turned to his brother. "Could I stay with you?

Father is very busy, and I wouldn't want to bother him."

Trey wrinkled his brow. "You're welcome to, if that's what you'd prefer."

"Thank you, I appreciate it." He couldn't possibly stay here. Not after what he had done last night. He didn't feel welcome here anymore. He wasn't even sure he felt like part of the family.

He left the house with Lichelle and Trey and walked through the raging snow to the other end of the road. The Liftsons owned the entire street. Between his brothers, aunts, uncles, and cousins, they filled most of the village.

They reached the house, and Felix went straight to the guest bedroom, which smelled strongly of stagnant flower perfume. The room was bigger than both of the rooms in his tower combined. It was simply decorated but, like most rooms in Chantendell, had a spot filled with books.

Felix crossed the room and pulled Samuel's story from the shelf. He fanned through the pages and watched Ravelyn's name fly by. The crippling guilt within him increased, and he slammed the book closed, storing it back onto the shelf and out of sight.

Earlier he had told Merrick he was sick. He would know Felix had lied when he returned and Felix wasn't there. He likely already knew. He tried to push Merrick out of his mind. He was a reminder of how he was always acting a part that didn't fit him. When he was around Merrick and Victoria—and even his own family.

Chapter Twenty-One

"FATE, IT'S COLD OUT THERE," KARIELYN SAID AS SHE closed the door behind her. She pulled off her coat and hung it by the door. "My mother gave me more translations this morning."

"Really?" Excitement sparked through Xenia despite not having read all the last translations. She had spent her free time attempting to put them back in the correct order over break.

"Here they are," Karielyn said, handing her a thin envelope.

Xenia opened it, pulled out the translations, and spread them across the table. There were only five pages, and a note that she read first.

Dear Karielyn,

I sent this package containing more translations from your book! As you read through the pages, please take into consideration the consequences of your choices.

- Love, Mom

P.S. I'm having a delightful time translating this!

The note was a bit strange. Mrs. Height didn't seem concerned by the book's content. Xenia set it aside and then read the first page.

To change your fate is to change your blood. To change your blood is to change you. To change you it will cost a price not all will want to pay. The name you bear will forever be in the hands of the fate you now seek. The choice is no one's but your own. Your fate lies in your hands, alongside the fates of those who will come after you. The choices of now affect the results of forever. The price that you pay is the blood in your veins.

Chills crawled across Xenia's body as she read the last line. She would pay with her blood?

"Karielyn!" she called, folding the other papers frantically and shoving them back into the envelope. "I think we need to go see Felix." She didn't want to read further without his help interpreting, these pages seemed important.

"We can't go now," she said. "The weather is terrible. Besides, Victoria entered her story this morning, I'm sure he went to the library with her."

"Fine. We'll wait." Xenia set the paper down onto the table, though the last line didn't leave her mind. She wanted to discuss it with Felix. How long would she have to wait? And if the weather was so terrible, would the streets be safe in time for the selection at the end of the week?

The final day of Yule would be celebrated, and then a new ruler would be decided at midnight. Xenia's stomach turned. In just two days she would be at the palace giving a speech. Her mother's future hung on her words. Most of the kingdom feared her being selected and putting Xenia so close to the throne. Their greatest advantage was the Court of Seven. Moira's new leader would be decided by representatives from each Moiran nation, and none of the other kingdoms honored Fate the way Chantendell did.

"Why are you pacing?" Karielyn asked.

Xenia snapped from her thoughts. She sat on the sofa by the fire, her shoulders slumped. "Stress, I suppose."

Karielyn sat down beside her. "What are you stressing over? You're on break for Fate's sake."

Xenia exhaled. "I don't know if you read the paper last week, but Samuel Liftson… *antagonized* my mother because of my fate. Then my mother asked me to give a speech this week to counter it. I'm nervous."

"I saw that… I'm sorry." Karielyn smiled sympathetically. "Do you want some tea?"

She stood up before Xenia could answer. While she waited for her to return, Xenia mumbled her speech under her breath. *Princess Xenia Safire of Chantendell.* She never longed for that title, but her mother had. If she were selected, Xenia would be one of seven Moiran representatives.

Am I ready for that?

"Here you go," Karielyn said, handing her a steaming cup of tea.

"Thank you."

"I'm sure your speech will be great!" Before Xenia could respond, she said, "Xenia, I really believe that. I think you'll do perfect."

Tomorrow was Selection Day.

Xenia had read over her speech close to a thousand times now, yet no one else had heard it. She paced back and forth between the kitchen archway and the sofas in the living room, clutching her journal.

The silence deserted the tower at a loud knock—she hadn't seen Felix since the night at the ruins. It could be him, or Morea. She didn't go to check; she continued pacing while reciting her speech in her mind.

"Hello, Height," Felix said when Karielyn opened the door.

"Liftson." Xenia could hear the annoyance in Karielyn's voice and met her at the door.

She smiled weakly. "I'm glad you're here. There was something I need to…" She trailed off. *Was* there something she needed to tell him?

"You look…" He pursed his lips. "Are you all right?"

She hadn't eaten all day—or the day before—and had hardly slept. As the selection drew closer, her panic grew more and more. She was only eight last time, but could still remember the crowd…

"I'm all right," she assured.

"Felix, she's not all right. She's worried herself sick over tomorrow," Karielyn said, disregarding her words. Xenia shot her a look.

Felix frowned. "It will be all right, I promise. And I'll be there the whole time if you need me."

"Thank you."

"What did you need to tell me?" he asked, following her to the table.

She knew she wanted to talk to him, but her mind had taken her everywhere this week. "I can't remember, I'm sorry, I've been a little—"

"That's okay. You can tell me when you remember. I came here to tell you something, anyway. It's important. Karielyn, can you leave—?"

"No. I know what this is about, Xenia asked me to help her, and I said I would."

"Fine." He took a deep breath. "I think my blood is cursed—no, I *know* my blood is cursed."

"What?" Xenia asked, staring at him with suddenly wide eyes.

"I asked my grandfather about Liz Eveyon, it's an old family secret. I shouldn't be telling you, Liz promised not to speak of it. When she switched her fate, it… cursed our line. Before, we were mostly villains, but after the switch, every one of Liz's descendants has been a hero. A Liftson can't be born anything else, it's impossible."

Xenia's mind spun at the new information. Switching would curse their blood. Felix's blood was already cursed, and that was the reason Liftsons were always heroes. Could this have something to do with the passage she had read last week?

The passage.

"I need to show you something!" Xenia started for the

stairs closest to her room to grab the papers, and Felix followed her up. The papers were on her desk amongst other notes that were scattered across the surface. She handed them to him.

"This is it," he said when he finished. "This is the curse."

If Xenia switched, her children would all share her fate. Was it fair of her to make that decision for them?

Fate isn't fair, she reminded herself. Her own decision had been stolen from her.

"It's okay if you're afraid," Felix said. "I would never make you do this."

"I'm going to do it," she affirmed. "I can't live like this forever."

"Then we should keep working. Have you finished sorting the papers?"

She shook her head. "I've started, but most of them are still out of order."

She grabbed the papers and carried them back downstairs. Behind her an argument had sparked between Karielyn and Felix.

"Maybe I shouldn't have offered to help," Karielyn was saying. "It's not like I want to be allegiant to you."

"Well, I certainly don't want you as my allegiant!" he returned. "We should do this at my tower," he added to Xenia when they reached the main floor.

"Oh, can you not handle me?" Karielyn asked, her voice suddenly softer.

Xenia glared at her, shaking her head. They would never

be able to work together if they acted this way.

"I don't know how *anyone* can handle you!" Felix retorted.

"I wonder the same about you..." She paused for only a second. "Oh, oh, wait, everyone loves you because your father's a famous hero."

Felix grimaced.

"Enough! This needs to stop!"

They both turned to look at Xenia.

"You both agreed to work together, but we'll get nowhere like this."

Karielyn crossed her arms and muttered under her breath, too quiet for Xenia to hear.

Even after Karielyn and Felix settled down, they didn't work long. Xenia struggled to keep her thoughts straight. They kept drifting back to the selection.

Felix didn't stay long, either. Once he left Xenia went back to reading and practicing her speech. The words were in her mind before she even saw them on the page.

I am ready for tomorrow.

Chapter Twenty-Two

SHE IS THE WORST! ABSOLUTE WORST!

Felix trailed home, the wind blowing through his hair and sending hard snow to his face as he walked down the path to the men's towers. He reached his tower and pulled open the door. Warm air rushed around him.

"Where have you been?" Merrick asked immediately.

Felix stopped himself from groaning. Why did everyone seem to care so much about his life? They didn't even know him. Not really.

"I was at my brother's house. Family affairs."

"I thought you weren't feeling well," he tested.

"It passed."

"You're fine now? You look kind of… flustered."

"*Flustered?*" Felix repeated irritably. "Yeah, I'm fine." He stormed past Merrick to his room and changed into fresh clothes. He had to get that flowery sent off him. Most of the clothes he owned cost more than he wanted to admit. He didn't shop for most of his own clothes, either.

After rifling through his closet, he reached for a white shirt and button-up coat. Then he cleaned his face in the washroom basin and looked up at his reflection in the mirror. His cheeks were hollow and his eyes rimmed with dark shadows. He had to remind himself to get real sleep tonight, something he'd been lacking since he made that deal.

He finished fixing himself and then returned to his room. Since the encounter with Karielyn today, her voice rang in his mind like an old bell. When they were together, she would visit him when his tower was empty. She would cuddle up next to him as they sat by the fire, and then she would say something sweet or funny and wait for him to laugh.

Her laugh.

He didn't miss it anymore, not like he used to. Still, he could remember their first clandestine date like it had been carved into his mind. Despite their secret meeting, she still dressed in a dazzling, golden dress. He didn't need a price tag to know it cost a lot.

Stop, he urged himself. He couldn't let himself think about their relationship for long, or he would fall into a trap he struggled to climb out of. He had made a terrible mistake, and after, she dropped him like a glass shattering into thousands of tiny, sharp, unfixable pieces. He thought they would recover—

But our minds never worked the same.

A knock snapped Felix back to the present. He jolted up and went downstairs to answer it. People visited his tower often, and usually, he let Merrick answer it; but now he hoped Xenia had come to talk more about what they couldn't earlier.

He pulled the door opened and stiffened. "*Height*, what are you doing here?"

The cold turned her nose pink. Her arms were crossed. She opened her mouth to speak, but Merrick cut her off. "Karielyn Height is here?" he asked, sending over a peculiar glance from the kitchen.

"Could you leave us a moment?" Felix asked, attempting to cover his harsh tone.

"Why? Is there a problem?"

"Maybe."

Merrick frowned. "Okay, I have books I need to return to the library," he said calmly before hurrying to his room to grab his things, leaving Felix and Karielyn alone in the doorway.

"Why are you here?" he snapped once Merrick was gone.

"I came to apologize," she started.

"For what, because I've got a whole list," he said, attempting to sound careless, though he was eager to hear what she would say.

"I'm sure you do." She took a deep breath. "I came to apologize for today. We shouldn't have fought. I want to make things right—well, things will never be right with you."

"You're off to a bad start."

She ignored him. "I want to work together. For as long as it takes."

"Good."

"*Good*, and…?"

He ruffled his brows. "*And* what?"

"Well, aren't you sorry too?"

Felix smirked and shook his head. "Height, has anyone ever told you that you're really bad at apologizing?"

Karielyn's face turned bright-red. "I'm trying! I want to help Xenia, but that means helping you too."

He looked away from her to stop memories from rushing back. Perhaps if he had been kinder, they wouldn't have ended so jaggedly.

There's another reason too, his thoughts urged. *There's another reason we split apart—no*, he couldn't think about that now.

"It's okay," he said, "you don't have to help."

"Felix!" she begged, struggling not to cry.

He looked into her tear-filled eyes, the same ones that had stared at him when she left him.

"How could you?" she said when he arrived at her house that night. Her eyes filled with tears, glittering in the late sun.

He stood in the door frame, his heart dropping to his stomach. "Karielyn, please—"

"I can't. I can't do this anymore!"

Felix froze as he realized what she meant. Rumors about their secret relationship were starting to spread, and he had publicly denied them. His father wouldn't let him visit her for days after. He had hoped she would understand.

"Karielyn, I had to, you know I had to. My parents——"

"You could have told me." She looked into his eyes. "You could have told me you would say that."

"It wouldn't have changed anything. My father made me——"

"Well, maybe if your parents can't accept me—accept us—there shouldn't be an us."

Her words felt like ice in Felix's veins. "Karielyn, wait. We can fix this——"

"No, Felix. We can't. I'm done." Her voice was broken from hurt, yet she still sounded defiant. Felix watched tears trickle down her face as she closed the door.

"Felix!" Karielyn repeated. "Are you even listening?"

"No."

She let out an angry snort and then said, "Can you get over yourself so we can work together?"

"It's not that easy, it's not *myself* I need to get over," he said, leaning into the doorframe.

"Are you saying you're not over me?" she asked, crossing her arms.

He straightened. "No, that's not what I'm——"

"Please, don't start."

He shook his head, glancing at the kitchen to distract himself from her lingering stare. "Listen, I'll try to work with you, but I won't pretend I'm your friend."

"No, I assume you're too tired from pretending to be

everyone else's."

Felix froze but his blood turned hot. Six seasons ago, Karielyn had been the only person in his life he trusted with his secrets and feelings—now she used them to strike.

"I think you've been here long enough."

"Yes. I think so." She put her hand on the door.

"Thank you for visiting," he said sardonically. "You're always welcome here."

She rolled her eyes and left without another word.

Felix sat alone in the kitchen, staring absently at his History of Heroes homework. Merrick joined him and filled the seat beside him.

"What happened earlier?" he asked.

"Karielyn and I don't get along."

"Were you two close before?"

Felix had never told Rick about his relationship with Karielyn. He was one of the many people that questioned why they ever spent time together.

"A long time ago," he said, hoping to end the conversation.

"What happened?"

"That's none of your concern." The words came out sharper than he had intended. It hurt him to recall that memory. It reminded him of the mistake he had made.

For weeks after their argument, Felix couldn't stop thinking of all the ways he'd messed up. In the past Karielyn called him rude. Then he had tried to ignore it. He *was* rude. And she was a villain. Did any of it matter?

But something else he did had upset her, and it had upset him too. His entire life Samuel did things for the public that caused Felix different kinds of pain. And he had done what he always vowed he wouldn't do to Karielyn: he had chosen his reputation over his relationships.

And I hardly care about maintaining my family's reputation. But he had done it anyway, because Samuel had told him to. Because he still hadn't learned to resist his father's demands.

He couldn't get that memory out of his head. It was something he tried not to think about often. Even if their jagged ending didn't hurt anymore, he didn't want Karielyn to know how much it had pained him then.

"Well, if you ever want to talk about it, let me know."

Felix forgot what he had last said and, not for the first time today, was lost in his thoughts. "Thank you," he said. "But I don't think I'll want to."

Merrick studied him for a minute. "Okay," he said finally. "That's all right too."

Felix's throat tensed. He would never do it again. He would never risking his own happiness to appease his father, who never did anything for him.

Chapter Twenty-Three

XENIA'S HEART RACED. SHE HAD NEVER BEEN INSIDE THE palace before today. Would this be her last time?

Madam Hezlyn stood behind her, adjusting the dress she had made for the Selection tonight. Xenia eyed her reflection in the mirror. With all the extra work on her hair and makeup, she was almost unrecognizable.

"You're done," Hezlyn said, stepping away from her.

Xenia wore a white dress that trailed across the floor when she walk, with it she wore white gloves that were nearly long enough to be sleeves.

"Thank you," she said, releasing a breath.

Hezlyn didn't stay longer than she needed, leaving Xenia alone in the dressing room. She moved the curtains to peer outside. Even though the event didn't start until dark, the number of people already outside frightened her.

I'll have to speak in front of all of them.

"Xenia, are you done, dear?" her mother said from the

hallway.

"Yes," she called back nervously. She didn't *want* to be done. She wanted to stay in the dressing room all day—all *night*. Her stomach turned at the thought of her speech tonight.

"You're welcome to join me outside."

"Okay, thank you," Xenia said, dropping the curtain. Taking a deep breath, she pulled open the door. *I can't hide forever.*

Outside in the courtyard, party guests filled the rows of seats and tables and any space between. Not only was every notable person from Chantendell here, but the other six nations also had guests.

Numerous conversations ensued around her, and she couldn't make out a single word. She didn't know who to talk to, or even if she wanted to talk to anyone, so she sat alone on the marble railing that surrounded a rose garden behind the lines of tables. The roses were all dead and covered in frost.

"Hello."

For a second, she thought the voice belonged to Felix, but this voice was a bit softer. Instead, it was his oldest brother, Trey, who sat down next to her.

"Hello," she said without making eye contact. *Why is he talking to me?* Didn't he feel the same way about her that Samuel did?

"Why are you sitting alone?" he asked, frowning. "Surely you know someone here."

"No one I care to talk to," she said.

"I'm sorry."

She expected him to get up then, but he stayed beside her. "Has your break been nice?"

Xenia nodded. He didn't know how nice it had been. Aside from the stress today brought, the holiday break had been wonderful. Breaks from villain training always were.

"Can you believe it's the end of the year already?"

She knew he meant to be nice, but she struggled with conversations, especially with people she didn't know well.

"Hardly." Each year that passed filled her with more anxiety. She didn't have a lot of time to enter her story. What if she didn't get permission soon? *What if I don't get permission ever?*

"Are you nervous?" He watched her with knowing eyes. They made her feel so young. What had his story done to him? Had it changed him? After she received her fate, Xenia lost interest in the Liftsons' stories, but she recalled one of Samuel's sons killing his villain.

Wasn't it Trey? The thought made her dizzy.

"A little." She said it quietly, hoping that he wouldn't ask anything else.

"Don't worry. It's always a bit scary the first time you give a speech, but you'll do fine." He smiled, adding, "I don't think you have anything to worry about. After listening to my brother talk about you all week, I think you'd make a great leader."

Her heart beat in her throat. Felix had talked about her *all week?*

"Thank you."

After a few moments of silence, she stood up and walked towards the rows of tables filled with delicacies. Glass domes covered each plate of food to preserve it for tonight's celebration. She filled herself a glass of water and drank every drop. She wasn't very thirsty, yet her mouth felt dry. Her imagination, probably—something to stop her from giving that speech.

"Xenia!"

She turned around to face a woman she had never met. Her gown and jewels suggested she had a role in court.

"Can I help you?" Xenia asked, nearing the woman.

"I wanted to ask if you could give your speech about two hours 'til." Her slurred vowels identified her as a Nesalyn native, one of the farther kingdoms.

Xenia nodded quickly. "That will be fine," she said, trying to appear calm, as if she gave speeches in front of thousands of people often.

She felt sick. Before she could ask anything else, Xenia hurried away.

Felix didn't arrive until dark. He found her sitting in the front row of chairs reserved for her and her mother behind a velvet rope. "How are you doing?" he asked, stepping over the rope and next to her.

"Fine," she said dully.

"Are you ready for tonight?"

"No, of course not."

He looked at her sadly. She turned away so he couldn't see her face.

The crowd fell silent, and it took her only a moment to

figure out why. Samuel Liftson now stood at the front of the stage. Why was *he* giving a speech? This event had nothing to do with him!

Xenia stood up and started for the gate.

"Where are you going?" Felix called.

"I'll be back later—I don't want to… I'll be back." She didn't want to hear what Samuel had to say. *Not now.* She had made it this far and didn't want anything to stop her. And he would.

She paced around the wall of royal guards outside the palace gates. The snow was pushed into two piles on either side of the walkway. It didn't sparkle the way snow usually did; it was gray with dirt mixed into the mound.

Occasionally, she heard the crowd pick up in a round of applause. Each time sent a bit of dread her way. *What are they applauding?* Why had her mother thought her word would be any good against his? He was *Samuel Liftson*. And she was just a young girl destined to be a villain.

Once she was sure he had finished talking, she walked back to the palace. Before returning to Felix, she found her mother. "How bad was it?" she asked. From the worry pulling at Estelle's eyes, she wasn't sure she wanted the answer.

Estelle stayed quiet for a while. "There's nothing we can do to change what he said, but we can try to change their minds. You wrote that speech, correct?"

"I hope…" Xenia trailed off. *What do I hope? I hope it works? I hope I can do it?*

Estelle smiled. "It will be fine." She said it calmly, contradicting the frantic expression on her face.

Xenia walked closer to the spot she had left Felix at. People looked at her in a different way here than they did at the Training Center. Some people looked wary around her. Others looked at her like they hardly noticed her. They must have been from other nations. Xenia hadn't spent a lot of time out of Chantendell, but she knew other people didn't view their fates as seriously as they did. That could work to her advantage since six of the seven people voting tonight were from other nations.

It's almost my turn.

The night got colder as time slipped away. Before long she was asked to wait by the stage. Felix kept his eyes on her and smiled while she waited. When the woman motioned her forward, her heart raced faster, and her thoughts became fuzzy.

How can I give a speech when I can hardly stand?

The crowd wasn't silent for her like they had been for the previous speakers; they whispered and jeered as she made her way to the front.

Xenia blinked back tears. *Don't cry! Not now!*

"Good evening," she said, her voice cracking. A moment of panic passed as the words she had spent all week reading left her mind and lost themselves in the wind.

I can do this, she told herself as she stared into the crowd.

"I am Xenia Safire. I'm sure most of you know who I am. If not, I'm Estelle's daughter. As many of you know, I am fated to be the villain of my story. This has caused a lot of people to worry about my mother being selected."

She noticed that Samuel Liftson's eyes didn't leave her.

His mouth stayed in a tight line. She found a different set of eyes to focus on and smiled back at Felix.

"I would be too. I didn't ask for my fate, I never wanted this. I spent my entire life fantasizing about my story. When I was given my fate, I felt like I was an imposter—like my whole life meant nothing. Could I really be a villain?" The crowd blurred through the layer of tears coating her eyes. "I love Chantendell so much, I really do. And hurting some-one—anyone—I don't want that. If my mother is selected, I will do everything I can for the better of Chantendell.

"I was raised by a woman who loves this kingdom dearly. She knows how to lead a kingdom, and even more she knows how to lead one *well*. I can only aspire to be the kind of woman she is. I've tried my hardest to deny my fate, I know it's what I will one day face, but when I am in Chantendell, it's not who I am. It never will be. I want to be there for the children who are feeling the same way I did. I want to be there for the people who need me. You deserve a leader who can truly respect the kingdom and everyone in it. I believe that my mother is the one who can give you that, and I will fully support her in leading Chantendell."

The words weren't exactly what she had meant them to be, but they still felt right. She just hoped the people would feel the same way.

The crowd was silent when she finished and walked hurriedly off the stage. Tears rolled down her face. She didn't want to think about how people had taken her speech, or how her mother had taken it. She didn't want to worry about any of it right now.

"Nia, that was incredible," Felix said, grabbing her wrist to stop her from getting too far away.

She tried to thank him but couldn't. Tears still flooded her eyes.

He led her behind the stage to a dark passage between a palace wall and the back wall of the stage. "It's over now, you don't have to worry about it anymore. You did wonderful," he said, pushing a strand of loose hair out of her face.

"Here, take this," he said, handing her an empty glass. He popped the top of a bottle of red wine and poured it into the glass in her hand. Then he poured himself a glass and raised it.

"I've never done this before," she said, holding the glass a safe distance from her mouth.

"Make a toast?"

"Drink."

He laughed. "Of course you haven't. I didn't think you had."

"What do you mean?"

Still smiling he said, "It means you never do anything that could be looked down upon. You're *too* good." He watched her as she slowly brought the glass to her lips. "It's just juice. To a new beginning."

Something told her he wasn't talking about a new year. She emptied the glass into her mouth.

He finished his glass and then grabbed the bottle and swirled the liquid around. He moved it to his mouth and took another drink. Xenia smiled when she remembered what Morea said. *I'm sure if he didn't have a status to maintain, you'd find him hiding in the shadows drinking with the rest of the villains.*

They walked back to the party together hand in hand and sat in the seats reserved for Xenia and her mother. Dendilor's wife was giving her speech when they got back. Xenia heard her own name mentioned.

"Don't worry about her. You did great," Felix said. "Things will work in the end, even if your mother isn't selected, I promise."

"Thank you." She gripped his hand tighter.

"Felix!"

The voice sent dread coursing through her body. She didn't want Felix to leave her side when his father called, and Felix didn't move. He ignored his father as if he had never heard his name.

Samuel made his way through the crowd of people until he was arm's length away from them. "What are you doing?" He asked it casually, yet Xenia could hear the irritation in his voice.

"Nothing, why?"

Samuel kept his eyes fixed far from Xenia, but occasionally his stare wavered, and she could practically feel his gaze. It made her skin crawl. The way he looked at her made her want to fade into the night.

"You should sit with the family."

"Thanks for the offer, but I'm already occupied," Felix said, turning to her with a wicked grin hiding in his eyes.

"Felix, not in public, please—"

"What do you mean?"

Samuel kept his mouth in a tight line as he came closer.

"Don't do this here," he whispered. "Everyone is watching us, and everyone is watching *her*. If people see the two of you together, they'll get the wrong idea—"

"I don't care what idea—"

Samuel gripped Felix's upper arm. Xenia's breath stalled as she watched them.

When Samuel spoke again, his voice dropped so low, she hardly heard him. "Felix, you are risking our reputation. I don't want to face more rumors about my son having an affair with a villain. This family represents—"

Felix pulled his arm away, making no attempt to hide the motion. "I don't care what our family represents. I am here for Xenia."

"Fine. Enjoy your night," he said, returning to the rest of his family.

Felix's stare followed his father all the way back to his table before turning empty. "I'm sorry about him, he thinks... I'm sorry."

Xenia frowned. "You don't have to apologize—I'm used to it. *Very* used to it. Not everyone is as willing to be with villains as you are. I don't blame them—I used to be the same way." She was suddenly grateful for the dark; maybe he couldn't see the tears in her eyes. "You're the only friend I've had for almost four years."

"I'm sorry." He placed his hand around her waist and pulled her closer. For once she wasn't afraid. She leaned her head against his shoulder. "Sometimes I don't think I have any friends. They feel more like admirers. And they're not mine, they're my father's." He paused, taking in a deep breath. "I am honored to be your friend."

Was it possible that their situations weren't as different as they appeared? He seemed to understand her better than any villain ever had. Better than *anyone* had. She watched his breath freeze in the air. Was it chance that had brought them together? Or something more?

No. She pushed the thought out of her mind. Magic was never wrong. Magic determined their fates. There was no way she and Felix could be together.

Is there? Does our fate have to be as demanding as we let it?

"I never considered how heroes felt about their fate. I assumed they took it as an honor," Xenia said, pulling herself from her thoughts.

"I think most do."

"I've been told that's how I should feel about my fate, like it's an honor. I'm not sure…" She trailed off. He wanted to be a villain. Would he be honored to have such a fate? She didn't want to ask.

Midnight came much faster than Xenia wanted. Her mother stood on the stage next to Vanday and Dendilor, and the announcer stood in the middle of the stage, holding a small envelope. The Seven Representatives had decided tonight who would rule, and their choice was on the card.

Xenia stood in front of the stage in the same spot she had ten years ago when Blake held her hand instead of Felix. The crowd around her was counting, but she wasn't. Her heart raced, and Felix's support was the only reason she still stood upright. As the number shrank to ten, the announcer pulled out the paper inside the envelope and unfolded it.

Clearing her throat, she said, "The next ruler of Chantendell will be… Estelle Safire!"

Xenia screamed. Tears streamed down her cheeks as people around her clapped. Some shouted their names to the wind and yelled victoriously.

"What did I tell you, Princess?" Felix said, smiling.

His hand moved to her neck, and then his lips were pressed gently against hers. The space between them disappeared, and Xenia placed her hands around his neck. The crowd around them quieted as if they also felt the strong current of emotion. Xenia pressed herself closer to him as he moved his lips to her neck. When they parted, he grinned, and she hid her face against his chest.

"Xenia?" her mother called from behind her.

She stepped away from Felix and threw her arms around her instead.

"We did it!" Estelle whispered happily.

Tears still trickled down Xenia's chin, but she laughed. "We did, Mother! We did it!"

Chapter Twenty-Four

THE REST OF THE NIGHT FADED INTO A FEVERISH BLUR. Before Xenia realized the party was over, she and Felix climbed into a carriage to take them back to the Training Center.

Shock still muddled her thoughts. Her mother had won the selection. Xenia would be Princess of Chantendell. She had kissed Felix Liftson.

Fate, she had kissed him.

Her body trembled and tears rolled down her face. Felix put his arm around her, whispering words of comfort.

What had they done?

No one lit the lantern, so they rode back in the dark. Xenia let Felix hold her. It would hardly do more damage. Maybe tomorrow they could forget, and their relationship would stay the way it should. But did she really want that? What did he want?

They arrived at the Training Center and clambered out

into the cold. The courtyard was deathly still. Wind whistled through the trees in the otherwise grave silence. Every tower was dark, and every lantern had burned out.

"We should talk," Felix said when they reached the division in the path to the men's and women's towers.

Xenia could only nod.

"Let's go to my tower," he said, turning down the trail to the men's towers.

They walked in silence, leaving Xenia dizzily anticipating what he might say. He stopped at the door and pulled out a key. "Merrick should be asleep—we'll need to be quiet." He pulled open the door, and they entered the dark tower.

They took the curved stairs up to his room, and he locked the door. He turned and met her gaze, and even in the dark she could see the pain in his eyes.

"We kissed," she whispered. Tears ran down her face. "Felix, we *kissed*."

"I know," he said, stepping towards her. "Fate, I know."

She wiped at her tears. She had finally found someone who made her feel like who she was, was enough. Someone who never needed her to prove she was more than her fate. And she could never have him. So why did she have to come so close—why did she have to taunt herself this way? Why did she want Felix Liftson?

He picked up her hands and squeezed them. "We can figure this out—"

"No, we can't."

"We're already defying Fate this much."

"Felix—"

He moved closer to her, his grip on her hands tightening. "Can't we go further?"

She closed her eyes. She didn't want to want this. When did any of this happen?

"Please, can we try?"

Xenia tore away from his stare, glancing at the window behind them. In only a few hours, the sun would rise. What would tomorrow bring?

She turned back to him. "Fate will never let us."

His throat tensed, and he swallowed. "I can't—I can't go back now. I can't pretend nothing happened tonight. I can't pretend I don't want you."

Her stomach knotted. *He wants me.* How could she say she would try when she knew there was only one ending for them?

"Fate may be certain, but we don't know our ending yet," he said, as if reading her mind. "Some stories end in ways we'd never expect."

And some end in tragedy, Xenia thought, but she couldn't say it out loud. She wished her life were a book and she could flip to the end, just to glance at their fate.

She took a breath. Some chapters ended in heartbreak; she couldn't prevent that.

Felix's brown eyes were gentle, unlike his grip on her hands. He held her like he would lose her if he let go.

He was right. She didn't know the ending yet. And she really wanted to try.

Chapter Twenty-Five

THE WEEK FOLLOWING THE SELECTION, WORD OF XENIA and Felix's midnight kiss spread to every news press and was printed into every issue of the daily paper. Xenia never imagined her personal matters would reach so many people.

Today was her mother's coronation—and the first day she had seen her since the selection. The last thing she wanted to worry about was her relationship with Felix.

The court had decided that Xenia wouldn't be coronated until she returned from her story, and the former princess would maintain her status until then. Xenia was relieved at the news but couldn't help wondering if this was a way to keep her from the throne entirely. After all, could they give a villain a place in court? They weren't even allowed in the kingdom boundaries except to teach at the Training Center.

The ballroom in the palace had been transformed for the coronation. The once open space used for dancing was filled with rows of seating for guests. Golden accents adorned the white walls, and marble pillars supported the high celling. Rows of crystal chandeliers brightened the room.

Guests were quickly filling the room, reminding her of how close the event was. It would start any minute.

At the start of the week and new year, Xenia extended invitations to Karielyn and her family so they could attend. The Liftsons already had access.

"Xenia, do you mind standing up there? Your mother will be out shortly," one of the palace servants said, ushering her to the front of the room, in front of the rows of guests. Before her was a glass box with a golden crown resting on a velvet cushion. The sight of it took her breath away. The history books said it was as old as the kingdom itself, preserved by Fate's magic.

The crowd grew, and the seats filled quickly. Xenia scanned the crowd for Karielyn and Felix and spotted their faces amongst many others. Felix smiled in her direction from the row with the rest of his family. Karielyn stood next to him. She couldn't spot her parents anywhere. Across from them, the Cedars waved at her. Estelle would never let them miss an event like this—there wasn't a high number of people she trusted more than them. That was one reason why she had lived with them when Estelle was in her story. Xenia waved back, giving herself a reason to stop twiddling with the ring on her finger.

The pause in the music notified her that the ceremony had begun. She turned her head to watch her mother stride towards her like a bride. Her beautiful, golden dress wrapped tightly around her torso, bleeding into numerous layers of fabric that trailed a pace behind her. She stopped to the right of Xenia, a graceful smile spread across her face.

The priest, who stood between them, passed her mother and unlocked the box. The dominant religion in Chantendell varied from their own beliefs, but it was tradition that the same priests crowned the leaders. He pulled out the crown carefully and stepped towards Estelle.

"Safire, please take the oath of Chantendell."

Her mother cleared her throat and began, "I, Estelle Safire, having been chosen to rule the nations of Moira, will dedicate the coming years to the good people of this kingdom as their loyal queen. I, Estelle Safire, vow to never see the kingdom in a lesser state than the people now know. I, Estelle Safire, bind myself to the rules of leadership this kingdom holds. My kingdom I will serve for the remainder of my days." Her words were smooth, and she spoke them with ease. She bowed slightly, and the man placed the crown on top of her head. When she rose, the crowd cheered in approval. Xenia joined them.

Once she was dismissed, Xenia submerged herself into the crowd to find Felix and Karielyn. She found them quickly, and Felix pulled her into an embrace. "You look gorgeous today."

"Thank you."

"Where's your mother? I want to congratulate her," he said, peering past her.

Xenia followed as he weaved in and out of the crowd to find Estelle. When they spotted her, she was deep in conversation with one of the representatives. She stopped and turned to them as they approached.

"Mrs. Safire, congratulations!" Felix said. Karielyn echoed him from his side.

Estelle smiled politely. "Thank you… Have we met before?"

Felix shook his head. "Not properly," he said, holding out his hand. "I'm Felix Liftson."

Her forehead creased. "*Liftson?*"

Felix straightened himself and let out a deep breath. "Yes. I'm sorry about… I'm happy you won."

Estelle's lips were pressed in a line. Xenia knew her mother was thinking of everything Samuel had said against them—and possibly about their kiss as well—so Xenia grabbed Felix's wrist and pulled him away.

"Did I—?"

"You did nothing wrong," she said, guiding them to an empty table, "she's angry with your father. Not you."

He groaned. "Everyone associates me with him in some way I don't understand—"

"You *are* his son," Karielyn said.

"But I'm not *him*." A few heads turned at his raised voice, but the loud crowd didn't let his words travel far. "One day people will see us differently. Soon."

"No, you're not him," Xenia said. Felix was far kinder than his callous father. Yet he believed himself a villain.

This switch means as much to him as it does to me, she reminded herself.

"I understand how you feel. I've never felt like I fit my

fate, either," she whispered.

She grabbed his hand, and a smile touched his eyes. "We'll figure something out."

"I know we will."

They rode back to the Training Center, and Felix walked with her to her tower door.

"Thanks for being there today," she said as his hand dropped from hers.

"Of course. I'm so sorry I was late. I should have cleared my schedule. I'm sorry."

"It's fine." She hadn't realized he was late, but she had spent most of the morning in the dressing room. What had Felix been doing? He never mentioned anything happening before the coronation.

"No, it's not," he said forcefully. Before she could add anything else, he was walking away, the wind whipping his bangs off his face and ruffling his white shirt. His fists were clenched at his sides.

Karielyn opened the door before Xenia could. Her brows pinched together when Xenia didn't follow her in. "Are you all right?"

Xenia nodded slowly. "I don't understand why he's so upset."

Karielyn shrugged.

Since she knew Karielyn didn't have an answer, Xenia moved on. "Where were your parents?"

Her eye dropped and color rushed to her cheeks. "Oh, they… I think they were busy."

Something pulled at Xenia's chest. Did anyone want to be there today?

Inside, Karielyn offered to make dinner, but Xenia refused. The meal at the coronation was enough to fill her for a week. They settled down in the living room, filling out extra homework to turn in when training started again.

"What were your parents doing?" Xenia asked, watching Karielyn.

She hesitated. "They were very busy this morning, that's all. Nothing… personal."

What had they been doing to miss a *coronation*? An event like that only happened every ten years, and few people who received invitations missed it. Xenia couldn't shake the suspicion that something else had happened this morning. Something no one wanted her to know about.

Chapter Twenty-Six

Mrs. Height hadn't sent any new translations for weeks, and without them, they had no answers. Since Felix's discovery of the curse on his family, they weren't sure if he even *could* switch.

Perhaps the curse only stopped Liftsons from being *born* anything but a hero, but they couldn't ignore the possibility that it might prevent Felix from switching as well.

Xenia wouldn't let herself believe they couldn't switch. It felt too much like fate pulling apart their plans.

Since Yule break ended, Xenia and Felix hadn't spent much time together, aside from meeting once a week to discuss the translations. Her teachers had been sending her away with so much extra work, there was hardly an empty spot on her desk, let alone her schedule. Along with training, she had been signing papers at the palace. She wasn't the princess yet, but she still had plenty of things to occupy her attention at the palace in the meantime.

Felix was just as busy—if not more—even though he had already earned permission to enter. His brother, Trey, was his trainer, and though Felix had passed his hero training in only a few weeks, he kept him busy.

Estelle's calendar was more than full, and Xenia hadn't talked to her since the coronation a season ago. She had hoped things would slow down once Estelle settled in and formed a more secure schedule. But she didn't see that time coming soon.

She, Karielyn, and Felix had planned to work on the translations tonight. It was the only day no one had somewhere to be. They didn't have any new translations, but there was plenty to think about. Karielyn said her mother worked fast, but Xenia assumed she had other projects too. She didn't mind taking things slow. It meant she had more time in Chantendell. And more time to get permission from Ravelyn to enter.

Felix arrived shortly after class let out. Xenia and Karielyn had already laid out all the translations on the table. They had finally finished arranging them in what they believed to be the correct order.

Felix picked up one of the papers and cleared his throat. *"To change your fate is to change your blood. To change your blood is to change you. To change you it will cost a price not all will want to pay.* We know this is the curse. If you switch, your family is bound to your fate."

"But—will it curse your direct line, or will it affect your brother's children as well?" Karielyn asked.

Felix lost himself in thought as he ruffled through the

papers.

"Could you imagine if the Liftsons switched to *villains*?" Karielyn said with a laugh.

Felix glared at her. After a few moments, he set the papers down. "Well, Liz had no siblings, so it was only her direct line, but Rendon had a few nieces, and their fates varied, so it must only pass through direct relation," he answered.

Before Karielyn could respond, Xenia said, "We still don't know what the jewel looks like. It'll be hard to find something we've never seen before."

"What do you mean?" Karielyn asked.

Xenia glanced at her, her brows pinching together. "The Jewel of Fate, the one we need to find."

Karielyn shook her head and said in a correcting tone, "We know what it looks like."

Xenia and Felix both stared at her. "We do?"

She nodded. "It's also called the *Lafin Crystal*."

Lafin? Xenia had never heard of that, and by the look on his face, neither had Felix. When had Karielyn learn this?

"Where does it say that?" Felix demanded, picking up the pages again and flipping through them.

"Everyone knows that."

They both gazed at her as if she spoke in a language they couldn't understand.

"Everyone knows that!" she repeated.

"Apparently not everyone," Felix said, still scanning the pages.

A faint smile touched her lips. She was clearly pleased to know something Felix didn't. Without warning, she rushed to her room and came back carrying what appeared to be a schoolbook. She set it onto the table in front of them. "This is my… It's a Chantendell history book from a few years ago." She flipped through the pristine pages, studying each one.

"I never got that one," Felix said, mirroring the thought that lurked in the back of Xenia's mind.

"Obviously," she said, stopping on a page near the center of the book. "This was my Chantendell history book from *Enria*."

"You've been to Enria?" Xenia asked. Enria and Moira fought in the War of Chantendell centuries ago. After Moira won, the nations remained enemies, and rumors of a new war were always sweeping the kingdom. Enria was a huge nation, but it was far from Chantendell, and a boat was needed to get there. Xenia had never left Moira.

"That's where my parents are from—well, my father. My mother is from Dallova. They were only traveling through the kingdom when I was born. They never intended to have me in Chantendell, but a storm kept them there longer than they had planned to stay. I've spent a lot of time in Enria, but we moved here so I could get my fate and train."

Despite her unease, Xenia smiled. She had never been close to anyone from another nation. And Karielyn had nothing to do with the war. "You're Enrian!" Xenia said. "Can you speak the language? How come you don't have an accent?"

"I'm half-Enrian. And yes, I can speak the language

fluently, I grew up speaking two languages. I usually use it in the warm seasons. And I don't have an accent because I've spent most of my life in Chantendell." She answered with a hint of pride in her voice. Most people that came to Chantendell from Enria weren't proud of their heritage.

"Why in the warm seasons?"

Felix leaned back in his chair; he likely already knew this. He paid her no mind and went back to reading the translations.

Karielyn happily answered Xenia's question. "Because I always spend the warm seasons there. My parents own a house in Silvermere," she said, flipping over a few more pages. "Here, the Lafin Crystal." She pointed at the open page. On it was a drawing of a blue crystal with ridges and shallow dips that covered the entire surface. Underneath the drawing were a few paragraphs in Enrian.

"Why didn't you show us this sooner?" Felix asked, finally putting down the papers to look at the new one.

Karielyn shrugged. "I thought you knew."

"Why would we know? We never went to school in Enria!"

"I'm sorry, I assumed that we would still learn the same history!"

Xenia loved Chantendell's history. What school didn't teach her, her mother did—why hadn't she learned this?

"I had never even heard of the crystal until I met Xenia! You could have said something!"

"It's okay, we're not running out of time!" Xenia said, grabbing his hand.

"We don't have forever, either!"

Chills trailed across her back. They *didn't* have forever. They had less than six years.

Xenia met his eyes, and he breathed out slowly.

"I'm sorry," Felix said, his tone deflating. "Karielyn, can you read it to us?"

She nodded and picked up the book. "*The inner energy of the Lafin Crystal has the power to end a story if released. The Lafin Crystal also has a less popular ability: it possesses the power to switch the fate of two participating persons. This uncommon act is rarely performed successfully and hasn't been attempted in nearly three decades. The Lafin is rarely seen by anyone aside from select authorities.*"

Xenia's head spun at the facts contained in the short paragraph. Karielyn knew this all along? And the jewel must have contained magic. Magic could be dangerous if not properly concealed. When released in the air, it was called *open magic*. Xenia had never been around magic because Chantendell did nearly a perfect job at keeping it concealed and out of inhabited areas.

"Who switched recently?" Felix asked.

"It was almost thirty years ago—" Karielyn started.

"I thought 1403 was the last time anyone switched."

"It never said they succeeded." Xenia cut in. "And we don't know when the other book was written. Dozens of people could have tried to switch since then."

People might have switched since 1403. Even if they hadn't succeeded, Karielyn's book still confirmed the existence of the jewel. She never thought of it as a fable, but now she *knew* it existed beyond the book.

"But this is the only record of switching in Chantendell. How come other countries *teach* this?" Felix said, eying the drawing of the jewel.

"I don't know!" Karielyn snarled defensively. "Maybe you didn't pay attention in class!"

Felix looked on the verge of shouting, so Xenia grabbed his arm again, attempting to calm him. "It's not her fault we didn't learn about the crystal."

He pulled his arm away and ran his hand over his face. "Yeah, I know." He paused and exhaled.

"What we need to figure out is why we never learned this but Karielyn did—when she was in Enria. Did they teach you anything else we might not know about?"

Karielyn shrugged. "I don't know. He—my teacher wasn't fond of Chantendell."

Xenia grabbed the book and closed it to find the author's name. There wasn't one.

"He wrote this," she said, placing her hand on the teal book.

"You said he didn't like the subject," Felix said.

"He didn't."

He shook his head. "Then why would he write an entire book on it?"

"He—"

Xenia stopped listening to whatever they had found to argue about now. "Karielyn, what was your teacher's name?"

She stopped bickering with Felix to glance at her. After a few moments, she opened her mouth. Then closed it again. Then, finally, she said, "*Zarius Al.*"

Zarius Al. The blood in Xenia's veins turned ice cold.

"Was he from Chantendell?"

Karielyn didn't say anything for a moment; her thin brows were pulled in confusion, or thought. "He might have said that."

It can't be him. There must be more people who share his name.

"Do you know who your teacher is?"

Karielyn's face turned very pale. She looked as if she had seen a ghost. "Xenia, I don't know what you're talking about. He… He…"

Felix gave Xenia a wary glance. He must have recognized the name too.

"I'd never heard of the jewel until I got this book, but it has answers to questions no one here could ever answer. I once asked my mother how she got back to Chantendell after her story, but she didn't know. What if we aren't supposed to know?"

Karielyn's face was a confused copy of Felix's.

"Listen!" she begged. "If your teacher is against Chantendell… he must know things he shouldn't and—"

"Xenia, *seriously*?" Karielyn said. "You haven't even met him." Something had changed in her voice. The fear hadn't gone entirely, but it was masked now. "You are overthinking this."

"I'm not overthinking anything! I remember the name from one of my history lessons—" Then the missing piece fell in place.

Worry painted Karielyn's face.

"I know who he is. He was banned from the kingdom

years ago!"

Chapter Twenty-Seven

XENIA SLAMMED THE DOOR TO THE TOWER, WALKING AT A brisk pace towards the Training Center stables. Felix matched her pace. The news of Zarius Al's presence in Enria had left her shaken. She needed to take the information to her mother—or anyone at the palace who would listen.

"What do you plan to tell her?" Felix asked.

"I don't know yet," Xenia said. Enria was a large nation, and she had failed to get any details more specific than Silvermere from Karielyn. "But she'll need to know—"

Her words were cut short as she came to a sudden stop. Two strong-built men dressed in black stood in front of them. She stepped to go around them, but the man closest to her cleared his throat, and she froze.

"Safire. Liftson. You're just who we've come to see."

Felix put his arm around Xenia's waist, pulling her close to him as he assessed the men. "What do you want?" he asked.

The second man glanced between them. "To stop *this* before it becomes a threat."

"There is no reason for the two of you to have any sort of relationship. Unless you plan to defy fate. You are a hero, and she is a villain—it's best the two of you remember that," the first man said.

Who were these men? Did they suspect what they planned to do?

"I would never forget it," Felix said, taking a step past them.

One of the men gripped Felix's shoulder. "I don't think you understand the severity of what I'm implying. If either of you should attempt anything that would keep your fate from being fulfilled, our men would be forced to meddle. And you wouldn't want that."

"No, I don't think we would," Felix said coolly. "If you will excuse us, we have an urgent message to relay to Her Majesty."

The man let go of him, and they continued to the stables.

Neither Felix nor Xenia spoke until they closed the carriage door and left the stables.

"Who was that?" she asked.

"I have no idea." He shook his head. "But I think they suspect what we're doing. We need to be careful."

She leaned against the bench, fear stopping her from saying anything else. They had hardly begun, and already people had grown suspicious. How would they ever succeed?

The encounter with the men managed to distract her

from the reason she was currently riding to the palace: Zarius Al was teaching Chantendell History in Enria. How had no one turned him in?

Am I being foolish? Is there any way someone as dangerous as Zarius Al could teach history without being caught?

The rest of the trip was quiet. They pulled into the palace stables and climbed out.

They crossed the gardens, where snow still hid the grass and topped the trees, to the grand entrance.

The guards bowed at Xenia's presence. She hadn't even been crowned yet!

"I need to see my mother. Is she available?" she asked, trying not to focus on the kneeling guards.

"I don't know, but I can let you in so you can find someone to help you."

"Yes, that will be great, thank you."

The guards opened the gate and let her pass through. They stopped Felix before he could follow.

"He's with me," Xenia said.

The guard shook his head. "I'm sorry, my lady, but he is not allowed inside."

She took in a deep breath and turned to Felix. He nodded, urging her to move on, but she didn't want to leave him.

"He isn't going to do anything. This is Felix Liftson."

The guard still didn't look convinced, but at the mention of his name, he ushered Felix through anyway.

The castle halls were chaotic, people dashed back and forth and wove through and around rooms. Xenia tried to remember where her mother's office was located. She hadn't spent a lot of time in the palace, and it seemed to go on forever.

A grand set of stairs spread across the end of the foyer. She remembered taking them last time she came here. The landing at the top of the stairs overlooked the foyer. She struggled to remember which way would lead her to her mother's office from here and risked a turn.

"Could you help me?" she asked no one in particular. Her words were lost among the chaos.

After a few moments, a middle-aged man found them wandering down an empty corridor. "Xenia, can I help you?"

She didn't know this man, and previously she would have found it strange that he knew her name, but everyone seemed to know her name now.

"I need to speak to my mother," she said. "It's urgent."

"Of course, follow me. She's just gotten out of a meeting. Today has been busy."

They followed him through the halls to the palace's west wing. He left her at a door guarded by two men with swords at their hips. She spoke with them for a minute before convincing them to let her in.

Xenia called for her mother as soon as they opened the door and she rushed into the room.

"Hello, Xenia!" Estelle said, looking up from a stack of papers behind her desk. "Felix."

"Good evening, Your Majesty."

"I need to speak with you," Xenia said. "It's about Zarius Al."

Estelle's face lit in shock. She motioned for them to take

seats. Her dark eyes locked on Xenia's. Having experienced it before, Xenia was sure Felix felt invisible. When her mother wore this expression, everything and everyone else disappeared.

"What do you need to know?" she asked carefully.

"Who is Zarius Al?"

Her mother only stared at her, so Xenia added, "And what do I need to know about him? I know he was banned from Chantendell, right?"

Estelle thought for a moment. "I've mentioned him before," she said, choosing her words with evident caution. "He gained fame when I was young—he was a guard, in his story and later at the palace. He was a loyal guard, but one night he got into a fight with the king. He believed that the people of Chantendell shouldn't be forced to live out their stories in such an... *intense way*." She paused as if her next words were a struggle to say. "He tried to burn the Hall of Destiny."

Xenia gasped. Every fate scroll was kept in the Hall of Destiny. They needed their scroll to enter their story and fulfill their fates. Without them, what would their kingdom be like? More like Enria or Elisora? Life was fairer here. She believed that until she got her own fate, and maybe she still did after. It was her fate—Chantendell didn't change that.

"And he wasn't arrested?" She barely managed to get the words out.

Estelle shook her head. "He disappeared. No one knew where he went. He had the king's entire army looking for him. When they couldn't find him, the king banned him. He said that if he were to ever show his face within the boundaries of Moira again, he would be executed on sight."

Xenia and Felix exchanged a worried glance. "He's in Enria, he's a history teacher! A *Chantendell* history teacher!" she shouted.

Her mother turned pale. "How did he…?" She stuttered over her words and clenched the arm of her chair tightly. "Enria?"

Xenia nodded.

"Thank you this, but I don't think I'll be able to talk any longer. What you have told me is extremely worrying, and I must schedule a meeting immediately with my advisors. Was there anything else?" she asked, tossing her gaze between the two of them.

Xenia shook her head, too dazed to speak.

"All right," Estelle said, rising to her feet. "I need to ask you two not to speak of this to others, I don't want to strike panic."

They agreed, knowing fully well that Karielyn would hear what they had learned. At least the parts about the past.

They left the castle and rode back to the Training Center without saying a word. How had he gone so long without being turned in? Surely the news had spread to Enria. How could he have gotten away with teaching *their* kingdom's history?

Felix followed Xenia back to her tower, and Karielyn sat at the table with the stack of papers and books they had left towering near her.

They filled the seats next to her and explained what they

had learned.

"Are you sure it's the same person?" Karielyn asked, a trace of fear wrinkling her smooth face.

"Nia was right about Al. He tried to *burn* the Hall of Destiny."

"I—I'm not doubting you, but… I know him."

"I know," Xenia said, "but everyone has secrets."

"Are you okay?" Felix asked, meeting Karielyn's still wide eyes.

She looked up at him. "My *history teacher* tried to burn down the most important building in the kingdom!" she shouted, then attempted to apologize.

"I understand. Finding someone's kept secrets from you hurts."

"Shut up!" she snarled. "I bet you wish he succeeded!"

Felix frowned. "No, I'm glad he didn't, and my scroll wasn't even in there at the time."

Xenia looked away. Would her life be simpler if her scroll had burned that night?

Chapter Twenty-Eight

OVER THE NEXT WEEK, XENIA READ ZARIUS AL'S STORY. He was just a guard and hardly mentioned. After that, she tried not to focus on him. He didn't concern her, or even Chantendell anymore, but it was still hard to keep her mind off him. And part of her believed he *was* still dangerous. Her mother wouldn't have reacted the way she had if he weren't.

A knock sounded from the front door, and Xenia hurried to answer it. The woman standing on the other side of the door had thick, blond hair and brilliant, blue eyes. She looked to be around her mother's age, and she possessed a very familiar gaze. "Is my daughter, Karielyn, here?"

"Yes, she is."

Xenia shouted for Karielyn, and she came down the stairs and to join her mother by the door.

When Karielyn reached her, Mrs. Height said, "I'm terribly sorry, I don't mean to be rude, but would you mind… leaving us for a moment?"

Xenia nodded and left the tower. She hoped Felix would be free.

Past the fountain in the courtyard, two trails met. Parting from the previous trail, she hurried down the one to the men's towers.

Before she could knock, the front door swung open. "Nia! I almost did it again!"

She laughed. He was teasing, but it didn't show.

"I was actually on my way to see you." His expression was grim and his eyes dark. "I have something I need to talk to you about. Come in."

He led her through the door closing it swiftly behind her. He sat on the couch by the fire and motioned for her to do the same.

"Are you all right?" she asked, frowning.

Exhaling, he said, "I don't know." He glanced around the room, ignoring her gaze. "I've been thinking... we aren't supposed to like each other—I mean—you know what I mean." He stopped to look at her, but his stare didn't linger for long before he glared at the floor again. "If—sorry, when—we switch, I can't fight you. I'm not sure what I'll do." He looked on the verge of tears.

She didn't have any words that felt right. All this time Felix seemed so eager to switch. Why had he hidden this part of him from her for so long?

She placed her hand on his back. "We don't know the ending yet, remember?" she whispered.

"I—I think I know how it's going to end."

Tears burned her eyes. "And what will you do now? Will

you—?"

"I *can't* do anything now. Leaving and pretending I hate you will help nothing."

Xenia closed her eyes, letting her tears fall. If he wanted to leave and forget about her, was it too late?

His brown eyes narrowed, but he still focused on the ground. "I want… I *need* to be the villain, but I don't want to be your enemy."

She tilted her head to look into his beautiful eyes. "You are *not* a bad person," she said strongly. "I know you feel like you need to change who you are, but that does not mean you need to do something bad." Tears made their way down her cheek. She hated seeing him like this.

"I don't want to fight you," he murmured. "As a hero or a villain, I don't want to fight you." He looked up, and his eyes locked on hers. "I would rather fight the whole world than fight you."

Felix and Xenia walked back to her tower together. When they arrived, Mrs. Height had left and Karielyn occupied the table with a worried expression.

"You look upset. Is everything okay, Height?" Felix asked, welcoming himself to the seat next to her.

"My mother dropped the rest of the translations today." Her words left Xenia with a sudden emptiness that filled quickly with a flight of butterflies. Or moths.

Felix and Xenia exchanged nervous glances.

"Then I suppose I can stay late," he said, slipping into a seat at the table. Xenia sat beside him, and he grabbed her hand. His grip was so firm, yet it hardly steadied her.

"Did she say anything about the book? Or what she thought of it?" he asked as Karielyn set out the papers.

Her expression twisted until she was glaring at Felix. "No, no she didn't."

Xenia took a deep breath to prepare herself. "Let's start." Saying it this time sounded final. Like it was the beginning of the end. It felt like everyone was holding onto a single breath. *This is it.*

She picked up the papers and turned her attention to the words printed across the top page. "There's a foreword." She cleared her throat and shuffled the papers. "*Dearest reader, if you are holding this book and wish to continue your life the way you live now, then put it down. If you don't have the guts to set fire to your past life, move forward, and see the person that you truly want to be, set it down! The dangers in this book are grave. The challenges that come with completing the tasks within are not for the average peer. If you are still reading this text and have not yet set this book down, then have this warning: the actions covered on these pages may not be undone.*"

They began at the beginning despite having already read it. Now that they had the complete book, it felt right to start on the first page. Xenia was numb as she read and frozen when she reached the parts they'd never seen.

"Keep reading," Felix insisted.

She handed him the papers, shaking her head. "You read."

He took them and cleared his throat. "*Few get the prize*

they wish, and those who do rarely find the same satisfaction they sought for."

He stopped to turn the page, beginning the new section of the book. "*How do you successfully switch your fate? The steps are few: enter your story, seek the capital of magic and retrieve the Jewel of Fate, and then travel with your partner to a peak above the clouds and switch. Of course, everything can be simplified in words, but the reality is never quite the same. The task you are taking on is not simple. But you have this book to help you along the way—*"

Felix read several chapters deep before stopping to let Karielyn read and grabbing Xenia's hand instead.

Karielyn cleared her throat. "*Fate is a strange thing. It's carefully selected by magic especially for you. However, you might believe that your fate is not truly yours. But know that even then fates are significant. If you are destined for a different fate, then you should have the will to switch. You weren't given a fate you can't fulfill, and you are strong enough to change it.*"

As they read, pieces began to fall into place. The puzzle's gaps gradually started to fill.

Xenia chewed the inside of her lip to steady herself. She felt light. Despite the answers, something wasn't adding up. The fate givers used magic. Magic was never wrong. If this book were true and her fate was meant to be changed, then why had no one taught this?

Magic is never wrong. She repeated the phrase planted in her mind since she was young. There must be some other key, something the book didn't say.

Desperate for answers, they read deep into the night. It was only a few hours before dawn that Felix left. They read the entire book and, by the end of the night, came to a final conclusion: *We will switch our fates. We're destined to.*

Chapter Twenty-Nine

"I THINK WE SHOULD REGISTER THIS WEEK," FELIX SAID suddenly.

Xenia's heart jumped into her throat. They'd been working for nearly a month since they got the full translations, and Felix had subtly suggested they enter their story soon. She wasn't sure if she was ready. She had been making a mental list of the reasons she should and shouldn't enter yet. She knew once she entered, she couldn't turn back. That *terrified* her. If they failed, they would be killed. She also knew Blake was in their story right now. She had lost years with him and longed to see him again.

She hid her tense hands under the table in the dining hall, then using the same excuse she had every time he said something about entering, said, "I don't have permission yet."

"I may have fixed that." He smiled slyly, pulling out a pristine envelope with a shimmery surface. He handed it to her, and she broke the elegant seal. The note inside took her breath away. She had never seen the necessary permission slip before, but she had no doubt this was it. Her name was written at the top, and sprawled in neat handwriting at the bottom was Ravelyn Kage's signature.

Xenia clasped a hand to her mouth.

Felix's grin still shone, and his eyes now hosted a wicked gleam.

"How did you…?" she stammered.

"Maybe we should ride to the library after our training today."

"I…"

He reached under the table and grabbed her hand. "I'm nervous too, but we have to do it eventually." He was far braver than her.

"Karielyn?" he asked. Recently, she had stopped avoiding them in public and started sitting with them when they ate.

"Yeah, the sooner the better," she said flatly. The urge to argue was evident in her eyes. She didn't want to do this anymore than Xenia did.

They finished their classes, which felt strange now that they were training for the wrong fate, then the three of them met at the school stables.

Karielyn climbed in, but Felix waited outside, staying at Xenia's side. He pulled her into him and brushed his fingers through her hair.

I can't have this, she reminded herself. *It can never last.*

"You seem tense today. If you aren't ready, then neither

am I."

She wrapped her arms around him, breathing in his fresh, papery scent. Taking in a shuddering breath, she said, "I'll be fine. I've had more time to prepare than most."

"But if you change your mind before we—"

"Felix, I will be fine. Thank you."

He helped her in and closed the door. The horses pulled them slowly away from the Training Center. The weather today had stayed nice; Chantendell was finally starting to warm up. The late sun peeked through the trees, glowing softly through the windows.

Xenia had always wished the trip into the kingdom from the Training Center weren't so long, until now. She wouldn't mind riding for hours and hours to avoid entering her story, but it had to happen eventually. She knew that. She also knew the alternative.

They pulled up to the library and stepped out of the carriage. Felix pulled open the heavy, wooden doors to the tall building, and they walked in. The inside of this library was far different from any other library. It had books and seating, but the back room was called *The Portal*. It was where people went to be transported to their story.

They approached the front desk. A short, elderly woman with hair as white as clouds, wearing a pale-blue dress, came to the desk. "May I help you?" Her pale skin didn't show it, but she must have come from Elendore, or possibly even farther. The way her words drew out was proof that she had at least spent a great deal of time there.

Felix moved closer to the desk to meet her eyes. "My

friends and I were wondering if we could register to enter our story this week," he said with ease.

The lady straightened herself in attempt to see farther past the marble. "Of course. Can I have your names?" she asked, grabbing a pen. "And I'll need to see your permission."

"I'm Felix Liftson," he said slowly. "That's Xenia Safire," he said as he watched her write down their names. "And this is Karielyn Height."

The lady finished writing their names and then looked up. "Liftson and Safire? The two of you are entering together?"

Felix smiled, putting his arm around Xenia. "We are."

It can't stay this way. Now that they were entering their story, their time together would become more limited. *We can pretend all we want, but we're destined to destroy each other.*

The woman looked up from a paper and then said, "How about three days from now?"

Xenia's heart skipped a beat as her brain jerked it into reality.

"That's perfect!" Felix said, quoting the word at the bottom of the list of the ones Xenia would use. "Thank you."

The woman requested basic information that she wrote down and placed into an envelope that she sealed with a wax stamp. "I will send these to the fate givers and request access for your scrolls, then you'll be ready!"

Xenia wanted to thank her and tell her she couldn't wait, but she didn't want to lie, so she simply smiled. It was all she could manage.

The sky only had a few remaining streaks of light by the time they left the building. The days seemed to slip from Xenia like hours. It was nearly Lush season, but she wouldn't be here to see the colorful flowers bloom or take part in the Day of Victory festivities. No one knew what the new realm would be like, and there was no way to know until they got there. They could have already had their Lush season. They may never have a Lush season.

When they got back to the Training Center, Xenia glanced around her room, taking in the stacks of schoolwork she would never finish and the window Felix had broken all those weeks ago. She crawled into bed, but not into the covers. She just buried her face into the pillows like she did on her fourteenth birthday. She strained to suppress her tears, but couldn't help it. She had never been good at hiding her emotions, and right now they were crashing upon her with the weight of a waterfall.

She harbored an overbearing fear of entering her story, and she didn't want to leave her mother or Chantendell. Once she came back, she wouldn't have any need to go back to the Training Center. When she got back—if she got back—she would either be living down the street from the Liftsons in a fancy mansion or stranded on a far-off piece of land, not even allowed in the kingdom. Only time would reveal Fate's answer.

Chapter Thirty

IN THE MORNING, XENIA DRESSED IN A RED TOP AND black corset tied together with ribbons in the front. Her first class was Chantendell History. Her teacher briefed the class on the challenges of the first story. Despite being a villain, her teacher had made it clear that she was his favorite student. And it only became clearer after her mother became queen.

Her next, and least favorite, class was Villain Studies. Thank Fate she was almost done with this class.

She sat behind Merrie, who tipped back in her chair, and pulled out her book, turning to the page written on the board.

"Good morning, class! Today we will be reading a chapter from *The Way of a Villain*, if you could all turn to page 207. This chapter is about Ravelyn Kage."

They read the chapter, and at the end of class, their teacher asked them to choose a villain, preferably one in their line, and write about them—though Xenia wouldn't need to, since she wouldn't be there to turn it in.

After training, Xenia, Felix, and Karielyn walked to Mrs. Grimmlyn's office to let her know they would be entering. After verifying they had permission, she would log their departure and notify their trainers.

"We leave in two days," Felix said.

"You three?" she confirmed, reaching for a quill. "Do you all have permission?"

Karielyn handed over a small piece of paper with her villain trainer's signature sprawled across the bottom line. Felix pulled his own out of his pocket with one of his brother's names in fine script. Mrs. Grimmlyn took Xenia's and then stamped each one with golden ink before sliding them into a wooden box. She leaned back in her chair and grabbed three files from a nearby drawer. After a moment of assessing the files, she said, "Okay, that's everything I need. You're ready to enter!"

"Great, thank you!" Felix said happily.

Xenia couldn't believe how quick it was; she had expected it to be difficult. It all seemed easy. Easy and fast. Too fast.

Once they were in the hall, Felix said, "Are you okay? You're very quiet today."

"Just nervous," she said, taking a deep breath. "I still haven't told my mother—I should do that today."

"I'll go with you—I need to tell my family too."

"Let's go to your house first," she said. Despite not wanting to see Samuel again, she wasn't ready to give the news to her mother yet. It would feel final.

Karielyn decided she would do the same, but she refused to travel with them and see the Liftsons.

They left the building that held Mrs. Grimmlyn's office and started for the stables. White clouds swirled overhead, shielding them from the sun and setting the tone for a dull day. When they reached the stables, no one else was there, so they had no delay in getting a carriage. Felix climbed in first and pulled her in next to him. His hand glided across her wrist as she stared out the window, watching buildings pass by.

Xenia couldn't stop herself from thinking about all the things that could happen while she was away—especially with her mother in the palace. If history had taught her anything, it was that palace politics was a dangerous game to play.

She perked up as they neared Hero Village. The ride to the Liftsons' mansion was beautiful. Trees warped overhead, and the roads were made of smooth, dark pavement, unlike the normal dirt streets in Chantendell.

Inside they passed rows of stunning mansions. Even though she had visited numerous times—and even lived there for a few years with Blake's family when her parents entered their story—the beauty still stunned her. It was so different from the rest of the city.

When they arrived at the Liftson Mansion, a servant welcomed them inside. They found Felix's parents in the same room they had the night of the Yule celebration.

Samuel and Sybella Liftson sat on the settee nearest the

door. Felix and Xenia took seats opposite them.

"Felix. I didn't expect you," Samuel said with a tone like steel. Before Felix said anything, he turned to Xenia and said, "What makes you think you're welcome in my home?"

Xenia bit her tongue to stop herself from saying something she might regret. *I should have waited in the carriage.*

Felix put his arm around her. "Father, please don't do this. You know she—"

Samuel's eyes narrowed. "Felix, this is ridiculous. You are a *Liftson*—"

"She's not what you think."

"I think her fate tells me exactly what she is."

Xenia stared at the polished, wooden floors and velvet rugs beneath her feet and tried not to hear what Samuel said about her. No matter what she did, she knew he would never feel different about her.

Felix moved closer to her, his arm steadying around her. "We came here to tell you something."

Samuel grunted. "Get on with it."

"We're entering our story this week. Two days from now," Felix said.

Xenia silently thanked him for getting to the point—she didn't think she could bear another second of his argument with his father.

Samuel's brows rose. "Both of you? *Together*?" he asked. His tone changed and he added, "Well, you are behind. Your brothers all entered long before they turned eighteen. Trey was back before he turned as old as you!"

Felix scoffed, not bothering to cover it up.

"How old are your brothers?" Xenia asked, hoping she could ease the tension in the room.

"Trey's the oldest, he's thirty-three. Elden's twenty-nine and Lance is twenty-five," Felix answered.

Xenia hadn't realized there were so many years between them; they all looked very young. "I never would have thought Trey was older than twenty-five."

"It runs in the family," Samuel said with a force that didn't belong with his words. He did appear nearly ten years younger than his wife, although Xenia knew they were the same age.

"You're leaving in two days," Mrs. Liftson said, then added, "Together."

Felix nodded.

A ghost of a smile pulled at Samuel's lips as he said, "You understand you won't be able to stay together, don't you? Felix, you'll need to fight her."

Felix grimaced, but it was slight and left his features quickly. "We both understand perfectly well what our fates mean."

"Good."

Samuel's reminder pulled at Xenia's heart. *He's going to leave me. He'll have to.* Everyone always left.

"I think we should leave now," Felix said.

He moved his arm and rose to his feet. Xenia did the same. They walked towards the archway that led out of the room, and Felix pulled it open. Before she could leave, a hand closed around her arm. She spun around to face Samuel Liftson.

"You are making a mistake with my son," he whispered through gritted teeth. "You don't belong together. I suggest you leave him alone before things get worse."

Xenia pulled her arm free as Felix stormed past her until he stood a span away from Samuel. "Don't you dare touch her."

Samuel didn't get the chance to say anything else before Felix stormed down the hall. Xenia couldn't imagine leaving her family with an argument like that, though Felix didn't seem to care.

The air seemed lighter outside the mansion. An invisible weight lift from Xenia's shoulders. Felix talked to the coachman while she climbed into the back of the carriage. As soon as he joined her inside, he said, "Nia, I am so sorry. I—he shouldn't have treated you like that." He covered his face with his hand and sighed.

"It's not your fault. That's just the way people have been told to treat me—you can't help that."

He slid his hand down his face. "That's horrible. No one should act that way towards someone because of their fate."

She went silent as she leaned against his shoulder.

"Let's go to the palace now," he said, then mumbled something about not visiting his brothers.

The drive to the palace from the Liftsons' house wasn't a long one, and once they stopped at the gate, she felt a sense of peace to mix with her worry. She hoped her mother would be able to see her. Their conversation about Al was the last one she had had with her in person, and it wasn't the last attempt she had at speaking with her. After the same process as last time, the guards pulled open the gate for the two of them, repeating their bow. She ignored it and darted into the castle.

This time, she managed to locate Estelle's office on her own. She reached for the handle, but the guard watching the door stopped her.

"Xenia?"

She looked over at the man, and he embraced her. Confusion pulled her featured. He removed his helmet. "It's me."

"Akron?" she asked. He nodded. "What are you doing here?"

Akron had worked for her mother when they lived in the Dwelling. She'd known him most of her life.

He smiled. "Your mother got a promotion, and I came with her. Did you think I was going to guard an empty castle? We're all here, Xenia."

"I'm glad… I mean—we're getting ready to enter, but—well, when we're back—"

"You're entering? Xenia, that's wonderful! I can't wait to hear your story," he said, dropping her shoulder. "That must be why you're here, isn't it? To tell your mother? I'll let you to it, then." He unlocked the door and pulled it open, ushering them inside.

When the door opened, her mother rushed toward her.

"Mother, how are you?" Xenia asked, holding her in a hug.

She had dark spots under her eyes, and her face

reflected her tiredness. "I'm fine, how are you?"

"Fine, I suppose. Felix and I are planning on entering our story in a few days!" She surprised herself with how cheerful she sounded.

Estelle looked at the two of them in silence until tears formed in her eyes. "A few days?" she whispered. She took a deep breath and then said, "I'm proud of you, Xenia, I'm proud of the woman you are." She picked up her hand and squeezed it. "I know that you're destined to be a villain, but you will always be my hero," she said softly, stroking her fingers with her thumb.

"Mother… I'm going to miss you so much."

"It will be all right—I will be waiting for you when you get back," she said slowly. "And once you're in your story, you can find Blake. He will be happy to see you and he'll look after you." She paused and glanced toward Felix. "Though I'm sure you're capable of that."

Felix smiled. "Nothing will happen to her under my watch, Your Majesty, I swear to it."

The promise was supposed to comfort her mother, not Xenia, but it did, even though she knew it wasn't true. Eventually, they would have to fight each other.

"Thank you, Felix, and please, call me *Estelle*," she said, letting go of her hand.

"How have things been at the palace?" Felix asked politely.

Her mother sighed heavily. "Not well, I'm afraid." She pointed at a stack of letters on the table. "Chantendell is being threatened. We've been receiving warnings by mail for months now." She folded one of the papers over, hiding the figures from view. "I shouldn't say much more, not yet, at least. We must wait until more is confirmed."

Felix's brows pulled in concern.

Threats? Perhaps the rumors of war against the western kingdoms were more than rumors.

"Will you two be joining us for dinner? Ariela makes a splendid roast."

Before Xenia could change plans by answering for them, Felix shook his head. "No, Karielyn's cooking for us tonight, but thank you."

"Your roommate?"

Xenia nodded.

"She seems very nice."

Felix scoffed. Estelle gave him a peculiar glance, so he attempted to pass it as a cough.

"Are you al—?"

"He's fine," Xenia said, rolling her eyes.

He smiled, and she caught it from the corner of her eye as she turned back to her mother. "Akron's here," Xenia noted, watching Estelle sort through a stack of letters. They all bore the same seal: black wax pressed with an inflamed crown and two crossed swords running through the inside.

"And Hezlyn—oh, Xenia, it's wonderful here. I'll be anticipating the day you return, and your coronation, oh, it will be perfect!"

Xenia smiled, not letting herself think of what else the future might bring. "I'm sure it will be."

Chapter Thirty-One

SLEEP, XENIA KEPT TELLING HERSELF. *I NEED SLEEP.* Yet every time she repeated the phrase, she felt more and more awake. Today wasn't a day she wanted to spend miserable and tired. But she couldn't sleep. Not with thoughts flooding her mind like a city after a dam broke.

There were so many ways their mission could fail.

There were so many things she never learned about Zarius Al.

There were so many things that could go wrong in Chantendell while she wasn't there.

There were so many things she wouldn't be prepared for in the new realm.

There were so many—

"Xenia?" Felix called from outside her bedroom door.

What time is it? Panic seeped through her. She hadn't slept the entire night. "Are you ready?"

"I will be—in a minute, I just need to…" Her words

trailed off as she jumped from her bed and changed into different clothes. She grabbed her bag from the floor, threw it over her shoulders, and glanced around the room to make sure she had everything. Most of her things were stored in boxes now. When she left, they would be taken to her mother's house in the Dwelling until she returned.

"What time is it?" she asked when she met Felix and Karielyn in the hallway.

Felix shook his head. "We need to leave now, or we'll risk being late."

His words sparked another round of panicked thoughts. What would happen if she arrived late? They would surely wait, right? Did she want them to wait? She didn't mind rescheduling—

No. I am doing this.

"Are you ready?" Felix asked when they made it downstairs.

"Yes."

"Do you have the book?"

"Yes, both versions. I wouldn't forget it."

They walked out into the crisp morning air. It was still dark, and she suddenly felt less guilty for not being ready on time. The three of them climbed into the back of the carriage reserved for them, and the horses pulled them toward the library.

If she weren't so worried, she would have fallen asleep then and let Felix wake her when they got to the library, but if last night was sleepless, she certainly wouldn't sleep now. The cool air chilled her to the bone, yet she was sweating from nerves.

When they arrived, her mother and several of her guards, Morea, the Liftsons, the Cedars, and the Heights were already waiting. "Sorry we're late," Karielyn apologized. "Someone slept in." She jerked her head towards Xenia.

Xenia's mother laughed, and she rolled her eyes. "I was *not* sleeping."

They walked into the building, and three fate givers led them through a door at the back of the building.

The room sparkled like the night sky. The walls looked like mirrors, though instead of her own reflection, Xenia saw the glow of endless stars. Yet as she studied them, she couldn't tell if they were there at all. The room was round, and the walls were split into panels, tarnished around the edges of each one.

She stared, too stunned to speak. No one ever spoke of the portal, or what exactly happened when you entered. Perhaps this was why: she couldn't find words to place the room's details. She wondered if the walls contained magic.

"Isn't it beautiful?" Felix said.

She nodded, still entranced by the starlit walls.

Karielyn and Morea were already hugging each other and crying. It reminded Xenia of the day Blake left. She hoped she would find him soon. It would be one thing to make the worries this week held dissolve.

"Are you doing all right?" her mother asked from behind her.

"I suppose."

"Are you sure?"

"I'll be fine. I'm just afraid."

"I understand. I was terrified when I left, I had never been a queen before, I didn't know what to expect." Estelle pulled her into a hug, and Xenia broke into tears.

She pulled away and rubbed her puffy eyes.

The fate givers each held a scroll of yellowed paper. *Their* scrolls.

Tears streamed down Xenia's face as the fate givers scanned the room, their stare lingering on the three of them.

"Xenia Safire?" one of them called.

She embraced her mother and friends one last time before walking up. The fate giver nodded and held his hand out to give her the scroll. All she had to do was touch it, *one* touch.

She reached her hand out and carefully placed each finger on the paper. Slowly, her vision faded, then her hearing. Everything became muffled. She could feel her head spinning and feared she might fall over, but she could no longer feel the ground beneath her feet. All she could feel was the bag on her shoulder weighing her down like all the contents had turned to heavy stone.

Xenia imagined she had fallen over, but she couldn't tell. It felt as if the air had left the room. If she was even in a room. She felt light, yet heavier than ever before.

Everything was gone. Panic trickled its way inside her. She was nowhere. She didn't know where to go and, more pressingly, *how* to go anywhere. She couldn't rely on her senses. All she had as a reminder of her existence were her thoughts. But even those were hard to hold on to. She couldn't concentrate on one thing. Her mind felt like gelatin, bouncing this way and that. She was like a gust of wind, only in one place for a second. Or she was being blown by the wind and trying desperately to stand her ground.

Then, suddenly, she could feel her toes and then her legs, as if she were melted wax being poured into a mold. She regained feeling in her legs and began to feel capable of holding her body again. She could feel again, her hands and fingers rubbing against each other in a desperate attempt to send a message of reality to her brain. She still felt as if she was nowhere, nowhere reachable to anyone but her, but slowly, she became more aware of her surroundings. She could smell pine and hear birds singing a song in the high distance. She could taste her stale, dry lips. When she opened her eyes, she could see.

She was no longer in Chantendell.

PART TWO

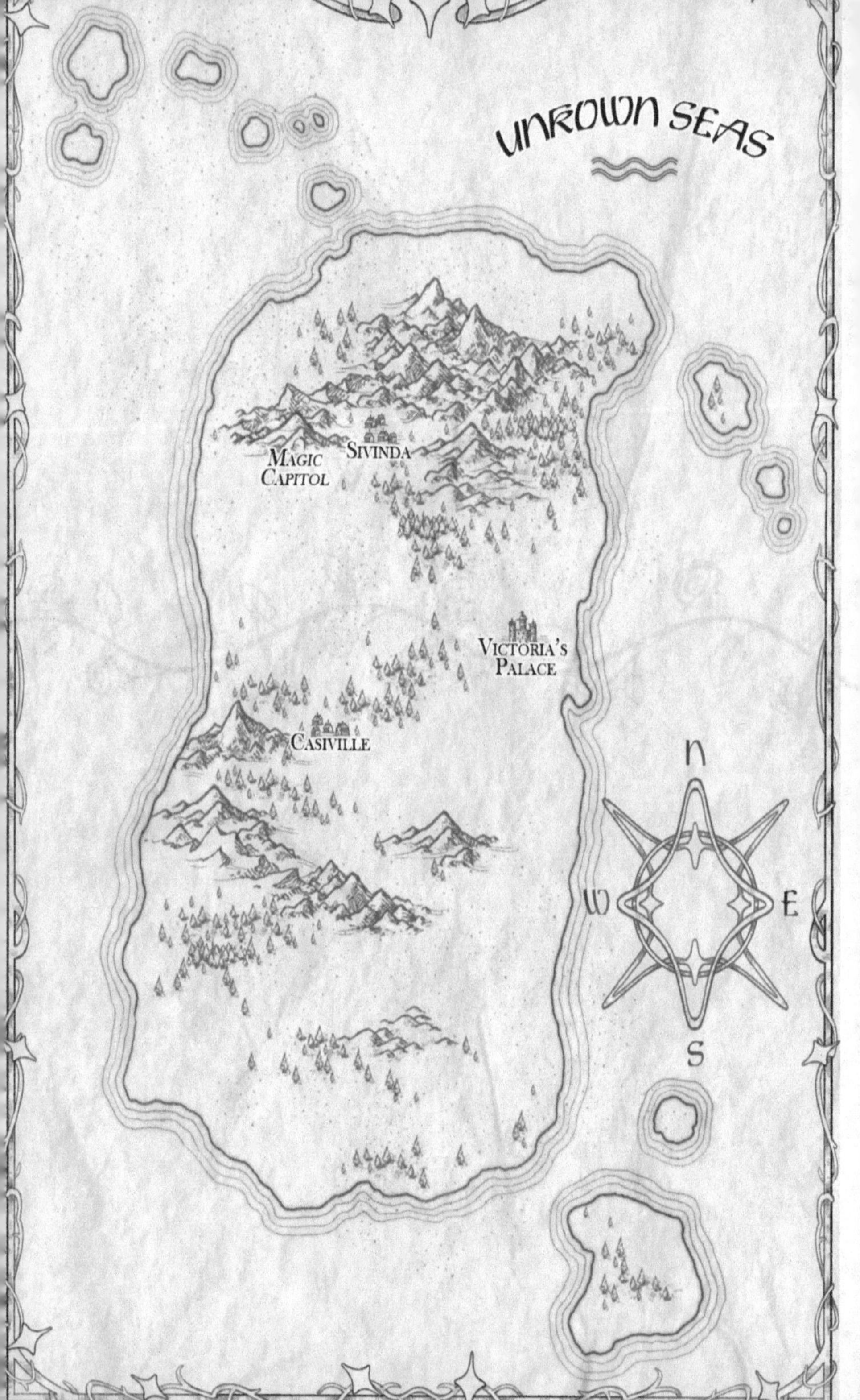

UNKOWN SEAS
SIVINDA
MAGIC CAPITOL
VICTORIA'S PALACE
CASIVILLE
N
W
E
S

Chapter Thirty-Two

THE NEW WORLD CAME INTO FOCUS AROUND XENIA AS she recovered from traveling through worlds. An experience she would never forget, yet never quite remember. Like a dream. She could feel it, but she would never know it as she did.

Rich, emerald-green trees behind her hugged the clearing she stood in. A dirt trail ran into the horizon where the sun should've been rising, but instead sat high, indicating midday.

Distracting her from the view, a sharp pain in her head blurred her vision. She grabbed her temples to sooth the ache. Her fingers shook, and her body trembled. Groaning, she fell to her knees and took in shuddering breathes.

Behind her, Felix called her name. His body slid next to hers, and he wrapped an arm around her. He mumbled something about the effects of magic, but his words were lost beyond the pain.

The searing pain passed, replaced by a string of awful, cruel thoughts. Thoughts foreign to her mind but that *felt* true.

"Felix," she whispered, trying to keep the thoughts at bay. "I…"

"Nia?"

Clutching his hand, she rose to her feet and forced the thoughts away. "It's nothing." Dirt stained the bottom of her skirt, and she brushed it off. "I'm fine."

"Are you sure?"

She nodded. The pain had passed; there was no reason to worry Felix now.

Karielyn appeared behind them and rushed to their sides. "I never want to do that again," she said, her body trembling.

"We should look for a town—or someplace to stay," Felix said.

Xenia numbly agreed. Where had those thoughts come from?

"We should go that way," Karielyn said, gesturing ahead of them. "There's a trail, that must mean there's a town close."

"Let's see," Felix said, already walking away from the mountains and down the trail.

Xenia and Karielyn glanced at each other before smiling and darting off after him. Wind rushed through Xenia's hair. Beautiful forest sounds whispered in the trees.

Xenia took a deep breath, letting the breeze carry away her anxious thoughts. She had made it. For now, that was all that mattered. She would worry about Fate later.

They passed through fields of plain, yellow grass and weeds. Occasional black birds speckled the sky. There was nothing unusual about the land, but every detail held her attention. It didn't look any different from the world she was used to, which could be an advantage. Some stories varied drastically from their world. Xenia used to dream of exploring a strange world, but adjusting to a new living condition would complicate their mission.

They walked nearly an hour before reaching a small town. Xenia had never seen a town like the one surrounding them. The gravel they'd been walking on blended into a light-yellow, cobblestone road that ran through a narrow aisle packed with crooked buildings. Each one had unique properties: the one to her left stood taller than the one to her right, and while some sported stained glass, others only showed warped windows. In front of them, the stone buildings merged into an arch with a clock built into its base.

The town was still, unlike Chantendell. The streets were entirely deserted, and the building doors were closed just as the curtain drawn windows were.

"Is this a real town?" Karielyn asked. The question seemed senseless, but Xenia secretly wondered the same thing.

"Yes, it's just really small," Felix said, walking farther in. "The only people here are the people who have entered our story, and this is only *one* town."

"Do you think Blake lives here?" Xenia asked. There may not have been many people, but how big was this world?

He could be *anywhere*. Surely they'd find him; he was Felix's allegiant, and Fate had a way of bringing heroes and villains together in their stories.

"He might," Felix said resentfully. "But I want to start soon, and it'll be difficult to—"

Karielyn didn't give him the chance to finish. "If we find him, he might be able to help us navigate—"

"I think we need to be careful who we give our plans to. And I know you have other intentions for finding him, so don't bother coming up with further reasons," Felix snapped as they made their way down the street.

Karielyn's face burned red.

"Is there anything your brothers told you? About their stories?" Xenia asked, to keep her mind off Blake.

"To expect anything, I suppose. Elden's story was filled with magic, like an old fairy tale. But Trey's and Lance's were like Chantendell, magic wasn't accessible to everyone."

Xenia already knew this. Most of the kids in Chantendell—possibly all of Moira—could retell any Liftson story from memory.

"Do you think there's a lot of magic here?" Karielyn asked.

"I'm not sure, but whatever magic there is we'll find," Felix answered. "We have to."

They crossed under the small arch—if it were any shorter, Felix would have needed to bend over to make it through. Past it, the buildings branched out, showing off the town's foliage: bright-green grass and neatly trimmed bushes, unlike the path into town. The brilliance of the green put

Xenia in a Lush spirit.

Felix ran across the emerald path and pulled at the branch of a pink Malus tree. He tossed a small red apple in Xenia's direction. She surprised herself by catching it. Before she could take a bite, a sharp scream pierced the quiet air. She winced at the sound.

"Hey!"

Xenia turned around to face the girl who had screamed.

"Those are *mine*! You're stealing!" she shrieked from the doorway of one of the buildings Xenia had presumed empty.

Felix backed away from the tree. "I'm sorry," he shouted back. "We just got here—we don't have any—"

"Felix?" The girl stopped him mid-sentence and ran toward them. "You're here!" she squealed. The way her arms wrapped around him made Xenia uneasy. Did all girls think he had feelings for them?

Felix pulled away and stepped closer to Xenia.

Xenia met the girl's soft, olive eyes with her own sharp, green ones. The girl's brown hair curled perfectly at her side, lining up with the hem of her sleeve. Xenia pushed her own black hair behind her ears.

"I don't think I know you," she said.

"Xenia." The girl spoke as if it were a punishment just speaking her name. Did she ever do anything to prove that she was worth their fear? "I'm Sierra. We had astrology together. Don't you remember?"

At the name, she rushed back to Xenia's mind. She was one of the apparently many girls to have a crush on Blake. Did girls swoon over all heroes?

She didn't know why the thought of Blake finding someone made her uneasy. She'd never wanted him herself; growing up together made him feel like a brother. But once he found someone, she would be reminded of how much things had changed.

"Sierra," Xenia said dryly. "Yes, I remember now."

"Well, welcome to Casiville. If you need anything, let me know! That's my neighborhood over there." She pointed at an unseen location hidden behind the green hill.

"Actually, I have a question, does Blake Cedar live nearby?" Karielyn.

"Of course! Until Victoria showed up, he was really the one who led us. Everyone in Casiville knows him, he's my neighbor."

"Really?" Xenia exclaimed.

"He might be working now—he owns the meet—"

"We should look for him," Karielyn said.

Felix's fists tightened. "I'm really not sure that's the best idea," he whispered, a hint of distress in his smooth voice. He started down the hill, motioning for Xenia and Karielyn to follow.

Karielyn put her hands on her hips. "Is there something you're afraid of, Liftson?"

Felix shook his head. "If we find Blake, we'll need to explain our plans. And I don't want to risk anyone finding out. Now that we're in our story, we'll be watched closely. A small slip could cost us everything."

Karielyn rolled her eyes. "And what do you propose we do? Blake lives here, and right now we have nowhere to go.

He can help us!"

Xenia glanced beyond the hill at the cluster of log cabins Sierra had referred to. She understood the risk that involving Blake came with, but she couldn't stand being so close to him and leaving without him.

"I think Karielyn is right," she said. "We'll need to be careful, but he can help us."

Felix went silent.

Xenia turned around, studying the houses in the distance. Beyond them was a forest filled with trees that waved in the gentle wind. A deer left the trees, taking slow steps across the clearing.

This was where Blake had been for the past four years.

As she watched the deer, her thoughts began to tear away her mind's peace. *What if he changed and we don't get along anymore? Have I changed? I've changed a lot. Will he still accept me? Did he leave to get away from me?*

"Xenia, are you okay?" Felix asked.

She nodded, pulling herself from her thoughts. It was so peaceful here. The only sound was an occasional crow flying out of a nearby tree, rustling the leaves as it spread its wings.

The silence broke, replaced by their screams as a silver arrow ripped through the air, striking the center of the deer.

Xenia grabbed Felix's arm. Karielyn's hand wrapped around her other wrist as she turned her head frantically, searching for the shooter.

"Xenia?"

She squinted her eyes to see where the voice had come

from. The branches of a tree in the grove across the clearing shook as a figure emerged. Xenia recognized him even from where she stood. Without hesitation, she ran to him.

Chapter Thirty-Three

"I MISSED YOU SO MUCH!" XENIA CRIED AS HER ARMS found their way around Blake. He had grown taller, and his curly, blond hair crept slightly down his neck. Though he looked different, his eyes still filled her with peace like they used to, and his smile put her whole mind at ease. Even before speaking to him, she could tell he had changed. Matured. Everyone said your story would do that. Change you. Force you to grow up.

"I missed you too! Fate, I'm so happy you're here!"

The sound of his voice rang in Xenia's ears as memories flooded her mind. He hugged her tighter.

"Nia!" Felix called from behind her.

Forcing herself away from Blake, she turned to Felix. He flashed a quick glance in Blake's direction before turning his attention to her and pressing a quick kiss on her lips.

Xenia blinked in surprise.

He pulled back and placed his hand on her shoulder,

glaring at Blake.

Blake's eyes narrowed as he glanced between them. He seemed to be weighing his words before settling on, "Did the three of you enter together?"

Xenia nodded. "We just arrived. We still need a place to stay."

"You can stay with me for now. My house is over here."

He left the deer behind in the field and threw his bow over his shoulder, leading them to his house.

The structure was simple: no elaborate furniture or unnecessary decorations. He had a small table behind a gray couch in the living room. To the other side of the cabin was the kitchen. The only separation between the two living spaces was a tall, wooden counter.

Blake offered to cook them a meal as they caught up, though Xenia knew it would take longer than one meal to catch each other up. This entire world had practically been built while Blake was here—he had a lot to tell her. And she had plenty to tell him as well.

When Blake finished cooking, he set the table the way they would at a palace: the plate in the middle, knife to the right, and fork to the left. Xenia taught him that, years before they received their fates. He set a plate of meat, potatoes, and bread on the table for each of them.

While he was in the kitchen, Karielyn leaned towards Xenia. "Are you going to ask him about…?"

Xenia nodded, glancing hesitantly in Blake's direction. "Yeah, I just don't know how. I haven't seen him in years… but I'll think of something."

Karielyn didn't respond as Blake slid into the chair across from Xenia's. His smile had been consistent since he started cooking—unlike Felix, who had hardly spoken upon arriving at Blake's house. Xenia slid her hand over his to see him smile. He did, but it looked forced. She made a list in her mind of things she could say to him, but kept them on her tongue.

She had never eaten deer meat before, and she couldn't bring herself to try it. Blake watched as she picked at her potatoes and toast, and when she finished them, he took her meat with his fork.

After dinner, Karielyn offered to clean the dishes while Xenia and Blake talked. Blake gave her a tour of his house, which didn't take long since she'd seen everything aside from two bedrooms and a bathroom—which lacked the fixtures found in Chantendell. The Training Center towers were larger than his house.

"So, what's happened in Chantendell?" he asked, now wiping the table clean with a damp cloth.

"So much! I don't know where to begin." Xenia leaned into one of the ladder-back chairs, watching him. In the four years they were apart, it felt like everything had happened— yet life seemed to move slowly. "My mother won the throne!"

Despite being eight and not fully comprehending the idea of Estelle being queen, Blake was crestfallen when she didn't win ten years ago.

"Really?" he said, eyes wide. He set down the cloth. "That's amazing! So, you're princess now?"

She shrugged. "I'm not technically princess yet. They'll hold the coronation when I get back."

Blake's smile wavered slightly. "Will they coronate you with your fate? Won't that violate their laws? They don't even let villains into the kingdom." His voice lowered to a whisper as if he were frightened one of the others would hear them and disapprove of their conversation.

Xenia lowered her voice too. "There's something we need to tell you. Regarding that."

She gestured to Felix, grabbing his attention. "Yeah?" he asked, joining them at the table.

Xenia redirected her attention to Blake. "Do you remember the book I found in my tower when I moved in?"

Blake nodded. "What about it?"

"It's not a journal. It's a guide."

"Guide for what?" he asked, taking a step away from the table. Karielyn left the kitchen, grabbed the translations from Xenia's bag, and handed them to Blake.

He took it cautiously as if the words alone could cause damage. After he read the first page, he looked up, his face pale.

"You can't do that," he mumbled, shaking his head. "That's why you're with him? You two want to—"

Felix clasped his hand over Blake's mouth. "They're listening!" he hissed.

Blake grabbed hold of Felix's wrist and slammed it hard enough to send him staggering into the wall behind him. Xenia flinched.

Felix's caution was well meant. There were two

branches of magic. The first was open magic, found in natural elements. It contaminated the air and must be contained to safely use. The second was Fate magic—what Chantendell used to monitor stories from the kingdom. It was similar to open magic—it was natural and must be contained—but it was stronger, only worked in relation to stories, and was only found in Chantendell.

There were people in Chantendell who used Fate magic to monitor their actions. Xenia didn't know much about it. It wasn't something they were taught.

"I'm sorry," Blake said, looking behind his back as if expecting to see someone. He turned back to Xenia and frowned. "This is forbidden!"

"Say it again, in case they didn't hear you," Felix said, rolling his wrist around in his hand.

Blake ignored the comment. "Nia… why? You'll be risking your *life*!"

"This is what I want. You know this is what I want, it always has been."

"Please, Nia. If you do this… I could lose you," he said, his voice gentle. He picked up her hand and squeezed it. His fingers were rough and calloused.

"You won't lose me. You'll never lose me."

The words were empty. They all knew the chances of her dying on this mission were high. Chantendell already suspected them. If they revealed themselves too soon, they wouldn't stand a chance.

"Will you listen to me?" The gentle was swallowed up now by the sharp ring in Blake's words. "We both know how dangerous this is. You more than me, I'm sure. I don't care what's written on your scroll, you will never be a villain in my eyes. You do not need to do this."

"Blake, I—"

"Cedar,"—Felix cut in—"she's already made up her mind. She made it up seasons ago. Stop trying to change her decision." A strong force hid behind his words.

Blake's face hardened and his fists tightened. He looked ready punch Felix, and with his build, he could probably knock him out. "Will you let me speak to her?"

"This isn't your choice. We've already made up our mind. Nothing *you* say is going to change that!" Felix shouted, making his way to Xenia's side. They reached for each other's hand in unison.

"I'm trying to protect her! You're not foolish, Liftson, you know this is dangerous."

He nodded. "I do. I know perfectly well. But this is our only chance. We're choosing the course of our future!"

"Exactly! Do you want to live alone and spend life away from everyone because people are too afraid to come near you?"

"Do you want *Nia* to live like that? This is better for *her*."

Xenia and Karielyn glanced at each other. If anyone was listening it wouldn't be hard to piece their plan together now.

Blake's lips settled into a firm line. He glanced between the two of them before saying, "I want Nia to live."

Felix nodded. "Me too, and I won't let her die. Clearly you haven't noticed yet, but I care about her!" He stepped even closer to her.

"You've already put her in danger." Blake looked in Xenia's direction, but was careful not to look at Felix. "Nia, I can't lose you, I've known you my whole life. You're still my closest friend. This is a really bad idea…" He stopped talking and stayed quiet for a moment as if he weren't sure if his choice of words were the right ones. "Will anything I say persuade you?"

Xenia's cheeks reddened as she shook her head. "Don't you understand what this means to me?" Her voice was a strained whisper. "This… this gave me the first bit of hope I've had for years. I can't go back now."

Blake remained silent as he watched her. His blue eyes did a well enough of job of conveying his confusion and fear without any words.

"You don't have to help me," Xenia said, breaking the silence her last statement left. "I'd never want to put you in danger. But I have to do this."

Blake's lips pinched. He looked at Felix, as if assessing him, then at Xenia. Pain wrinkled his features. "I couldn't let you do this on your own and live with myself after. You have no money, no weapons—and from what I've heard, it's only a matter of time before you're discovered. You'll need more help… Fate, this is a terrible idea."

Xenia's solemn expression softened. "So, you'll help us?"

"If it's really what you want."

Chapter Thirty-Four

BLAKE'S COLLECTION OF MAPS WAS SPRAWLED ACROSS the table. As the sun sank lower, they lit candles to see them.

"There's no way to tell from a map where magic is," Blake said. "And certainly not where it's most. At least, not my maps. But Victoria entered a few months ago. The palace will be stocked with maps and charts of all kinds. If we can manage to talk to her—"

Felix didn't wait for him to finish. He leaned back in his chair and said, "That'll be easy. She might even invite me over herself."

Blake made a mark on the parchment and wrote *Victoria's Palace*. "If we manage, she might lend us a map."

Xenia tensed at the thought of telling Victoria what they planned to do and asking her to help them. *We're only going to borrow a map*, she told herself. They didn't need to tell her what it was for.

"Wonderful." Felix bristled.

"Once we do that, we find the jewel, correct?" Blake asked. "Do we know what it looks like?"

"Yeah, I'll show you," Karielyn said, reaching under the table for her bag. She pulled out the page she had torn from her schoolbook and handed it to him.

Blake unfolded the paper and narrowed his eyes as he examined it. "What language is this?"

"Enrian."

"Why do you have this?" he asked, studying the strange letters.

"I'm half-Enrian. I lived there for a few years," Karielyn answered with a touch of pride in her voice.

"Really? That's—"

"Can we stay focused?" Felix snapped, grabbing the paper from Blake and tossing it back to Karielyn, who scoffed. Her face showed the disappointment Xenia knew she meant to hide.

Blake glared at Felix as if his feelings echoed Karielyn's. Surely they didn't. Xenia pushed all the thoughts from her head, silently scolding herself for thinking in that manner.

"Is there a problem?" Blake asked, still glaring at Felix.

"This is serious," he said. "We need to stay—"

"He hates me." Karielyn broke in. "That's all." She picked up the paper and pushed it into her bag.

After seasons Felix and Karielyn were still marching on thin ice around each other.

"Then why risk so much to help him?"

Karielyn opened her mouth to speak, but she seemed to think twice about her words and quickly closed it.

"We should keep working," Xenia suggested, attempting to break the tension.

Blake nodded. "What else do I need to know?"

"Once we find *it*, we need to find a peak above the clouds," Felix said. "That's where the guide said we need to be for it to work."

"Victoria might have something that can help us with that too." Xenia didn't like how much of their mission's success relied on Victoria. Blake remembered what had happened between them, didn't he? Did he think she'd be willing to help? "Anything else?"

"I think we covered everything we need for now," Felix said, taking the translations and slipping them into his bag. "Are you sure you have enough room for all four of us?"

"I have two rooms. You and I will have to sleep on the couch."

"That's fine," Felix said flatly.

Blake rolled up his map. "Oh, Nia, I should warn you— the rooms are small, and the windows don't open."

A slight shiver tickled her spine at the thought. The arrangement wasn't much different from her room at the Training Center, but she didn't mind switching places. She couldn't imagine how both boys would fit on the couch anyways. "I can switch with Felix."

"Are you sure—?"

She nodded.

"I don't need a room, either," Karielyn said.

Blake glared at Felix as if it were his fault the girls wouldn't have beds, but he didn't argue further.

"I have extra quilts in my room. I'll go grab them," he said, rising from the table. Karielyn offered to help and they disappeared into the small room behind the kitchen.

In their solitude, Felix reached for her hand. She laid hers on top of his and his fingers closed around it.

Everything had become real. She had anticipated this day her entire life and it had finally come. Yet all she could think of was everything that would follow.

Karielyn and Blake returned carrying stacks of dull quilts and pillows. Karielyn's cheeks were glowing a wild shade of pink.

"I didn't realize you spent so much time in Enria," Blake was saying. "They regard Fate different there, don't they?"

"They don't regard it at all."

Xenia let go of Felix's hand and rose from her chair. "I'm a little hot, I think I'll go sit outside."

"Do you want me to come with you?" Felix asked.

She shook her head. She hadn't had a moment alone since she left Chantendell.

"I'm fine, I'll only be a minute."

"All right. Tell me if you need anything."

Xenia nodded and then started for the door. She pulled it open and walked around the house. The sun's rays lay cross the lawn, painting yellow across the ground and purple across the clouds. She leaned against the wooden logs of the house and watched the sun slip beneath the horizon.

She breathed in the crisp air, thankful to finally be clearing her mind. She closed her eyes and focused on the warm glow of the fading sun against her face.

"It's pretty out here, isn't it?"

The broken silence made Xenia jump. Blake neared her, carrying two cups. He handed her one and took a sip of his own.

"Yeah, it is." She took a drink of the tea and shivered. The warm liquid made her realize how cold it was outside. Her arms and legs were coated in small bumps from the wind that danced through the trees.

"Is something wrong?" he asked, raising his cup to his lips.

"No, I just needed to clear my head." She moved over, giving him room to sit down beside her.

"What is it?" he urged, sliding closer.

"Nothing, really."

He grinned. "Fine, I didn't want to know, anyway." He took another drink and then said, "How long have you been with Liftson?"

She tensed. Was that what she and Felix were? Together?

"Not long. The end of the year," she said, trying to keep her answer brief.

He said nothing and replied with a simple *hm*.

The sun's final light drifted away, and the starlight gradually grew stronger. The night air was cold and refreshing. Something about being outside after dark satisfied her. It reminded her of the night she had spent with Felix.

She took a drink. "Do you like it here?"

The amount of time it took Blake to answer convinced her that he hadn't heard. Instead of repeating the question, she let it go. He might have avoided it on purpose. She twirled the leaves around in her drink. Silence like this was rare when they were younger.

He cleared his throat. "Yes, to an extent. There's nothing wrong with Casiville, but… I miss my parents. And you. Life's been pretty lonely. A lot lonely, actually." He practically choked on the last word.

Lonely. He had been lonely too. The spiteful feelings Xenia had felt when he left simmered inside her. He had left her alone for years when he could have waited for her and spared them both. She imagined at least he was happy, but was he?

It's not important. We're together now.

"About Felix," Blake said, "do you really like him, or are you only with him to switch?"

She opened her mouth to speak and then closed it, realizing she had no answer. For weeks she had sworn that nothing would become of her and Felix. But somewhere between the night she met him at the fountain and the selection, she had found something more between them. Something in the way he spoke to her. In the way he understood her better than anyone else ever could. And she knew he felt the same.

"I—I do really like him."

"You're a villain. He's a hero. Do you really think—?"

She frowned. "Blake—"

He shook his head. "I'm serious, Nia." His voice was suddenly grave. "No matter which side of the battle you fight, you'll be fighting him. He knows that, I'm sure. Do you?"

She rose to her feet. She and Felix both knew perfectly well what they were getting into. She knew Felix didn't want to hurt her. "This is what you have to say to me? I haven't seen you in four years, and all you want to do is tell me where I've gone wrong!"

Blake stood too. "What I'm saying is that a battle isn't over when you take a hit. It's over when you have no hits left. Do you think Felix plans——?"

"I don't care!" she shouted. "I don't care what Felix plans to do!"

"This all seems incredibly reckless."

"*Reckless?*"

Before Blake could respond, Felix appeared from behind the wall. "There you are! Are you all right? I heard shouting."

"She's fine," Blake said coolly. "Go back inside."

Felix glanced in Xenia's direction. "No, I think I'll wait for her to answer."

"I'm fine, Felix."

Before either could speak, Xenia started towards the house. Blake grabbed her wrist.

She pulled her arm away. "Don't touch me!" she snarled, folding her arms against her chest.

"What in Fate's name did you do to her?" Felix shouted, rushing to her side.

Blake didn't respond. He only glared at them.

"I'm going to bed," Xenia said, turning towards the door. She wanted this to be over. How had this even happened? She and Blake always got along.

Felix grabbed her hand and stopped her. "Hey, hey, what happened?"

When their eyes met, tears pricked her eyes. Blinking them back she said, "Nothing. I'm fine."

They hugged and kissed before pulling away. *Again.*

"Good night, Felix."

Before he could say anything else, Xenia pulled herself away from him and returned to the cabin.

The house fell silent long before she was actually ready to sleep. Her hair hung over the arm of the couch as she stared at the celling, listening to Karielyn's steady breathes.

Despite the seasons of preparation, she didn't feel ready for what waited ahead.

Chapter Thirty-Five

BLAKE MOVED XENIA'S ARM AGAIN. "KEEP YOUR BODY straight." He shouldn't have had to remind her as many times as he had. He had insisted on teaching her how to use a bow, as he said it would be good for finding food if they got separated. She hoped that never happened. If it did, she didn't even have a bow.

And she didn't want him to think this time meant anything to her. Their argument last night continued to make her feel uneasy every time she met eyes with Blake.

"Lower your finger so you don't—"

"I know," she said, sliding her finger down to avoid the fletching. She let go of the arrow. It flew through the air and disappeared within the mass of trees. The wooden target Blake had made hung in front of her, untouched.

He smiled despite her miss. He might have been trying to get her on a better page, but she was still stuck on the last one: reading over the same lines, wondering how things

280

could go so wrong. And like most stories, she feared it would get worse. Until the end, at least. If she made it that far.

"You'll figure it out." He raised his own bow and positioned his arrow. He let go of the arrow, puncturing the board directly in the middle. "It takes practice."

She glanced at the bow in her hand. He crafted it himself. The markings from his knife were evident on the stained wood. She stoked the carving at the bottom with her finger. *Cedar.* He told her it was only there so he didn't sell it with the others by mistake. Xenia thought he did it as a mark of his work. A signature.

"Try again," he said, handing her another arrow. She took it from him hastily and placed the arrow on the rest, then securing it to the string in the back. She drew it towards her face and held her arm steady for a moment. Then, she took a deep breath and let go. It struck the wood near the middle stripe. She dropped the bow carelessly and ran to it.

"It hit!" she said, pulling it out to examine the hole the arrow had left behind.

"That was great," Blake said, following her to the tree.

Xenia realized that for a few moments she had let her guard down, and he had noticed. She quickly put her stern face back on and moved her attention from the wood.

He pulled down the target. "That's enough for now."

She helped gather the arrows and placed them into Blake's leather quiver. They walked back up the hill to his house, away from the place they'd found Blake hunting yesterday. They hiked back to his house to drop off the archery equipment before going into town. Blake said he wanted to show them around.

Even when living from one bag, Karielyn managed to look her best. She had dressed in a light-pink sundress that craved attention. "Is there a bakery in town?" she asked once Xenia and Blake met her and Felix by the front door.

"I own the meat deli. But yes, there's also a bakery," Blake said.

Fateless could pick from many courses to help survive in their story. Medical, architecture, and baking were a few. Blake had a fate, but he still took an elective class on weaponry. And apparently, he had learned to hunt too.

They walked down the path they'd taken to find Blake yesterday, into the small, empty town. "How many people live here?" Karielyn asked, moving gradually closer to him.

"Exactly—I'm not sure. Around fifty."

"I would love to live in a town like this," Felix whispered to Xenia.

She shrugged. Though she wouldn't mind living in a town this small, it wouldn't be her first choice. "I don't mind a place like Chantendell."

He shook his head, smiling. "You're only saying that because you're the princess."

"No. I love cities." The lights in windows and chatter in town at night could ease the loneliness she felt most nights.

The twisty, yellow road held a series of beautiful surprises, now that she took the time to enjoy the details and examine each shop. In a dust-covered window, a display of wool-knitted scarfs caught Karielyn's attention, and Xenia stopped to admire them with her. Karielyn muttered softly to herself about the cost, and Blake handed her a small, silver coin with a ring of crowns around the edge. It wasn't Moiran currency.

She smiled at him and then disappeared inside. When she returned, a heavy, off-white shawl lay in her arms. She thanked Blake, and he mumbled a compliment.

Another window greeted them with a collection of plump loaves and muffins. But Blake kept walking, leading them across the street to a small building decked with wooden signs, each featuring carefully carved or burnt letters. The largest one read *Cedar's meat market—Fresh meat & produce; Hand crafted weaponry; tent rentals.*

How had Xenia missed his name the first time they passed by?

Blake opened the front door and led them inside. The wall to their left held six bows, each one slightly different from the other. Stacks of paper packages lined the back wall from top to bottom.

"You own this place?" Xenia asked. "This is really nice!"

He ignored her, though his cheeks glowed red. Xenia rolled her eyes and took a closer look at the hand-stitched quivers by the door. Blake had done all this?

"Things here are very different than in Chantendell," he said. "There wasn't any place to buy food when I got here. There was hardly a hundred people who had entered."

A hundred students were required to register before anyone could enter. Blake had been one of the first to leave Chantendell from their year.

He picked up one of the parcels in the back and pulled

it open. He handed them each a stick of dried meat and took two for himself.

The door swung open, and a couple made their way to the front counter. Blake rushed to assist the customers; two people Xenia knew from school before training. She smiled and waved at them, but they ignored the gesture.

"Do you think we'll come back here after the… switch?" Karielyn said.

"I'm not sure," Xenia said. "I hope."

"We might have different plans," Felix said, joining the conversation. His voice was jagged.

"What are our plans now?" Karielyn asked slowly.

Felix pursed his lips. "We don't have any, and I think it's best to not get any ideas."

What did that mean? Xenia turned her attention back to Blake's shop to keep herself from overthinking. She'd been solving far too many puzzles lately.

Xenia stared at the celling, battling her thoughts. She shifted, careful not to wake Karielyn, and slipped off the couch.

They had blown all the candles out hours ago, yet a sliver of light bled from under Felix's door. She took slow steps towards it. The wooden floor creaked beneath her.

She placed her hand on his door handle and twisted it open. Felix's head snapped in her direction. He sat on his bed, candles lit, peering over a page of translations. There was only a bed and nightstand, yet the room lacked space.

"You're still awake?" he asked.

"I couldn't sleep."

"Me neither. Come in."

Xenia closed the door and then sat beside him on the bed. She glanced at the page he had been reading. It was about the Jewel of Fate.

It waits where magic guards the most. Once found submerged in mer-lands deep, other times guarded by dragons at peaks.

The grave dangers of the jewel are battled at every last page. At the end of each story, the Lafin Crystal must be broken in order to return home. Anyone who breaks it before then will suffer arrest and execution.

"What are you doing?" Xenia asked.

"A bit more research. I want to make sure we know what to do when we find the jewel. And what not to do." Felix grabbed the papers and set them on the nightstand.

"Are you all right?" she asked, standing up next to him. "You've been different since we arrived."

His eyes fell to the ground. He shook his head idly.

"I'm afraid too," Xenia whispered.

"I don't want to lose you." He looked up and placed his hands on her waist. "I'm going to find a way to—I won't fight you."

"How?" Xenia could hardly say more beyond the lump in her throat. Was there a way? If they refused to fight each other, they would be replaced and executed.

"Trust me."

She closed her eyes. How did she get here?

"There is a way, but you'll need to trust me."

"I do," she breathed. "I trust you."

Felix's eyes shone like glass against the candle light. His lips parted, but before he could speak, Karielyn screamed from the living room.

Felix ran past her, throwing open the door. Xenia darted after him. Her blood turned to ice as she reached the doorframe.

Five men stood in the center of the room, each armed with swords and daggers.

Chapter Thirty-Six

KARIELYN THRASHED, FAILING TO FREE HERSELF FROM the man's grip. He held her arms behind her back while another struggled to fasten metal shackles to her arms and legs.

All five men wore black uniforms sporting the Chantendell emblem in purple thread: a crown surrounded by a circle of seven stars. They must have been from the palace—they were too old to be part of the story—but Xenia had never seen guards dressed like this. They weren't wearing the standard coats and swords guards wore around Chantendell.

They know what we're doing! They already know!

"Help!" Karielyn shouted. At her words blood rushed from her split lip.

The man behind her moved one hand to her mouth and pulled her closer as she thrashed her arms to free herself. "Be quiet and stand still!" he ordered.

"Karielyn!" Xenia darted to her and grabbed her arm, ripping it away from the guards. Karielyn pulled her other arm away and kicked the guard's calf with her bare foot.

The man closest to Xenia snagged her upper arm. She let go of Karielyn as he pulled her towards him. His fingers clawed into her skin while the other man unlocked cuffs for her hands.

Felix rushed towards her. A guard blocked his path and lunged his fist towards Felix's face.

The door to Blake's room swung open, and he darted in her direction. He threw a punch at the man, narrowly missing Xenia's face. The man let go of her and tossed her to the ground as he turned his attention to Blake.

"Nia, get out!" Blake dodged a punch. "Get out!" he yelled again. "I'll help Karielyn and Felix."

Xenia squinted in the dark to find the door. She ran for it, but one of the men reached out and grabbed her arm. He yanked her towards him and grabbed her other arm.

Felix broke away from his fight and grabbed her arm, pulling her out of the guard's grip. "We can't fight back like this!" he said. "We need weapons."

"I'll get some!" Blake shouted, breathless. "They're in my room!"

While he fought against the guards, Xenia ran towards his room. She squinted, surveying the space. She pulled open a closet filled with linen shirts, and dropped to her knees, sorting through a crate on the ground. Her heart raced as she pulled out a roll of knives.

She jumped up but hesitated before returning to the fight. *What am I doing?* She wanted to help the others—but what could she do about it?

The thought of helping them was quickly replaced by the same feeling that had accompanied her when she first arrived. *Why should I help them? I want to see them suffer.*

The malicious thoughts that filled her mind hurt her heart. She took a deep breath. The thoughts were suffocating.

Blake ran through the doorway, stopping beside her. "Nia, are you okay?"

She couldn't answer him. She didn't trust herself to speak. What if she voiced her cruel thoughts?

A dull thud crashed against the wall from the living room. Karielyn screamed. Xenia pushed past Blake back into the fight.

She nearly fell back as she crashed into another guard. Shakily, she reached for one of the knives. He yanked her arm, and the knives flew across the room. Blake ran after them.

Xenia kicked the man as hard as she could before chasing after Blake. She peered through the dark. Felix lay unconscious on the ground, blood trickling down his head.

"What happened?" she shouted. "What happened? Is he all right?"

No one responded.

She slid next to Felix and grabbed his hand. "Felix!" She pressed her fingers to his neck; he had a pulse. Her fingers ran along his blood-stained cheek.

"Grab her," a guard holding Karielyn ordered. "And get him too," he said, pointing at Felix.

The other two jumped to the spot where Xenia kneeled.

One grabbed her arms and pulled her up. She thrashed and fought his grip to no avail.

Across the room, a guard grabbed hold of Blake. Tears streaked Xenia's cheeks. She could do nothing but watch.

Do they really matter? She screamed at the thought.

She twisted her arms in attempt to free herself. "What did you do to him?" she shouted as a man bent down to pick up Felix. "Please, leave him alone!"

"Hold still!" the guard holding her ordered.

"Prepare to travel," the man in the center of the room said. All the guards pulled off their left glove, revealing a silver ring with a small, blue jewel. "Three… two—"

As the guard holding Blake moved his arm to pull off his glove, Blake freed himself and sent a punch towards the man's face. Blood streamed from his nose. The man cursed while Blake turned one of the knives over in his hand.

"Surrender or—"

"I am protecting my friends."

The man Xenia presumed to be their leader shook his head. "Your friends are criminals—even the Liftson. They will be punished as such, and so will you."

"They are not criminals—"

"They're breaking the law."

Guilt twisted like a knife in Xenia's chest. She and Felix were. But Blake wasn't. Not really. He hardly even knew what was going on.

Felix groaned, and Xenia screamed. "Felix!" She tried again to break free. The guard held her steady without batting an eye. "Please, leave him alone! If you take me, he can't switch! Please, leave him alone—"

The man covered her mouth with his hand. "Maybe you should have considered Mr. Liftson's safety before you pulled him into this," he whispered.

Blake's frown deepened. "Get out!"

"Prepare to leave. Three… two—"

Blake's knife tore through the air. The leader fell to ground, blood gushing from his side. Blake reached for more knives. He grabbed another dagger and launched it at Xenia's captor.

The knife soared past her cheek, barely missing her skin. It struck the man's shoulder. He groaned in pain, releasing her.

Blake handed Xenia a knife and launched another at the next guard. The man threw Karielyn out of the way and dropped towards the already wounded men.

"We need to return him to Chantendell!" the man called. "He won't survive much longer!"

"We need to take care of Liftson and Safire!" the man holding Felix returned.

"They won't get far—we can come back. Two of our men need immediate medical attention."

The man cursed. "We can take them with us—"

Blake's fist smashed into the man's jaw. He staggered back, losing his grip on Felix. Xenia flinched as he fell to the ground. Blake pinned the guard against the wall with his forearm and held a dagger to his throat with his other hand.

The man grabbed a fist of Blake's golden hair and shoved him aside.

A blade ripped through the air, striking the man's shoulder blade. Xenia spun around to see Karielyn stumbling into the wall behind her, her hands trembling.

Cursing, one of the uninjured men reached for the ring on his finger. Xenia could hardly make it out in the dark, but she could see the faint outline of an oversized gem.

He pressed the gem, and a thick, blue smoke formed around him. The others followed his lead, and blue smoke filled the room. When it cleared enough to see, all the guards were gone.

Chapter Thirty-Seven

EERIE SILENCE FILLED THE HOUSE AT THE GUARDS' ABsence.

Blake leaned back and pressed his head against the wall. Xenia couldn't move. Her head spun as she processed what had happened. She fell to the ground and cried.

A gentle hand dropped to her back. "Are you okay?" Karielyn's voice was uneven.

Xenia didn't respond. She couldn't.

She heard Blake slam his fist into the counter and curse to himself. After a few moments, Karielyn stood up and walked over to him instead.

"Karielyn, please—don't."

Xenia looked around the room. A pool of blood lingered where the guard had lain, and Felix still rested on the ground. She edged towards him. "Felix," she whispered, shaking him gently. His eyes opened slightly. "Felix, are you all right?"

He groaned. "Nia? What happened, are they gone?"

"Yes, they're gone. What happened to you?"

"One of the guards slammed him into the wall," Karielyn answered.

"Should we get him to a medic?"

Blake shook his head. "In Casiville? There are no medics here." He left the kitchen and returned to his room without another word.

"Did something happen?" Felix asked, attempting to pull himself up.

Xenia pushed him back down. "Be careful."

"I'm fine—"

She shook her head and ran her fingers through his golden-brown hair. "Do you need anything?"

"I'll be fine. You should make sure Blake's all right."

"Are you—?"

He nodded, urging her to leave. She stood up and walked to Blake's room. At her knock, he said nothing, but she opened the door anyway.

"Hey," she said, sitting on the bed beside him.

He ignored her and gazed ahead at the window, though it was too dark to see anything.

She put her arm around him. "Blake… I am so sorry I involved you…"

"They would have attacked you either way. At least this way I was there to protect you."

"But I've put you in so much trouble."

"I made my decision, it's not your fault."

She had expected him to say something like that.

"I'm sorry," she said.

"Me too. I'm sorry about the other night. I guess I was just a bit… surprised at how much you've changed."

She wrapped her arms around him. "I forgive you."

"Thank you." He broke out of the hug and started for the door. Xenia followed him back into the living room with the others.

Felix was standing now, but leaning against the wall. Karielyn stood close by with her hand on his arm.

"Get ready to leave," Blake directed. "I don't know how much time we have before they come back. We need to start moving now."

"You're right," Felix said. "But I don't think we'll be safer somewhere else. They *will* come back. And next time they'll be more prepared." He paused. "Why did they leave?"

"We attacked them—or—Blake did," Karielyn answered.

Felix glanced around the room. "Where did they go?"

"This… blue smoke… took them," she said.

Confusion painted Felix's face, but he didn't question her further.

Blake found matches and began lighting candles, giving them enough light to find their things. "Karielyn, grab that case by your feet," he ordered without paying her a look.

Karielyn glanced at Xenia, brows drawn, but bent down anyway and picked up the canvas case. "What is this?" she asked.

"A tent," he said.

Xenia hated tents—they were so *small*.

"You all right, Liftson?" Blake asked.

"Yeah, I'm fine, thanks."

"Good. We need food too. Nia, help me with that."

Blake walked into the kitchen and pulled open a cupboard. He started pulling out items and tossing them onto the counter: various loafs of bread, a sack of dried meat, potatoes, and a few apples. Xenia shoved them into her bag and gave Felix and Karielyn a few for theirs.

"Let me grab my things," Blake said, disappearing into the bedroom.

At his departure the three of them shared a wordless moment. They had spent seasons preparing for this, yet it didn't feel real. Maybe that was why: the wait was finally over. Xenia suddenly felt like a short timer threatened her life.

When Blake returned, he held another bag identical to the one Karielyn had and a few other things—some of which Xenia couldn't name.

"Do you need help with that?" Karielyn asked.

"No, I can handle it," he said as he dropped a small bag.

Felix laughed, and Xenia tossed him a dark look as she bent down to pick up the bag. Blake reached for it, but she didn't give it back.

"Can someone grab those quilts?" he asked.

Karielyn folded the blankets and picked them up.

"I don't think we'll be any safer if we leave Casiville. That's not going to stop them from finding us, they always know where we're at," Felix said.

"It will help if we have room to run—we can't be cornered again," Blake said, fixing his grip on the items in his arms.

"I guess."

"I'm right."

"Humble, aren't you?"

Blake ignored him. He used to be very humble; it must have been the stress getting to him.

Xenia's mind flashed the memory of her thoughts from not too long ago. What was *her* problem? What was getting to *her?*

Once they gathered all of their things and blew out the candles, they left Blake's house.

Casiville was a whisper of its already quiet self in the night. They passed a few small shops on the way out of town. All the windows were dark.

"Where are we going?" Felix asked when they reached the outskirts of town.

"Just as far as we get before we need rest," Blake replied. "I don't know how fast they can travel. Until we figure out how they travel back and forth, it's best we assume they're right behind us."

A cool breeze spread bumps across Xenia's skin. The sun wouldn't rise for several more hours. She already knew they had a long day ahead, but she hardly worried about the walk. Other things filled her thoughts. What was happening back in Chantendell? How much time did they have before they were attacked again?

They continued walking along the same trail for hours. By the time the sun rose, they turned, making it to an area with slightly taller trees to block the bright rays. Birds Xenia had never seen before flew overhead and sang songs far smoother than most in Chantendell. Excitement flooded her at the thought that they might only be found in this world.

As they walked, Xenia tried to spot differences between the two worlds. This world was definitely warmer than Chantendell at the time. There was far more vegetation—likely from the lack of people and buildings. And the sky seemed to shimmer. Before, she had convinced herself that she was imagining it, but now she was certain something was different. It looked as if extra stars shone in the daylight, practically unnoticed.

Blake led the way without looking at his map for reference the entire day. He would stop at turns and nod his head when he spotted landmarks. He even pointed them out to Xenia, explaining a bit about each one.

"I used to live down that way," he said, pointing at the trail opposite the one he'd picked to lead them down. "I moved to Casiville once I started earning more." He promised her that, if possible, after the mission he would take her to his favorite locations.

Felix tried to sway their plans. He said they shouldn't make any. Just like he had back at the deli. He reminded them how much plans could change on their mission. Xenia had read enough books to know not to set her mind on the ending. There was always a plot twist—but it was still fun to dream.

They stopped long before the sun set. By the time they picked a camp site, Xenia felt she might pass out from fatigue. She hadn't slept since the night before—and hardly even then.

Once the fire was lit and the tents were up, Blake approached her. "Will you be fine tonight? Sleeping in a tent, I mean?"

Xenia frowned. Small, enclosed spaces made her heart race as if she'd never escape. "I—I'll manage."

Settling in for the night, the four of them sat by the fire to warm up. Felix took a spot on a dead tree stump, and Xenia sat at his legs as he twisted her hair. Blake threw more wood onto the fire to keep it ablaze as he told them stories from his past trips.

Xenia went to bed after Felix left the fire and crawled into the canvas tent. Karielyn, still awake, sat on the ground with her head in her hands, crying.

"Are you all right?" Xenia asked, sitting next to her.

Karielyn glanced up, her eyes irritated. "Since I've been here, I can't help but feel…" She didn't finish, but Xenia already knew what she meant to say.

"Like a villain?"

Karielyn groaned. "Like a terrible, cruel villain."

Xenia fought back tears at the memory of the thoughts she'd had towards Felix and Blake. "Me too."

Ravelyn's words flashed through her mind. *Love. Fear. Hate.* She said passion drove a villain. But Xenia wasn't a villain. She was an innocent girl posing as one. What drove her?

Xenia woke when the sun bled through the tent the next

morning. She and Karielyn met the boys outside, and they packed up camp.

Once they finished, they started hiking farther away from Casiville. Weeds and tall grass now covered their path, the blades trampled with their steps. Morning light glistened between the leaves of the tall, arching trees.

Since agreeing to help them find the jewel, Blake had taken over the journey. And he hardly let them stop to rest. "We don't have any time to waste," he kept telling them. Xenia's legs burned, and she knew that everyone would appreciate a break. Blake was right, though; they didn't have time for a break. Not now that Chantendell authorities knew what they were doing.

When Xenia was younger, she felt safe around Royal Guards. Her mother had taught her to respect them, and she did. Estelle would be furious with her now.

The others stayed as quiet as Xenia—lost in their own world of thought just like her, she assumed. The canopy of trees was behind them now, and grass spotted with thousands of dandelions crept up Xenia's legs. As they walked through the field, the fluff separated from the plants and danced around their legs.

Xenia bent down and plucked one. "Felix!" she called. He spun around to face her. "Make a wish."

She handed him a dandelion. He took a deep breath and blew the seeds towards her. The wind carried them in the opposite direction, and were lost behind them. Laughing, he grabbed her hand, and they walked through the field together.

Miles of pale, green grass spotted with white accompanied them for most of the day, providing no relief from the beaming sun and attracting swarms of bees—and, as the light dipped behind the distant mountains, mosquitoes.

When the flowers disappeared, a forest wrapped them in more evergreen trees and moss-covered rocks. Xenia inhaled deeply, relishing the fresh smell. The forest continued for miles, and they stopped to camp in its heart. The site Blake picked was only slightly smoother than the previous options, but the trees spread farther apart, leaving an opening large enough for their tents.

Before the sun set, he left to find water. The rest of them stayed back and rolled out the canvas tents. Without Blake, they struggled to put up the tents, and still hadn't finished when he returned.

Judging by the pressed expression on his face, he expected the tents up. "Do you need any help?"

"We're almost done," Karielyn said, securing the last corner. Xenia rushed to her side to help.

When they finished Karielyn hurried to help Blake start the fire.

"Will this be okay?" Felix asked. "Blake told me you don't like small spaces."

Xenia stared at the tent. Somehow it looked smaller than she remembered. But she wouldn't be trapped inside. The ties on the door came loose easily, she reminded herself. "I'll be fine. I managed last night."

He smiled. With the late sun hitting his face, his brown eyes glinted like gold. It made her heart flutter the way it had when they met at midnight. "If you need more space, you can always throw Karielyn out."

She laughed, shaking her head. "Yeah, I could definitely do that."

"We still have to put up the other one," he said tiredly.

Xenia opened her mouth to respond, but closed it quickly. Suddenly the butterflies that filled her chest when she gazed into Felix's eyes were replaced with kindling anger.

Fate, he's an arrogant hero! Why am I with him? Her eyes must have projected her thoughts.

"Are you all right?" he asked. "You look upset."

"I'm fine," she rasped.

Avoiding his gaze, she bent down to pick up the first piece of the boys' tent, and Felix helped her push it through the sleeve. An urge to scream settled itself deep within her, and she didn't want Felix to feel its wrath.

"I'm going by the fire," he said when they finished. "Will you sit with me?"

"I—I think I should get some rest."

He frowned but assured her that he understood before leaving her at the tent. As soon as he turned his back, she untied the door and hid inside.

In one of their training sessions, Ravelyn told her this: "Our stories have a way of bringing out the worst in us. They focus our minds on the things that are hardest to control— we let those things take over. And once we do it's hard to come back. Like jumping into an untamed ocean. The waves crash constantly against us, drowning us in their unwelcoming wrath."

Chapter Thirty-Eight

"We should reach Victoria's palace in three days—two if we keep a steady pace," Blake said the next evening, staring intently at the fire. "Liftson"—every time he said Felix's name, he acted like it was bitter on his tongue—"says Victoria will agree to let him in. If so, we'll ask her about viewing her maps, then we'll start our journey."

"You can call me *Felix*. I prefer that," he said calmly.

"I could."

"But he isn't going to, *Liftson*," Karielyn said.

A trace of a grin touched Blake's face. Xenia rolled her eyes and leaned against Felix's shoulder.

Three days. She hoped that wasn't long enough for another attack. If the guards attacked again, they would come better prepared. They wouldn't let them go twice. The thought made her pick up Felix's hand and squeeze it. If they failed, they would be taken back to Chantendell as prisoners. But if they succeeded, their fates would still force them apart.

It had been several days and Felix still hadn't presented her with his plan to prevent their destined battle. She had to trust him. He believed there was a way to stop it. Would his plan be stronger than Fate?

Would it really be so bad if Fate kept us apart?

Xenia stiffened and the thought. Felix turned to face her, shooting her a questioning stare.

Blake glanced between them and then rose to his feet. "I think I'll go hunting. See if I can find meat for dinner tonight. Karielyn, would you like to join me?"

Karielyn's brows pulled together. "I—I suppose."

Blake grabbed his bow and quiver and made his way back to the path with Karielyn right behind him. Xenia stared at the two of them as they walked off.

"Is everything all right?" Felix asked.

Her stare broke and she nodded, even though she was *not* all right. She was far from that. Her fate was taking over—how long could she resist before she acted on her thoughts?

"I—" A lump formed in her throat, stopping her words. How could she explain to Felix something she didn't even understand herself?

He cradled her closer. "It's okay. Whatever it is—you can tell me. And if you're not ready yet, I'll listen when you are."

Tears blurred her vision. Sparks jumped from the fire, twirling to the ground before losing their faint glow.

"I haven't felt the same since we arrived," she finally mumbled. "I feel like—like a villain."

Xenia wished she hadn't noticed the way he turned rigid

at her words. "What do you mean?"

Tears spilled down her cheeks. "I get thoughts. Thoughts that make me want to…" She couldn't finish.

Felix caressed her cheek, brushing away her tears. "What kind of thoughts?"

"Thoughts about… about you. Thoughts that try to convince me this is all a mistake. That I shouldn't do this and I shouldn't be with you. That I want to be a villain." She trembled from crying. "I wish it would stop."

"Nia…"

"Why is this happening to me?"

"I don't know. Your story can't change who you are. And magic can't, either. But I know you're stronger than it, Xenia. I know you are."

She stared deep into the heart of the fire until her eyes stung. Bitter thoughts fought their way into her head, tempting her to shout at Felix and defiling his gentle embrace. She stayed silent in his arms, resisting.

She straightened when Blake and Karielyn returned nearly an hour later. Karielyn held the water flasks, her face pale. Beside her, Blake carried a dead turkey and a blood-slicked arrow.

"Is anyone hungry?" he asked.

Karielyn tossed the flasks on the ground by Xenia and Felix's feet.

Felix smirked. "Weak stomach, Height?"

Karielyn grunted, and her fists curled.

"She actually did considerably well," Blake said. He pulled a knife from his bag. "I might take her with me next time. If she wants, I'll teach her how to shoot."

"I think I'll find something else for dinner tonight," Karielyn said, starting for the tent.

"Will you help me, Liftson?" Blake asked as he began skinning the turkey.

A slight grimace wrinkled Felix's features as he rose to help Blake. Xenia's lips curved into a smile. Something told her Felix didn't want to help any more than Karielyn had, though he would never admit it.

The turkey took the rest of the night to prepare and cook. By the time Blake took it from the fire and served it, Xenia didn't think she would make it through the meal.

She pushed past the image of Blake skinning the turkey and ate enough to make up for lack of food she'd had since they left Casiville. She hardly realized how hungry she was before she started eating.

As soon as she finished, she joined Karielyn in the tent. She secured the knots holding the door closed, and then Xenia climbed into the blankets and lay still.

"Xenia!"

I spin around to locate the voice.

In front of me Felix stands, a plead in his eyes. Around him are villains from every story. He calls my name again, but this time Ravelyn Kage places a hand over his mouth, muting him.

I want to help him, but I can't. I can't. Heroes don't help villains. I hold my scroll tightly in one hand—I don't need to look at it to know it says hero. Felix begs for my help, but I ignore him. Instead, I walk up to Blake.

"I warned you, Xenia. He's a villain. But you're the true villain."

I want to cry. I want to tell Blake that he's lying. If only he were.

I run to Felix, but blue smoke forms around us, blocking my view of him. When it's gone, so is he.

Xenia woke to her heart beating out of her chest. She found herself in the tent and calmed herself enough to lie back down.

It was a dream. Felix wasn't in danger. He wasn't with Ravelyn Kage. He was a mere pace away, asleep, like she should have been.

Before she could shake the nightmare and fall back asleep, the tent flap lifted, and a figure neared her. She screamed, but a hand reached out and covered her mouth, muffling the noise. Karielyn turned to the other side but didn't wake.

"Nia." Felix moved his hand and backed away.

"You scared me!"

"I'm sorry. I didn't want you to wake Karielyn. Come here."

She followed him out of the tent and into the crisp air. Leaves rustled from the breeze in the distance. She tugged at the sleeves of her satin pajamas to keep herself warm.

"Look up."

She did as he said, and gaped. The stars shone twenty

times more than in the kingdom. She wanted to say something, but decided against it. Instead, she lay against his shoulder.

"You are *extraordinary*." He kissed her head and, when she looked up, her lips. It felt real and raw and perfect.

The chill air suddenly didn't feel cool enough. One hand wrapped around her waist, and with the other he pushed her hair behind her ear and placed his hand on her neck. Every part of her wished she could freeze time and live in this moment. When they pulled away, she felt dazed. Felix smiled before turning back to his tent.

Xenia stayed outside a minute longer, gazing at the stars. She took a deep breath of the night air as if it were a cure. For once, she thought her story might be a fairytale.

Chapter Thirty-Nine

THE GROUP PACKED UP CAMP FIRST THING IN THE MORN-ing. Everything had happened so fast since they arrived. Xenia wished she could go back to that moment with Felix last night. Her stomach tightened at the thought that they might not have many more moments like that—he hadn't even mentioned his solution since the night at Blake's house.

Xenia helped Karielyn stuff the tent into its bag and tie it closed. Then Karielyn picked it up and pulled it over her shoulder.

They followed the boys down the trail in silence for a what felt like hours. The sun peeked through the trees. It hadn't found its highest point yet, giving them a sense of time.

They walked along the same path most of the day. The air was cooler today than yesterday, and they seemed to take more frequent stops. It also helped that they were reaching higher ground. It didn't make it easier on their legs, but it helped them stay cool.

By midday, the sun burned directly against Xenia's face, reddening her skin. She missed the shadows the thick trees cast over them. Currently there were few trees, and they didn't provide much shade. Small bushes and weeds littered their path instead.

Chantendell had been a wooded area before a kingdom was built in its place. The kingdom's outer roads were still guarded by plenty of lush plants of all sorts. The more Xenia brought to mind the kingdom's farther destinations, she started to crave living within the green forests. Villains lived there. She could too. She was a villain. What was stopping her from acting like one? If she switched Felix took her place. *Her* place.

She stopped walking and waited for the rest of the group to notice.

Blake turned to face her in annoyance. "We really shouldn't stop."

Xenia sneered at him. *This isn't right*, she thought. Yet she didn't stop.

Worry spread across Karielyn's face. They were both villains, shouldn't she understand? She ran towards Xenia and grabbed her arm. "What are you doing?"

Shrugging her shoulders to break her grip, Xenia said, "Reconsidering. Why should I give my fate to Felix?"

At her words Felix's expression changed. The look on his face snapped her. She had done it again, jumped into the ocean.

"I'm so sorry," she whispered, burying her face into her

palms.

Felix darted to her and picked up her hand. His fingers laced with hers. "It's all right," he soothed.

Blake's forehead creased. "What's going on?"

Karielyn glanced at Xenia before answering. "She's felt… like a villain, since we got here—so have I." Her explanation matched Xenia's understanding of what was happening. Their stories didn't change who they were. They *couldn't*. That was impossible.

Blake's eyes widened.

"We don't understand it, either," Xenia said, letting go of Felix's hand to keep walking. "But Ravelyn, she—"

At the mention of her, Felix's face lost color.

"Are you okay?" Xenia asked.

He nodded quickly. "I'm fine, I just… I'm perfectly fine."

He still looked sick. Xenia didn't finish speaking. His father would have raised him to be terrified of Ravelyn. She could only imagine the things he had told his sons about her. Why did the thought make Xenia nauseous?

"Let's keep walking." She didn't want to dwell on the subject. The others followed closely as she started hiking down the trail.

Karielyn grabbed her wrist and leaned towards her ear. "Are you all right?"

Xenia nodded. She wasn't eager to discuss it.

By late afternoon the forest broke away entirely, leaving fields of dry weeds and sage brush. A new quietness took over now that there wasn't anything for the wind to blow.

Small stones and pebbles made a trail beneath their feet. The trail comforted Xenia. It let her know they weren't far from civilization. She imagined Victoria's palace wouldn't be in the middle of an empty desert.

"Do you want me to carry you?" Felix asked.

She shook her head, smiling wryly. He picked her up anyway, throwing her legs over his arms.

They found trees again by the time they decide to stop and set up camp. She never thought she'd walk so far in a day. Even against their circumstances, she loved exploring so much of a new world.

Felix and Karielyn skipped dinner to sleep early, but Xenia stayed with Blake by the fire.

"I can hardly believe your mother is the queen now," he said. "I've missed so much being here."

"There wasn't much else to miss. Chantendell was incredibly dull without you there."

He frowned. "I never should have… I should have stayed—"

"Please, don't. It won't change anything." Xenia sighed. She couldn't think about Blake leaving her now; he was with her here, she hoped it would be enough to close the gap between them.

"I missed you," he said, watching her closely.

"I missed you too."

"Let's go to bed." He stood up. "We need to wake up early tomorrow."

Xenia agreed, and climbed into her tent. She lay awake until the evening light no longer seeped through the canvas.

Yesterday's nightmare still lurked in her mind. What was that blue smoke? Had it taken the guards back to Chantendell, or somewhere else? The questions eventually carried her mind to sleep.

Xenia woke before anyone else and crept quietly out of the tent, careful not to disturb Karielyn. The tree next to the dead firepit's roots grew out of the ground, forming a place to sit. Multiple times she caught herself checking behind her—surely the guards would come again. Her mother may have found a way to delay their next attack, but even if she had, Xenia knew Estelle was furious with her.

She struggled to keep herself awake despite the blinding gold that peeked above the horizon, so she stood up and stretched to wake herself.

"You're already up?"

Startled, she glanced at Blake. "You told me we needed to be up early."

He eyed her suspiciously. "All right. Will you wake Karielyn for me?"

Xenia crawled back into the tent and kneeled next to her. "Karielyn," she said, shaking her softly. "It's time to leave."

Karielyn stretched her arms and yawned. "Already?" She sat up and grabbed her bag from behind Xenia to dress.

Xenia climbed back out of the tent, cool air rushing around her.

"We should be there by tonight," Blake said, pulling a bag over his shoulder. Victoria's palace was only part of their journey, but it reminded Xenia of the progress they had made. A smile accompanied her as they started walking again.

The trees around them now were pines, coating the trail with their needles. They stretched high into the air, casting large shadows across the ground that hid their own. Xenia closed her eyes and listened to the birds singing softly to each other and the sound of every steady, quick footstep.

Karielyn sang softly under her breath. Xenia didn't recognize the melody; she assumed it was Enrian. At her side, she heard Felix humming quietly to Karielyn's voice.

Edging herself closer to him, she said, "Do you know this song?"

His face glowed red. "I… She loved it, it's the only thing I know in a different language." He went quiet, and just as she convinced herself that he had finished speaking, he continued. "We used to sing it together."

"Oh."

"What's your favorite song?" he asked quickly.

"I don't have one." Growing up, the only music she had heard was classic piano songs played by musicians her mother would hire on special occasions. She knew many songs, but didn't have a favorite. Even if she told him one, she was sure he wouldn't recognize it. The songs she enjoyed were written hundreds of years ago.

"That's okay, neither do I," Felix said. "What's your favorite fairy tale?"

He quizzed her on all of her favorite things as they walked until they got stuck discussing a story they both loved. Spending the trip laughing with Felix made the time pass easily.

Their conversation came to a sudden stop as they reached the top of a hill, revealing a kingdom. Victoria's palace crowned a lush, green peak. The kingdom's homes and buildings wrapped around the palace, accessorizing the hill like a rich painting. If they weren't racing from the Chantendell guards, she would want to see and do everything the small kingdom could offer.

The town's slight activity piqued her curiosity. She wanted to know how people lived in this world. If only she had time to enjoy the different culture.

"Have you been here before?" she asked Blake.

"I've been practically everywhere. Casiville's my favorite, it's peaceful. I wish you could have spent more time there. It grows on you."

"How long do you think our story will last after the switch?" She wanted to ask if he thought they would return, but her voice revealed more of her feelings than she had meant to share.

Blake grimaced. "I… I don't know."

After the switch, would she and Blake leave the others? She focused on her steps to distract herself from the thought. They used to dream about being heroes together, but now that that might happen, she longed to be with Felix.

Would this switch benefit either of them enough to justify everything they were risking? What difference would it make the part she played in the battle now? She wouldn't be fighting evil; she would be fighting *Felix*.

"Felix!"

"What's the matter?" he asked, turning to face her.

"What are we doing?" Emotion broke her words. "We'll fight each other no matter what. How will the switch help us now?"

"It will help both of us in so many ways. Don't forget, it's always been about more than which side we fight for. If we succeed, you'll live a better life. And Chantendell needs you as their princess."

"But what about you?" Xenia was vaguely aware of Karielyn and Blake standing beside them, but all she could focus on was Felix.

"Nia, this switch is every bit important to me. This is an opportunity I've waited years for. I want people to know that I don't live by a fate I didn't choose." His hand swept her hair. "And if I get to grant your wishes in the prosses, trust me, it's worth it."

"Thank you." She lifted herself to her toes and threw her arms around his neck. In case they didn't have much longer together, she would make now count.

Chapter Forty

THE PALACE WAS MORE BEAUTIFUL UP CLOSE THAN FROM afar. The sight of it stole Xenia's breath. The tall towers and arches made of white stone seemed to glow against the deep-green plants growing around the walls. Each window featured carefully cut glass framed like art. A large, rushing waterfall ran ruthlessly beneath the stone bridge built in the palace's foundation.

They followed a winding trail up the peak the palace sat on. Green overgrowth snaked onto the trail. At the end of it, a gate enclosed the castle, surrounded by royal guards. Silver helmets hid their faces, but Xenia knew the people underneath. And despite their age, they were dangerous. They wouldn't have earned permission if not.

"State your name and business," one demanded as they approached the gate.

"Felix Liftson. I've come to request a meeting with Queen Victoria," he said, stepping forward.

"Felix Liftson," the man repeated as if he hadn't heard the name before. "Does she expect you?"

"No, sir. I've just arrived. May I speak to Warren?"

"Warren Fallon, the chief?"

"Yes."

"Fine." The guard called to a man on the other side of the gate, who left his position and walked over to a group of men standing near the edge of the waterfall. He spoke to the one on the far left, who quickly abandoned the water and rushed to them.

The man took off his helmet, exposing a head of curly, black hair, accompanied with sharp, green eyes. "Felix! You're here." Warren beamed. His smile fell when he noticed the rest of the group. "You brought *them*?"

"They're allied with me—for now, at least," he said. "We need to borrow maps."

"I'm sure you'll find something here that will satisfy you. I'll take you inside. Victoria will be ecstatic when she hears you're here."

He ushered them towards the gate. Another guard turned a metal crane attached to a rope, and the gate fell open. Felix and Blake walked through the gate as two guards grabbed Xenia's arms. Two more grabbed hold of Karielyn.

"Hey," Felix said, breaking away from the others. "They're coming too."

Warren leaned his head close to Felix's ear but hardly whispered. "Felix, they're villains. I can't bring them—"

"They're with me."

Warren surveyed the girls for a moment before saying

in a steely tone, "Fine, but I'm trusting you, Felix."

Felix didn't respond.

The guards didn't let go of Xenia and Karielyn, but escorted them through the courtyard and into the palace.

The foyer inside glittered with gold and shone from white, marble floors and walls. A curved staircase led to a landing surrounded with golden railing. Velvet carpet led up the stairs and trailed through the upper halls. Xenia expected to turn up the stairs, but instead, Warren pushed open a set of grand double doors with golden handles. At the end of the wide room, Victoria sat on a throne, wearing a ruby-covered crown.

At the sight of them, she jumped out of the tall seat. "Felix!" she said, running in their direction. Felix grimaced as her arms twisted around his body. "You're finally here!"

"Yes," he said, pushing her off. "And I need help with something."

"With what, love? I'll help you with anything."

Why did Victoria believe she could treat him that way? Bitter thoughts bloomed in Xenia's mind like roses. She bit on her tongue to keep herself from releasing words she'd later regret and took deep breaths to distract herself.

"We're looking for something, but we aren't sure we'll be able to find it with the maps we have," he said carefully.

Not now, not here, she told herself.

"How can I help?"

"We need to borrow a map, one with a lot of... detail."

"You need a detailed map?" she repeated, tossing confused glances towards Karielyn and Blake. She ignored Xenia entirely.

Deep breaths.

Victoria's arm slipped back around Felix. He grimaced.

"Of course, I have too many." She moved her body closer to his. "Anything for you—"

"Please leave him alone," Xenia said, straining from the effort of fighting off her thoughts. If she upset Victoria, she would spoil their chance at earning her help.

Felix's frown only deepened at her words. Victoria pulled back, and his shoulders relaxed. She stepped closer to Xenia.

"Excuse me?" Victoria sounded both taken back and amused.

"Don't touch him," Xenia said.

She smiled grimly. "Oh, Xenia… you still believe he wants you?"

Felix groaned. "Victoria, please—"

"Trust me, darling, I know him far better than you. It's just as I told you before. You are amusement, he enjoys playing with you." She stood only a few spans from Xenia now.

Xenia twisted against the guard's holds. She wavered in their grip and stumbled away, heart racing.

Warren made a sudden move for the sword at his hip, but Victoria put her hand up to stop him. "I'm sorry, I didn't mean to touch a nerve."

Xenia's emotions mixed with her villainous urges, muddling her thoughts. Her breath became short, and her mind spun.

"We're only here for maps," Felix said behind them.

"Then we'll leave."

"Right," Victoria said, tearing her icy glare from Xenia. "Warren, constrain her, please. And take care of Height. I'll take Liftson and Cedar to the observatory."

Warren reached for Xenia. She fought against him, kicking and thrashing until his silver sword rested against her chest.

"I won't use this so long as you comply," he murmured.

She closed her eyes, attempting to clear her mind and settle her thoughts.

"Warren!" Felix shouted, darting across the throne room to his side. "Don't hurt her!"

Warren shook his head. "I don't understand what's gotten into you, Felix. She's just a villain."

Felix slammed his fist into Warren's face. He shouted in pain and then moved his sword up to Xenia's throat, tilting her chin back with the blade. Xenia's heart pounded like a war drum.

"Let her go," Victoria snapped.

Slowly, Warren withdrew his sword and pushed Xenia away from him. Blake rushed to her side, wrapping his arm around her shoulders.

Victoria strode past her and stopped in front of Felix. "Let me talk to this… rogue."

"*Rogue?*" Felix said, a stunned expression touching his face.

She studied him with stern eyes. "Yes, rogue." Exhaling deeply, she said, "You have violated my law, Liftson. Attacking palace guards is punishable with up to six seasons in solitary confinement."

Confinement. The word alone turned Xenia's body hot.

Felix smiled, yet a trace of fear crept onto his face. "Solitary confinement?"

Victoria nodded.

"That won't work with our plans."

She looked at him pitifully. "Oh, won't it?"

Felix shook his head slowly. "No, I'm afraid not. But I will take the maps."

He didn't wait for Victoria's response before darting in the opposite direction, back towards the foyer. Blake directed Xenia to follow him and ran towards Karielyn, breaking into a fight against the guards restraining her.

"Grab the rouges!" Victoria ordered, picking up her skirts and running away from the fights erupting around her. The throne room echoed with shouts that bounced off the marble walls.

Warren caught Xenia's arm and pinned his sword against her throat, struggling to keep her steady. Adrenaline coursed through her.

Two more guards started for Blake and Karielyn. Blake knocked Karielyn out of the way as he dove into a fist fight with the men. Karielyn pushed herself to her feet as a guard's metal glove smashed into Blake's face. Blood streamed from his nose.

"Nia!" Felix shouted, spinning back around. "Don't touch her!"

Fear weakened Xenia, but every muscle in her body stayed tense. Warren swiveled out of the way around to avoid

Felix. Xenia screamed as the blade pressed deeper into her skin.

"Let go of her!" Felix shouted "Please! You don't have to hurt—"

"Actually, I do have to. We're in our story now, Felix. I respect my fate and I respect my queen."

All her life, Xenia's mother told her how serious her story would be. *It's not a game, Xenia—it's real. Our stories need to be written, not ignored. You'll do your best to make that fate your reality, as will everyone else.*

Every Chantendell story she read had been real. They weren't staged, and they weren't fake. Hers included.

"Escort her to the dungeon," Victoria called.

Warren drew his sword back, grazing Xenia's neck as he did. Blood trickled down her chest. He yanked her arms behind her and pushed her towards the doors. His grip on her faltered, and he yelped in pain as he crashed to the ground on top of Xenia.

Behind them, Karielyn breathed heavily. Blood gushed from Warren's leg. Karielyn smiled slightly, turning a knife over in her hand. She dove next to him and slid the blade against his neck.

"Don't touch her, understand?" Karielyn jumped up, leaving him helpless on the ground. "We need to hurry," she said, stretching out her hand to pull Xenia up.

"Thank you," Xenia said over a heavy breath. Karielyn had stabbed Warren. *Fate.*

"Where do you think the observatory is?"

"I don't know," Xenia said, following her past the

throne room. Karielyn handed her another knife and wiped the blood from hers on the sleeve of her pants.

"What about the boys?"

"I think it's best if we leave them and look for the map," Karielyn said, spinning around to climb the stairs. "Then we can get out of here sooner."

In Chantendell, guards watched every doorway and hall in the palace. Here it seemed the guards only monitored the most important areas since not all of the guards had entered yet, leaving gaps in security.

They slowed down at the top of the stairs and walked quietly through the hall. Torches lined the walls, lighting the empty corridor. Wooden doors stood every few feet apart from each other on either side of them. Karielyn tried the first door and cursed under her breath when it didn't open. The second door was locked as well. The first door that wasn't locked led to a flight of spiral stairs curving within a round room. They climbed in a near run and pulled open the door at the top. The evening sun shone against their faces in blinding, orange light. A bridge connected this tower from one on the other side of the palace.

"I don't think this is—"

"Let's cross," Karielyn said, running out of the tower. "I want to get away from this side of the palace." She ran across the bridge and disappeared inside, Xenia right behind her.

Inside the other tower, they took a set of stairs identical to the ones in the last tower, ending up in a deserted hall similar to the one they had roamed previously.

Boots clattered down a nearby hall. Xenia darted away from the door. She tried opening the doors as they passed, but the locks rattled.

She reached for another one. The handle turned, and she and Karielyn hurried inside.

Dark-blue silks draped across the wall between the spaces taken up by charts mapping constellations. A round window on the celling gave view to the darkening sky. Strange, metal sculptures sat on shelves, next to journals, books, and pots of ink. Compartments filled with paper scrolls lined an entire wall.

"I think we found the observatory," Karielyn said. She pulled a map from the compartment and unrolled it.

"Let's take a few—just in case," Xenia said, pulling rolls of paper down and stacking them in her arms.

Karielyn grabbed one of the cases and pulled off the lid for Xenia to slide them in. She checked the maps, assuring they contained the details they would need, and then slipped them into the cylinder case.

Karielyn closed the top and threw it over her shoulder. "Let's go find the boys."

They hurried through the castle back to the throne room, where Blake stood by a stone pillar with a knife pressed to a guard's neck. A cut in his sleeve, stained deep red, revealed a gash in his bicep. Felix was using a stolen sword to combat Warren.

"We got the maps!" Karielyn shouted, snagging Blake's attention.

"Thank Fate," he said through a pant. He blocked a

punch and then ran in their direction, followed closely by his attacker.

The guard made a quick movement towards Blake, sending Xenia into the wall instead. Her head hit the marble, and a sharp pain shot across her body. A daze overcame her mind, taking her vision and consciousness with it.

Chapter Forty-One

XENIA WOKE IN FELIX'S ARMS. HER HEAD ACHED FROM the hit and throbbed with every jolt from his quick steps. She focused on his heavy breathing and buried her face in his chest. His heart beat fast against her swollen cheek. She couldn't see where they were going, but she didn't care as long as it was away from Victoria's palace.

"Are you all right?" Felix panted.

She nodded, unsure if he noticed. He ran faster, and she feared he might drop her.

"Hold on."

She groaned softly as his steps increased. He breathed sloppily but didn't stop. In the distance, Blake muttered something about taking turns and breaks, but Felix ignored him.

Eventually, he stopped and laid her on the grass next to a bushy, green tree. She glanced around. Trees surrounded them from all sides, hiding them from any paths.

"How are you feeling?"

"I have a headache, that's all."

"Well, I hope it passes soon." He smiled sympathetically. "I wish I had something for your eye, hold on—Blake, get me some water and a cloth."

Blake did as he said and brought over the flask, along with one of his shirts. Felix poured the water, wetting the shirt, and dabbed it around her neck and cheek. Then he cleaned the blood off her collarbone. He poured more water and continued cleansing her skin. He let the water run down her forehead, wetting her hair. "Is that all right?"

She nodded. "Thank you."

"Of course. Do you need anything else?" he asked, ringing out the shirt.

"No, you've done enough, thank you."

He kissed her head and then pulled her against his chest, stroking her hair. "Is *this* all right?"

Smiling, she said, "Yes, thank you. I can't repay you."

"You don't have to—this doesn't cost me anything."

The sun had gone. She needed rest for tomorrow. They would need to get as far away from Victoria's kingdom as they could in case she sent guards after them.

She closed her eyes and tried to sleep, only feeling more awake. Her mind recited the day's events over and over. They had the map, and tomorrow they'd start their journey to find the jewel. She still needed to close her eyes occasionally to remind herself that this was reality. *Her* reality.

The next morning, they laid the maps out across the emerald grass. It spread out longer than Xenia had realized when she picked it out, showing off detailed illustrations of each land-mark.

"Here's the key." Blake pointed at a small box at the bottom of the map. "But I don't see anything indicating where magic is."

Xenia studied the map for anything that might help them find the magic capital.

"I think I may have found it," Felix said. *Already?*

She followed his finger down the map. He traced a mountain range, stopping at an illustrated cave. There was no name, only a warning in bold letters: **Open Magic**.

"*Open magic?*" Xenia said, as if hearing what she read out loud would change its meaning. They were seeking magic, what was she expecting? It to be *safe? Concealed?* Of course not. "Open magic is dangerous."

Her words carried little sense; everyone already knew how dangerous it was.

Karielyn turned white.

"I know," Felix said. They were both thinking the same thing. Humans couldn't be exposed to magic—not unless it was concealed.

Few people were permitted to use magic for a reason. It got its name because when not concealed, it settled in the air like an invisible, poisonous gas. Chantendell used magic more than any other nation. Magic could be controlled and used properly, but if not, it could be deadly. Their bodies couldn't handle it.

"How—how will we…?"

"I don't know," Felix said, reaching for the map's case. "But we have time to think about it. It'll take us a little over a week of traveling at best."

"Are you ready to go?" Blake asked as he rolled up the map and slipped it into the case in Felix's hand.

Xenia stood and brushed the dirt off her legs. "Yes. I want to get as far away from Victoria's palace as I can." She rummaged through her bag for a ribbon and used it to tie back her hair.

"Then let's go," Felix said, tossing his own bag over one shoulder. Without the tents to take down, it didn't take long to pack up camp.

Blake walked at Xenia's side, but stayed silent. She wanted to say something but couldn't find words. The thought that they had gone so long without information on each other's life made her heart ache. What may have mattered three years ago had no meaning now, and he would never know. She couldn't imagine how many untold stories he had to share.

"What's wrong?" he asked, bumping her side with his arm.

"Nothing."

"You're lying."

Why did he have to know her so well? Even after years of separation, he hadn't lost his touch.

"I… have a lot on my mind."

"Me too. What are you thinking of now?"

"I suppose that everything feels real now. I am *really* going to switch my fate."

Assuming we aren't caught before that happens.

He didn't say anything, so she continued. "What if I'm not good enough to be the hero? Fate isn't chance."

He exhaled. "No, it's not, but I was reading your book, and it's my understanding that some fates aren't meant to be, but they're not mistakes." He paused. "I could never understand why you were the villain, but I think I do now. You need to change your fate. *That* is your destiny. I think everyone's fate has a meaning, but some don't mean what we think. I think you have a… *broken* fate. You need to fix it."

They stopped in a field of tall pine trees just off the trail they had been walking on. The clearing was barely large enough to pitch their tents. They set up camp quicker today than the previous days and still had the sunset to enjoy. As the others settled down by the fire, Xenia slipped out of their company and hid herself in the tent.

She pulled open her bag and took out the guide. She flipped through the translated pages to find the part Blake had referred to.

Fate is a strange thing. It's carefully selected by magic especially for you. However, you might believe that your fate is not truly yours. But know that even then, fates are significant. If you are destined for a different fate, then you should have the will to switch. You weren't given a fate you can't fulfill, and you are strong enough to change it.

Too many thoughts spun in Xenia's mind, distracting her from the ones falling into place. Maybe fates weren't selected for the better of a story, but the better of a *person*. Was her fate there to help her grow beyond her story? Maybe their fates were merely an obstacle on the path to finding themselves.

Xenia looked up as Felix climbed into the tent and sat next to her. "What are you doing?" he asked, leaning over her shoulder to read the page.

"Do you think I'm the villain by chance?"

His eyes narrowed. "Fate isn't chance… Why?"

"What if I'm not the villain for the purpose of the story? What if my fate was selected so that I could overcome it?"

He eyed her strangely and then grabbed the book. She pointed at the section. He stayed quiet for several moments. "I've never considered that. If that's true, then why is this illegal? If the point was to help us, why would they make it so… *difficult*?"

She considered his words. It didn't make sense that something so important would be made so difficult by the leaders if they wanted them to do it, but maybe they had changed. Was it possible they didn't want them to *anymore*? At the thought, her heart pounded as if trying to escape.

"I don't know…"

Was she just making up excuses for herself? Was that all Blake was doing? Making up an excuse for her?

"I'm not dismissing the idea, only thinking."

The tent door pulled open again, and Karielyn came in. "Felix, did you want—?"

"Not now." His voice was sharp.

Karielyn's brows ruffled, and she looked at the guide. "What are you doing?"

"Xenia?" He turned the explanation to her, handing back the stack of papers.

She took a deep breath before starting. "Blake thought maybe our fates aren't for our story, that they're more about our own life."

"Yeah, they're personal, right?"

Xenia traced her finger along the paper, thinking about how to reply. "Yes, but not in the way he's suggesting. He thinks my fate may have been chosen *so* I could change it."

"But they don't want you to change."

Xenia hesitated. "Well, our fates aren't anyone's choice. They're determined by magic. *There are no mistakes in magic,* remember?"

"Unless you don't know how to use it," Karielyn countered.

"Well," Felix said, "Chantendell knows how to use it. We use it more than any other nation. And the fate givers know what they're doing, they don't make mistakes. Not when it comes to magic."

Karielyn went silent.

The tent opened again, and this time Blake clambered in. Xenia took a deep breath. Quilts piled around her, and the tent barely had enough space for the four of them.

He glanced between the three of them and the book. "What are you doing?"

"We're discussing your theory," Xenia said, making

room for him to sit next to her.

His brows ruffled. "My theory?"

"The one we talked about on the way here."

"Oh, that one." His expression softened. "What is there to discuss?"

"A lot." She paused, then lowering her voice to a whisper. "It questions Chantendell's leaders."

His brows raised, and he glanced at the others as if looking for an explanation. "It… it does?"

She nodded absently. If he was right, the rulers of Chantendell were trying to hide something. His name flashed through her mind again: *Zarius Al.*

In need of fresh air, she climbed out of the tent without another word.

Xenia knew how dangerous it was to be out alone at night—especially with the risk of Chantendell guards arriving at any moment—but right now she didn't care. Her mother's words rang in her ears all evening. *He believed that the people of Chantendell shouldn't be forced to live out their stories in such an…* intense way. Did Al have the same theory as them? Perhaps he believed their fates had a different meaning. And when he couldn't convince the king, he decided to get rid of them completely.

Xenia asked herself countless questions, but the answers seemed untouchable.

She had walked far enough now that she couldn't see

camp. Even though she knew she should turn back, she didn't want to. Here she could get her thoughts in order. It was quiet, but she heard things like wolves in the distance and cricket wings. It put her at ease. Part of her wanted to keep walking forever, to never go back. But Felix kept that thought from becoming her reality. She couldn't leave him yet, and she couldn't give up on their switch.

By the time she returned to the tent, she dreaded the coming day. Since they entered, she hardly had any peace. And she knew the worst had yet to come.

In the morning she didn't want to get up when Karielyn called her name. She pulled herself up and rubbed her eyes.

"The boys already have their tent down—hurry!" Karielyn said.

"Okay, I'll be out in a minute," she replied through a yawn. She folded the quilts, grabbed her bag, and then left the tent.

"Good morning," Felix said as she climbed sleepily out of the tent door. His voice was dim, like a shadow working to conceal. He attempted a smile, but he looked as if he had gone the entire night without sleep.

"Morning," Xenia replied, leaning closer to hug him. He took a step away, his eyes on the ground.

"I'm going to take your tent down now," Blake said, giving Xenia a quick side hug. "You can have one of the potatoes I cooked if you'd like."

Disappointed in Felix's lack of response, she hardly hugged Blake back.

"Okay, thanks." Xenia didn't feel like eating—there

wasn't much she felt like doing. She wished she could talk to her mother. Or Al.

Her stomach fluttered at the thought. *Not him. Never him.*

She helped Blake pull down the tent and fold it into the case. After they picked up, they started moving again. She longed for a break, but it wasn't the walking that tempted her to stop; it was their destination. They didn't have a plan for the open magic. And what if they were wrong? They didn't have any definite signs that the open magic would be their final destination. If the jewel wasn't there, where would they go next?

They walked through a forest of pine trees the entire day, making little conversation. Xenia was grateful when the sun began to fade, knowing they would stop soon.

"Are you okay?" Felix walked beside her, matching her pace.

She ran her words over in her mind a few times before letting them escape her mouth. "We still need a plan, we can't just… expose ourselves to open magic."

"We can for a few minutes."

She shook her head, stopping to face him. "You don't know that, it's too risky."

"Yes, I do, actually…" Felix lowered his voice to a whisper and leaned closer. "My family's been exposed to it before."

"What?"

He raised a finger to his lip. "I personally haven't, but my father… It was when he was young, he was exploring a cave in Elisora. The cave was on a restricted site, but he went in anyway. Nothing happened. He told us the story but made us swear we would never share it, though I don't know why it matters."

"That's a big risk."

"I know but—"

Out of irritation she left his side and darted ahead to catch up with the others. Why couldn't he take this seriously? *Heroes! He thinks he knows everything, well—*

Xenia trained her eyes on the dirt and plants beneath her feet to keep herself from arguing further.

"What's wrong?" Blake asked when she reached his side.

"We still don't have a plan for when we reach the magic," she said in a low tone.

His face fell. "Oh. Yeah, I've been worried about that myself."

At least he understood its danger. *But he's a hero too.*

"We can't be exposed to it," she said. "At least, not for long."

"No, but there are four of us, maybe we can look for it in turns."

"That sounds…" *Dangerous.*

"It's just an idea, we still have time to figure something out."

She rolled her eyes, turning the necklace Karielyn had gotten her around in her fingers to keep herself distracted. Just because they had a better way of showing their fear didn't mean they weren't worried about it.

Or they don't care. They're prideful heroes.

"You're not taking this seriously!" Xenia shouted, voicing her thoughts. They stopped walking and faced her. "Do you even care? Why are we even attempting this switch? It risks everything, and for what? Maybe I like my fate now. You haven't asked me—"

"Xenia." Felix grabbed her wrist and looked into her eyes. His grip tightened as she tried to pull away. "Don't let this control you. Remember who you are."

"I'm sorry," she said softly. "I'm so sorry, I can't… I can't help it."

His finger slid gently across her hand. "It's okay—promise me you won't lose yourself to it, all right?" His gentle voice was quiet and cracked.

"I'll try not to," she whispered. She had already been trying so hard to fight this. Could she last any longer?

Chapter Forty-Two

THE GROUP STOPPED FOR THE NIGHT NEAR A RAGING river with no plan of how to cross in the morning. Xenia helped Blake set the fire while Karielyn and Blake pitched the tents.

Once burning, red flames licked the firewood, Xenia left Blake and joined Karielyn and Felix by the tents.

"If we do it well, it could work." Felix's voice was lowered to a faint whisper.

"What are you talking about?" Xenia asked before Karielyn could respond.

"Felix had an idea. We can discuss it later," she said. Her thin brows were pulled together.

"Is it about the magic?"

Felix placed his hand on her shoulder, squeezing it. "No."

She tilted her head back to meet his gaze. "What is it about?"

A frown pulled at his eyes as he leaned closer so that his lips brushed her ear as he spoke. "It's about *us*."

"What do you mean?" She pulled away to look him in the eyes. His twinkled softly under the last light of the sun, resembling glass.

Behind him, Karielyn bit her lip and tucked her hair behind her ear. Her eyes drifted far from them. What had they been talking about before?

"Xenia." His voice hardly sounded as kind as usual. Or possibly more so—either way, her body tensed in anticipation of his next words. "I don't think this is a good idea anymore."

"What isn't a good idea? Switching?"

"Yeah, that too." He breathed out, his eyes drifting to the ground for a moment before locking on hers again. He shifted, sending his familiar aroma in her direction. Beneath the sweat and smoke, she still smelled the part of him that made her think of new books and mint. "I don't think we should be together."

The declaration gripped her heart and left her breathless. He didn't want any of this anymore?

A large lump formed in her throat as if it wished to suffocate her. *Of course. I always knew he'd leave.*

Tears pricked her eyes, stinging them the longer she refused to blink. Her heart fluttered as she tried to determine what had happened. She wanted to ask a question, to hear an answer that would save her from the despair his first statement was drowning her in. But she wasn't sure she could manage speaking. And even if she could, she knew his answer would offer her no relief.

After a moment, she regained control of her voice and said in a feeble tone, "Why?"

He frowned and cleared his throat. "I'm sorry. I…" He glanced towards Karielyn and then back at Xenia. His words begged her to hear what they left unspoken. "I don't trust you anymore."

She narrowed her eyes and pinched her lips, resisting tears. He didn't trust her.

"You've changed. I don't know how much longer you can resist, and I don't think I should stay near you anymore."

Xenia looked away so he couldn't see the tears trickling down her face. She dried her cheeks with the hem of her sleeve and started taking slow steps away from him.

"Xenia!" he called after her.

She didn't turn around; she didn't want to look at him.

"I'm not done talking to you!" He cursed, shouting for her to listen to him.

She kept walking. Her eyes stayed fixed on the ground. More tears rolled down her cheek. She had trusted him. After everything he had told her, everything they had been through, she had believed him worthy of her trust.

What would happen now? Would he go against his word and fight her too?

"Are you crying?" Blake asked, approaching her. "What happened?"

She avoided his gaze. Telling him what had happened would pour salt into her fresh wound—she didn't ever want to repeat what Felix had said. The thought alone wrenched her heart, and she shuddered from tears.

Blake put his hands on the front of her shoulders to stop her from walking past him. "What's wrong?"

"We… split up." Felix answered for her.

For a moment Blake just stared. "What?"

"We split up. I can't trust her anymore. We're done."

At his words, Xenia cried even harder.

Blake pulled her into him, nestling her in his embrace. "Nia, I'm so sorry," he said, brushing her hair with his rough fingers. She held him tighter to stabilize herself as she fought off a scream and settled for a long string of tears. He moved his hand to her back and stroked it.

"Hey, Xenia." Karielyn's voice was soft. She grabbed Xenia's wrist and pulled her away from Blake. "I think we need to leave the boys since you aren't switching anymore. It will be safer."

Xenia's chest seized. How could she leave Blake? How could Felix leave her?

Memories of Felix flashed through her mind—the image of him standing on the balcony at the forgotten palace. The smile he had flashed the night he slept in her room. His voice echoed around her mind. *Mistletoe.*

Why did he do this? All her pain, anger, fear, and sadness seemed to form together, leaving her with a hopeless burning in her chest.

He did this to me! Fate-forsaken hero! He did all this just to hurt me!

Her face must have reflected her grim thoughts, because Karielyn steading her grip on her arm. "Xenia, calm down.

You don't have to be a villain. Not at heart. Don't let your thoughts control you."

Karielyn had said she felt like a villain too, but she hadn't acted on her thoughts. Why could she control herself so much better?

"Everything will be fine," she continued. "Don't act yet, you'll regret it."

She cleared her throat, drawing the boys' attention. "Xenia and I will be leaving in the morning."

Blake glanced between them, livid. "*What?*"

"We're not switching anymore," Felix said loudly, as if exaggerating to make her feel worse. It worked—she pinched her eyes closed. "It's better they leave."

"After all this?"

My thoughts exactly.

"What about us?" Blake asked.

"What about us? We'll stay together, you are my allegiant."

Blake frowned. "Are you——?"

"Yes, we're sure," Karielyn answered. "I think it's best we… distance ourselves from *heroes*."

"Fate, you can't be serious! We traveled all this way for Liftson to cower?"

Felix's hands formed tight fits. "I am not *cowering*! I am doing what I believe is in all of our best interests."

More tears forced their way down Xenia's cheeks. He couldn't truly believe this was in her best interest. She felt like a tower built high only for the pleasure of being knocked down. Victoria's words withered her mind. Were her warnings true?

"You think leaving the girls to wander the forest alone is in their best interest?"

"It's what I know you've believed from the beginning, Cedar. She's better off without me, our fates will result in this either way." The sun was hardly visible now, shadowing Felix's face.

Karielyn crossed her arms. "That might be the only sensible thing you've said, Liftson. She'll be far better off without *you* to burden her."

Xenia imagined the fire flickering at her feet spreading across the camp and swallowing her in its flames. That was what it felt standing in the midst of their argument. Like every word spoken was a flame burning her body.

"We're leaving as soon as the sun rises tomorrow morning no matter what either of you think about it," Karielyn said, spinning towards the tents. When she left, Blake began shouting at Felix. Xenia didn't want to listen any longer. She followed Karielyn into the tent and did her best to ignore their shouts.

Every part of her hurt worse than any injury ever had. A scream lingered inside of her that she refused to let out. Felix couldn't know what he had done to her. She wouldn't let him know. He knew he had hurt her; he shouldn't get to see her like this.

Is this what he intended all along? Her heart ached at the answers that filled her mind. Every interaction they'd had, every late night, every kiss—had he meant *any* of it? Did he mean *this?* Xenia replayed his words, desperate to find another meaning. After everything that had sparked between them, would he really leave her on behalf of her fate? Perhaps their story was attempting to twist him into a hero as much as it tried to force her into a villain.

Karielyn didn't say anything when she climbed in. She only lay under the covers and fell asleep. Xenia silently thanked for that. She didn't want to talk about anything right now.

She lay beneath the quilts, shaking from trying to keep everything in. She needed fresh air, but she didn't want to leave the tent—Blake and Felix were still arguing outside. She didn't want to face Blake's questions, or let Felix's stare find her for a second.

All she wanted was to be alone. And luckily for her, when she got back to Chantendell, that was all she would ever be. Alone.

Chapter Forty-Three

THE MORNING CAME TOO FAST. XENIA DIDN'T WANT TO get up for countless reasons when Karielyn woke her. One being the dread of leaving Blake again. Another was being reminded of her pain. Sleep numbed her emotions, easing her heart from its grief.

"I'm sorry. I tried to let you sleep, but we have to go now," Karielyn said.

"Okay, I'll be out," Xenia said softly. Everything had happened so suddenly. Yesterday morning, her future and fate were still uncertain and jumping with possibilities. Possibilities that had disappeared like the sun before a long, cold night.

When Karielyn left, Xenia pulled herself up and took a deep breath. She didn't want to split up and leave Blake, but what choice did she have?

She dressed in the best outfit she could manage from her single bag. She didn't want to show Felix how she really felt. Growing up her mother told her that the best way to feel good was to treat herself well. Xenia didn't feel good, but Felix didn't have to know that. If their relationship never meant anything to him, she didn't want him to know that it had meant everything to her.

Xenia climbed out of the tent. The others were already dressed and working to pack up camp. Before anything could snag her attention, she turned and started taking down the tent.

Blake joined her. "How are you feeling?"

She said nothing.

Once they finished taking down the tent, she gathered all of her things. Without Karielyn telling her, she knew it was time to go. The camp's solemn quiet wouldn't let her believe she could stay longer than necessary. After yesterday, she didn't feel welcome anymore.

Blake stopped them before they left, giving them a tent, a sack of coins, food, a map, and several knives. Even while separated, he would be the reason she survived.

Xenia threw her arms around him. He held her steady, making her wish once again that she weren't leaving.

When she pulled away, he said, "My biggest mistake was leaving you. I regretted entering as soon as I did, and I'm really sorry I left you for so long."

Xenia's heart stalled at his words—at the reminder. She couldn't tell him the truth—tell him how hard his departure had hurt her. When he left, she didn't have any other friends, without him she was lost.

"I *really* am sorry. I can't believe I'm losing you again.

I've already lost so much time with you. You're more than a friend, Nia, you're family. I love you the way I would a sister. Don't ever forget that."

Before she could respond, he turned away and left her standing by the trail.

"Goodbye, Blake!"

He glanced over his shoulder. "Goodbye, Nia."

Karielyn said nothing as she started walking down the trail, and Xenia darted towards her. Before she reached her, Felix gripped her arm.

Trust me, he mouthed.

Was he taunting her?

She yanked her arm away and continued down the trail without another glance.

"Ready?" Karielyn asked, grabbing hold of Xenia's hand as if she expected her to run in the other direction.

Maybe I should.

"I have to be, don't I? Where are we going?"

Karielyn hesitated before saying, "I know where we're going, but I... can't remember the name. It's a mountain town."

"Is it far?"

"It will take a few days to reach."

Xenia shielded her swollen eyes from the sun. "What are we going to do once we're there?" She should have been the one taking control—but Karielyn seemed to know what she was doing, and Xenia had no idea. Not anymore.

"We'll have to... I don't know yet."

Xenia couldn't find anything else to say, so she tried to

focus on her steps.

"There's a town nearby, maybe we can get a room somewhere," Karielyn said. A room would be a blessing after all the nights spent on the ground in a tent.

They walked the overgrown path until they reached the river. Trees caved above it and rough water sprayed mist in their face as it crashed against jagged rocks. Xenia took a deep breath, letting in the fresh air.

"We'll need to jump stones to cross it," Karielyn said. "The current is too strong."

They walked along the bank, searching for a place with even a few stones. The part of the river they stopped at was slightly lower, and a few rocks peaked above the water.

The rocks were slick from the water splashing against them, and they weren't very flat, either. Karielyn stepped to the edge of the water and attempted the first jump. She landed on the stone, throwing her arms to the sides to balance herself. When she jumped to the next stone, Xenia stepped up to the water's edge. She tried to copy Karielyn's movements but almost fell in after the first jump. Fear stalled her next jump. The water roared beneath her with its threatening current.

She held her breath as she jumped onto the next stone. Her feet grazed the edge, and she fell to her knees but didn't fall in. Shakily, she stood and jumped to the final rock before sending herself towards the bank.

The path on this side of the river looked the same as the other. She could easily imagine she still stood on the opposite bank as Felix's words rattled her world.

Karielyn reached for her hand, shaking her head. "I don't like this," she admitted. "We won't be very safe on our own."

Xenia took her hand, and they walked down a narrow trail. Trees arched above them, blocking out the daylight. Karielyn had seemed so eager to leave them yesterday. The confidence she had paraded then had faded now. Her fingers tightened around Xenia's.

The road narrowed after several hours, the trees around them thinned enough to see buildings in the distance. Relief washed over Xenia. They would stop there for the night and have beds for the first time since leaving Casiville.

They started searching for an inn as soon as they made it to the town. It should've been an easy task, but Xenia was easily distracted by everything around her. And she let it divert her attention. The town only had a dozen homes, but each one was stunning. They were all made from stone with vines tangling themselves between windows and leaves that covered entire walls. In the center of the small square, a set of steps carried the town's buildings up a hill.

At the top of the hill, they found an inn advertised by a hanging, wooden sign. The owner greeted them at the door and led them inside.

"We need a room please," Karielyn said, already reaching for her money. While she paid, Xenia glanced around the room. Brown furniture and stone walls. Even though the colors weren't bright, the space still let in enough sun to feel light.

"Just one room?" the girl asked.

Karielyn nodded.

"Here's a key."

When she finished paying, they walked down the empty hall to their room. One of only five. In Chantendell, inns had rows of rooms and several floors. This one also lacked a bar and stage.

Karielyn unlocked the room. It had simple, unpolished, wooden floors and white walls. There were two thin beds covered in linen sheets, and a broad window between them.

"Thank Fate there was somewhere to say," Karielyn said once she closed the door to the room. "I don't want to sleep alone in the woods yet."

Xenia tossed her leather bag onto the ground and fell back onto the bed to the right of the window. "And we have beds."

Karielyn laughed. "And maybe we can get dinner somewhere instead of compromising another meal."

"I never thought I'd miss the Training Center," Xenia said, remembering the meals she had had in her last few seasons there. She never would have risked going to the dining hall without Felix. Until she met him no one had ever had a kind word to say to her.

Tears blurred her vision.

"Are you all right?" Karielyn asked.

"I should have listened to you." Tears slipped past her temples into her hair. "I miss him so much." If she had listened to Karielyn, she might still be in Chantendell and not in the middle of a nameless town with a heart that was missing a piece yet felt heavier than before.

Karielyn bit her lip. "I'm so sorry, Xenia." She sat down beside her. "Perhaps Fate has something better ahead of you."

Xenia shook her head. "Fate doesn't care about me. I'm destined for isolation and discrimination."

"There's an Enrian proverb that goes, '*One's future is limited not by their fate, but their ability to fight for their destiny.*' Fate cannot turn us into something we don't want to be if we don't let it."

"We aren't in Enria, Karielyn," she said, though she committed the words to memory. "In Moira, we're told magic is never wrong. And magic is inseparably connected to Fate."

"We aren't in Moira, either," she said, standing. "It's getting late. Why don't we look for a place to eat?"

"I'm not hungry," she said, pulling herself into a sitting position.

Karielyn rolled her eyes. "I'll pick something up for you."

Xenia groaned but didn't protest. Maybe she was a little hungry. But she'd rather stay in her room than risk facing anyone who remembered her from training.

"I'll be back soon." Karielyn grabbed her bag.

As soon as the door closed, she curled herself up on the bed and started crying again. She had no idea where she was at, what town she was in, or what the others were doing. Did she want to think about any of that? What if she never saw Blake again?

No, that's ridiculous, of course I'll see him again.

Is it?

She caught herself wondering whether she'd see Felix again too. *I don't want to*, she told herself. *I don't want to.*

But of course she did. She wanted to see him again more than anything. And she wanted him to want the same thing towards her.

Her unsteady breaths started to gain control over her, so she forced her mind to linger on something else. The light spilling across the bed and onto her face was enough for a second. She pulled herself up to stare out the window and watched a few birds peck at seeds on the ground.

Did it even bother him? If it did, he didn't show it.

Why couldn't Xenia control herself? She pressed her head against the glass. Would the Chantendell guards still be after them? Calling off the switch eliminated their reason to punish them.

A storm twisted in her stomach. Had Felix considered that? Perhaps this *was* a part of his plan.

A knock sounded the door, cutting the thought short. Xenia rose from the bed and pulled open the door.

Fear crashed over her as if she had stepped through a waterfall. Victoria stood on the other side of the door, escorted by several royal guards.

Xenia tried to shut the door, but Victoria held it open. "Xenia," she said steadily.

She didn't say anything back as Victoria pushed her way into the room, holding the door open. Three guards followed her in.

They're only eighteen, she told herself. *They're only eighteen!*

Though, it didn't change anything. They may have been young, but they were well trained. One grabbed Xenia's arms as Victoria moved closer to her.

"Where's the other rogue?" Victoria asked.

A voice inside her urged her to give up his location, but she knew it wouldn't fix anything. A lump formed in her throat as she tried to speak. "I don't know."

"Why are you alone?"

Why do you care? she wanted to yell back, but she had already gotten herself into this much trouble, and she didn't want to make things worse.

"Answer me!"

She couldn't let Victoria know that Felix had left her. What could she say to explain their need for a map while also explaining his absence?

"We… we're looking for something." She could borrow parts of the truth without revealing it. "Once we got the maps, we thought it would be better to split up, to cover more ground."

"You're lying," she said. "I came here to get you and Liftson in custody. While he isn't here, I don't doubt you know where he is, and you *will* tell me."

"I don't know where he is, we left him this morning, I—"

"*We?*"

What had she done now? Karielyn had attacked Warren, Victoria wouldn't let her go.

"I'm with Karielyn, she insisted we leave them after…"

No, she wouldn't let her know what had happened. It

would make the situation worse.

"After we left your palace."

"So, you abandoned Felix and Blake?" Victoria didn't need to say anything for Xenia to know she didn't believe her. "What really happened?"

Xenia remained silent until Victoria motioned to her guards, and the man holding her tightened his grip. He forced her to the ground and kicked her hard in the back. Pain dulled her vision. He grabbed her hair and yanked her head back so she faced Victoria.

"Lying to Her Majesty is another offense to add to your sentence, Miss Safire," the man said.

Victoria kneeled beside her, her burgundy skirt pooling across the wooden floor. "Tell me the truth, Xenia, or this will only get worse."

Xenia's eyes filled with tears.

Realization lit Victoria's face. "You split up, didn't you? Felix left you, didn't he?" She was smiling now.

Xenia nodded, unable to speak.

"I tried to warn you," she drawled. "How about we make a deal? I will let you and the others go free in exchange for Felix's location."

Her even voice sent chills down Xenia's spine. She *couldn't* tell her where he was. She knew she couldn't, but there was more of her arguing why she should. The villain in her argued a stronger case: if she told her, Xenia wouldn't have to worry about fighting him. He had hurt her; couldn't she do the same to him? She was a villain, after all.

"He…"

Can I really do this to him? Would he betray me like this? More tears filled her eyes. *He already has.*

"The last time I was with him, he…" She took a deep breath. "He was nearly six—"

The door to the room swung open, and Karielyn froze at the sight. "What's going on?" she shouted. "Fate, I shouldn't have left you!"

"I'm fine." That couldn't have been further from the truth.

"Go ahead," Victoria urged, "where is he?"

She felt empty as she surrendered Felix's location. "He was six miles from here. He may have moved. I haven't seen him since this morning."

Karielyn's glare turned to ice. "What are you—?"

"Six miles in what direction?"

"South—"

"Xenia!" Karielyn shouted above her. "You can't do that! Felix doesn't deserve this!"

Her words sent a pang of guilt coursing through her body. She knew she was right, but it was too late.

"Let her go," Victoria ordered.

The man dropped Xenia and bowed his head apologetically.

Karielyn rushed across the room and grabbed Xenia's arm. With her wrist in a tight grip, they started for the door. The guards didn't follow them. Xenia had kept her end of the deal.

Chapter Forty-Four

FELIX PACED BACK AND FORTH ACROSS CAMP, SWEARING aggressively under his breath. Had he made the wrong choice?

No. He knew things would be better this way.

"You've been at this for hours. May I ask what your problem is?" Blake asked, pushing himself away from the trunk of a thick tree. They still hadn't left the campsite. The girls had left hours ago.

"How upset do you think she is?" Felix asked abruptly. He stopped pacing and rested his cold stare on Blake, as if he had answers. Wrongfully, he had hoped to elicit a reaction from Xenia. Something to make this more believable. But he never wanted to hurt her, and he feared that that was exactly what he had done.

"I'm sure she's devastated," Blake replied idly. After a moment he added, "You left her."

Enflamed anger burned in Felix's chest at Blake's

words. "You want to talk about *me* leaving her?"

"You asked a question and I answered. You hurt her." The last words rattled with bitterness. Felix knew Blake was angry with him. He was angry before he left Xenia. Even when they shared a tower, Blake never liked him. People who spent a lot of time with him never did. Except Xenia. Even after he showed his cards, she showed him love.

Not all of my cards, he thought.

"If you didn't want to hurt her, you shouldn't have left her," Blake snapped.

"*You* left her first. You left her *knowing* that she had no one else. *Knowing* that people would mistreat her. You left her alone for four years!"

"Don't you dare bring that into this! You left her knowing it would break her. You knew. You knew all along what you were doing. You knew once you left——"

"Shut up!" Adrenaline coursed through Felix's veins. Blake didn't understand their relationship——how dare he accuse him of false intentions?

Felix put a hand to his temple. *She's gone now. That's what I wanted, right?* He started pacing again. This plan would have benefited from more thought, if only he'd had more time. The Chantendell guards could show up at any moment. Would this be enough to dissuade them?

"Did you ever care about her?" Blake continued. "Or did you know from the moment you met her what you planned to do? How much of your relationship was real?"

Every bit of it, Felix thought. But he couldn't say that out loud.

"I knew you didn't have good intentions the moment I saw you with her. How could anyone believe a *Liftson* would want to be a villain?" Blake stepped closer to Felix. "What you did was not heroic. You're an evil—"

"Stop talking about things you don't understand, Cedar!" Anger burned Felix from the inside.

"I never should have let Xenia follow through with this," Blake mumbled.

"You were never in control of her. We found hope together. Did you really think after four years your word would still be better than mine?"

Something ignited in Blake's eyes. His fist slammed into Felix's face. Felix stumbled back, his head throbbing. Though he hurt, all he felt was numb. Numb from anger. Numb from longing. Numb from regret.

Regaining control, he pulled his arm back swiftly and punched Blake in the chest. The contact made his knuckles sting. Blake stumbled back, but Felix wasn't strong enough to do nearly as much damage. Before he could prepare himself, Blake's fist slammed just beneath Felix's chest, knocking out his breath. The impact sent him backwards into a tree. The bark scraped his back, but he pushed himself forward, already balling his fists.

He aimed his next punch at Blake's face, but Blake blocked it with his forearm. Felix cursed as pain shot through his fingers. Blake charged for him, hooking his arm around his neck and slamming him back into the tree. Blake's hold loosened. He spun around and punched Felix in the stomach before stepping back.

Groaning, Felix slumped to the ground. Every part of him ached. He glanced down at his hands. Each of his fingers were split and bleeding, as well as his lip and nose. He leaned against the tree behind him and attempted to catch his breath. He could never win a physical fight against Blake, he knew that. But Blake started it, and he had to defend himself.

Blake stared down at him, the dangerous flame in his eyes still glowing. Felix hated being slumped against the ground while Blake stared down at him, but he couldn't get up. He could hardly move.

Kneeling, Blake gripped his chin and gazed into his eyes. "Don't talk to me like that." He pulled his hand back, then stood and turned away.

Finally, Felix caught his breath and attempted to push himself from the ground. He got to his feet and placed his hand on the tree for support while he searched for his balance.

He turned to face the trail. "We should start walking now."

"I said that six hours ago," Blake said.

"We didn't need to start walking ago six hours ago," Felix replied, pulling off his shirt. He used the fabric to wipe the blood from his face and fingers. His chest sported a series of bright-red bruises.

"It's getting late now, we should wait for tomorrow," Blake said.

"No, we'll leave tonight." *I can't get too far behind.*

Blake ran his fingers through his curly, blond hair. "Fine."

Felix had no plans to leave later whatever Blake said. He touched the top of his cheek and flinched. Bruised too.

"Grab your things," he said, reaching for his flask. "We'll be walking all night. There's a town not far from here, but we won't stop."

"We didn't pass a town close to here."

"We're not going back."

Blake's expression changed again. "Then where are we going?"

Felix ignored him and poured the water over his shirt. He dabbed it across his face. "Hurry up, I want to leave before dark." Once the blood from his lip and nose slowed, he pulled the blood-stained shirt back on.

Blake shook his head and picked up his bag and the case with the tent. The thick trees blocked out plenty of light on their own, but the rich, orange rays that were slipping behind the horizon reminded him that it would only get darker.

"I'd really like an explanation," Blake said.

Felix shook his head, dismissing the request. "You'll get one eventually," he assured, focusing on the distance. Even if he could explain things to Blake now, he wouldn't. He didn't want to speak to Blake at all.

The wind had picked up, and the temperature dropped consistently, but Felix didn't care. He wouldn't upset his plans by waiting for the morning. His fight with Blake had already cut into their time.

"This is dangerous," Blake said.

"No part of this trip has been safe."

At his words, an icy breeze brushed through their hair,

as if adding to the flaws in Felix's plan. He clutched his arms and rubbed them for warmth.

"I think we should pitch our tent somewhere and—"

"Shut up," Felix ordered, listening carefully to the sounds hidden in the wind's howls. "I hear…" He strained to identify the sound over the wind. "Hooves."

Before he had time to think more of it, a small light emerged from the trees, illuminating a carriage. The light wobbled as the cart hit the bumpy road. The horses slowed to a stop, and the two of them moved aside to give the carriage room.

"Be careful, it might be—"

"I'll be fine," Felix said, ignoring Blake's warning.

He approached the carriage. The door opened and Victoria smiled, leaning towards him.

"So, she wasn't lying." She held a lantern that lit her face. "I'm talking about Xenia. She gave me your location in exchange for her safety. I thought you might want to know that."

Would she really do that? His head spun. Why would she betray him so easily? The thought hit him harder than any of Blake's punches.

Before he could react, the guards held him steady, pushing him into the carriage. He twisted his arms, trying to free himself from their grasp.

The guard on his right pressed a knife to his skin. "Get in, and don't resist," he said.

Felix stilled, and the guard pulled it away carefully. The guards pushed him further and he climbed into the carriage cabin.

"Felix!" Blake shouted, running to the carriage. "What's going on?"

"Keep walking until you get to the town, I'll meet—"

Victoria placed her delicate hand over his mouth. "Shh," she whispered. Then, raising her voice, added, "He won't be doing anything of the sort." She glanced at Blake. "If you want to keep yourself out of trouble, then I suggest you move along." Her level voice possessed a grave warning.

Felix nodded, urging him to do as she said.

Blake grimaced, but he stepped away from the carriage. When Victoria pulled her hand away, Felix buried his face in his palm.

The carriage moved forward slowly, rocking its passengers up and down. "I'm sure you have questions, and I'll let you ask them," Victoria said, hanging the lantern on the latch above their heads.

From the tone in her voice, Felix didn't want to know the answers.

He leaned back against the bench, closing his eyes. Fate, he didn't want any of this.

A memory he thought he'd buried surfaced in his mind. He had returned home for the Yule celebration, only fifteen at the time. After spending an entire day reading in his room, Samuel came to speak to him. He asked how training had been. Felix had already received permission from Trey but stayed in Chantendell anyway. Samuel asked if Felix had made friends.

"Not real ones," he had answered. "There's this girl,

she's the queen of my story."

"The queen? That's good."

Felix shook his head. "Every time we speak, she acts like we're lovers. And she touches me that way too…" Felix's words failed then.

Samuel set his hand on Felix's knee, smiling. 'She must really like you. Keep her close."

Tears welled in his eyes. "Father, I can't…"

"She'll make a valuable ally in your story. You need her."

Felix had used his father's advice on how to appease the press and admirers to endure Victoria for four years, but he couldn't do it anymore.

"Did she really betray me?" he asked, ripping himself from the memory. He had more questions than Victoria would be able to answer, but that one was the most persistent.

She laughed under her breath. "Felix, you betrayed her first. Can you blame her?"

He fought the tears stinging his eyes and cleared his throat. *Don't worry about her, not now.* "You're going to arrest me?"

"You're a threat to my people."

Felix scoffed. He wouldn't have started a fight if she hadn't threatened Xenia. And the things she had told her…

Fate, I hope she didn't believe any of it.

He scanned the carriage and the surrounding areas. There was a river in the distance. He couldn't see it in the dark, but he could hear the rushing water and remembered it from the map he had stolen.

He leaned past Victoria and pulled the lantern down. "Get ready to jump," he said tersely, whisking the smile off her face.

"What?"

He threw the lantern against the floor, shattering the glass and spilling the melted wax across the carriage. The flame flickered in the dark as it spread across the carriage floor. Felix pushed on the door until it came open as the flame picked up, eating at the wooden cart. He jumped out of the carriage and onto the cold ground outside.

He hit the dirt and the jarring impact sent a wave of pain through his already sore body. Looking up, he watched the horses carry the smoking cart to the river. He pulled his leg out from underneath him to release some of the tension. When his breathing steadied, he looked around for the other passengers.

Victoria stood a few paces away, already brushing the dust off her dress as she made her way towards him. "Fate! Why did you do that?" she yelled. She straightened the crown on her head. "You could have killed us!" she said, pointing at the smoking carriage. "And now we're stranded!"

"Maybe you are, but I know how to walk," Felix said as he pulled himself to his feet. A sharp throb pulsed through his ankle, sending a jolt of pain through his leg. He attempted a few steps, slowed by a limp. He stumbled towards a tree and leaned against it for support.

"I cannot believe you!" she shouted. "This is—this is treason! I should have you locked up until our story ends!"

"Really?" Felix tested her. "You should be more careful, Victoria. Step any closer to the line, and they'll write you as a villain."

"Perhaps I don't care about that. You know, I used to be so careful with my reputation. I wanted everyone to know which side I was on. But these were my father's rules. I don't have to live by them." She moved closer to him until they were a span apart. "You've never been brave enough to do that. Break your father's rules."

Felix winced. Just a few more days, and she would see how very wrong that was.

"You can't change your side, Liftson, but I can. I can be whatever I want, and I don't have to be your ally."

"You act as if you need me for years, only to turn against me now? What changed?" he snapped.

"I don't need you anymore," she said plainly. "After what you've done, you'll only mar my name."

He pushed past her, narrowing his eyes in search for the trail. He didn't know what reaction Victoria had hoped he'd have, though he was sure he wasn't giving it to her.

Victoria shouted at her guards, who rushed into action. This time, they didn't hesitate to attack. The one closest to him swung a sword at him. He managed to move out of the way before it could pierce his skin.

Another guard knocked him to the ground, sending him crashing back onto his injured foot. Felix grimaced as pain spread across his leg. A sharp rock had sliced his jaw. The cold wind whipped his hair across his face, and he shivered from the bitter air.

Victoria shook her head, making her way to him. She kneeled next to him and ran her fingers along his jaw, pulling away as red blood painted her fingers.

"Don't touch me!" he shouted.

She sneered as she pulled herself to her feet. His glare followed her. He knew she used to be friends with Xenia—when she was known as the daughter of a royal—and stayed near him after Xenia was titled a villain. The only reason she had cared about Felix was because he could give her things other people couldn't: approval. Credit. Never really friendship. He had become a mere accessory used to flaunt her status.

"Felix?"

He lifted his head at Blake's voice, squinting in an attempt to see farther into the dark.

Blake rushed through the trees over to the spot Felix lay, pushing guards out of the way.

"You!" Victoria shouted to one of her guards. "Go retrieve the horses from the carriage before they're injured! We need a way back to the palace."

The guards nodded and ran towards the burning carriage in the distance to rescue the horses.

Blake slid next to Felix. "Can you walk?"

"Probably not." He clenched his fist as a sharp pain crossed through him. "My leg…"

"I'm going to help you stand, okay?" Blake said, wrapping an arm around his shoulder. "You can hold my arm to steady yourself."

Once up, Felix clutched Blake's arm for support. The

pain overwhelmed him with the added pressure of his body resting above this leg. He groaned as his weight shifted. Blake slipped his arm under his shoulder to keep him up.

A guard grabbed Blake by the arm from behind. He spun around, letting go to face the guard. Felix groaned in pain as Blake pulled away.

Blake pulled his knife out of his pocket and held it ready. The guard pulled out his own dagger. Blake dogged his attempt to stab him and pressed his own knife into his armor, clanking in attempt to find his skin. Swiftly, he lunged his fist at the man's face.

The other guards returned, guiding the horses behind them.

"Felix," Blake called, "try to take one of the horses!"

"How do you expect me to do that?" Felix shouted, struggling just to stand. He forced himself to walk towards the horses. The guard lunged at him, dropping the horse's reins. Felix dove out of the way, stumbling back into the other guard. He abandoned his horse as well and reached for Felix.

Felix spun back around to face the horse. There was no saddle and no stool to help him up. He grabbed ahold of the horse's neck and attempted to pull himself up. As he let off the ground, his leg throbbed. The guard below him clutched it. Felix grabbed the horse's mane and kicked his leg free. Swinging his good leg over, he rested on the horse's back, breathing heavily.

"Start moving, I'll catch up," Blake ordered.

Felix grabbed the reins and leaned forward. The horse

started galloping away from Victoria and her guards, towards the trail. He was moving. He hoped in the right direction, but for now, leaving Victoria mattered more than anything else.

He reached the trail and braced himself as he approached the river. Dark clouds of smoke emitted from the carriage stuck in the current. Felix held his breath as the horse leaped into the lake, splashing him with ice-cold water.

In the distance, he heard another horse galloping towards him. Relief washed over him. Blake's horse chased his for what felt like miles before running off the trail and stopping within a grove of trees. Blake pitched the tent as Felix tied the horses to a tree.

Even though Felix knew Victoria wouldn't find them this far and hidden within the trees, fear kept him up all night. Fear of the future. Fear of things he couldn't discuss with anyone. Fear of returning to Chantendell.

He told his mind to shut off and calm down, but it wouldn't. He spent the entire night wishing for peace of mind, but it was sent further away with every thought.

He had never been so thankful to see sunlight.

Chapter Forty-Five

HE DIDN'T MEAN IT.

Fate, he didn't mean it.

Xenia felt numb. Upon leaving the inn, it was all she could think about. Felix hadn't meant what he told her. It was a ruse to buy them more time. It had to have been. He had asked her to trust him, and she still did it.

What have I done?

"Really, Xenia?" Karielyn snapped once they made it out of town. "What in Fate's name where you thinking? How could you be so careless?"

Xenia couldn't bring herself to look at her. Guilt already laced her thoughts. Since leaving, the deep cavity in her heart left from Felix had been filled with guilt.

"I didn't realize..." she mumbled. "And with the thoughts. Fate, I'm so sorry." Her tears returned.

Karielyn's eyes gentled. "You understand now."

Xenia nodded.

"They'll be all right," Karielyn said, walking closer to her. "They're strong. And Blake is a good fighter. If they find them, they can fight back."

Her words did little to comfort Xenia. No matter what happened, it didn't change what she had done. She had betrayed Felix for her own safety.

Xenia cried harder. Karielyn dropped her things and threw her arms around her. "You made a mistake," she soothed. "Everyone does. You didn't know. And it isn't fair that our story has so much control over your mind."

"But you haven't done anything irrational because of it."

"Xenia, don't—I've also been struggling, but I wasn't placed in your situation. Victoria is cruel, if she wanted Felix's location so desperately… I might have given it up too."

Xenia turned back to the trail ahead of them. Even if Felix had lied about not trusting her, he had reason not to. Would he forgive her for what she had done?

They kept walking down the trail. She had no idea where they were going. If Felix had been lying, that implied he still intended to switch. Were they going to the magic capital?

The same birds she saw before swooped out of the trees past her, singing their elegant song. Their paper-white wings fluttered as they dove onto a branch on the other side of the trail.

Xenia and Karielyn roamed into another grove of trees, some sporting thick canopies of leaves and others naked to nothing but bark. In Chantendell, the Lush season would just be taking over, leaving small flowers rising out of the frosted grounds in the mornings. It already felt warmer here, like this world was ahead in the year cycle.

Karielyn stopped to pull out the map Blake had sent them with. It was far smaller than the one they'd left with the boys, but the markings matched. As they walked, Karielyn sang softly in Enrian. It was a beautiful language. It was hard to imagine such a graceful culture being the same one that terrorized Chantendell and continued to threaten them now.

"You never seem upset at your fate," Xenia said after a while of walking in silence. "I don't understand how."

"I just don't believe I would be any different without a fate. It doesn't change who I am, and I know I'm not a villain. And I suppose it might be an Enrian thing. Fate is regarded very differently there." Karielyn looked ready to say more, but then she bit her lip and fell quiet.

"Aren't you afraid of life when you return? They'll punish you whether you believe you're a villain or not."

Karielyn's thin brows pinched together. "I like to believe Fate will save me from… unjust punishments," she said carefully.

Xenia frowned at her friend's remark. No villain had ever evaded their punishment. What made Karielyn believe she could?

They continued walking until midnight, at least. Xenia's legs burned, but somehow, they hadn't failed her yet.

They pitched the tent and unfolded their blankets, spreading them from one end to the other. Karielyn sat up, examining the map and calculating something under her breath.

Spending their first night without the boys kept Xenia up late listening to the wolves howling and the critters rustling the plants near the tent.

As she tried to sleep, ghosts of Felix haunted her—his smile, his laugh, his touch. She longed for him. What had she gotten him into?

In the morning, Felix lay motionless, stopping himself from waking Blake. They needed to leave, but he didn't want to risk upsetting him again. So instead, he lay, staring up at the tent and feeling each precious moment slip away.

When he knew it would be bright enough to see, he climbed out of the tent and sat next to an overgrown tree, his bag in his hand. The morning wind painted bumps across his skin, but he ignored it.

He pulled Liz Eveyon's story from his bag and flipped through the familiar pages, distracting himself as best he could from the pain he felt each time he thought about leaving Xenia— and the fear he felt each time he thought about *her*.

The tent flapped opened and Blake climbed out. From the shadows under his eyes, he hadn't gotten much more sleep than Felix.

Without invitation, he sat next to him. After releasing a long breath, Blake said, "About our fight… I'm sorry. I—I shouldn't have lost control like that."

Felix stayed silent, and Blake continued. "I know Xenia

wouldn't have wanted that. Not only because she's a good person, but because she cares about us. Both of us."

"I know. And you're right, she wouldn't have approved of the way we acted. Of the things I said… I'm sorry."

"I'm not a very good allegiant, am I?"

Felix shrugged. "I'm not a very good hero."

After a moment of nothing but silence, Blake said, "Why…? Why did you leave her?"

Felix held his breath. *Should I tell him?* That could ruin everything. That *would* ruin everything.

Lacking an appropriate response, he shook his head. Thankfully, Blake didn't press. Felix had grown so used to people relentlessly searching for information about his life he didn't want to give. He wasn't like his father; he didn't like the thought of his life being as accessible as a story. Though, Samuel did manage to keep some things from the public. Keep them from his family, even.

Without Xenia, he never would have known what had happened with his family in 1403. He would never have questioned his family's legacy further. Things would have gone the way he had always imagined. And they would have ended with another hero to add to the Liftson glory. Though, he knew he wasn't anything glorious.

Rising to his feet Felix said, "We should get moving again."

"Are you sure you don't want to rest a while? I beat you pretty hard yesterday."

Felix grimaced. "I'm fine."

His words stretched far from the truth. *Fine* would be

not worrying about binding deals or dangerous gambles. *Fine* was a word foreign to him. But letting Blake know that would be a mistake.

He wished he didn't feel the need to act stronger than he was around Blake, but everything from his strong arms to his history with Xenia made Felix feel weak.

Blake stood. "What about Xenia, do you think she's all right?" he asked as he began to take the tent down. "Do you think Victoria will find her too, I mean?"

Felix shook his head, wishing Blake hadn't unearthed the topic he wanted to keep buried. "No, Victoria promised her safety if she gave up our location."

Blake shifted. "Would she really do that?"

"Apparently."

As the words escaped his mouth, a hand of grief pulled at his heart. *What have I done?* Clearly, he didn't have time to waste. What else could Xenia do in such a short time to disrupt his plan?

"She did, and it's my fault. Let's go. Kari—we need to go." His body tried to lock up. He scolded himself silently; how could he make such a simple mistake?

Blake glared at him, placing a hand on the brown mare. "What about Karielyn? She and you are—"

"Keep your voice down. Don't forget, someone is listening," Felix said, checking over his shoulder as if someone were watching him.

He positioned himself atop the other horse. "The longer we wait here, the more time they have to find us again," he said.

Blake followed suit, and the horses started pacing forward, kicking a trail of dust and dirt behind them. The sun was still rising to its highest spot, warming the crisp morning air.

There were no distractions, nothing to pull Felix from the busy mess of his mind. Not only did his stomach churn from the thought of Xenia betraying him—but he was also worried about his family. If he followed through with his plan, his family could get hurt. Severely hurt. Could he live with himself if something happened to one of them? Any of them? Whatever happened, it was too late now to prevent it.

Chapter Forty-Six

"WE'RE NOT FAR," KARIELYN SAID, FOLDING HER MAP into her pocket.

The morning sun illuminated what Xenia hadn't been able to see the night before: big boulders and trees. They must have been getting higher.

"From the… mountain town?"

"From Sivinda. It's a small town along the way."

They took the tent down. This time Xenia took a turn carrying it. They started moving as soon as the tent was in its case.

The path became harder to walk the closer they came to Sivinda. The ground was uneven from rocks and the trail winded around the mountain.

They reached Sivinda after several hours. This town was the smallest and dullest one they'd seen yet—simple buildings and houses, some of which were incomplete. The most notable thing was the mountain it was set on.

"We can't stay long, but I want to check something while we're here. We'll be back on our way to the cave soon."

Cave? What was Karielyn talking about?

Xenia opened her mouth to question her but thought better of it. This was more information than Karielyn had given her yet—if she brought it up, she would become more cautious.

The magic capital was located in the mountains in a cave. Were they ever going to a mountain town?

Xenia followed her down the dirt streets and watched as she peered through each window. Finally, she spotted whatever she had come for and darted quickly into a brick building. Xenia joined her inside.

"You don't have anything covering last night?" Karielyn asked.

The young man she spoke to stood behind a desk littered with papers and pots of ink. "Ma'am, it takes several days for the paper to be delivered, I'm sorry—"

"You haven't heard anything?"

"No, you're the first person I've spoken to all morning. Word takes far longer to spread here than in Chantendell."

Karielyn cursed under her breath in Enrian. She spun around and walked to Xenia's side.

"What are you looking for?" Xenia asked.

"I want to read the paper. If anything happened to Felix, the press would cover it. But I don't have time to wait for yesterday's coverage."

"We aren't in any rush—"

"Actually, we are. I suppose we'll just have to hope he left early enough to miss Victoria."

Xenia blushed. How had she been so careless? What would Victoria do to Felix if she found him?

She felt her eyes fill with tears and glanced at Karielyn. "I—I'm so sorry. I shouldn't have told her where they were. Yesterday I was so caught up. I didn't want to fight Felix and—and with—"

"Xenia." Karielyn grabbed her hand. "Listen to me. It's too late to fix it now. The only thing we can do now is keep going."

Xenia nodded and blinked away her tears, even though she didn't want to keep moving—she wanted to give herself time to rest while she thought things through.

As they left the small town, a string of painful thoughts pulled its way through her mind. She remembered Felix's arm creeping over her shoulder. The memory brought a warm feeling, almost like he stood next to her, about to kiss her—then she remembered what he had said to her. She remembered that he had left her. She tried to push the memory of him out of her mind to keep herself from falling apart. But she couldn't. He stuck like a permanent tattoo running across her brain.

"Karielyn," she started carefully. "How much farther do we need to go to get… wherever it is we're going?" She knew Karielyn couldn't give her too much information now. Not if they wanted to keep the guards away.

Karielyn hesitated for a moment, looking over her shoulder as if she expected someone to be behind them.

"Maybe two days."

Two days. Two days, then she could rest.

As the evening progressed, gray clouds swirled overhead. Soon, a single raindrop hit Xenia's cheek, quickly followed by more. The soft wind sprayed the water in their faces. The rain increased, soaking their dresses. Xenia's arms wrapped around the bag, pulling it close to her chest to guard the translations.

The rain poured down harder, obscuring their path and softening the ground. The longer they walked, the more the rain mixed with the dirt, making thick mud that stuck to their shoes.

"Should we stop?" Xenia asked.

"Not yet," Karielyn said, raising her voice to be heard over the rain. "We need to keep walking. I'd like to get there as soon as possible."

The rest of the night was cold. The rain damped the air long after the storm passed. No wind was left to blow through the trees. The only sound was the soft shifting of the rocks beneath their feet as they walked. The gray clouds hadn't moved yet. They still shaded their path from the setting sun, adding to the mix of grief and guilt that was already heavy on Xenia's heart.

The next day passed in an uneventful blur. They hadn't found any towns since Sivinda. The weather and terrain had slowed their pace, and they covered far less ground than the previous days.

Several times, boulders fell from above, threatening to crush Xenia and Karielyn. When the land became rocky, it seemed they stepped on every unsteady area. By the time they reached sold ground, their hands were torn and covered in blood and dirt. Cuts ran across Xenia's dress, and her hair was matted with mud. Karielyn didn't look any better. They kept walking, even though Xenia's heart still raced from nearly falling off the trail.

The rest of their hike wasn't much easier. Once again Xenia wondered if Fate was attempting to stop her and Felix from switching. Heavy rain and fog obscured their view, making staying on the trail even harder. Her wet, black hair stuck to her face, and her dress clung to her legs, complicating each step.

Xenia gasped for breath as they came to a stop at the mountain's summit. They stood in a clearing, beside a large rock that formed a peak. The fields they'd spent days hiking through were all visible from here. The edge of the mountain was guarded by trees that would offer little protection were she to fall. They filled the spaces between large rocks spiraling all around the mountain, decorating the beautifully steep way to death.

"This is it." Karielyn panted. She peered around a large rock, standing on her toes as if looking for something, or someone. "This is our destination."

It was beautiful, and Xenia didn't want to go any farther, but this wasn't a cave or a mountain town. "Why here?" she asked. "What's going on?"

"This is where we're meeting."

Chapter Forty-Seven

FELIX WAS COMING *HERE*. XENIA WOULD SEE HIM SOON.

She leaned against the rock to steady herself. The thought of seeing Felix excited her at first, but did she really want to see him? Would he know what she had done to him? Her heart ached at the thought of him suffering on her behalf. If only she had let Victoria take her.

I was so selfish!

Would Felix forgive her?

They had scarce food left, and the only weapon Blake had left them with was a set of knives, though neither of them knew how to hunt by any means. Xenia didn't trust herself to find safe wild berries to eat, so they did their best to ration what little food they had left.

They set up their tent and spread out their blankets for another night. The sun went down, and storm clouds darkened the already black sky. Once again, Karielyn fell asleep long before Xenia's mind calmed enough to sleep. She felt like there was an empty hole inside her where butterflies had died.

Even though she desperately wanted to see Felix, she wasn't ready for tomorrow. Would he even be able to stand her? She wouldn't be able to stand herself. He had a good reason to leave her. What if his words hadn't been entirely false? Had he saw the villain that hid inside her? She buried her face into the quilts and cried herself to sleep.

It rained through the night, waking Xenia and Karielyn to find their possessions soaked. In the morning—or the dark hours before the sun—they took apart the tent and hung the canvas over a tree branch to dry. By the time they finished ringing everything out and spreading them across the ground to dry, the sun had started to peek over the side of the cliff. Xenia laid the translated pages of the book out on a rock in the sun.

When they finished setting everything out, she began pacing back and forth across the cliffside clearing. She massaged her temples, trying once again to distract herself. Karielyn watched her as she braided a small portion of her hair to the front of her head. What would Xenia say when she saw him? Maybe he wouldn't want to speak to her at all.

What if he doesn't arrive at all? Victoria could have arrested him.

The dead silence that had been haunting her brain and trapping her in her own thoughts finally broke. In the distance, horse hooves crushed weeds. Her chest ached from her heart's complicated beating.

Two horses carrying Felix and Blake rounded the

corner and appeared in the clearing.

Xenia stood like a statue as Blake helped Felix off his horse. Every thought she had had before escaped her mind. The only thing that mattered now was that she was seeing Felix again. She didn't care how things would end.

She ran for Felix, throwing her arms around him and hiding her face in the shoulder of his button-up shirt. She shouldn't have been doing this—he had said he didn't want her anymore. But he was so familiar, and in that moment, she couldn't remember why her arms shouldn't be around him. He loosely wrapped his arms around her, carefully placing his hand on her back as if he'd never hugged before.

"Careful, my leg is injured." He pulled her off him and limped towards Karielyn.

Xenia didn't stay to hear what Felix told Karielyn, she hurried behind the large rock and slid against the stone, hiding her face in her knees. Had she been wrong? Had Felix meant what he told her before they separated? Or was he still acting?

Blake slid next to her. He shoved her shoulder with his own. "Are you all right? This isn't about Felix, is it?" he asked, wrapping an arm around her.

"Is he angry?" she asked, looking into his soft, blue eyes.

He smiled and laughed a little, shaking his head at the ground. "No," he said slowly. "Well, he might be. But he still cares about you." He leaned closer. "He missed you. A lot."

A spark of hope jumped in her chest.

The horses in front of her flapped their tails in the wind. Xenia leaned her head against Blake. His breathing remained steady, and his heart hammered even beats against his chest.

"Why… why did you really tell Victoria where we were?" he asked.

Her heart raced at the mention. *She told them what happened.* "I… I was afraid—I know that's not a good excuse, there is no good excuse. I didn't know how things would end. I thought we would have to… I thought if…"

Tears trickled down her sunburnt face. She tried to wipe them away, but it wouldn't help anything; she couldn't wipe away her mistakes like a spill, they had already stained the surface of her relationship with Felix and soaked into the roots.

"You thought you needed to do something villainous?"
She nodded.

He stood and extended his hand. She took it, and he heaved her up. They started walking away from the camp, behind the peak.

"You know I'll love you no matter what, right?" he told her. "Nothing you say or do will change that. You *are* my family. I know you as well as them. I worried that you might not receive that same appreciation from Felix. I didn't want him to hurt you. I thought I knew him well enough when we were roommates, and I wasn't fond of him—of course, we were only fourteen and I'm sure he's changed, but I knew him as rude."

They cut through a field of yellow and white flowers. "I don't think you would put yourself in a dangerous relationship—though sometimes they're the hardest to resist. But I assumed if you were with him, he'd changed. What I didn't understand was *why* he left you the way he did."

"He faked it," Xenia whispered. "Didn't he?"

"That's what I believe," Blake said. "I don't think he ever wanted to hurt you—he thought he *had* to. I think he wants you back. He was worried *you* wouldn't want *him* back, and he lost hope when you…" He didn't finish, and Xenia was thankful for that.

Blake cleared his throat. "But if he is upset—well, sometimes we need to fight for things we want—and for the people we love. We don't always get things easy, and that's all right. If we never tried for anything—truly tried—we would never feel satisfied. Not really. Without pain we can't find peace. And if you show him your love and he doesn't accept it, remember that sometimes things change, but sometimes they come back, and if they don't, you'll come to accept that it wasn't meant to be. At some point we need to move on—or even just push forward."

"Thanks, Blake."

Xenia had made a grave mistake. She didn't know how that would affect them, but she would do all she could to fix it.

When they walked back, Felix and Karielyn were talking. "Oh, good you two are back. Should we go now?" Felix asked, looking over at them, then turning back to Karielyn.

Xenia frowned. He already wanted to move again? Couldn't they rest for at least a day?

"Sure." Karielyn reached her hand out to help steady him, and Xenia darted over to help.

"Are you all right?" Xenia asked.

Felix looked at her sadly. "Yes, I'm fine." He tried to force a smile. His face resembled his father's when he tried to act like he thought of her in a way he didn't.

Karielyn helped him as he stepped onto a rock for elevation and swung his leg over the horse's back. Once he was on, she climbed on behind him.

Xenia stared at the ground to keep her eyes off him. Blake grabbed her arm and helped her onto his horse, a brown mare with a matching mane and tail. Once they were all on a horse, Felix started leading them away.

Xenia leaned her face closer to Blake's. "Where are we going?"

He shook his head. "I don't know."

She looked ahead to see if she could spot where they were going, but she couldn't see anything different from what they were leaving. It had begun raining again, harder than before, and she couldn't see far ahead.

They were spiraling back down the mountain. As they passed a rocky wall, her heart stopped.

A cave.

They were at their alleged magic capital.

Felix stopped and slid off his horse. Xenia shielded her eyes against the rain and climbed off the horse. On her way to Felix's side, she found a shimmery residue on a few of the rocks and plants despite the rain.

When she reached Felix's side, he said, "I think this is where the jewel is." A breath broke his speech. "I still want to switch, I lied to keep the guards away from us."

The breath left Xenia's lungs, and she couldn't seem to

get it back. All she could do was stare at him.

He grabbed her hand and squeezed it. "Are you ready?"

Before she could respond lightning struck above them, and the ground shook.

We're here. After seasons of preparation, they were there. Her chest burned, and her thoughts were stopped by a fog. Yet she nodded.

They were going in.

Chapter Forty-Eight

XENIA'S AND FELIX'S HANDS WERE SEALED TOGETHER AS they walked towards the cave—a cave contaminated with *open magic*.

We're exposing ourselves selves to magic. Her heart wouldn't slow down, and her thoughts wouldn't, either.

They got closer to the entrance and a metallic smell lingered in the air. Xenia held her breath and tightened her grip on Felix's hand. "Are you sure—?"

"Yes," he said firmly. "I told you before, it will be fine if we're fast."

A lump formed in her throat as they reached the entrance, making it hard to breathe evenly. She didn't like caves—especially ones filled with magic that could kill her. What if it caved in on them?

The daylight faded inside the cavern's stone walls, enveloping them in darkness. Rain no longer blew against them, but Xenia felt no warmer. Their footsteps bounced off the walls. Already she felt lighter. The light had faded away entirely now, and though she couldn't see the walls, she felt like they were closing in on her.

Thunder shook the cave and stones fell around them. She screamed. The cave would close her in. She would never breathe fresh air again. Fear fought to paralyze her. Panic made her thoughts spiral further from her mission. She tried to take deep breaths to assure herself of the air around her, but she couldn't even focus on breathing. Her shallow breaths turned her head light.

Deeper into the cave, she shielded her eyes from a blue glow. Was she imagining it? Hallucinating? The light seemed to draw her in, pull her towards its rays. She kept walking, following Felix closer to the glow. She couldn't help but feel as if the magic was seeping into her skin. At the thought, shivers spread across her body.

Her head was spinning—or she was. She felt like a child after twirling around in mindless circles to dizzy herself. The ground shifted from left to right like a scale. Still, she kept walking towards the blue light.

She tripped over a rock, losing her balance, and stumbled to the ground, grazing her knee.

Felix helped her back to her feet. He placed his other hand on her back and guided her closer to the glow. The light came from a small jewel.

The jewel. It sat upon a stone cog with carved markings running around the inner circle.

Felix reached for it, but it didn't move. "Help me turn this," he said as he placed his hands on the gear's notches.

Xenia followed his example, but her hands trembled and she couldn't push it.

Felix muttered something about numbers lining up. Carvings numbered the stone by each gear. He turned them until each one was lined up in numerical order.

The stone clicked.

The sound echoed around the cavern. The entire cave shook as Felix lifted the jewel. Debris showered upon them. Xenia screamed; the sound was lost beneath the rumbling stone.

She lost her balance and fell against the stone wall behind her. She cried breathlessly from pain. Her vision was muted. She couldn't tell if it was an effect of the magic or hitting her head. An ache spread across her body, steadily increasing in pain.

"Felix…" She could barely hear herself, and she knew he didn't hear her, either. She wished she could call for him again, but she could hardly breathe. Each breath sent a stronger shot of pain to her chest. Thoughts no longer roamed her mind. She could focus on only three things.

Pain.

Breathing.

Felix.

It was dark when Xenia woke, aside from the stars that gleamed overhead, out of reach. When she was younger, she thought of the sky like a barrier that kept her from leaving.

Maybe it was true. She was told it wasn't, but did anyone really know what lay beyond their world? Her mother was beyond *this* world. Could she be an inhabitant of one of the distant stars she saw now?

Quick whispers sounded beside her, but she couldn't make out what the words were or even who each voice belonged to. She didn't pull herself up to see. Her head throbbed and her body ached.

Felix emerged from the darkness as he neared her. "Nia! You're awake! Are you all right?" His voice was thunderous—she didn't think he had meant to be loud, but his words cut through her skull like a knife. She groaned.

"I'm fine, I suppose." Her voice came out raspy and quiet, and her mouth was dry, making it harder to form the words properly.

He placed his hand on her head, then moved it to her neck. "You're really hot. Are you feeling any better?"

She nodded, though she couldn't remember the pain well enough to say if she had improved.

"We got the jewel!"

They did it. They'd found it. All the moments before she passed out rushed back to her. The glowing blue light, the cogs and numbers, the ground shaking. *The jewel.*

"We're still switching," she said.

He nodded as he leaned closer to her. His fingers drew across her wrist. "Nia, it was all fake. I didn't want the guards to attack while we looked for the jewel, so I thought it might help if we weren't together. I do want to switch, but more importantly, I want to be with you. Everything I've done in the past week has been to keep you safe, but it was foolish of me to think we could handle the magic. I thought if we were quick enough—"

Confusion creased her face. "What happened?"

"You passed out from the magic, I think. We got the jewel, but we weren't prepared. The magic didn't affect me, though."

She wanted to say something else, but it required too much effort, so she simply stared.

"I don't know why," Felix said in response to her silent question. "It just affected you more than me."

Why had it affected her so much? Was there something wrong with her?

"Why?" she asked. "Why did it affect me and not you?" Her voice cracked.

"I really don't know, Nia, I'm sorry. I wondered the same thing." He smiled. "We're both human, right?"

She grinned. "Right. Right?"

More footsteps sounded in the distance. Blake, followed by Karielyn, strolled over to them. Blake handed Xenia a flask filled with water and laid his hand on her forehead. "Are you okay?" he asked. "We need to get your fever down. The affects should be wearing off soon—you shouldn't have gone in there like that. If I had known what you were doing, I would have stopped you."

Karielyn sat down at Xenia's other side. She pushed the hair out of Xenia's face and tied it back with a piece of ribbon.

"Where are we?" Xenia asked.

"We traveled a few miles after you passed out, we wanted to get you as far away from the magic as we could," Karielyn explained.

Blake folded the quilt down so it only covered beneath her waist. She knew he wanted to reduce her fever, but the ground was cold, and the evening wind didn't help.

"We won't be able to move until you've regained your strength," he said, noticing her movement for the quilt.

"It's cold!"

He shook his head, rolling his eyes. "You'll be fine. Drink more water," he ordered, standing up and walking away so she could only see the outline of his body in the dark. He picked up a quilt and threw it at Felix. "I'm not setting up the tent tonight, get comfortable," he said, throwing another quilt to Karielyn.

Karielyn spread her quilt out a few feet from Xenia's and crawled under it.

Once Karielyn and Blake fell asleep, Felix moved closer to her. "I'm sorry," he said. "For lying to you."

Xenia sat up, propping herself against her elbows. He may not have wanted to leave her, but by lying he had used her emotions as a tool to dissuade the guards. And she had surrendered his location so Victoria could arrest him.

"I'm sorry too. I shouldn't have told Victoria where you were—"

"It's all right," he whispered. "I forgive you. I just want you back, if you'll have me."

"Of course I'll have you," she breathed. *Even if it's just for another day.*

Felix had never spoken to her again about the plan he'd mentioned in Casiville. Did he really have one?

He pulled her close, pressing his lips against her. When they separated, he unrolled his quilt and lay beside her. His eyes lingered on her until they both drifted asleep.

Xenia felt ready to keep moving in the morning, but Blake insisted they wait a few hours to be sure. When she had fallen in the cave, she'd ripped her dress and scraped her back—nothing threatening. Most of the side effects from the magic were gone when she woke up.

Felix hadn't left her side since she woke up, which made her feel even better. *It was all fake*, she reminded herself. Maybe she could spend one more good night with Felix before they switched.

"We need to find a peak," Blake said, rolling the map out. "The guide doesn't have too many requirements, so long as it's *a peak above the clouds*."

Xenia, Felix, and Karielyn joined him by the map. "I think we should pick a mountain and climb as far to the top as we can," Felix said. "Just in case."

"I agree," Blake said. "Any should work so long as you're high enough. Which you choose is up to you."

Xenia studied the map, her eyes catching on an illustrated mountain along the same range they were at now. She traced the line of mountains with her finger, stopping on the peak several miles from their current location. "I think we should go here," she said. "It feels right."

Felix smiled. "Then we'll go there."

Blake rolled the map up and returned it to its case. The rest of camp was already packed up.

"I want to see the jewel before we leave," Xenia said. She hadn't seen it since the cave, which now felt more like a fever dream. She wasn't entirely sure which parts of it were real and which parts *were* a fever dream.

Felix grabbed his bag and pulled out the blue crystal. "Here it is." He placed it in her outstretched hands.

Xenia gasped. It sat lengthways in her hand, and her fingertips barely grazed the edge. It wasn't glowing anymore. It looked like stained glass. It wasn't as heavy as she had expected.

"It's… magical," she said, mesmerized by the dull shine it possessed. It was strange to finally hold it in her hands after all this time. She imagined all the magic contained inside. Enough to send the entire world back to Chantendell if she were to break it. Enough to manipulate Fate.

She handed it to Felix, and he placed it back in his bag.

"Worth the risk?" Felix asked.

"We'll see."

"We should start walking if we want to reach the peak by morning," Blake said.

Xenia's mind translated his words: *If you want to switch by morning.*

Chapter Forty-Nine

THE MOUNTAIN THEY INTENDED TO CLIMB WOULD TYP-
ically take two days to reach the top, but they rode through
the night so they would arrive by morning.

Tomorrow morning. Chills blanketed Xenia's body. She
needed to push the thought out of her mind to keep herself
from locking up.

A distraction came easily.

"You thought your little charade would fool us?" A cold
voice sounded behind her.

Felix pulled the reins on their horse to stop. A group of
Chantendell guards stood behind them.

No. They were so close.

"You're lucky you have friends in high places, Liftson,
or I'd kill you right here." One of the guards said, fingering
the sword at his hip. "But your father has paid for our mercy
so you will be gifted a trial as soon as we get back to Chantendell. Same goes for you, *Princess.*

"As for you two," another man said, motioning to Karielyn and Blake. "Let's just say, your parents couldn't afford to save one of you if they put their gold together."

Xenia had never thought of guards as mean; she was surrounded by them when she was younger and thought of them as loyal and dedicated. She was never on the other end of their work.

"Please!" Xenia cried. "Please don't hurt them!"

Felix muttered curses under his breath, urging the horse to pick up again. The guards fired arrows at the mare, driving it to the ground. Xenia choked on a sob as the abrupt drop sent her and Felix toppling to the ground. She groaned as she pulled herself to her feet.

Blake jumped from his horse and rushed to help them. Arrows flew in his direction, narrowly missing him.

Karielyn screamed as arrows showered down around her. She jumped away from the horse and bent out of the way.

Blake reached for his bow and pulled an arrow from the quiver on his shoulder. He notched it and sent it flying towards the guards. It whizzed between two men, missing them.

Xenia searched for her bag. It had been thrown across the trail when she dropped from the horse. She ran for it, slightly avoiding an arrow that rushed past her ear.

"Nia!" Felix shouted. "Move!" He grabbed her arm and pulled her away from the arrows aimed at Karielyn and Blake.

One of the guards leaped in front of Xenia—Felix

pulled her closer, but the man didn't strike. He held out his arms *shielding* her.

"Return to the kingdom now! Queen Estelle's orders!" His voice was strikingly familiar.

"We don't take orders from—"

"You will if you wish to keep your life and position." The man's voice was grave. *Who is he?* Xenia battled the fog of fear stopping her from thinking straight as she struggled to place his voice.

Despite his threat, the guards reached for their weapons. As a guard advanced towards Xenia, the man jumped into battle with him.

Xenia untied her bag and grabbed the knives Blake had given her. She handed one to Felix then spun to face the guards.

The man closest to Karielyn drew his knife from the holster at his side. He lunged it towards her chest. She dove out of the way, her arms guarding her face. Blood spilled from her forearm.

Blake fired more arrows. Each missed their targets, who jumped out of the way, already notching their own.

One of the men lunged at him, knocking the arrow from his hand. Blake punched the man in the chest. He promptly returned it, knocking Blake in the stomach. He crashed to the ground, groaning.

The man drew a sword. Xenia threw her knife—it struck the man in the shoulder, and his sword clattered to the ground. He dove to grab it, giving Blake enough time to rise to his feet.

Two men stepped behind Xenia and Felix, yanked their arms back and fastened chains to their wrists and ankles.

The man from before spun around, sword at the ready. "Don't touch her!" He swung his sword at the man nearest Xenia who met it with his own, barely stopping the blade from hitting his chest.

Blake locked eyes with Xenia and mouthed, pointing at his hand. She frowned, shaking her head. His face turned in frustration.

He jerked his arm back suddenly, into the stomach of the man beside him. It wasn't hard enough to cause damage, but enough to cause a distraction. He ripped the man's glove from his hand and tossed it aside. He grabbed the guard's wrist and pressed against the blew jewel on his ring. The same smokey blue substance from the last attack swarmed around him.

Blake smiled, wiping sweat of his forehead. When the smoke disappeared, so did the guard.

Karielyn nursed her wounded arm but spun around in time to kick a man who had crept up behind her.

Xenia wrestled with her chains to no success.

Blake grabbed the guard he'd sent away's fallen sword. He lunged towards one of the men. Xenia winced as their weapons met one another's flesh. Blood soaked Blake's light hair. He rose his sword again, this time knocking the other man's weapon from his hand. He stumbled to the ground to grab it, and Blake dropped down next to him, thrusting his knee onto the man's chest. He pulled off his glove and then broke his ring as well.

Felix spun around and slammed his body into one of the guards, causing him to trip over his feet. The cuffs around Felix's wrist clattered against the chain as he tried to free himself.

Another arrow was fired in Karielyn's direction that passed her and flew towards Xenia, who dropped to the ground to avoid it.

A guard grabbed Blake from behind, thrashing a dagger in an attempt to stab him. Blake dodged forcefully, resulting in the knife tearing across his bicep. He groaned in pain, reaching for the cut. The guard snatched his arm, and he screamed. Before Blake had time to recover from the man's grip, he shoved his free hand into the man's ring. He cursed angrily as the blue took him.

There were only three guards left. The familiar man turned to them. "You will return to Chantendell this instant!" His voice had grown more dangerous than before. His words alone were sharp enough to pierce. He thrashed his sword at one of the guards, knocking his weapon out of his hands. The man pulled off his glove, breaking the ring and vanishing with the smoke.

The guard that now held Felix stood still. "I was ordered to—"

"Return to Chantendell at once!" he shouted, nearing the man.

He didn't move.

The man stepped towards him, and the guard let go of Felix, pulling out his own sword. "We had orders!"

"And I'm following mine," he replied. Their swords

clashed in the air. The guard swung, and the man blocked the attack with his own sword. The guard pulled his sword back, and the other's clanked against it. The sword flew through the air, landing with a clash on the side of the trail. The guard reached for it, but the man moved quicker and pointed his sword at the guard's chest, ready to press into his heart.

"You leave now, or I swear you will never see Chantendell again."

The man's fingers trembled as he pulled off his glove and, with the smoke, disappeared.

Once he was gone, the man removed his helmet, revealing a head of short, brown curls. He turned to face Xenia. Akron Vanhild. Her mother's personal guard.

He reached into his pocket and held out a key. Blake took it cautiously. "Thank you," he said through gritted teeth, a strange gaze set on Akron.

"Don't mention it—to *anyone*," Akron said, drawing a sword.

Blake rushed towards Xenia and Felix and unlocked their chains. They fell to the ground with a dull thud.

Xenia threw her arms around Akron. "Thank you," she said softly. "Thank you so much."

"Of course, Xenia." Emotion split his words.

When they separated, he picked up Blake's wrist and examined the cut across his upper arm. "You and the girl need medical attention. Do what you can to tend to the wounds, then take the horse to the nearest town."

Blake nodded and went to assist Karielyn.

Felix grabbed Xenia's arm. "It only needs to be us."

She nodded, not wanting to speak.

Karielyn ran in her direction and gave her a fierce hug. "Good luck, Xenia! I love you." She paused. "And I swear, if you don't make it back alive, I'll never assist you in anything like this again."

Xenia laughed. "I love you too. Be careful."

She shared her laugh. "I'll try."

"Xenia, you should keep moving," Blake said. "I'll help Karielyn. We'll be fine."

Felix picked up his bag and handed Xenia hers. "He's right, we need to keep moving."

Before continuing farther, Akron stopped and turned to face her and Felix. "Xenia, please. You know this isn't right. It's against Fate's path for you—please, *stop*. Now, before it's too late." His desperate, brown eyes bored into hers.

Felix acted before she could respond. He reached for her wrist and led her away from Akron. She had nothing to say, anyway. It was too late to give up.

Felix squeezed her hand. They left the poor horse on the road, and Blake and Karielyn took the other.

Xenia closed her eyes and breathed in the crisp air as they continued down the trail. This was it. In mere hours, her and Felix's fates would reverse.

Chapter Fifty

XENIA AND FELIX WALKED THROUGH THE MOUNTAINS in silence. The trail twisted into a steep climb as the night progressed. Dark storm clouds lingering above them threatened to soak them at any moment. Lightning webbed across the sky and thunder clapped, shaking the ground.

The mounds of snow around them now made it hard to believe that a week ago, she had complained about the heat.

More thunder shook the ground beneath them. Rocks tumbled form the side of the mountain, missing them and falling off the cliff.

"Fate." Felix cursed as rain began pounding against them. Xenia used her free hand to shield her eyes from the drops crashing down. They obscured the distance, fading the path ahead from view.

The rain and icy wind chilled Xenia to the bone. She trembled from the cold that soaked into her clothes and skin.

A sudden scream escaped her as the ground beneath

them flaked away. Felix hooked his arm around her waist and clung to a rock peeking out of the cliffside. He pulled them back onto the trail, panting heavily.

"Should we wait out the storm?" As she asked it, the ground trembled beneath them. Stones rained down behind them.

"Run!" Felix shouted.

They darted forward as hundreds of heavy boulders tumbled down where they had stood moments before. They kept running as the wall of stones beside them crumbled down. Lighting lit the sky.

"In here!" Felix shouted, pulling her into a cavity in the side of the mountain. Trembling, she leaned against the wall of the stone hollow.

He shuddered from the cold beside her as they watched the storm rage outside.

Would they even make it to the peak?

"I-I'm scared." She heard her voice before she realized she had said it out loud. "What if we don't make it back?"

Felix faced her, sincerity working up its own storm in his eyes. "We're going to, Nia. We'll make it."

Failing had always been a possibility, but now that she was close enough to suffer the consequences, fear held her in an inescapable embrace. "But we might not." Her words were broken. "And if we do… I'm not ready to fight you. Or leave you."

Felix picked up her hands and his eyes locked on hers. His wet hair stuck to his face, and his teeth drummed together as he shivered. "We are going to reach that peak, and when we do, I'm not going to fight you."

She pressed her eyes closed and hot tears mixed with the cold rain on her cheeks. "But you'll leave. You'll have to. Everyone always leaves. I lost years with my mother, and Blake, I'm not ready to lose you too."

"I don't want to lose you, either." Felix's voice was coarse and uneven. "Nia, losing you—losing you is losing everything." He stopped, looking up at the cave ceiling, his throat taut. When his gaze fell back on her, tears slipped down his face. "It's losing the only person I *truly* care about. My… my family never had time to know each other the way a family should. Their life wouldn't allow it—it convinced me I wanted the opposite. Lonely, isolated, hated. Until I met you, I hadn't realized what I truly wanted. I want to be loved. Really loved. And you make me feel like I am."

All the fear that had engulfed Xenia moments before had faded. She should have felt hopeless. Hopeless to have found something so beautiful just in time to lose it. But she couldn't look into Felix Liftson's eyes and feel hopeless. Because when he looked at her, when he spoke to her, he reached parts of her soul no one ever had before. Standing beside him returned parts of her she believed her fate had stolen away. He made her feel whole again.

"I thought I knew what I wanted," Felix said. "Until I met you. I'm not going to fight you, I'm going to fight *for* you. Because I love you, Xenia. I love you more than I've ever loved anyone."

"I love you too," she whispered. "Felix Liftson, I do and always will love you!"

His lips pressed against hers, and rich joy coursed through her body, washing out the pain and grief she'd carried for the past week. She didn't know how this night would end—or even if they would survive it. But the way Felix held her now made her believe she had forever to spend with him.

Despite everything, this was a moment for her best days to envy. A moment of pure bliss and love. The moment belonged only to them, perhaps a gift from Fate for the pain they had endured to be there.

When they pulled away, she pressed her head against his, resting her forehead on the brim of his nose. His breath warmed her face. She didn't want him to ever move. She would have stayed there forever.

Xenia wished she could forsake everything else for this moment, yet one more question lingered in her head. "Do you really have a plan?"

Felix flinched as if her words stung. "Yes. I have a plan. I won't fight you. And I—I'd never want to leave you. Not unless I have to. I love you. And no matter what happens, don't let yourself believe for a moment that I don't. My love for you is as sure as Fate—it's written in the stars, if you only remember to look."

Xenia fumbled closer to him. "I love you, Felix."

As his arms wrapped around her, she closed her eyes and let herself feel the weight of every one of his words. She had fallen in love with him despite every time she tried to stop herself from letting it happen. She loved him, yet spent so much time telling herself she couldn't in fear of losing him. Even through her attempts to keep herself from him, they ended up together. She couldn't evade all of Fate's plans for her, and she didn't have to hide from everything that would bring her happiness in fear of the day she would lose it. For years, she'd hidden from the possibility of love. Still, she stood here, perfectly in love with Felix Liftson. Despite the uncertainty of their fate, the love between them now felt like enough to carry them through forever, even when they were too far apart to touch.

They spent another minute in each other's arms, holding each other steady against the uncertainties ahead of them. When they pulled away from each other, Xenia wanted to return to the last moment, but she knew if she stayed there forever, she would miss every other beautiful thing Fate had in store for her.

They held each other's gaze, the silence smoothing over the uneven moment.

Above them, the stone cracked.

Felix grabbed her arm and pulled her back into the violent rain. In moments, the cavity caved, filling the hollow space with debris. Fear shook her.

"We need to hurry," Felix said. "If we can reach the top… we'll be safe soon."

They broke into a run, struggling to see ahead. Felix limped, but it hardly slowed them.

"We should gain elevation," he said. "We just need to get as high as we can."

The higher they climbed, the thinner the air became, and Xenia struggled to breathe steadily. Occasionally, she caught glimpses of the land beneath them, reminding her of how far they had come.

The rain eased, and they came to a stop at a wide patch of flat land, overlooking everything. A layer of fog settled between the sky and hills, above miles of river and forest.

Felix turned to a snow-crowned peak beside them. "Let's… climb it," he said, chattering from the cold.

Climb that. We're going to climb that!

He rummaged through his bag and pulled out ropes and a few other things from Blake. He passed Xenia a set of leather gloves, and she pulled them up her arms.

Calm. Stay calm.

Felix placed his hand against the hidden rock, brushing away snow. He threw his leg up and climbed as if there was an unseen ladder.

Xenia placed her gloved hand on a wedge of rock and found a spot to rest her foot. Her heart pounded violently within its cage as she pulled herself higher.

She screamed as her foot slipped from a patch of ice coating the piece of rock she'd set her foot on. She swung herself towards the rock and gripped the stone in her hand tighter as she repositioned her foot.

"Are you all right?" Felix said through a pant from above her.

Xenia fought for breath, shrugging off the feeling of falling. "Yeah."

She kept climbing, applying extra caution to each movement. Her lungs felt as if the cold air had somehow set them on fire. Her chest stung, stretching into her throat. Her wet hair froze to her face, and ice stuck to her lashes. She slipped a few more times, catching herself only barely.

When she was finally close enough to the top, Felix grasped her hand to help her up. Her teeth beat together. She had not the slightest idea how she would get off the cliff, but that was a matter to deal with latter. Right now, she stood at the top.

Felix wrapped her in a warming embrace. "Let's do this," he whispered.

He stood at her side as she pulled the book out of her bag and flipped to the very last page. The words had been splotched from the rain, but she could still read it. She recited the words in her mind until they were rooted in her brain.

Felix handed her the jewel; her hands trembled. She didn't want to drop it. If it broke, all of their effort would be for nothing, and the slip would earn her a spot in prison.

"Ready?" he asked, placing a hand on the stone.

She nodded.

They spoke in unison: "Two fates—two souls—one decision. Your duty, I will fulfill as my own. May your title no longer be a burden to your name, but an addition to my own. With you will I ever be connected. With you will I forever stand the light of my own choice. With you, I convert."

The jewel began glowing a brilliant blue. Xenia closed her eyes. When she opened them, everything looked the same, but she felt as if a heavy jacket had fallen from her shoulders. She took a deep breath and blinked away her tears of relief. After everything, she stood next to Felix, their places reversed. Their fates fixed.

Felix threw his arms around her and lifted her to the

sky, spinning in a circle. His lips found hers and they kissed. She was free. Free from her fate, from Chantendell. No fate defined who they were. They did. No one else could choose who she was. And she chose to be standing with Felix Liftson atop an icy peak. They didn't belong to a fate or a title; they belonged to each other.

He met her gaze and then said, "I love you." His eyes filled with tears as he added, "And I need you to forgive me, but I have to do this. I don't want to, but I have to."

"Do what?" she asked, ice slipping into her veins. He pushed her hair behind her ear. His fingers dropped, and he stroked her hand with his thumb. Then he grabbed the jewel.

Panic shot threw her. "Felix, what are you doing?"

Tears fell down his face.

"What are you—?"

"I'm sorry." He closed his eyes and took a deep breath. "It's better like this, I'm sorry."

He lifted the stone in one hand.

No—

No, he couldn't do this. It would cost him everything! He would get himself in even more trouble. He would get himself *killed!* She couldn't live with that. Without him.

"Felix, no! You can't—"

"I'm sorry."

He threw the stone to the frosted ground. It shattered into thousands of sharp, blue pieces, scattering across the snow. The same smoke she had seen so many times filled her lungs and covered her body.

It seemed to pull the thoughts out of her mind and leave

her blank. Once again, her senses were stripped from her, leaving her with only her fleeting thoughts. She fought to hold on to what little bits of reality she had left but eventually they all slipped from her too.

Finally, she let go, embracing the emptiness around and inside her. Letting it swallow her up until she no longer remembered where she was or where she was going.

When the world began to form around her, she was reunited with the fear that fought to consume her. She didn't want to know what happened next. She didn't want to open her eyes, but she forced herself to anyway.

When she did, she was back in Chantendell.

# Epilogue

XENIA'S MOTHER WAS BY HER SIDE AS SOON AS SHE opened her eyes. One hand fingered her hair, and the other held her steady as if she expected her to collapse. She fell into her mother's embrace, and Estelle's gentle arms wrapped around her body.

"Xenia," she whispered, "you're all right."

Xenia pulled away and watched silent tears slip down her mother's cheeks. Turning her gaze, she surveyed the room. She had never been here before, and she wasn't alone. Hundreds—possibly thousands—of people filled the wide hall.

Xenia jumped to her feet, surveying the room, but she couldn't find her friends.

"How are you already here?" she asked, facing her mother again.

"I was informed the jewel broke this morning. I've been waiting for you all day."

All day? How long ago did me and Felix switch? How long have I been here?

She glanced around and noticed that all the people around her were slumped against one another or a wall. Some groaned softly, and others were slick with sweat.

"What's wrong with them?" she asked.

"It's the magic, this always happens when people return."

The magic didn't seem to have affected her, but why not? Why were they struggling while she wasn't? Last time she was so sensitive. But Felix wasn't.

Felix.

"I need to find—"

"Felix is gone."

Her heart tumbled. *Gone?* She clasped a hand to her mouth to stop from gaping. "What do you mean? Did—?"

Estelle shook her head, silencing her. "Xenia, the magic has a terrible effect on humans, but the two of you don't seem affected. Him especially. He fled as soon as he got back. I've already sent guards to find him, but no one knows where he went."

"What are they going to do to him? You can't let them kill him, Mother—"

"I have no choice," she said firmly.

Xenia shook her head. Felix couldn't die, she couldn't let him.

Her mother grabbed hold of her hand and squeezed it soothingly. Xenia froze, noticing for the first time that Estelle's wrist was branded. Her skin bore seven stars dancing around a small crown. The symbol of Chantendell.

"What's that?" she asked.

Estelle's eyes were wide as she said, "That's not for you to worry over. Not yet, at least."

Xenia's head spun as questions flooded her mind. Her mother was branded. Felix was missing. Her entire future had been altered by her switch of Fate.

Her story was supposed to end there—but something told her it had just begun.

ACKNOWLEDGEMENTS

Being here right now, writing the acknowledgments for the story I started four years, ago is surreal.

I've always enjoyed reading the acknowledgments and seeing how much work and love went into a single book. Often, I read them before I start the story itself. However, they're the last thing I can write. Even now, I feel as if there's enough time between writing this and the book's publication to miss a few thank-yous. So, to everyone who has helped me, and everyone who's yet to help me: thank you.

There's only one way I can start this. Thank you to my Heavenly Father. This story was from You. I know it in the way I learn from it every time I decide not to give up. Thank You for placing this story in my heart, and for seeing me through it to the end.

Thank you to my family. To my parents for believing in, supporting, and encouraging me. It means everything to me.

And it's very likely the reason this book is here at all. Thank you to Kayla, for every late night you spent with me, helping me through plot holes—all those girl talks were much needed. To Ashlyn, for always making me laugh when I'm taking things too seriously. To Zarik, for your sweet spirit helping me through hard moments. To Cambrie and Ariel. You're too young to read this now, but one day I hope you find this and know I love you.

To Nana and Papa. You've always shown me unbelievable amounts of love and support and I appreciate that dearly.

Thank you to Chey, for spoiling me with your support. You keep me going. Thank you. I appreciate every late-night call, every text. You are a blessing.

To London. Thank you for always supporting me. Seeing and hearing from you brightens my day. I'm so glad we're cousins.

To Brooklyn. Wow. Your work on the cover still blows me away. I am so, so grateful to have you as a cousin and cover artist!

To Sydney. For so long you were the only other writer I knew. Thanks for supporting me from the beginning and continuing to now.

To Izzy. What would I do without my cult bestie? Writers are often told not to quit their day job, but we already burned ours down, so… Thanks for everything.

Thank you to the Instagram writing community. Where would I be without y'all? Thank you for supporting me these last four years.

Thank you to Paris, for being the first outside my family to read this story. It's changed a lot from the version you read in 2021, but you were supportive of it even then. Thank you.

Thank you to Ariana. You have been such a blessing in my life. Your advice has changed this story for the better. I couldn't have asked for a better editor. Thank you for being a wonderful friend and role model.

To Dana. Your support means so much to me! Every comment, DM, reel—you are so sweet and I'm so glad we crossed paths!

Thank you to the Laurels. Your constant support and love has gotten me through so much, and I wish you all the best.

There's so much more I could say to each of you, but I know these things are supposed to be short. So I'll close by saying this: thank *you*, dear reader. If you are holding this book in your hand, you are the reason. It wouldn't be here without you. Thank you for taking a chance on *Broken Fate*. And in case you're like me, enjoy the story.